The zombis closed in on both sides.

The one coming in the window would be through in just a few seconds, and the one at the door was stalking up the hall. Max spun toward that one and thrust his palm at it. He tensed, focusing—golden energy flared like a bolt of heat lightning, and hurled the zombi backward to tumble into the broken doorway.

The other zombi caught its foot on the jagged windowsill and fell face-first into the room, into the back of the desk, with a mighty crash like a watermelon on the sidewalk. Undeterred, unhurried, it started to get right up. It was, or had been, a large man, like a football lineman. Pam bent down suddenly, scooped up books from the floor, and hurled them at the creature. They landed with solid thuds but had no effect on its progress. Max turned from the first zombi to battle the second but before he could do anything the second had reached across the desk and seized his right hand. It yanked Max forward, toppling the computer monitor. Max used the momentum to strike with the edge of his left hand at the bridge of its nose. He knew it wouldn't kill it as it would a normal man, but it might blind it.

No such luck. The zombi grabbed his left hand and now had both hands trapped in its own. Max jumped onto the desk to get freedom of motion. The zombi began to squeeze Max's hands, and Max's face betrayed his struggle—a losing struggle.

Turn the page for praise for the Max August books.

PRAISE FOR *THE LONG MAN*

"*The Long Man* adds another dazzling burst of story-telling power to Englehart's ongoing display of his brilliance."

—Michael Chabon, *New York Times* bestselling author of *The Yiddish Policemen's Union*

"Steve Englehart was one of the first authors I ever read. It was the first comic book that ever scared me. With *The Long Man*, he proves that even thirty years later, he still has the ghostly touch. Immortals, alchemy, and beautiful revenge. I'm young again."

—Brad Meltzer, *New York Times* bestselling author of *The Book of Fate*

"[Rising] over the top of Nob Hill in San Francisco, Juliana in Suriname, and Mount Hillaby in Barbados, *The Long Man* is an engaging thriller that is fun to read; just ignore credibility, especially of the throwback comic-book villains. Fast-paced . . . Max and Pam elude the enemy, while also killing some along the way; readers will enjoy the return of the Point Man."

—*Genre Go Round*

"Steve Englehart has finally continued the story of the Point Man, and it's about damned time. A crackling mystical thriller."

—Peter David

THE POINT MAN

"In a matrix of rock music, dizzy rock fans, the police, the Mafia, sex, betrayal, and innocent bystanders, the Point Man moves and performs his function. The magic is most magical, and enormous to boot, and the mystery and the tension will not release you. Or maybe this is enough: you'll like it."

—*Twilight Zone Magazine*

"Englehart weaves a roller-coaster ride of music, magic, and madness involving the USSR, the KGB, the FBI, the CIA, ESP, radio station KQBU, and all the rest of the letters of the alphabet as Max, possessor himself of heretofore unknown powers, helps thwart a plot to destroy the U.S. through sorcery in a Cold War Magic Gap. The writing is solid and compelling, evidencing all the skill of a craftsman who has spent the last decade learning how to build an episodic story in the to-be-continued environs of comic books, yet never giving in to cartoony excess. Sometimes when comic book writers write prose, we miss the luxury of the pictures to help carry our story along. In *The Point Man*, Englehart never lets the absence of pictures slow his story. It's a shame he hasn't written more prose since."

—*Bookgasm*

"Full of reach and astonishment . . . Few working writers alive have [Steve Englehart's] sense of sound and of scene."

—Theodore Sturgeon, author of *More Than Human*

The Long Man

Steve Englehart

TOR®
fantasy

A TOM DOHERTY ASSOCIATES BOOK / NEW YORK

This is a work of fiction. All of the characters, organizations, and events portrayed in this novel are either products of the author's imagination or are used fictitiously.

THE LONG MAN

Copyright © 2010 by Steve Englehart

All rights reserved.

Edited by James Frenkel

A Tor Book
Published by Tom Doherty Associates, LLC
175 Fifth Avenue
New York, NY 10010

www.tor-forge.com

Tor® is a registered trademark of Tom Doherty Associates, LLC.

ISBN 978-0-7653-5661-1

First Edition: March 2010
First Mass Market Edition: December 2010

Printed in the United States of America

0 9 8 7 6 5 4 3 2 1

This One's For
My Father
And Fellow Time Traveler,
Gordon Kerfoot Englehart

I think, therefore I am.

—RENÉ DESCARTES

He lives well who lives well hidden.

—RENÉ DESCARTES

An excerpt from the *Codex*, as it existed at this time.

The divine calendar of the Mayans is made of two interlocking cycles. The first, consisting of numbers, goes around every 13 days, while the other, consisting of images, goes around every 20. So each day's name consists of a number and an image. Altogether, there are 13 x 20, or 260, distinct day names. And each number and image has a meaning.

NUMBER	KEYWORD
1	Establishing
2	Encountering
3	Advancing
4	Encompasing
5	Empowering
6	Responding
7	Engaging
8	Connecting
9	Being
10	Personifying
11	Owning
12	Fulfilling
13	Managing

IMAGE	KEYWORD
Nipple	Reality
Wind	Possibilities
Night	A Private World
Corn Seed	The Public World
Serpent	Yáng
Death	Yin
Hand	Assertion
Star	Devotion
Moon	Transcendence
Dog	Embodiment
Monkey	Divergence
Tooth	Cohesion
Corn Stalk	Unison
Jaguar	Clarity
Eagle	The Storyline
Candle	The Matrix
Earth	The Universal
Flint Knife	The Unique
Milky Way	Alchemy
Sun	All

So, for example, 11 Wind has to do with Owning Possibilities . . .

The Long Man

11 WIND

His name was not Max August.

"Hey!" the guy with the cape said. "Aren't you Max August?"

The questioner was not the only one in costume, because tonight was Hallowe'en and the night would be here soon. All the kids coming home from school past Mount Davidson Park, and some of the more-alive adults, had gotten started early. But the guy with the cape wore his backpack under the cape, so he looked like the Hunchback of Notre Dame.

He for his part was looking at a man in his midthirties, dressed normally: jeans, flannel shirt, tall, blond, athletic. A high brow, high cheekbones, large, intelligent hazel eyes, and the full mouth of a guy who talked for a living—very much like Max August. That mouth smiled wryly as the blond man said, "Sorry. You've got the wrong guy."

"Really?" The caped guy was peering at him, eyes narrowed against the low sun. "You look just like him."

"I hear that," the blond man said, "though not so much anymore; it's been like twenty-five years, right? Max August would be in his fifties."

Suddenly the caped guy felt very stupid. "Yeah. Sure. Sorry." Then, hopefully, "You a relative?"

"Nope. Just similar genes, I guess."

The guy shifted his weight from one foot to the other. "Ah, well—sorry, dude. I was just rememberin' watchin' him do his show inside his window at KQBU. We all did, back in the day; we'd duck out of school for it. The coolest thing in San Francisco—if you were a teenager. He called himself Barnaby Wilde then, but anybody *cool* knew his real name. He played the best music, great music, an' danced like a lunatic, right in the window, y'know?"

"Nahhh. I lived in Miami when I was a kid, so I never heard the guy live. But I've had a crash course on him since I moved out here, I can tell you that."

"You know what happened to him?"

"Been working on the East Coast, I think. He's got some new air-name; 'Barnaby Wilde' doesn't make sense anymore. I don't think he's ever used his real name on air."

"Huh. I probably wouldn' even know him if I heard him now," the caped crusader said. "Or saw him. But I just had this picture of him in my head, up in that window, all these years, and bam! you were it." He shrugged. The wind was picking up and his cape ballooned, mimicking the gesture.

"I'm sorry I missed him," the blond man said.

"Yeah. Hey, I'm sorry I bothered you."

"No problem, man. Happy Halloween."

The guy grinned suddenly, remembering his cape, his character, and the night ahead. "Happy Halloween!" He walked jauntily away along Dalewood, heading west, while Max turned into the park.

Among the shadows of the eucalypti, Max's smile died, his face turning cool, if not cold, and utterly self-contained. He gave a sharp, impatient shrug.

Time *was* passing. But it was still madness, coming back to San Francisco. He'd been so huge in the '70s, the king of all rock, and he *had* done his show from a window studio right on Sutter Street. How could he have known that one day he'd lust for anonymity the way he'd lusted after fame?

How could he have known he'd turn *Timeless*?

OCTOBER 31 - 5:00 P.M. PDT

11 WIND

He'd been a normal guy once, if you called having a feel for music and getting famous for it "normal." One night that normal guy had done yet another rock-star interview and had met the rock star's manager. He turned out to be Cornelius Agrippa, a wizard close to five hundred years old. By the time Agrippa died five years later, he had taught Max how to become Timeless.

Timeless was just this side of Immortal, but the difference was significant. Timeless meant you didn't die until something killed you. Agrippa went five hundred years before he was overpowered by a sorceress called Madeleine. He didn't get older for five centuries, didn't even get sick, but then he died. The same could happen to Max at any time. He was just a normal guy who had a feel for music and, as it turned out, the music of the spheres. But none of that would have had him looking at five centuries and beyond if he weren't a normal guy in one other way. Like a lot of guys from back in the day, he'd spent some time in a shooting war, and he had a feel for self-preservation.

At sunrise on the Autumnal Equinox of 1985, exactly one hundred days before Agrippa left the world of the living, Max had taken what Agrippa had taught him and stepped out of time. He was barely thirty-five years old then, and he was barely thirty-five years old now, and he'd be barely thirty-five years old until somebody took his life away.

That life stretched before him like a highway in the desert. After years of being Timeless, he no longer thought in terms of the next year, the next five years, the next ten. He was looking at a horizon a hundred years ahead and beyond. And the more he looked out there, the more he saw of the world that could be coming. He was going to walk through the entire twenty-first century if he could survive it, then on through the twenty-second, the twenty-third . . . Soon enough, no one would have actual memories of the twentieth century except him, and a few others like him. People would ask him "What was it like?"

But the highway stretched out behind him, too. His particular route ran through Howdy Doody, color television, *The Twilight Zone*, the Kennedy assassination, the Beatles, Motown, drugs, *The Prisoner*, Vietnam, Watergate, *Star Wars*, Agrippa, AIDS, Atari, Timelessness, Iran-Contra, the first Iraq War, TransNeptunian Objects, the Internet, *The X-Files*, O.J., Ken Starr, the new millennium, 9/11, the fake Iraq War, blogs, global warming . . . and whatever was happening *now*. The past, the present, the future, it was all one route, and it all mattered. He was here *now*, to do what he chose to do *now*.

And still, he remembered what it was like to be dancing in the window of KQBU, his earphones on, his mind a million miles away *and* right there on the air. He was *into* it, and people got that, so they filled the sidewalk outside the window every weekday, four to eight, to watch him at his work. Damn right he danced; he'd pull something from the side bin that fit the mood precisely and lay that disc of vinyl on the turntable and lay the needle in the groove and hold the cork circle on the disc so it wouldn't move until he let it go, which he did when the disc he was already playing spun to its end. It was all feel, talent, and craft. He danced below the neon BARN-ABY WILDE, people's minds were expanding, and Freedom was marching down Time's highway. Neptune in Sagittarius and Uranus in Scorpio was one explanation; "that's just the way it was" was another. Who needed an explanation? The world was welcoming, everyone was pushing their envelope and enjoying the fruits of the others' push—it was a golden age, and he was the golden boy, and he danced in his window studio because he couldn't *not* dance.

But he didn't dance now.

DECEMBER 31, 1985 - 11:51 P.M. PACIFIC STANDARD TIME NEW YEAR'S EVE

6 STAR

Nine minutes till midnight and the Happy New Year of 1986, Anno Domini. Reagan had been President for five years, Nintendos were red hot. In twenty more days, the first Martin Luther King Day would take place.

Cornelius Agrippa, who had met da Vinci and drawn a horoscope for the first Queen Elizabeth, would miss MLK Day. At the stroke of midnight, he'd be dead.

"*If* you believe in the Gregorian calendar!" Max told him forcefully. They were standing in Agrippa's Victorian mansion, sprawled across Mount Tamalpais above San Francisco Bay. The only thing in the black sky over the city was the Virgo moon, rising in the east. "Cornelius, tonight means nothing to the Chinese or the Muslims or Mayans! It's Twenty Eleven or Eighteen Rabi' al-Akhir or Six Star. Six Star means Responding to Devotion, for God's sake! Your calculations are all off! You just have to believe it!"

Agrippa laughed easily, faintly mocking. Wearing his well-tailored black suit, standing at ease, he was the picture of successful equanimity even now. The only outward signs of a change in him were his hair, which had finally turned from gray to white, and a voice that had grown a little reedy. "You don't think I'm responding to *your* devotion, Max?"

"If you were, you'd fight this! You're a wizard! You're *the* wizard! Take control of your life like you always have."

"Max, you've decided to pursue alchemy. An alchemist shapes himself in order to shape the world. But you are correct that I am a wizard, and a wizard shapes the world itself, working the tides of history. I shaped the world quite well in my time, but I have never controlled it. The tide is going out tonight, whatever name you give it, and even if I *could* shape it, I couldn't stop it."

"All right, then," said Max doggedly. "I work in the here and now, where things actually happen. Let me try to keep you here."

"It would be like swimming up Niagara Falls"— Agrippa snorted, an old-world sound—"then on through the sky to the stars. I am a wizard, and I learned my art from the great Trithemius, who also taught Paracelsus. I may be European but I know the universe, and whatever the Chinese or Mayans say, it will come to the same thing. I tell you I *know* what the universe has in store for me, and I tell you I am content."

To show how content he was, he took a pull from the intricately-carved stein of Rheinländische Bitterbier he was holding, and smacked his lips deliberately. Then he went on: "Madeleine—or, to use her true name, Aleksandra—is a shape-shifter, and her lack of a defined *center* fooled me. I knew what I knew, but I did not know how to deal with such as her, and she exploded my mind. You know full well that Timelessness is not disrupted by sleep or even unconsciousness, any more than breathing is, but she tore my mind apart. When I floated back together, I had lost my control, and I could feel the decay beginning. I hadn't felt it for over four hundred years, so it was rather noticeable, and I was still wizard enough to calculate very quickly how long it would take to still my heart. The answer was five years to the day, a nice round number because I still have some harmony with the tides. Now, if you don't mind, I would like to enjoy the most beautiful voice of the past five hundred years while I still have ears to hear it."

"I'm gonna punch you!" Val snapped. Both men turned their eyes toward her. There were six minutes left now.

Her sound was all around them, clear and sultry from the huge Bose speakers in the corners of the vast room overlooking the bay. It was the final track of her latest album, a long concept piece from her biggest seller yet. Standing there, wearing tight acid-washed denim, lace, and piles of costume jewelry, she was everything a true rock diva should be. Her loose, fluffy hair, almost black with deep auburn highlights, hung heavily to frame her face and her huge hoop earrings. The only thing wrong was, that rock-star face was a study in grief.

Agrippa took her fist in his hand, tenderly. "For the sound track to their last moments on Earth, many men, especially a European and *especially* a German, would choose *Der Rosenkavalier*. But this is what my world sounds like, right here and now. It makes me so happy, and so proud of what you accomplished, dear Valerie."

But she had a rock star's drive. "C'mon, Corny, fight it!" she pressed him over her amplified voice. "If you won't do it for yourself, or for Max, do it for me."

He sighed. This wasn't easy for him, either, no matter how blithe he appeared. "I would do anything I could for you, Woman, but I can't do this." He squeezed her hand. "You know that."

"I *don't* know that," Val said stubbornly, "and I don't like it, and nothing you say can *make* me like it."

"You don't like it because you know me, and you know me because I extended my life till it overlapped yours."

"I know you because I loved you."

"And I loved you, but those are the tides I speak of." He spread his hands, reasonably. "By rights, we should have missed each other by four and a half centuries. Instead, we had each other for a time, and because we did, there are two wonderful people to take my place—which justifies everything I did in my life. So how can anyone in this room be sad?"

"You're leaving Max in your place, not me," Val said. "I need you, Corny. I need more time. I haven't learned *everything* you had to teach me."

"You'll do fine without me," Agrippa answered confidently. "I know this, too. You're a different person from Max, and you have a career, so it takes a little longer. But you will get there, if only because you have a better soul than he does."

Max laughed. "Hell, everybody knows that." He put a comforting arm around his wife's shoulders. If it had been up to him, he'd have let her continue, but he had to rein it in now. They'd fought the good fight to keep Agrippa here; it was time to honor their mentor's wishes and ease his passing. It was time for Max to start moving toward taking control.

Agrippa, however, had gone in the other direction. "I'm very serious about her soul," he told Max. "Valerie has a purity you and I have never had. You can hear it in her voice; it's what makes her a star. But we all have what it takes to master the occult, and I leave this world with full faith in both of you. Cornelius Agrippa, born fourteen September 1486 in the Julian calendar, dies thirty-one December 1985 in the Gregorian. That's four hundred and ninety-one years; should I cry because I didn't get five hundred? I might cry for not seeing you become Timeless, Valerie, but Max has a soul that gets things done. He'll take you there."

"I'll get it all done," Max said seriously. "I'll carry on your fight. Five years ago you told me, 'In the year 2000, another new era will begin. I believe it will involve this world's emergence into the solar system, but Wolf Messing believes it will see the final triumph of totalitarianism.' You killed Wolf and I killed Aleksandra, and from fourteen years out, it looks like Russia's going to fall, but totalitarianism is a powerful drug. Someone else will pick up the needle, and 2000's coming faster than we think."

Agrippa was still the master. "So you must remember

that creatures with no center are almost impossible to discern. Because nothing is cut and dried in magick, you beat her face-to-face—"

"Or something like that," Val muttered, nudging her husband just a little bit harder than was necessary. His magick had been sex magick.

"You beat her, but others may be even better. So you must be better, too. You must devote yourself to your new life, Max. Grow every day."

"I will," Max said, and somehow those words seemed to echo off the high, vaulted ceiling. It was Agrippa's house.

Two minutes. The Val in the speakers reached the end of her album, leaving only the soft hiss of the tape. The Val in the room asked quietly, "What will I do, Corny?"

"Max knew almost nothing when he faced her. You are far stronger now than he was then. So just remember that you can rely absolutely on your soul and your will." For the first time, his parchment face grew intent. "Wizardry is nothing but wisdom and will."

"So you always say."

"Good, then. You two love each other. Make many children and teach them alchemy from birth. In that way I'll continue through Time by other means, and so will you." He took a last lusty swallow of *bier* and put the stein down. He clapped Max on the shoulder and shook his hand. "Good-bye, Max."

One minute.

"*Wiedersehn*, Cornelius," Max said. Time was falling in on them so fast, so relentlessly. Nothing could slow it down.

"Corny—," Val said, her voice breaking, and he took

her shoulders and hugged her. It was meant to be a tight hug, but she could feel the tremors in his arms as he held her. "Good-bye, Woman," he said. When he released her, she turned to Max and hugged him even more tightly as Agrippa walked just slightly unsteadily to the couch. She had her face buried in Max's shoulder, refusing to look, as Agrippa sat down carefully, gave them a final confident smile, closed his eyes, and died. The clock struck midnight. Fireworks erupted over the bay.

Max's eyes were fixed on his mentor, taking in everything about the moment. On one level, it was no less than Agrippa deserved, and on another, it would add to Max's store of knowledge, which was the best they had now that Agrippa's work was falling to him. The deaths of Magi were not common things. On another level, simultaneously, Max saw Agrippa's soul rise from the forehead, a golden nimbus. It didn't so much *look* like Agrippa as it held his *scent*. It didn't so much *fade* as it *expanded*. Even Max, the professional motormouth, couldn't find the words for it, but he felt it as it filled him . . . and then filled the night. Now he knew it. Agrippa had left the building.

He stood in silence, digesting everything about it, following each train of thought. After long moments, he returned his attention to Val . . . and realized she was no longer holding him. No longer at his side.

"Val?"

No answer.

He called her name again, and when still no answer came, he began to hunt through the mansion's rooms. But she was not there. Alarm leapt sharply within him. He ran out onto the deck, underneath the moon and firework stars. At the base of a railing post, sharp in the moonlight, was a black loop of rope. He went to the railing, looked down.

Saw his wife hanging by the neck above the steep hillside, slowly turning in the chilling wind.

He ran to the end of the balcony where it came closest to the ground, jumped off the edge, hit the slope, and rolled ten feet before he could regain control. Then he scrabbled along the profound drop to reach her, dirt spitting from beneath him. He grabbed her legs, raised her to get the pressure off her neck.

Her legs were cold. She'd been dead for hours.

It was like a sledgehammer square between the eyes. *Someone else* had stood beside him in that room, accepted Agrippa's kisses, kissed his own neck. A shapeshifter!

"Now we're even, Max."

He spun to spot her hovering in the black abyss.

Aleksandra!

She was gone.

OCTOBER 31, 1986 – 10:30 P.M. EASTERN STANDARD TIME
ALL HALLOWS' EVE

11 TOOTH

There is a moment—*the* moment—when death occurs. The veil between the Earth World and the Death World is thin to the point of nonexistence, and the soul crosses over. The Tibetans, the Mayans, and the alchemists, to name three, trained for that moment, so that in the rush from one World to the Next, the rush *of* one World to the Next, the adept would not succumb. The adept would enter the Death World on his own terms, alive in his soul, and become something like an angel—Timeless in the Dark. The Mayans called those who have done this Jaguars. The alchemists call them Men and Women in Black.

Had Val grabbed that moment?

That was the question that haunted Max in the bleak months after her death. It was not something he would have thought she could have done, considering her skills in wizardry, and he knew her better than anybody. But he understood that he hadn't known shit when he'd pulled something from deep inside him and beaten Aleksandra five years before. Wisdom and will. Val knew all she needed to know to do it, even if she didn't realize she knew it, and as Dr. Johnson once said, "The prospect of hanging concentrates the mind wonderfully." (When Max's monkey mind spit out that thought, he cringed.)

Would Val have done it? He thought she would, but he didn't *know*. His best efforts at necromancy were pretty pathetic back then, and the few friends of Agrippa's he'd met were no better. It was not a common skill. But the Celts—the witches, the druids—believed that the veil between the Earth World and the Death World grew thin on All Hallows' Eve. On that night, as the darkness of winter engulfed the living, the dead were as close as they would ever come. And so Max put himself in training for the next Hallowe'en, to see if he could contact her. To see what they could do next. He wanted her back, badly, but she would be living in a new way now. She would have adjusted no matter how it had gone, and she might not even want to return. But he would find her, to find out what she wanted. To bring her back if that was best, to help her if it wasn't.

If she were there.

If he could reach her.

• • •

He'd gone deep underground, cutting himself off from anything that could lead back to him. No credit card, no telephone card, no car registration, no bank account, no San Francisco. He paid cash to rent small houses in medium-sized Southern cities, moved on no set schedule, and worked day and night to prepare himself for October 31. Agrippa had said that alchemists, unlike wizards, didn't have long-term plans, but he had one now. And it was shaping him into an alchemist such as the world had never seen.

As Hallowe'en neared, he rented the empty split-ranch house in Louisville where Val had lived as a girl. He wanted to make it easy for her; if she were trying to reach across from the other side, this would be her first attempt, too. He could have used Agrippa's house, or their house, but both of those had been subjected to Aleksandra's evil. His instincts were telling him her first home was best.

The old house was silent as he entered in the late afternoon. Outside, the humidity turned the sunlight ruddy, so it streamed through the blinds in red rectangles. White dust danced in it.

He raised his left hand, held it palm-outward near his right shoulder. The scar on his thumb was a pale line in the gloom. Then he swept his hand in an arc from right to left, as if wiping it across an invisible sheet of glass, and peered closely through the area he'd "cleaned." Satisfied that no trap awaited him, that Aleksandra hadn't found him, he began to search the house.

From Val's descriptions over the years, Max reached her old bedroom easily. There was a metal bed frame with no mattress now, and a chest of drawers. Empty. Occasional paper triangles on the wall showed where taped posters had been torn down. Other people had lived there after she'd gone, but still, he felt her here, close by.

The Mayan day was 11 Tooth—Owning Cohesion. It was a good day to bring them back together.

There were other places in the house she'd told him about. She'd loved to lie in the sun streaming in through the huge front window. She'd loved the back porch, where she used to sing. He'd have had to conjure cover all around the building even if it weren't Hallowe'en, with kids and parents coming around. But cover is one of the simpler tasks for an alchemist, so by the time night fell on Kentucky, the house looked so deserted and dark that no one would even think of approaching it.

Inside, however, four grinning pumpkins threw their angular orange lights on the hardwood floor of the dining room. They marked out a twelve-foot diamond, with Max sitting quietly at the center. A large crystal ball rested on a low table before him. A ritual sword lay close to his right hand. The scent of burning nutmeg filled the air. He could have done much more, to protect himself from what might come tonight, but he didn't want any extra barriers between himself and Val. Which isn't to say he forgot about Aleksandra. Her approach would trigger alarms; she might startle him, but she could not completely surprise him tonight. He hoped she would come; he wanted to see her almost as badly as he wanted to see Val.

As the four flickering lights played through the glass sphere, a burning, golden glow he'd always felt in times of action, long before he'd learned the ways of magick, played through his mind. The four carved faces loomed and dwindled, and he let his glow meld with theirs, so that his mind was drawn down into that crystalline world. He passed through its surface, into its solidity; there was no air and yet he hovered. He existed in crystal. Lowering himself to the bottom, where the world curved up in all directions, he saw the world as an elongated distortion, stretching away. Distorted shadows hung in it, and he went among them, hunting.

It was familiar to him, more familiar than strange, though he'd never walked through glass before. Being a point man in Vietnam had shaped him for life; hunting was hunting, and he was good at it. He moved uphill, along the curve of the ball, and when he passed the hanging shadows he saw himself reflected dimly in the dark. The lights grew fewer, but eye-watering when he found them in the gloom . . . and suddenly, he felt Val run her hand along his cheek!

It was a lover's touch, that heightened sensitivity that he knew in his soul to be the essence of Valerie Drake August. He reached for her in crystal, and was drawn forward, up into the other world, back to his pumpkin lights. He willed himself with all his soul to be sure he was really feeling what he thought he was feeling, that it was really her and not a dream or a trick. Then he saw her, clearly, Val, standing in front of the huge front window. The light from Jupiter shone through the windowpane, and through her, and still she threw a faded shadow on the floor. She looked at him, so thrilled to be back, joy radiating from her face. He ran toward her. But it was too much, too soon. As he reached for her she evaporated, holding out her hands to him, her eyes screaming dismay. He called her name and the old house echoed with it. But she was gone.

She was gone, but he would find her. Every Hallowe'en for as long as it took, he would make himself stronger, force himself closer, just as he knew she would. And one Hallowe'en night they would take hold of each other through the veil, and they would keep hold, and their long nightmare would be over.

OCTOBER 31, 1991 - 9:30 P.M. GREENWICH MEAN TIME
ALL HALLOWS' EVE

4 FLINT KNIFE

He was standing in an Atlantic gale, in the center of Cobawnus-ne, an ancient stone circle on the Bodmin Moor, at the westernmost tip of England. The grassy expanse was seventy-eight feet from one end to the other, marked out by nineteen gray stones averaging four feet in height. A twentieth, twice as tall, trimmer, phallic, at a raised angle in the center, pointed toward the sunrise of Midsummer Day. Pagans were never subtle.

It had once been the main druid circle in England, but, England being England, he'd only had to hike in over the dark and desolate land, into the teeth of a thin but strengthening rain, to reach it. He was still thirty-five years old and the hike was refreshing. He had seen no one else and met no fences along the way. But when he finally came to the circle, he'd had to maneuver slowly and carefully through the thick halo of brambles and gorse that surrounded it, to reach the solitude within its ring. The Leo moon had been just visible, a gray shard setting in the gray mid-afternoon. There would be no light for All Hallows' Eve, which was also 4 Flint Knife—Encompassing the Unique.

After Louisville, he'd sifted toward Asia—"drifted, but with intent." He knew that any overt action on his part might set off some alarm, so he went with the flow so long as the flow went east. In Bangladesh, he let himself wash up against three men. One was Tashi Tsering, a Tibetan monk in the Dalai Lama's loose circle of advisors. The second was Dà Zhuàng, of the Shaolin Kung Fu monastery, and the third was Ricky Sing, a legendary street fighter. He studied with all three for two years, bracketing Hallowe'en in the shadow of Everest. When he was done he was a master of the *Book of the Dead*, and he had a bastard UFC style of mixed martial arts. He'd also brought the three men together as unlikely friends. The members of that cross-cultural trio had twice stood him in good stead since then.

He also began his deep immersion in the other systems of hidden knowledge, as he sifted back out into the world. Agrippa had specialized in Western magick, descended from the Jewish and Moslem masters, and Max's own energies had worked what his master knew, but now he devoured knowledge of asteroids, runes, and shamanism, of palmistry, color, and aromas, of the Knights Templar, the Holy Grail, and the Grays. He discovered a real feel for the Mayans. He also discovered a lot of mystic crap out there, a vast body of information that made no sense if you tried to actually work it, so clearly the writers hadn't worked it, they'd just wanted to get paid. That discovery led Max to work everything, to learn not just the letter but the spirit of the magicks, and in so doing, he discovered many, many things that had been lost over the centuries. Not just facts, but how the facts fit together. At first he had expanded his knowledge, ravenous for new systems to work. Then he had focused his knowledge, as he found that every system had the same truths at its core. Sages around the world and through the millennia had seen those truths in different ways, and each system was exquisite in its own way, but each system fit with every other system, and each system magnified all the others. The universe was coherent; it's the nature of a universe. So Max's wisdom and his will both grew, not just longer, but wider and deeper, too, and each Hallowe'en he made his way closer to Val.

Each year he'd chosen a new power spot that felt right to him. Last year he'd stood in the intersection of the Queen's Chamber Passage and the Grand Gallery, at the center of the Great Pyramid of Giza—a place they'd once been very happy together. Very distinctly, he had *sensed* her in the vast stillness of the carved-out stone, *smelled* her scent, *heard* her rustling movement. Finally, he had *seen* her, a beautiful, pure white translucent figure where there was no light at all. She smiled at him, her growing strength showing in her face where weariness had once been. Her lips moved as she spoke his name, but in all that silence he still could not hear her. Nevertheless, he said her name, as he reached his hand for hers. This time the touch was electric, the energy pulsing up his arm, and he could see she had the same reaction. He could *see* the connection from shoulder to shoulder. Their other hands reached out to complete the circuit. She wanted to bridge the gap just as much as he did. This was their year—

No! The energy climaxed and dimmed. Before their hands could touch she slipped back into darkness, her face showing almost comical frustration. Val was nothing if not feisty, no matter how long it had been.

The energy in the pyramid became absolutely still; nothing moved at all in that eternal stone. Maybe the solution this next year lay in having external energy to hand, to push them both along. So he walked out onto the Bodmin Moor, to stand on the open, flat, green land, in the fog and rain and wind of the Atlantic, where nothing was ever still. The ancient magick of England and the work of many druids through the centuries could well make Cobawnus-ne the place where he and Val would grab hold at last.

It was then, as the clouds above the heath let a momentary patch of starlight through, that he saw a figure walking his way. In the gloom it was hard to tell at first, but the figure resolved itself to female, visible above the gorse, coming down a gentle hillside. This was public land so it was not necessarily unexpected that another seeker would come to this sacred spot, but he could have wished it otherwise. Well, he thought, if it was a tourist, she wouldn't stay with a strange man, and if it were a witch, he'd share; it was a large circle. But if it were someone else . . . He wiped his left hand across his line of sight, and the nimbus of her hair, which should have been plastered to her head, blossomed with a lurid red light to outline the beautiful shape of her face.

In the moment of knowing, his fury almost overwhelmed him. He had the will; he had the knowledge; he hurled his power at her with everything he had. But she crouched on the hillside, raised her own hand in the evil-eye gesture, and gave it right back. As the wind whipped her raincoat around her, it blew open down the front, flew apart. She was naked. She was perfect! The most beautiful woman ever created, revealed in tantalizing glimpses by the whipping fabric and the flashing lights. Perfect breasts, perfect hips, perfect legs, perfect face, in that order—and she was proud of it. Max knew all of that too well. He felt it even now, even as he hated her more.

She raised her arms in a houri pose and a cloud of lightning swirled around them, above her lurid hair. The cloud grew, spitting fire like striking serpents. There were eyes in it. It loomed above Aleksandra as far as the horizon, dark and muttering.

It struck! A flash of scarlet lightning burnt the space between it and Max, driving for his life. Max took the blow, crashed to his knees, his face, but rolled over. It had been muffled, diffused. In that instant, Max and Aleksandra both knew the circle's power, added to his own, had saved him. He was still too weak to withstand the cloud otherwise. But he *was* in the circle. Max took that ancient stone power, that dark druid power, that deep witches' power, brought it into his fire-lion power, and threw back as good as he got.

His golden flame surged against her scarlet lightning, lighting the entire heath with their phosphorescent discordance. Below, a broad swath of grass was burned to a crisp, even as the rain poured down. Max refocused his fire and all the grass surrounding Aleksandra burst into flame, engulfing her. She snarled, waved her hand, and the rain around them grew stronger, becoming almost solid water, drowning the flames. A gesture and the plunging water became ice, pounding down on Max like a collapsing building. He flipped a palm over, hurled fire at the skies, and the storm over his circle ended, though ice continued to plummet outside it. But not where Aleksandra stood. She thrust her left arm forward, the fingers twisted like claws, and a crimson mist billowed in his direction. It crept across the blasted heath like blood from an artery, toward the nineteen standing stones. But when it arrived, its tendrils slithered away. The circle would have none of it. This was not friendly territory for her.

Aleksandra watched the mist dissipate . . . then lowered her hands gracefully, laying them along her hips. Her defenses were firmly in place around her but she was standing down. The raincoat fell back to hang vertically, leaving just one thin glimpse of her body. Max had to admit: one hell of a body. Which was interesting, because the last time he'd seen her looking like this, that body had rotted right before his eyes. That was a once-in-a-lifetime thing, a freak occurrence, as his battering tonight proved. He knew he'd been lucky both times. But he also knew, as an alchemist, that luck could be cultivated. He withdrew his own power, but stayed balanced on a wary knife-edge.

Aleksandra was watching him greedily, her thin brows intent over her blue-black eyes, her scarlet mouth smiling in pleasure. She looked exactly—no, she looked *better* than she had eleven years earlier, which was really hard to believe. The only word that fit was "perfect." The perfect woman.

But her voice, when she spoke, came from within something far larger than that perfect female form.

Hello, Max. You understand that I had to know what you've been doing with yourself.

She looked like a woman, but she was something more. Not too much of a surprise, since the woman had died. And if this woman could come back from the dead— He blocked that line of thought for now. "So now you know you can't take me, Aleksandra."

Call me Maddy, Max. It's what you used to call me, when you fucked me on my desk.

He remembered, but with the gut-wrenching clarity of a near-death experience. "I was young and stupid then."

You're still young and stupid. But now you're afraid. I've surrendered to your power, just as I always have, Max. A man would come out of that circle and face me.

"Good thing I'm more than a man, then."

But I haven't seen you in six years, Max. And you haven't seen me in eleven.

He gave her no satisfaction, saying flatly, "Either way, I've never forgotten you."

Who could? Even if I hadn't hugged poor Agrippa before my power killed him. Even if I hadn't hugged Val's throat with these very hands, and felt the small bones breaking, the eyeballs popping . . .

He was so close to Val on these All Hallows' Eves that the idea of Aleksandra strangling her almost drove him forward onto the bitch. It was only his long years of seasoning that made him remember he was an alchemist as well as a husband. An alchemist with a mission.

She laughed again, watching him flat-eyed like a cat.

But I haven't forgotten you, either, Max. We're just alike in that.

"We're nothing alike."

Oh yes we are. We both kill.

She slowly drew her hands apart, and the effect was of opening curtains: soft light spilled out, enough to illumine them both and paint harsh shadows on the stones. He weighed the light and found it benign, a simple glow, as she continued.

We kill because we have to, for our own personal higher cause, but it amounts to murder, just the same. You killed my people; I killed your people. You have no moral high ground, Max. We're equally guilty.

"Forget it," he scoffed. "Save the psy-ops for the rubes. I've seen you up close and personal, and I know the difference between you and me. You could be fronting for the Virgin Mary and you'd still be evil. I'm not evil. That's the difference."

That was then, Max. You've been through some changes in the past eleven years. You've moved deeper into the Magick. You've moved in my direction.

"And I told you over dinner at Ernie's, Allie, that I'm a point man. Early on in life, I went into the dark jungle full of unknown dangers on my own—and I not only survived out there, I prospered."

That was a sexy night, Max. It was wonderful.

"Not as wonderful as the last night we met wearing our own faces."

When you "destroyed" me? It felt good, didn't it? But I was already leaving humanity behind; you just expedited the process.

"As I recall, you didn't look happy about it."

I wasn't happy. It's a long leap. But I survived it. Here I am. And now I'm not human at all.

She cocked her head insinuatingly.

I walk the fringes of your world now, Max. Unseen, unfelt—now and then forgotten. It will be in one of those times you forget me, even if it's just for a moment, when I'll surprise you just as I surprised Agrippa and Valerie. And so another Timeless man will die.

He grinned at her, an utterly savage grin. "Never happen. You'd have crushed me if you could, but you couldn't. You'd crush me now. But I know you like no one else does."

Oh no . . .

"Oh yes! You went too far, Allie. Much too far. You can't get me when I forget you, because I never forget you now."

She laughed.

Well then, the devil with surprise. You have other vulnerabilities. For example—how did I find you here?

"I'm sure you'll tell me."

*And **I'm** sure you're already thinking, you'll pretend disinterest, but you'll rectify the error and make yourself even more secure. But no, Max, it's only this: I saw that you'd spend every Hallowe'en trying to find your lost little sheep, and there are only so many places you would go to do that. I have the people to watch those places. Your surreptitious entry of Giza fooled not only the guards but also my watcher last year, or I would have had you then, but this year you were seen. And I was called.*

"Sounds to me like I *can* rectify that error. Next year I'll do Hallowe'en at a Holiday Inn."

*You miss my point. Whatever you do, however strong and clever you are, humans inevitably make mistakes. It's human nature. You **will** slip, I **will** be there to catch you when you're down, end of story. We both have all the time we need for it.*

"Then why are you here?" Max snapped.

Meaning . . . ?

"Why track me down if I can't possibly win?"

To change your point of view.

"Meaning . . . ?"

To this point you've fought me, and you've lost

your wife and your mentor. It's time to take the other road. Join me and I guarantee that I will bring Val back to you, as good as new.

That struck home, but he kept his face still. "It's a great offer, Aleksandra," he said coolly, "but unfortunately, you have no credibility whatsoever."

*How can you be **sure**, Max?*

"Because you're *you*."

*But I'm not **just** me. I have another organization. We can always use a man like you, just as you can use our extensive resources. Think about it, baby. To this point you've devoted your life to enhancing the wizardry Agrippa taught you, and to finding Val. Well, what would you do if you had her back? If she were beside you every day and night, just like it used to be? I can make that happen.*

She threw her hands wide and the illumination on them was as bright as day.

*Then you'd have only one goal: enhancing the wizardry Agrippa taught you. Would you rather do that on your own, on the run, or would you rather live in comfort, in **splendor**, and help drive the fate of this planet with it?*

"Fuck—"

***Think** about it, I said. I know your quick answer: "No, never, I'm a point man." But you're going to be here a long time if things work out for you, Max. Decade after decade, century after century, possibly even millennium after millennium. You could live forever. Does it even make **sense** to wake up **every one** of those endless, endless, endless days in **conflict** with **the power that runs the world**?*

"Your Russians never did run the world, and they certainly don't now—"

The Russians were always a front.

"It doesn't matter. You killed Val and you killed Agrippa. There's no way in hell I'd work any way *but* against you!" He laughed again, and this time sardonically. "*You* don't want me working against you, and that tells me I most definitely want to spend the rest of my endless, endless, endless life on your ass!"

You could have that, too. Now I can be any woman you want.

"Fish or cut bait, bitch. You can take me or you can't, and if you can't, I've got people to see."

Val won't be coming back to you, Max.

"Yes or no?"

Well then, no. I'll leave you to it. But the offer stands, and time will change your mind.

"I," said Max, "am time-*less*."

She was gone. In the moment he could see the hole in the rain where she'd stood as it fell diagonally to earth. Then all light was gone.

• • •

That night, for the first time, he could not feel Val at all.

The dawn came. Still he felt nothing.

And he never had since.

OCTOBER 31, 2007 – 5:45 P.M. PACIFIC DAYLIGHT TIME

11 WIND

The Pacific sun was beginning to descend on San Francisco, throwing the eucalypti into deepening shadows, and the fog was threading its way through those shadows. Every Hallowe'en since that night in 1991, he had gone somewhere, done his best to find Val again, and every Hallowe'en he had come up empty. But he'd never had the first thought of stopping. He'd paid a heavy price to get this far, but by getting this far, he had to believe he was closer to the breakthrough, the ending. And he was still thirty-five years old, so he had plenty of time. He just didn't dance, and he didn't much smile.

This year he'd leased a house on Rockdale Drive, which dead-ended on the northern edge of Mount Davidson Park, the highest point in San Francisco. He had rectified his 1991 error and had never again gone anywhere Aleksandra might be looking. He chose the sites randomly, based entirely on his alchemical intuition—i.e., what felt right. He rented them at random points in the year. This house had no connection whatsoever to any of the places he'd lived the last time he'd been in this town. There were very good memories and very bad memories here, and the danger of recognition, but this year San Francisco felt right to him, so here he was, first time in twenty-two years.

His house had sweeping views when the fog was out—which was seldom—but for Max its prime attraction was the huge backyard bordering the park. There was no view of him as he came and went on the steep hillside, thanks to the huddled, shaggy old trees. He did things that required both nature and solitude—things that made him enemies over time—so he lived a careful life.

The house was protected by his alchemy and by state-of-the-art electronics; he lived in both worlds, and he planned to keep living in both. Man does not live by magick alone, nor does he want to; there are powers and pleasures in reality, too. The physical and metaphysical scans confirmed his identity and kept silent as he moved between the two trees that framed his back gate. Inside, his backyard was completely framed by evergreens, whose massive branches were singing softly in the wind. The grassy rectangle of the yard, landscaped to be flat, was open only to the sky, which was darkening as he watched. From the far front of the house he could hear children heading out on the street to get candy. Making use of his absolute privacy, he stripped off his well-worn jeans, running shoes, and tan flannel shirt, and laid them on the stone bench set beneath the oldest tree. Since San Francisco's long hot fall runs out just before Hallowe'en, it was going to be chilly here in the fog, but goose bumps were part of his chosen profession.

He stepped into a twelve-foot circle of small white stones, took a moment to adjust to the ancient world conjured within—a world that could be opened and closed anywhere he happened to be. He moved around the circle, apart from San Francisco now, lighting the four carved pumpkins. At the center of the circle was a cauldron over firewood waiting to be lit, with nutmeg incense to hand. Beyond the cauldron, to the north, was an altar decorated with local boughs and apples. There were three candles: black, the tallest, in the center; red to the left; and white to the right. When lit, their three flickering flames would add to the four pumpkins' light to filter through the large crystal ball at the center of the altar. He had adapted and expanded, and grown every day, since that first Hallowe'en in Louisville. He had become a pro.

He stood quietly in the white stone circle, breathing in the gathering gloom. . . .

Night fell, at last.

His iPhone rang.

11 WIND

It did not ring often. He could count on one hand the people who had the number, and they'd all been sworn to secrecy—secrecy he never doubted. A phone call had to mean something, and if Max knew anything, it was to pay attention to alchemical intuition. He offered his mental apologies to the world within his circle, thankful that he hadn't begun the ritual, then stepped out of it, into the chill and the wind. Padding quickly barefoot back over the grass, he thumbed the iPhone's face, then held it to his ear.

"Hello," he said tonelessly, into the dark.

"Barnaby?"

For the second time today, that single word threw him back in time. There was only one living person who could reach him and use that name. Uncharacteristically, he swallowed before responding. But—

"Hello, Fern," he said evenly. "How are you tonight?"

"Not so good. Barnaby . . . I need to see you." Her voice was old, thin, reedy—barely living. He hadn't heard it in six years, and the years evidently had not been kind.

"I can't make it tonight, Fern. How about tomorrow?"

"Sooner is better."

He nodded in the dark. Something was definitely happening. "I'll be there in an hour."

Now it was her turn to be surprised. "You're in the Bay Area?"

"Yes, I am. Rest easy, Fern."

He put his clothes on again, thinking it over. He was doing something he'd never, ever contemplated—shutting down his search for Val on Hallowe'en—but why *was* he here, in the Bay Area, of all places? If he'd been on the other side of the world, he wouldn't have been able to respond to Fern, and that would have been that. But because he felt like returning to San Francisco for the first time in two decades, he was perfectly in place, and you didn't have to be an alchemist to think that wasn't just blind chance. *This* was the path he needed to follow this Hallowe'en. Wherever it took him, it was some sort of progress after years of utter standstill, and he would follow it gladly.

He trotted across the grass to the garage and slid into his leased Brera. From its console he opened the garage door onto Rockdale. Quickly but cautiously, he drove out onto the narrow street, which was filled with small children wearing costumes of witchcraft and monster, dragging their parents from house to house. He waved at them as he made sure not to hit them, and they waved happily back. Since he hadn't planned on answering the door this evening anyway, he'd already set a huge bowl of candy on the front porch.

He cued up his traditional Hallowe'en collection of medieval rock by Steeleye Span and, to the sound of Maddy Prior's dark minor keys, punched the Brera down the hills toward the witchfires of the bay. He would have laid good odds he would never come back to this house.

11 WIND

There were even more angels and vampires prowling Fern's middle-class streets. With all the parents home for supervision, Max had to park two blocks away, but he jogged back through the throngs, dancing around tiny Shreks, and when he reached Fern's house he rang the bell with a sharp push.

The response was slow in coming, but eventually a middle-aged Filipina nurse answered the door and looked him over. She was unimpressed, but that was probably true with everything she encountered. "Mr. Wilde?" she asked suspiciously.

"Close enough," he said shortly.

"Eh?"

He didn't have time for this, so he smiled at her, her BFF. "Yes, I'm Mr. Wilde."

She responded as he knew she would, softening her manner to match his. "Mrs. Jenkins is very weak. She's eighty-seven, you know, and I'm afraid she doesn't have much time left. She's insistent on seeing you, but please make it brief."

"I understand."

The nurse led him through the house, along the traversable paths that cut through cluttered rooms where the smells of old paper and old age hung. It was all too evident that no one lived in these rooms any longer. The lights along the way were low and yellow, throwing brown shadows flecked with dust stirred by their passage.

In the back bedroom lay Fern Jenkins, impossibly small, in an adjustable bed configured to raise her head slightly. The head had shockingly little hair, and what there was of it was stringy. Her face was gaunt, her lips shrunken from yellow teeth, her cheeks molded to her skull with skin pale as wax. And yet her eyes were sharp.

"That's good, Cortesia," she told the nurse. "Go away."

"I don't believe—"

"I don't care what you believe. I'm the one that's dying. Please leave us alone."

Reluctantly, the nurse withdrew. "Please make it brief," she repeated in an aggrieved whisper. Max closed the door behind her, then turned back.

He raised his left hand and made his wiping motion, cleaning the space between himself and his old friend. Only then did he approach her. "Hello, Fern," he said with genuine affection, and it surprised him. It made him realize how long he'd gone without feeling that sort of thing.

"Hello, Barnaby," Fern said. "I guess you weren't lying about living forever."

"I'd never lie to you, Fern."

"I know that, but I'm glad to see it with my own two eyes—while I can." She looked him over, and he could see it was an effort that cost her. At last, she said simply, "You have changed, though."

"Have I?"

"You had a hard shell before—a young man on the prowl. Now you're harder on the inside. Is that what magic does to a person?"

"In my case, yes."

"Maybe living forever's not so great."

"You could be right."

She wheezed, and a small dribble slid down the side of her jaw. "I'm just going to talk, okay?"

"Sure."

"You remember how we met. You came over and drank beer with Earl, even though he was so much older than you."

"Earl was one of the grand old men of radio, Fern. I took radio seriously, so I respected his place in it."

"We met—" Her voice cracked but she forged ahead. "We met, and not too long after, you got mixed up with Russian spies, and you got changed. Remember when Russians were the awfulest thing in the world?"

"I remember."

"Those spies killed Earl, and pret' near killed me. My blood was almost fried." For a moment he thought she'd used all her strength saying that much, but she picked up the thread after slowly filling her lungs. How long did she have left? "The doctors had never seen anything like it—the regular doctors. Then some new ones came from the CDC. They seemed to know something about it all, and they thought I should have died, like Earl. But since I didn't, they studied me. Every six months since that terrible night, I've gone in for tests." She raised her withered hand a few inches off the bed and studied it; Max imagined she'd had needles in its blue veins many times.

"After ten years, they decided I had permanently damaged blood, but not so damaged that I wouldn't live my full life, and it looks like they were right. Eighty-seven's a full life, I guess—though it seems like only yesterday . . ." She wiped her mouth with that trembling hand. "Anyway, the CDC doctors went back to whatever secret stuff they usually do, and they handed me off to another lab in Berkeley. Since then a series of young doctors has kept tabs on me. The latest, for the past two years, is Pam—Pamela Blackwell—Doctor Pamela Blackwell."

"I'm with you."

She gestured at a glass atop a bedside table. "Could I have a drink of water, please?"

"Of course." He held the straw in her glass to her thin lips and helped her drink. It took a while. When she was satisfied, she lowered her head to the pillow.

"This afternoon I got a call from a friend of Pam's. She said Pam had had an accident and wouldn't be able to see me today, even though Pam knows I'm about done for. She usually comes to see me every two weeks, and this week she's been coming every day. But the friend said she was just going through Pam's appointment book; Pam . . . wasn't conscious." An incipient sob caught in her throat; she turned her head to the wall, embarrassed at the naked emotion. But there was no artifice left in her, no social niceties. Doing what she had to do took all she had left.

"I like Pam—she's been very sweet—so I called the hospital—Pam's friend said she was at Alta Bates, over in Berkeley. I've been in there so many times, I know a lot of the people there real well, and I talked with a nurse I know. She said Pam seems to have been poisoned." Fern rolled her head back toward Max, the tendons in her neck quivering. "But nobody can figure out what the poison was. She said it was like Pam had been . . . struck down by magic. That's when I thought of you."

Max studied her. Her eyes were rheumy, but they were steady on him, saying what words wouldn't.

"Sure, Fern," he said. "I'll see what I can do."

"Thank you. I was worried. . . . Pam's been good to

me, Barnaby. She's very wise. She listens, and she cares. I wanted to help her, if I could, while I was still able. . . ."

"You have, Fern. Just describe her for me so I'll know who she is."

"Why? Somebody might impersonate her?"

"Stranger things have happened."

"Yes. Yessss—she looks kind of like Miriam Hopkins. Remember her?"

"Not the way you do, Fern. But I've got Turner Classic Movies. Blond—"

"Yes, but Pam's hair's cut that funny way they have today, so it always looks shaggy, raggedy. Like that Meg Ryan. She's got a really smart forehead—Pam, I mean. Big blue eyes that look right at a person. Pretty. Her mouth has got a little crook on one side, the left side, like she's always smiling. But she's usually smiling anyway. Except probably not now. Will that do?"

"That'll do fine. Now here's what you have to do for me: don't go anywhere until I tell you how I make out. Deal?"

"It's not really up to me, Barnaby."

"Oh, I think you can handle it. Deal, Fern?"

She smiled for the first time. "For you, Barnaby. Deal."

11 WIND

As he was driving across the Bay Bridge to get to the hospital, with community lights sparkling in all directions around the bay, Max's thoughts were inevitably drawn once again to the time when he'd been the area's AM King. It was like being the top manufacturer of buggy whips. Who could have imagined that what they had could be so big then and so gone now? Satellite radio was available, and FM was still viable; still, most folks bought an iPod. But back in the day, jocks picked from everything and strung it together with a purpose; the shuffle wasn't the same.

On impulse, he cut off Steeleye Span at the end of "Long Lankin," switched the Brera's sound system to AM, and punched 1390. That was the spot once held by KQBU, but his old station had switched to computerized rock, and then, over the years, to country, classical, soft rock, oldies, country again, rock of the '90s, Sinatra, smooth jazz, and finally wing nut talk. He hadn't been here for most of that, but he'd kept track in the trades. Right now some guy with a nuclear attitude was yammering on about witches (this being Hallowe'en) and their secret pacts with Hillary Clinton (this being any time). Max listened until he turned up Ashby Avenue. He liked knowing what hallucinations the bad guys had, but he was finally forced to slide some Chemical Brothers into the Blaupunkt to get back to reality.

Alta Bates hospital takes up a chunk of real estate on Ashby just above Telegraph, and Telegraph is the main drag headed for the UC campus, so now the people on the street were older, less costumed, and less tethered to reality than the little kids he'd seen earlier. That went with the guy on the radio. Nevertheless, Max parked the Brera on a side street rather than use the hospital's parking garage. He might want to leave in a hurry.

It was still half an hour till visiting hours ended so the front desk gave him Pam Blackwell's room number easily enough. They wanted to know his relationship to the patient but didn't question his assertion that he worked with her. The distinguished gentleman seated in the waiting room, on the other hand, listened to every word, and Max took note.

Up on the fourth floor, Dr. Blackwell had a private room, as befitted a sister member of the healing profession. The lights were low and the silence was broken only by the soft mews of a man in obvious pain around the next corridor.

Max entered softly. Pam Blackwell—it was definitely she—lay sleeping, vital signs monitored and emergency equipment at the ready. There isn't much medicine can do for poisoning after the initial treatment; it can only stand by for a crisis. By the looks of things, that crisis was not far off. Pam lay curled in a quasi-fetal position, her face once called "pretty" pinched, and her breathing coming in slow, irregular jerks. She was certainly not smiling, and her eyes were scrunched tight shut.

Nevertheless, he did not immediately approach her. He made his wiping gesture again. Only when he was satisfied did he move forward.

Her eyes flickered open. "Who are you?" she breathed, and gasped at the effort.

"A friend of Fern Jenkins," he answered evenly. "You're Pam Blackwell?"

"Yes." She tried to smile, but it was a death rictus. "You're a doctor?"

"In a way. I'm here to help. My name is Max."

"Whad'you mean . . . 'in a way'?" Suspicion flashed in her eyes. Max was impressed; she hadn't surrendered herself to the darkness, even though it was crowding close. Fern hadn't either, but Fern had been expecting it; this was a woman struck down in the prime of her life.

"I know a little about esoteric poisons," he said. "Fern says they haven't determined what yours is. Or have they?"

"No."

"Then let me take a look." When she continued to look dubious, he grew annoyed. "I'll only have to touch your hand."

"Psychic healing." She was trying to sound cynical but her breath caught in her throat, and she fought to get it out. "Well . . . you'd have to be . . . sicker than I am, to want . . . me now." She weakly held her hand out to him. It trembled.

He'd barely taken hold when her strength failed her and her body went limp. Her eyes fell shut and her hand was dead weight in his.

But there was a pulse.

Max concentrated on that pulse—concentrated everything in his own body. He felt the surge, surge, surge—the power of life passing through his hand, the march of Time—and he consciously surrounded it with his own energy. Sweat broke out on his forehead. This was not easy. It never was.

From the depths of her mind, Pam seemed to see things as in a dream—a bright, jagged fever dream. She knew her eyes were closed, on some level, and at the same time she saw a matrix surrounding her wrist—a golden sphere that also encompassed the man's hand. The sphere began to pulse in tune with her blood. The sphere began to grow, inspired by her blood, expanding like a balloon. The golden energy grew brighter, shinier. It encompassed their arms, visible through its swirling haze. The scene was in her mind, she thought . . . and her mind was in the scene.

As the golden ball filled the room, the room slowly dissolved. It was like fog burning away, to reveal a detailed background that seemed to burn with an inner fire—as if the background were somehow *more real* than what it replaced. It formed a chamber of tan stone walls, marked with Egyptian hieroglyphs whose colors were very *fresh*. The pyramidal ceiling rose to a golden point directly above her, but *through* the ceiling she could see stars burning brilliant patterns in a black desert sky. The patterns were clear to her, the connecting lines unmistakable, *saying* . . . something. Through the night, through the walls, the wind carried the scent of sandalwood and cedar. Unknown women called to each other, somewhere across the sands.

She lay curled on a pallet of reeds, hovering at the height she'd occupied when she'd been in a hospital bed in Berkeley, California. At her feet, a human figure with the head of a jackal stood somberly, and at her head, looming high, stood a man with the oldest eyes she'd ever known. Between those two, back and forth, flowed energy so powerful it crackled in the air. But each waited silently for the third man in the chamber. The third man bore the golden headdress of a lion, and from her angle she could not see his face. He stood where Max had stood, with his elbows at his side, his forearms forward, his hands palm-down above Pam's body. He might have been blessing her, he might have been feeling her energy, but all Pam could think of was the pose of the eternal Sphinx.

With the thought came a sliver of knowledge she *knew* she didn't know. It wasn't from her subconscious, it was just *there*, a part of what she was experiencing in what she *knew* was her oblivion.

The Sphinx was Harmakhis, an aspect of Horus, the sun—"Horus on the horizon," who ruled each day's new dawn as his golden energy expanded to fill the world.

Harmakhis turned his head to the right to stare above her face at Imhotep, Egypt's greatest physician—so wonderful in his results that he'd achieved deification. His vitality filled the room.

Harmakhis turned his head to the left to stare above her feet at jackal-headed Anubis, lord of the dead. Anubis breathed, in time with Pam's pulse. His breath was slowing.

Then Harmakhis turned his bright lion's eyes on the woman before him, studying her face, her skull, her mind. He extended his gaze deep inside her body and watched the red blood pulse from her lungs, to her heart, and on through artery and vein, turning blue as it went, gathering impurities. It pulsed, it pulsed, it pulsed, surging back to the heart, and on to the lungs, and nowhere in the network of blood was there any source of death—any poison he could recognize. But lying in her left side, below the ribs, was a jagged dart of midnight blue. The dart, like the room, like his mind, was pure energy; it was a bitter magick that occupied no space in the physical world, so no physical device could detect it. As

Harmakhis watched, it twitched forward a millimeter, upward, straining toward her laboring heart.

His eyes narrowed. The golden light around him grew deeper, like old gold. His head began to radiate in its own light, flinging deep shadows off Anubis and Imhotep into the Egyptian night. The gold washed deep into the minute blue light, dimming it, blinding it, but not quite obliterating it. For the first time, Harmakhis-of-the-dawn spoke, in a voice that vibrated through his own body, and hers, and those of the gods, and the room and world beyond. She couldn't understand it, or even follow it; it wasn't in English, and was never meant to be heard by human ears. For that matter, it wasn't meant to be spoken by a human larynx; it was far older than even an Egyptian god. But the vibrations were pure in his throat and the knowledge behind them was focused—

Suddenly, Pam felt all her pain wash away, like a wave sliding out to sea leaving wide, sun-warmed sand. She gasped, in stark relief at the end of the pain, and she was overwhelmed, savoring the gasp, drawing it on and on, because it was pain-free. At last her lungs could hold no more, and she opened her eyes to the world around her, and there was just a man in her hospital room. His face was flushed.

"What—did you do?" she managed to choke out.

"What I do," he said, and the pure English words sounded strange to her. Maybe to him, too. "Is there any pain at all?"

"No. None." She was bursting with energy now, as if she'd downed five Red Bulls. Her training told her it was illusory, just the reaction to the change in her, but what had caused the change?

For the first time she focused on the man with her,

forcing her training to work. His face had become cool, distant, impersonal. She thought of the doctors she knew who had that look. No bedside manner. But that didn't matter if you could heal.

"Was there something to do with Egypt?" she asked him, tentatively.

He shrugged. "I'm into Egypt."

Screw tentative. "Who *are* you?"

He studied her. Considered. And seemed to smile at his conclusion. "I don't usually answer that question, Dr. Blackwell," he said. "But my name is Max August."

"Why don't you answer it?" she demanded.

"Because what I do gets people talking, and I don't want them talking about *me*."

"Aren't you afraid I'll talk?"

"In your case, it can't be helped."

"Why? And what did you do to me?"

"I'll get to that," he said. "In a minute. First, tell me when and where you were when the pain first hit you."

But she sat up, feeling her side and still marveling at the lack of pain in her body. Uncontorted, it was a very nice body, as Max now saw. "Are you kidding?" she demanded. "Do you know I'm an epidemiologist?"

"I would have guessed something like that, from your work with Fern."

"Well, finding cures for rare diseases is what I do. You have to tell me right now how you did 'what you do,' Max August."

"After you tell me what happened to you, Pam Blackwell."

Pam's mouth tightened with stubbornness, but she saw the same stubbornness in him, and after a moment, with the practicality of a researcher, she decided to take the other path. "Fine. I was working at home this morning, dotting the i's and crossing the t's on my latest project. All the wretched paperwork after the fun is over. Ordinarily, I'd have been at the lab."

"Fern told me."

"Well, I got a package from the lab. It came by one of our messengers."

"Is that unusual?"

"Sort of, but I don't usually work out of my home so the whole situation was unusual."

"Go on."

"Well, I opened the package to see what it was. There was no sender listed, so I had no idea. And there was a terrible *flash*! I thought the package had exploded, and at the same time I felt a sharp pain hit me here, in my side below the ribs." She pulled the hospital gown away to examine her side with the frank unconcern of a doctor, scientifically revealing a tight waist and lush hip. Max, as he'd said, was not a doctor, so he was good with the view if she was. She used her fingertips to feel her flesh centimeter by centimeter, continuing, "This was all in the split second I was passing out. I remember thinking I was dead. But after some period of complete unconsciousness, I came to, just barely. I was weak, nauseated, in a lot of pain—but I saw that the package had *not* exploded. It was intact. I wouldn't have noticed anything right then, except that both the package and I were right down on floor level. It was in front of me as I crawled my way to the phone. I managed to dial 911. . . ." She finished her examination. "I don't see any mark, or feel anything unusual."

"Uh-huh."

She calmly dropped the gown back into place. "Well, when I came to again, I was here, in the hospital, and they told me I'd been poisoned. But they seemed very . . .

uneasy. I tried to talk to them doctor to doctor, but I couldn't keep up my end of it. I just asked them to call my friend Phyllis, and ask her to cancel my appointments. But I felt as if I were going to die."

"Did this package look normal to you? Like other packages from the lab?"

"Yes. Sure. It had a standard routing slip. But again, I haven't had that many."

"What were its dimensions?"

"Um . . . like several paperback books. Six, seven inches long, four or five high. I thought it was notes from one of my lab partners' work. Now can we get to what was really wrong with me?"

Max considered her again. As if she were a lab specimen, and she didn't like it. He said, "I'm willing to do that, Doctor. But you'll have to put your scientific mind in neutral while I'm doing it."

She cocked her head, eyes narrowing. "This is going to be a fantasy?"

"My answer's no, but you can make your own decision."

She sat silently for a moment, mulling it over, but really, what was she going to say? As Fern had said, her blue eyes were wise. So she lifted her right hand and dropped an imaginary stick shift out of gear. "Talk to me, then," she said. "I'm listening."

Max said, "Once upon a time, I was just a normal guy, a disc jockey on KQBU, and I got caught in a situation involving Russian spies. They were using some techniques that had been developed in the depths of the Cold War, when both they and we were looking for any advantage. Their techniques involved telepathy and telekinesis—what you might call low-level magick. 'Magick' with a 'k,' to distinguish it from parlor tricks.

This magick had been quantified in a Siberian lab with the wonderful name of Academgorodok, which means 'Science City.' "

"I'm still in neutral," Pam said clearly, "but I'm looking at reverse."

"I don't blame you, but I didn't name it, and it's all verifiable. Anyway, some bad guys who could actually do this low-level magick were in San Francisco, and I got in their way. But it turned out they had an enemy, too, and he not only saved my ass, he could do even better magick. He started teaching me what he knew. I happened to have a head for it, and after we busted the spies I kept at it. And once I'd added his magick to whatever other skills I had, I thought maybe I should try to make this world a better place, for want of a better expression." He rubbed his jaw, tired now, coming down. "I've been doing it for a while now. Usually I find trouble on my own, but Fern's an old friend."

Pam thought he looked sane—very down-to-earth, in fact. If he was nuts he was hiding it well, though that, she knew, proved absolutely nothing. All she could say for sure was that the pain and nausea were gone. So all she said was, "A spooky story for Hallowe'en."

"Yeah, and it's not over. I found a twist of magick in your side—kind of like a dart. You can't feel it or see an entrance wound because it's composed of pure energy. It was fired into you by what you took to be an explosion."

She started to say, "I saw that," but decided that was giving away too much. Instead she said, "A dart of energy—magickal energy. That I can't see."

"Exactly."

"Now how am I supposed to verify that?" she demanded.

"By how you feel," he said.

"You could have slipped me a drug to make me feel better."

"By what you saw, then."

Pam was getting frustrated, and angry. Everything in her life thus far was rebelling as his story hemmed her in. "How do you know what I saw? And *whatever* I saw, that could have been from a drug, too!"

Max just shook his head, quiet and composed. "You saw Anubis, Lord of Death, at your feet, and Imhotep, Lord of Health, at your head. You saw Harmakhis, Lord of Light. And, Pam—you saw the dart."

"Then it was *hypnosis*!"

"What about the package that blew up but didn't blow up? What about the result that made your professional brethren decide you were going to die?"

"Listen to me! I don't believe in magick!"

"No, you listen to *me*. The reason I don't want people talking about me is that pretty soon they'd be demanding I prove myself—prove something unscientific scientifically. Just like this. And it really can't be done. So either I'm crazy or I'm the sanest man on the planet, and you can't tell either way. So I do what I do and I walk away, leaving people to think whatever the hell they want. I *really don't care*—ordinarily. But this time I can't do that. And why? Because you didn't see me take the dart out of your side. Because I can't. And that dart is still trying to complete the spell that will drive it up to your heart and kill you."

Pam flinched; the memory of the pain washed back over her like a black tide. She took refuge in the pretense of a professional consultation—an exercise in dispassionate logic—but her voice was unsteady. "Why can't you remove it?"

"Only the person who sent it against you can do that. All I can do is hold it at bay, for a while. The spell is extremely powerful, from the Renaissance, and my counterspell will fade in time. At that point I'll have to renew it. So you and I have to stay together and find the person who hexed you, to undo his spell."

He brusquely chopped the air with his hand. "Apply your logic to this: if I had designs on your tender body, why would I go to all this trouble? Bombs, hospitals, a story you naturally disbelieve; I could have just bought you a drink in some bar. The odds are I'm telling you the truth, but you're not gonna know that for a while. Meanwhile, you have to get out of that bed and come with me now if you want to survive."

"Goddammit!" Pam exploded. "I'm not going to just run off with you!"

"Then get a second opinion. Call Fern."

"That's a good idea," she said, then backtracked. "Wait. She's dying. You knew that."

"Call her and find out."

"All right, I will!" She swung her legs over the side of the bed, this time making sure to keep her legs covered, and reached for the phone. She kept her eyes on Max while dialing the number by heart and wishing she were half as wise as people thought she was. *Could it possibly—?*

The nurse answered, "Jenkins residence."

"Hello, Cortesia. This is Dr. Blackwell. Could I speak with Mrs. Jenkins, please?"

"I'm sorry, Doctor. She's asleep."

Goddammit! thought Pam, near the end of her rope. But she forced her voice to stay level. "Will she be awake soon?"

"She sleeps in fits and starts. She's failing. I can't say."

Pam eyed Max. "Did a man come see her tonight? Midthirties, blond, tan flannel shirt?"

"Yes. A Mr. Wilde. Though I'm not sure if that's really his name."

"Really? Was Mrs. Jenkins happy to see him?"

"Oh yes. She called him in the first place. I told her she should save her strength, but you know how she is."

"Yes. All right." Pam gnawed her lip. "Thank you."

Pam hung up, and with that made up her mind. She really couldn't see why he would lie to her, but she really couldn't believe him, either. But she couldn't afford to be wrong (according to *him*). But she would keep her eye on him at all times, ready to react at the slightest wrong move. She had pepper spray.

"Okay, Max. I'll at least match the ante and stay for another card. Now go out in the hall while I get dressed."

OCTOBER 31 - 9:00 P.M. PDT
ALL HALLOWS' EVE

11 WIND

The distinguished gentleman who had sat in the hospital's waiting room had slipped away with no one noticing. He now stood at the end of a side hall where he could keep an eye on Pam's room. When he saw Max leave, he pulled back and took his cell phone from his pocket. He speed-dialed a number, but nothing appeared on the readout.

"The man's come out, Hanrahan," he said in a low tone, barely above a whisper. "Something's wrong."

OCTOBER 31 - 9:05 P.M. PDT
ALL HALLOWS' EVE

....

11 WIND

Five minutes later, Pam joined Max outside her room. She was wearing a navy blue turtleneck and gray cords. "I'll check myself out," she said, turning toward the nurses' station.

"Can't," said Max in a low tone, taking her arm.

"But I can't just walk out. They'll go crazy."

"There's no way around it. Here, don't make a big deal out of it, but have a look over my shoulder. See the guy at the corner of the hall?"

She raised her eyes. "He just stepped back."

"He was in the waiting room downstairs when I got here. We'll have to lose him, too."

"He's probably a cop. I *was* poisoned."

"Are you important enough for a cop to be detailed just for you?" he asked.

"I'm not important at all, outside of a lab," she had to admit. "So he's probably visiting someone else on this floor."

"Or he's the tooth fairy. Let's go." They started walking in the other direction, toward a cross corridor. As they turned the corner, Pam looked back and saw the man padding after them, and he saw her. He began to run. Max, his eyes on the hall ahead, snapped, "What's the nearest way out?"

"Stairway, in the next corridor."

By common consent they started to run as well, and Pam marveled again at how good she felt. Better than before she was attacked, and she'd been in great health then. As an epidemiologist it was her business to keep a watch on herself, and she was running flat out with no strain. Her endorphins must be peaking. If it was drugs, it was good drugs.

They slewed into another corridor. "Get ready!" Pam said. She grabbed him with her right hand and pulled open the door to a stairwell with her left. They pivoted inside, Pam darted down the steps, but Max spun back around.

"I'll meet you downstairs!"

"What?"

"Go!" He yanked the fire extinguisher off the wall.

She hesitated. Having thrown in with him she wasn't expecting him to leave—

The closing door flew open again. Max was swinging the extinguisher like a baseball bat, but the man wasn't coming in to meet it. Instead, he crouched in the doorway and snapped off a shot at Pam. The bullet struck the extinguisher and the sudden decompression ripped the container from Max's hands. It cartwheeled downward, spewing foam hard, and crushed the pursuer's foot, inches from Max's. The pain buckled the gunman's knees as he fired again, putting that bullet into the floor. Max reached into the doorway, grabbed him, and sent him flying headlong down the stairs, past a stunned Pam. The crack of his skull shattering marked his arrival on the landing below.

"What did you do?" she demanded, her voice too loud in the echoing stairwell.

"They already tried to kill you once. That gun wasn't bling. You figure it out."

She ran down the stairs, knelt quickly, and felt for the man's vital signs. There was nothing. She twisted her neck to look up at Max, her face a study in conflict. "Did you have to kill him?" she asked, but in a quieter voice.

Once again Max had the feeling he had a live one. Most people would have been riveted on the killing part, but she was already on to the whys and wherefores of it. He hurried down the steps, pocketed the gun.

"He's not a hit man, or he would've come through that door a lot more cautiously, but he's still a pro," he said. "If you didn't die from the dart, he was ready to kill you; they didn't think they'd need anyone better against a helpless woman. Let's go."

"You're going to leave him here?"

"Unless you want to have him stuffed."

"But what about the police?"

"You want to explain it to 'em?" He reached out his hand. "With a story you don't believe?"

She gave him a long look, seeking a final judgment. In the hallway above she could hear people gathering, gaining the courage to come through the door. She said distinctly, "Damn you!" and ran with him down the stairs.

No bedside manner.

11 WIND

"How did you do that so easily?" Pam demanded as Max wheeled the Brera through Berkeley's flat streets. Hallowe'en parties were in full swing on every block.

"Which part?" he asked.

"Killing that man."

"I was a point man in the war. I had my share of hand-to-hand, and I've learned a little since."

"You were a deejay, a magician, and a soldier," said Pam, still trying to fit this all together. "That's a lot of stuff."

"People have lives, go through changes."

"Sure, but that's all over the map."

"Why? I was a soldier through no fault of my own. I chose to be a deejay afterward. Then something new opened up, just as my kind of radio closed down. Life goes on. And what about you? You haven't always been a doctor."

"No, but I've done nothing half that glamorous so far. And what did you mean—?"

"Sorry," he said suddenly, braking for a yellow light. "But I want a look at that package you got. How do we get to your house?"

She took a look around, figuring out where they were. "You know where Avenida is?" She went on to describe the route and found him completely familiar with the twists and turns of the Berkeley Hills. They hurried onward past the Cal football stadium in Strawberry Canyon, then headed up the winding road to the heights. A small group of laughing goblins was partying in a glen to the side of the road, the pounding of Ghostface Killah rattling the trees.

As the Killah dropped behind them, Max asked thoughtfully, "Where would you be tonight, if you hadn't been attacked?"

"I don't know. One of the guys at the lab is throwing a party. Probably everybody else would be there, but I guess I would have called a guy I know and seen what he was up to. I like the people I work with but I don't like office parties all that much. If you let yourself go you'll never live it down, and if you stay buttoned up, what's the point of the party?"

"Is this guy you'd have called connected with your lab at all?"

"No."

"Then he doesn't figure in this."

"No," she said, "he doesn't figure." She was silent, thinking, then said slowly, "There was no magick in killing that guy."

"No," he agreed.

"So if you can do magick, why didn't you?"

"It's mental energy powered by will," he said. "It takes time to concentrate the power, and we had no time, so I handled it physically."

"What sort of energy?" she asked.

"You don't want to know much, do you?"

"Do I? I don't know. That's why I'm asking."

Uplit by the dashboard in the dark, he nodded wryly. "Yeah, okay, sure. I'll give you the answer, Doc. What you do with it is up to you." He downshifted for the final surge to the top of the hill.

"Here's the money quote: everything is energy. Science tells you that. Everything that looks solid is *really* made up of molecules, which are *really* made up of atoms, which are *really* made up of protons, neutrons, and electrons, which are *really* made up of quarks and leptons, which are *really* probabilities in the flow of pure energy. And for every probability there's an *anti*probability, so there's a complete range of *anti*matter particles, up to a complete *anti*matter universe as well. That's just standard science, circa now, right?"

"I haven't heard it put quite so baldly, but yes."

"Magick is like touching the energy directly—bypassing all those masks it wears. The pure energy that's the basis of everything puts on a mask, and then another, and then another, until finally, we, who are made up of those masks ourselves, can only see those masks around us. But underneath it all is something that *we really are*, and magick is finding the connection to that, strengthening the connection, and finally using the connection."

"Using it how?"

"Energy flows. We see its tides in the cycles of women, of the year, of history. We're part of it, but a minute part, so no one controls it. It flows where it wants to flow, and if we're just driftwood on the tide, we go where it goes. But a magician is conscious of the energy, and a magician can swim, so he can at least have some control over the ride he's getting. And at most, since he and the energy are truly the same, his will has some influence over where the energy decides to go."

She studied his face in the dim light. "The way I learned it in Sunday school," she said slowly, "that boils down to saying you pray to God, and sometimes He grants miracles."

"Magick's a little more direct, but yeah. Just remember that God lets both good and bad things happen to good people. The guy who put some energy under your ribs gets his power from the same energy I do."

"Isn't there black magick versus white magick?"

"Magick's magick. It's all one—that's what I'm telling you."

"Well, it sounds simple enough when you say it. Then I start thinking about it. . . ." She bobbed her head in annoyance, but her eyes showed he had caught her interest.

They drove past the Lawrence Hall of Science, perched on a plateau above the lights of Berkeley and the bay, and famous for playing a "science institute" in a dozen science-fiction movies, most recently Ang Lee's *Hulk*. (*"Academgorodok"* in *The Max August Story*? Pam wondered.) They turned left onto Grizzly Peak, which wound along the crest of the hills past homes with million-dollar views. There were no sidewalks here and few trick-or-treaters. They drove past a house Max had once owned, but he was no longer thinking about the old days. This was now.

Pam broke what had become a lengthy silence. "You mentioned the tides of the year. Does what's happened to me have anything to do with it being Hallowe'en?"

"It's a powerful night, but the spell worked on you is good any time."

"Powerful how?"

"All Hallows' Evening is all about death. Not a good time to get poisoned by magick, but as you can see, people don't die just because it's Hallowe'en."

"No, they die because they get thrown down the stairs," she said sarcastically. "But if Hallowe'en's about death, why do we send our kids out, sometimes alone, to gather up candy?"

"Because for most people, death is scary but inevitable, so we have to deal with it somehow. The human way to do that is to have fun with being scared; spit in its eye and party."

He turned downhill again onto Avenida, and followed the heavily shadowed streets at odd angles away from city lights. "Hallowe'en's kind of a rowdy wake, if you're looking backward. If you're looking forward, though, it's the beginning of the New Year for the Celts, the people we got fairies and witches from. Like most early peoples, the Celts began their days at sunset, but only the Celts began their year at the sunset of life. They started when life turned irretrievably cold and hard so they would have better times ahead, as the year unfolded. 'Now the strong must live through Darkness until the Light returns,' they said. It was a hell of a ballsy thing to do, facing the darkness squarely, but they got a better New Year's Eve party out of it. Better than any I've known."

He gave her an oblique look in the light from the dash. "We tend to think that people are born and sometime later they die. The Celts thought people died and sometime later they were born. We're both right."

"You know that for sure, Max?"

"Yeah, I do."

"So do you believe the dead exist?" she persisted. "You believe you can commune with them?"

"That's what I'd be doing right now if Fern hadn't called," he said, his tone suddenly sharp and final.

11 WIND

Pam's home was a neat brown shingle down one of the several canyons, backed up against a hillside of California live oak. It was a smaller, more rustic version of Max's house and the park behind it, across the bay; the trees that surrounded her house gave her even more privacy (but the winding road out front offered a much worse chance of escape if needed). He pulled the Brera to a stop on the steep hillside and got out, breathing the crisp, cool night air. The trick-or-treaters were done around here. There was almost perfect silence, marred only by the faraway, fragmentary murmurs of Berkeley below, and the occasional owl. High above the treetops Pisces burned in a pitch-black sky.

Pam led the way along redwood steps to her front door, but stood back when she actually reached it. Max easily took the lead and held out his hand for her key. She handed the ring over. Once more he *felt* what lay before him, inside the house, before opening the door. He felt emptiness. So he led them inside, and locked the door behind them.

Pam gave a small grunt, like a woman taking a tap in the belly. She stared at the package, which lay, still half unwrapped, in the corner of the room. Ripples in her entryway rug showed where the paramedics had wheeled her away and inadvertently kicked the package aside. Max held up a hand, keeping her back, and moved toward it with—Pam couldn't help but notice—easy grace. How could he be so cool, especially if he were right?

She wondered if she'd spent too much time in a lab; she really couldn't get a handle on this man at all.

He sat on his haunches before the package, holding his hand above it. *Could it be about to explode again?* Pam suddenly thought. Her rational mind tried to tell her that that was impossible, a mere fantasy born of remembered panic, but her rational mind also reminded her it had no answer for why it had exploded the first time—or why it *hadn't* exploded, since it still looked intact underneath its loose brown paper. All she knew was that she was walking backward, putting distance between it and herself, and to hell with knowing anything right now. Her shoulders banged up against the locked front door.

But Max seemed satisfied with his examination, and reached out to pick the package up. He hefted it, judging its weight—then turned it over and let something fall to the rug with a dull thud.

"What is it?" Pam asked, craning forward from the doorway.

"A talisman," he answered slowly. "Made of silver. This is what caused that dart in your side." He picked the piece up and turned it back and forth. It was about the size of an orange and shaped like one: planes of silver met at angles in the center to form something essentially spherical. Each plane was etched with arcane symbols and words in meticulous Latin, all the way into the center. "Fourteenth-century. At least, the design is." He held it closer to his face, studying it.

"For God's sake, be careful!" Pam snapped.

"Don't worry. It's done its work," Max said. But he continued to examine it, and his face grew grave. "This is odd, though."

"What?"

"It's never been touched by human hands."

"You're really beginning to creep me out, Max!" she exploded. But a new thought struck her. "Wait a minute! The delivery boy was human."

"He didn't handle the talisman; only the package."

"Okay, fine." She was beginning to feel ashamed for having backed away, in the face of his confidence. "But since I'm just an ignorant know-nothing, I can come up with a dozen explanations. Trained animals. Robots. Teleportation. Ghosts. Time travel . . ."

"I'd sense all of the above except the robots, and this attack is magickal, not mechanical."

She grimaced, then gingerly moved forward, to get a better view. "That thing's never been handled by humans—since the fourteenth century?"

"The design is fourteenth-century, but it was created in the past month. Created, packaged, but without any trace of the creator. And the creation of a talisman like this is no cinch; it requires a lot of patient work, at specified, separated hours of the day, over fourteen days from new moon to full moon. Look—the etchings down where the planes of silver meet are as clear as those near the outer edges. Could human hands do that?" He dropped the talisman back in the box, then stood up and faced her, setting the box on the entryway table. "Let's come at this another way, Pam: why were you attacked?"

"I've been trying to figure that out, and I have no idea. I'm an epidemiologist, studying *physical*, *real* threats to human life, like Fern's damaged blood cells."

"Fern's damage was magickal."

Pam was startled. "Really? Maybe I should have consulted you a long time ago. That would explain . . ." She shook her head. "But if that's the case, I should have been attacked a long time ago, or my predecessors before me. We've had her under observation for over twenty years and this never happened before."

"True. What else do you do?"

"That's it for work. I take a salsa dance class, I like calligraphy—"

"Stay with the work. No other epidemiology studies?"

"Sure, all kinds, but nothing worth killing me for. I made a small contribution to the vaccine for mad cow disease, I just finished developing an antidote for tetrodotoxin—that's what I was finishing up this morning—and I've been pitching in on the West Nile virus. Oh, and peer-reviewing one of my colleagues' work on Ebola."

"Tetrodotoxin," Max said. "What's that?"

"Something you don't know." She smiled; she realized with a sort of shock that she was beginning to get comfortable, back in her own house. For the first time, she had the conversational edge, and she unconsciously straightened her shoulders. "Usually when I expound on my work I can shut down a conversation in nothing flat. Attend: Tetrodotoxin is a poison carried by the fish order *tetraodontidæ*, meaning 'four-toothed.' That's fugu, or puffer fish to you. They're—"

"No shit," said Max softly.

"Stop interrupting; it's my turn. Fugu are found around coral reefs in the tropics, where they're dangerous to swimmers. Tetrodotoxin kills by blocking the voltage-sensitive sodium channels of excitable tissues; nerve impulses don't pass and the result is paralysis and death. We already knew that the fugu don't make the tetrodotoxin themselves; it's generated by bacteria that live inside the fish. Fugu grown in the lab don't produce tetrodotoxin until they're fed tissues from a fish that does produce it. But the fugu have developed a mutation that protects them from this effect." She looked him the eye. "I'm sorry this is all far away from your 'magickal energy.' I know I'm dealing with 'masks' . . . good old fish you can hold in your hand . . ."

"No, you're doing great."

"Well . . . thanks." Most outsiders got bored quick. "So—there were two ways to go: study the fugu's protective mutation, or, since there have been tremendous strides in the knowledge of genetics, take a fresh look at the bacteria. That's what I did. And I found a way to neutralize the poison they create. Anyway, I wasn't poisoned with tetradotoxin. So unless there are mad fish menacers out there, nobody's after me for that."

"Lady," said Max, "you don't know how right you are."

"What?"

"Your research is on your computer here?"

"Here, and at the lab."

"Show me."

Puzzled, Pam stared at him; then sighed and led him through the little house into her study, a spare bedroom lined with bookshelves. More books lay in piles on the floor, in a rough semicircle around a desk with a standard-issue Dell. The computer and a floor lamp beside the desk were still on from earlier in the day, since the room's one window was covered by a blind. A cup nestled in a heating unit, its contents gone but still scenting the air with coffee. Before the desk sat a comfortable old office chair, and several framed Ansel Adams prints hung on the walls. "Excuse the mess," she said.

"No, I like a mind like this."

"Like what?"

"Busy, and too focused to take the time to clean up."

"Ha. Whenever I finish a project I put everything away, and it's very nice to have a clean room when I do. But in the middle of things I never know what I want, and I don't want to take the time." Still, she was pleased to get the compliment. She hadn't had many ego-boosters today. She sat down in her chair and palmed the mouse; moved it back and forth to get rid of the swimming-fish screen saver; double-clicked a folder in the center of the screen. The folder opened.

It was empty.

"This is no good!" Pam said sharply. "I had everything here! Where is it?"

"First things first," Max said. He knelt beside the PC and unplugged the computer's DSL line.

"Why'd you do that?"

"Your computer could've been wiped by hand, but it's more likely to have been wiped through the Internet, with a worm. Disconnecting you from the Internet is locking the barn door after the horse is gone, but at least it *is* locked now."

"They erased my data on tetradotoxin? But *why*?" Pam's voice rose shrilly; that comfort she'd felt in her home was long gone. "It's *fucking fish poison*!"

"Let me see if I can resurrect anything." He motioned her to get up and took her place in the chair. He restarted in DOS mode, and once he had the text screen he began typing furiously. "Windows is useless for security," he said.

"I have a personal firewall," Pam said defensively. "I have Vista."

"Doesn't matter. In their quest to run everything,

Microsoft left all the doors wide open so anything can connect, and that includes hackers. Despite all the critical updates they issue, they refuse to close the doors."

"What do you know about it?"

"I got into computers early and I keep up. Sorry it's all far away from my 'magick,' but I live in this world, too. Still, you'll be happy to hear that it's not my primary field, so I keep a hacker named Dave on the payroll, to watch my stuff and keep me up to date." He grunted. "Nothing here. Let me try something else. How long ago did you get to a point where someone watching you would say 'She knows too much about tetrodotoxin'?"

Pam was astounded to feel a shiver run up her back. "They've been watching me? I hadn't thought . . ." But this girlish innocence was beginning to annoy her; she was tougher than this, wasn't she? "Well, I'd say, a week ago? I mean, they could have been watching me moving in the right direction. But if you mean when I saw it, when it made sense across the board to me . . . eight days ago. No, nine. Nine days." She touched his arm. "Did they come into my house?"

"No need for that. They probably sent a worm through the Net to relay your keystrokes. Then all they had to do was read your notes. But it's significant that they had a talisman ready, and it takes longer than nine days to make. They were anticipating your figuring it out." He leaned toward the screen, put his chin on his thumb. "Here's something I don't recognize. An exe called 'FileRecordCount.' That's not part of the standard OS—"

Something thudded hard against the front door.

Max and Pam looked at each other. "Was that a knock?" she asked, not able to believe it but hoping. . . . He held his finger to his lips, and waited. They could see the front door at the end of the hall that led to this room. Something thudded against it again, even harder this time. And then again. It was being battered from the outside, mechanically, by something strong. It was beginning to give just a little. Pam's gaze was held by the door; she was astonished and yet not astonished. It seemed as if it was all sort of inevitable.

Max rolled his chair back, got up, and said in a low voice, "Is there a back way out?"

"Yes. A back door in the kitchen. But we'd have to go past *that* door!"

The front door began to crack under the relentless pounding.

"Out the window, then," Max whispered—just as a fist smashed through the glass. Shards of glass and wood flew in all directions, ripping the shade down the center. The fist and arm behind it hung motionless in the room, glass embedded deeply in waxen skin. No blood flowed.

The front door ripped from its frame.

A man came through the wreckage, or at least it looked like a man, at first. But the broken wood gouged his skin without apparent effect, and his eyes were dull and staring. Slowly, he stood up straight and rotated his head to rotate his gaze. The blank unblinking eyes pinned Pam and Max.

Behind them, another man unfolded his fist and put his hand on the jagged glass protruding from the bottom of the sill. A second hand joined it as he shifted his left leg through the opening and began to climb inside. He moved with deliberate, inexorable resolve.

"You've gotta be kidding me," muttered Pam, not even knowing she was speaking. "Are those—?"

"Zombis," said Max, watching intently.

"Goddammit!"

"Well put," he said evenly. "This is weird even for Berkeley. Stay right here but be ready to run if I say so."

The zombis closed in on both sides. The one coming in the window would be through in just a few seconds, and the one at the door was stalking up the hall. Max spun toward that one and thrust his palm at it. He tensed, focusing—golden energy flared like a bolt of heat lightning, and hurled the zombi backward to tumble into the broken doorway.

The other zombi caught its foot on the jagged windowsill and fell face-first into the room, into the back of the desk, with a mighty crash like a watermelon on the sidewalk. Undeterred, unhurried, it started to get right up. It was, or had been, a large man, like a football lineman. Pam bent down suddenly, scooped up books from her floor, and hurled them at the creature. They landed with solid thuds but had no effect on its progress. Max turned from the first zombi to battle the second but before he could do anything the second had reached across the desk and seized his right hand. It yanked Max forward, toppling the computer monitor. Max used the momentum to strike with the edge of his left hand at the bridge of its nose. He knew it wouldn't kill it as it would a normal man, but it might blind it.

No such luck. The zombi grabbed his left hand and now had both hands trapped in its own. Max jumped onto the desk to get freedom of motion. The zombi began to squeeze Max's hands, and Max's face betrayed his struggle—a losing struggle. Golden light escaped from within the zombi's hands but the creature seemed impervious. Max's power had to be directed, and with his hands crushed inside the zombi's grip he couldn't do that.

Pam understood. She looked wildly around the cramped room. The other zombi was back on its feet by the doorway, coming forward again. In the other direction was the floor lamp. She stomped one foot on the cord and yanked the fixture upward. The cord ripped loose from the lamp, plunging the room into near-total darkness. Pam reached down beside her foot, unseeing, found the cord, and grabbed it in the middle. She swung the cord at the zombi holding Max, barely silhouetted against the pale starlit window.

The creature and Max both spasmed involuntarily as electricity shot through their bodies. But the zombi's grip loosened enough for Max to pull free. Stumbling backward, he, too, touched the cord, and jumped away from the second shock.

"Not me!" Max snapped. "Where's the other one?"

Pam's eyes were rapidly growing used to the dimness. She lived in this room and knew what each contour in the dark meant. She made out the frame of the doorway, the hulking form reeling through it—and she heard it slam the wall so hard the wall cracked.

She thrust the cord against the nearest zombi once more. No reaction. The first one had hit the power switch!

"They're smart, Max!" she cried.

But he answered, "No, he doesn't even know the lights are off. He wanted to disorient us, make us easier prey, and got lucky." He shot golden lightning from both palms. The zombi in the doorway all but flew backward, crashing and skidding down the hall, leaving his image impressed on their retinas as if seen in a real lightning flash.

"Run for the kitchen while he's down!" Max shouted.

But an immensely powerful hand closed on Pam's

shoulder. The zombi from the window was back in the game. "Max!" she cried out in pain.

He hurled his golden energy at her captor and it fell back. Grabbing her hand, they lurched through the door, into the hall. The zombi there was getting up inexorably, a shadow among shadows. His arms reached for them but there was just enough room to leap past them. There was not enough room to reach the door behind him.

They scrambled on, down the hall to the kitchen. A night-light in the stove hood there gave better illumination. Behind them, the zombi lurched from the front doorway to come after them, but so did the second zombi lunging from the hall. For a moment the two were caught in an impasse, with no room to get around each other and neither one smart enough to back off.

"Back door!" Pam told Max, pointing. But he grabbed her arm, held her back. A new shadow appeared against the window there.

"Get over in the corner!"

"No! I've had enough of this! I've got a gun in here!" She yanked open a drawer, reached way in the back, and pulled out a CZ-83 pistol.

"Hang on!" Max yelled. "It won't do any good!"

"What about a knife?" She came up with a turkey carver.

"Let me handle this, Pam! They don't care if they get cut!"

"But even a zombi can't do much with slit tendons!"

Max laughed—a genuinely delighted laugh in the midst of all this horror. "You've got a point there, Doctor. Go for it!"

The zombi at the back door slammed his fist through the glass. In a replay of the action in the computer room, its fist hung suspended for a moment, and Pam deftly sliced her knife along its wrist.

The fist came unclenched, the fingers lolling. But that didn't stop it. The creature threw his shoulders against the wood, and the door rocked on its hinges.

The zombis from the front of the house had managed to disengage themselves. They came lumbering down the hallway, crashing against the walls. Max sent both of them staggering with another burst of power, but it was clear they'd never stop coming on.

Pam stood in the middle of the kitchen, her thick knife up and ready, looking around for any other weapon. Max took the decision out of her hands. On the counter by the back door was her microwave. He picked it up and ran his hand along the back side; the now-familiar golden glow reflected off the metal surface and cast his shadow on the ceiling. He popped the microwave's door open, and as the third zombie thrust his head through the broken back door Max flipped the oven's power switch. He'd disabled the automatic shutoff. The device began to hum and Max jammed the open box onto the creature's head. Instantly, the room filled with the stench of roasting flesh. The zombi tried to dislodge the microwave but caught its good hand on the jagged window glass, and the hand with the severed tendons flopped around uselessly.

The creature spun around uneasily and ripped the door from its hinges, crashing to the floor in a shower of shattering wood, still trying to remove the box. The back doorway was open for escape.

Pam ran for the backyard with Max right behind her. From inside the house came the very first growl of pain.

A shot snapped past Pam's ear, the second thunked a tree just ahead. She spun, bringing her automatic up, and fired five times. A return shot's muzzle flash lit other trees across the yard, before a man's body—not a zombi's!—tumbled into the fitful light from the street.

Max dashed past her, pushing her back, blurred in the dark. He moved forward from cover to cover. Only when he was sure there was no second shooter did he approach the prone man.

"Now you've got one," Max said after a moment's inspection. "Nice shooting."

Pam said with seeming irrelevance, "I grew up in New Mexico."

"Cowgirl Pam." He bent to examine the dead man's wallet.

"I learned to shoot when I was eleven," Pam went on, looking deep inside herself. "Bottles. I never shot a man before. . . ."

The zombi in the kitchen roared in agony now.

"That's the game we're playing," Max said quietly. "This guy's license says he's William P. Kennedy from Fort Ross, California—something to look into later. The first one must have reported that you were okay, so they activated Billy the Kid and his three stooges."

"But I was supposed to die in the hospital. Why have a backup ready? Why have such a *massive* backup? *Why have zombis?!*"

"Because they want you massively dead." Max stood. "I hear the cops coming. Let's get out of here."

....

11 WIND

The Brera rocketed through the dizzying curves of Grizzly Peak, away from the houses, into an undeveloped stretch flanked by grass and trees. The streetlights below carved out paths in the dark, and in the distance the lights of Treasure Island, then San Francisco, were dim in a haze of fog. A few cars cruised the bridge from Oakland, crimson meteors in the night. On Grizzly Peak all was darkness save for their headlamps.

Rebounding from the shock of shooting a fellow human being, Pam was buzzing on adrenaline. "Get to the lab, Max! All my data could still be there!"

"Not a chance, Doc. If they could wipe it out through the Internet, they certainly wiped it out in the place where your attempted murderer works."

"You think—?"

"I try. If the package came from the lab, the murderer works there. Where's the party they were all going to?"

"Party? In Oakland. At Barry Leander's house."

"You know how to get there?"

"I think so." She forced her mind to work. "Go down to Broadway, first. But I work with these people, Max—"

He took the next turn hard, squealing at the edge of the precipice, with Pam holding on for dear life. His eyes were locked on the road. "The package came by lab messenger. How many people outside the lab can make that happen?"

". . . Nobody."

"All right. Then how could it *not* be someone inside?"

"Couldn't the messenger have been hypnotized, or—or the package made to *look* like a lab package—?"

"You tell me. How good's lab security?"

". . . Good."

" 'Good enough for government work,' " Max said automatically, like any former soldier. "Any process can be compromised, but the simplest answer is that someone in the lab did it, so that's what we look at first. Now, who could send you that package? Surely the number's limited."

"Yes. Okay. Sure," Pam said. "People outside my group could only route stuff in-house. To send a package to my home, it would have to be a group member. But I say again, I *know* them all."

"Good. Then you can tell me about them."

"I will," she said. "I promise. But first tell *me* why someone is trying to kill me. You know, don't you?"

He nodded soberly. "Because you can kill zombis."

"I'm serious, Max."

"So am I. You know how zombis are made?"

"No. Of course not."

"Well, I've never done it myself but I have friends in strange places. The main ingredient is puffer fish venom—your tetrodotoxin. That's the stuff that lowers the life force in the victims."

"You're kidding me. Please tell me you're kidding me."

"Sorry."

"But, speaking as an expert, tetrodotoxin would almost certainly result in death!"

"Well, that's where the art comes in. In much the same way that I'm keeping the dart from finishing you off, the zombi master keeps the venom from finishing the zombi off. Not that you and zombis have anything else in common, but the idea's the same." He braked for another sharp curve, then accelerated into it, headlights raking the fog. "Zombis are alive, so they actually eat, maybe twice a year, and breathe about once an hour. But there's no life force for their minds because it's all focused in their bodies. That's why they're robotic and slow, but horrifically strong."

"They're *not dead*? I cut that one's tendons and it didn't react."

"It would have, in the long run. You heard one with its head cooking cry out as we ran away; it took it that long to realize it was in pain. As you can well imagine, people don't usually stick around long enough to notice them noticing. People either run like hell or get killed."

"Sure." Pam was once again getting her emotional feet under her. The shocks were wearing off faster each time. Relentlessly, her medical mind was finding its way to the fore. "But this is all done by a primitive people."

"So-called primitive people are right down there in touch with nature."

"I'm just saying, it seems too complicated for people without science."

"They don't need science; they have art. And lots of uninterrupted time for trying things out. Puffer fish venom's just the main ingredient in a zombi potion. They also use the leaves of the consigné tree and the tcha-tcha bean, both of which slow the rate of the body's functions. That's mixed with leaves from the bresillet tree and bwa pine, maman guepes and mashasha, pois gratter and pomme cajou and calmador, all of which cause severe itching and irritation. That last part's sort of to taste; it's where the artistry comes in. But the zombi master gets some of this potion on his victim, the victim starts scratching, and soon he's opened up a dozen sores. The poisons enter the bloodstream, his energy sinks from brain to body, *et voilà*, as they say in Haiti. Then that body is open to command." Max pounded the steering wheel as a thought struck him. "That's why the silver talisman had never been touched by human hands! I meant, hands of a recognizable human. Zombis are just walking meat, so there was no recognizable life energy. And patience wouldn't be a problem for one, either. A zombi made that talisman under direction." He nodded, satisfied. "That's all zombis are. Cheap labor."

"Working stiffs," Pam said, and surprised herself. A joke?

"You're getting the hang of this life," Max said approvingly. "Couple more days—"

"I can't be telling jokes, Max! And I don't want to be doing this for a couple more days! Somebody's trying to *really kill me*, with magick talismans and armies of zombis."

"There were only three."

"That's an army when it comes to zombis! Max"— she put her hand on his arm, tightly—"with all this, this *shit*, can you really protect me?"

Uplit by the dash light, his face grew serious again. "I've been honest with you all night, Pam, so here's my answer. You're no longer in the world of the cut-and-dried, so there's no *sure* answer. Magick is constant verification. But I've got some power, and it's all at your service." He freed his arm and took her hand. "There's no reason in the world why I can't."

He accelerated onto Route 24, headed for Oakland.

11 WIND

The Berkeley police cruiser pulled to a halt and the driver, a youngish, dark-haired man, stared at the scene before him. His partner, a veteran close to retirement, made a noise almost like a growl, which devolved into a smoker's cough.

Blocking the driveway to the neat brown shingle house was a Contra Costa County sheriff's car. They were not in Contra Costa County.

The Berkeley cops got out and strode across the chilly street. The wind whispered in the trees.

"Some sort of Halloween trick?" muttered the young cop.

"It better be," answered the older.

As they neared the out-of-jurisdiction vehicle, two deputies in their khaki shirts and dark pants materialized from the shadows. Seeing the approaching men in dark blue, the deputies hesitated, looked at each other, then continued forward.

"Evening," said the older Berkeley cop in a neutral tone.

"Evening," replied the closest of the deputies. "Sorry to be on your turf, guys. We were chasing a stolen vehicle—came up over the hill and down into here."

"We didn't get a call," said the younger cop.

"It was happening too fast. By the time we crossed the county line we were in these narrow-ass streets, and then we thought we lost him—"

"Which we did," added the second deputy.

"Which we did. We didn't know if he'd stayed on your side or doubled back."

"So why are you out of your vehicle?"

"We thought he might have ducked into this driveway. But he hadn't."

"You should have called it in," said the younger cop. "If for no other reason than we know these hills."

"You're right," admitted the first deputy. "Can't deny it."

"Did you find anything in your search of the area?" asked the older cop abruptly.

"No car, no nothin'," answered the second deputy. "Why?"

"We're responding to a shots-fired."

"Not by us. And I didn't see any signs of it. Did you, Carl?"

The first deputy shook his head. "It's quiet as a tomb back there."

"We'll take a look," said the older cop. "Next time, call."

"Absolutely."

The two deputies got back in their cruiser and drove away. They seemed to be riding low. The older cop took out his notebook and wrote down their license and ID.

"Sump'n up?" asked his partner.

"Just doin' my job."

The two men took out their flashlights and took a look through the dark yard. They found nothing. But when they went to the house's front door, they found it broken off its hinges. They flattened against the wall, flanking it, and identified themselves loudly—then went inside fast. The house was a shambles.

But it was empty.

11 WIND

Nancy Reinking was dancing like it was Hallowe'en night. The tang of danger was in the air, the darkness was shiny like vinyl, she'd drunk three mojitos, and the music was hot. It didn't make any difference that the guy she was dancing with was dull, and the rest of the crowd was duller. She wasn't here for them. She was here for the dancing on Hallowe'en night. She was here for the party.

One of the other dancers struck her arm and the last of her drink sloshed free. It didn't matter. But when Amy Winehouse wound down on the amped-up iPod and Daft Punk got going, Nancy told Barry, "'Nother drink." He nodded, and they went to a kitchen crowded with party goodies. He poured her more rum and mix, and grabbed a Pacifico. Phyllis Noriega's delighted chuckle rose from a room farther back, followed by a deeper voice. Barry moved in close to Nancy and they shared a long, lingering kiss in the momentary solitude. His hand went to her curly black hair, below her pointy princess hat. But she broke it up. "Later, Barry. Let's dance now." He grinned. He knew her.

They went back out to the living room. The living room window was wide open with steam twisting from the edges, swirling out into dimly lit trees, and Timbaland was so loud the curtains should have been swinging, or maybe shredding. Their fellow lab rats were rocking the room, which would have surprised her before she got to know lab rats. Especially since the senior

staff was involved. But there they were, her coworkers,
all in costume, dancing, drinking, and more than a few
making out on the fringes. Said fringes were a mix of
light and shadow thrown by lamps covered in orange
cloths, and a bank of seven computer screens showed
visualizers pulsing in unison to the sounds.

"They make a nice couple," said Helena Dawkins,
the staff microbiologist, to Fred Castleton, everybody's
boss. Fred was over sixty but could still get it on. He
craned his neck to see past a man in monk's robes.
"Barry looks tired," he said.

"I'm talking about Nancy, too," Helena responded.
"You don't know her so well, up in your exalted tower"—
she and Fred had worked together a long time—
"but she's our touchstone in the trenches. We need a
behavioral scientist just as much as the folks we work
with."

"Maybe more," said Fred.

"Maybe more," agreed Helena. "She brings us donuts
every Friday morning. Reminds us that because we're
dealing with death on a daily basis, we've got to have
our own lives. She's fun but she's indomitable. So she'd
go well with Barry."

"If you say so, Helena."

Nancy drained the last of her mojito as Barry led her
back on the floor. They started dancing and the energy
in the room went even higher. The joint was jumpin'.

Then Pam and some guy appeared in the open front
doorway. A pirate of the Caribbean, looking past the
French maid with whom he was dancing, yelled
"Pammy!" Nancy turned, saw her, nodded—then
grabbed at her princess hat, which was about to topple
off her head. Barry waved. Fred craned his neck, seek-

ing a better view through the eyeholes of his Dracula mask, then took it off altogether. Helena, seeing his reaction, followed his gaze and saw Pam; she registered sudden concern. Phyllis, dressed as a milkmaid, was entering from the kitchen, followed by a cowboy. Both were straightening their costumes, both stopped short on seeing Pam, and Phyllis did an almost comical double-take. The rest of the room kept on dancing.

Now Nancy was able to concentrate on the man Pam had brought with her. He was midthirties, blond, good-looking—doing some weird wave with his left hand. But she didn't know who he was. Pam was introducing him to the pirate and the maid, apparently; she couldn't hear a word they said as the blond guy shook both their hands. Now Phyllis was there, gesticulating, but Pam just shook her head. Max took Phyllis's hand and appeared to say something soothing. Then he and Pam started to make the rounds.

After a few moments, they got to Barry and Nancy.

"We thought you weren't coming!" yelled Nancy over the din.

"Change of plans," Pam yelled back. "Guys, this is a friend of mine, Max! Max, Barry and Nancy!"

"Hi!" yelled Barry.

Max nodded shortly. "Hi, Barry!" he said, and took the man's outstretched hand.

Nancy said, "Phyllis said you were sick!"

Barry added, "She told *me* you were poisoned!"

Pam brushed it off with a nervous wave of her hand. "Food poisoning! It comes quick and goes quick!"

Nancy grinned. "And who would know better than us?"

Max stuck his hand out. "Hi, Nancy! I'm Max!"

Her grip was solid. "Hi, yourself! Where'd Pam find you?"

"She went trick-or-treating and it was me or a Snickers! Hey, where can we get a drink around here?"

"In the kitchen!"

"I need a guide! Can you show me?"

"Sure!"

Max turned to Barry. "Can I borrow her?"

"Be my guest! She's worn me out!"

Nancy punched him playfully.

"Then—ladies!" Max took Nancy on one arm and Pam on the other, as they threaded their way across the dance floor. Nancy gave Pam a solid nod of approval behind his back. Pam nodded back, but a little distractedly.

"Whew," Nancy sighed, as they passed through the doorway. "No more shouting." Pam was reminded of her own kitchen and what had just happened there; in this most mundane and inoffensive of settings, she shivered again. Nancy was conferring with Max and didn't notice. "So—there's wine on the counter. The Merlot's really good. Oh shit, it's gone. But there's some Zin. And rum—" But now she noticed that Max still had a hold on her arm, and was steering her toward a closed door on the far side of the kitchen. "What are you doing?" Nancy asked. Pam, too, looked at Max in confusion.

"It's a game," Max said, with his most engaging grin. It did not seem to engage Nancy, who tried to pull away from him, but by that time they'd reached the door. Fortunately, it was slightly ajar and Max could open it with a kick. Inside, in the dim light of a single candle, the curved staff of a milkmaid lay spilled across the carpet. The air was heavy with sex.

Pam, following behind, looked on perplexedly as Nancy finally broke away from Max, who in fact let her go to close the door completely behind them. He then moved his palm across the door in an easy but definite arc, two to ten on a clock. Nancy, rubbing her forearm, appealed to Pam: "What's he doing?"

"I don't know," said Pam slowly. "But I'm beginning to get an idea. Max—"

He ignored her, concentrating only on Nancy. "You're the one who sent the package to her, Nan."

"What package?" Nancy looked at Pam again. "What's he talking about, Pam?"

But Pam kept silent, which Max noted and appreciated. The ongoing debate about even the *existence* of magick was gone—zombis will do that. But Nancy was Pam's friend, and still Pam believed Max knew what he was doing. They were over a hurdle in their race toward whoever had twice tried to kill her, and that made it easier. Now they could move faster.

Nancy looked back at Max, said angrily, "What package are you talking about? If she won't tell me, you have to!"

Max said, "I've sealed the door so we won't be disturbed. Even if it weren't so loud in the living room, no one outside these four walls will hear what happens next. So, Nan, the only question is, did you know about the zombis?"

"*Zombis?!* Are you *nuts*?"

"Because if you knew, then you know what Pam and I survived—and then you know the level of power you're facing here."

"I *don't* know what you're talking about!" Nancy shouted. Her fists went up as if to beat on his chest, but there was fear in her eyes and she held her fire.

Pam said, "Max, I don't know, either. Can you give me a hint?"

"Sure," he answered easily, but kept his eyes on Nancy. "One of your colleagues sent the package, so he or she expected you to be dead. When we came in, the other four reacted with some measure of surprise; they'd heard you were badly ill. But Nancy here didn't react at all. It gave me the idea that she's had training in controlling her true emotions—training I've seen before, as for example with that guy at the hospital lobby. Now, a better operative would have faked some reaction to the shock of your arrival, and an even better one would have let her natural reaction come through—which was shock at seeing you alive. But our Nan isn't that high up the food chain. She was just a sentinel, to alert her bosses if anyone had a breakthrough with tetrodotoxin—and she was a hander-on of packages." He nodded. "After our Nan caught my eye, I shook hands with all of your coworkers, reading everyone's energy, and hers was decisive."

"But she's been with the lab ten months—long before I turned my attention to the fugu."

Nancy said, "Yeah! You *know* I'm innocent, Pam!"

Max was unmoved. "Your lab's a prime place to find what they didn't want found. And we've already seen that they cover all bases."

"But ten months just to watch?" Nancy challenged him, emboldened by the lifeline Pam had thrown her.

"If zombis were that important to your bosses, hiring you is chickenfeed for insurance."

"Pam," said Nancy, turning back to her friend, "please tell me this is all a—a trick-or-treat—"

"You're better off talking to Max," Pam answered,

finding herself no longer holding any line out to this woman, and merely noting it; not surprised.

Max said, "So tell me, Nan, did they tell you about the zombis? Did they tell you about the guy at the hospital? Or did they tell you it was all up to you? Because if they didn't tell you you had backup, they didn't trust you one bit."

Her eyes were angry, and her lips were tight. She didn't like all this talking-down-to, and was getting tired of hiding it. But she kept her lips shut, so it was Pam who again broke the silence.

"Backup?"

"It's a control-freak thing," Max said. "They put Nan in the lab, and when they used her to send you the amulet, they gave her not one but two levels of backup. They don't trust her, which is understandable." Nancy's eyes were furious now. "But she's a control freak, too, which is why she can't react spontaneously, and why she hates being out of the loop."

"Goddammit!" snapped Nancy. "This *is* a joke! You can't convict me for being too drunk to stare and shake hands the way you like!"

"I'm not Judge Judy. I'm sure you took into account that you might end up in court someday—though with the PATRIOT Act, who among us can be sure? But today is not that day, and I'm tired of waiting."

Nancy threw back her head and screamed for help, with every atom of her being. The shriek was harsh and violent in the small, enclosed room, and seemed to go on forever. When it finally ended she screamed again. But Max withstood it easily . . . and Pam's eyes narrowed. Whatever Max had said to Nancy, he hadn't threatened her physically; that scream was too extreme a reaction, unless she *did* know the kind of power he had.

In the next instant, he used it.

He raised his hand and made that half swipe through the air again, this time in front of Nancy's face, quick, left-right-left. To Pam, watching intently, knowing there was something to *see*, he appeared to be stripping Nancy of her makeup, or somehow making her clearer, sharper, easier to see in the gloom.

Revealing with each pass the fires banked behind those no-longer-innocent eyes.

Erasing her *mask*.

A luminous sapphire nimbus surrounded her, further blurring her features. And it was not just a nimbus of light. A bitter, malign intelligence radiated throughout the room, and there was a sound like the silence on the dark side of the moon. . . .

In the midst of which Nancy shrieked, *"You brought it on yourself, you stupid bitch!"*

"What?" Stunned, Pam took an involuntary step backward.

"You got in our *way*!"

Then the accumulated fury of the entire damn day exploded in Pam. *"Your* way? *Whose* way?"

The thing that Nancy was now snarled at her, slit-eyed. "You'll find that out the day you wake up to find us in charge, Pammy! Control freaks? Hell, yes! Because control is what we do! Do you hear me? Do you understand me? We will not lose! We'll have nothing less than full control of *everything*! Whatever power this man has is nothing compared to my masters' powers! You can do what you want with me but in the end, I'll not only be rescued, I'll be part of the *authority* that grinds all the rest of you to dust!"

Pam gaped at her, then looked to Max. "I thought *you* were weird enough. I thought the *zombis* were weird enough. But what the hell is *this*?"

"Our Nan's id," answered Max quietly, watchfully.

Nancy's next words came with brittle pride. It was that pride that gave Max access; there was a part of Nancy that wanted to talk to them. "You stupid, stupid fucks, I belong to the *Free Range Coalition*!"

"That's a group?" Max asked.

"You see, *you* don't know! But we control the world! The whole world! We're burrowing, assimilating, subverting, and you don't know! One day we will be *all* around you, and you'll have no place to run. We have money, we have mastery, and we have magick, too! Whatever you do with me now, we will prevail!"

"You wouldn't tell me twice if you believed it, Nan."

"You *will* die, both of you! And I'll be there to watch!" She turned her glare on Pam. "I'm good at watching, bitch! I *like* to watch!"

Max said, "Who's your master?"

Again, pride. "Miller Omen!" She grinned.

"I know that name," said Pam in surprise. "He's on Lou Dobbs sometimes."

Nancy spat. "He's CEO of Meridian Pharmaceuticals, you cunt! He rules legal drugs in this country, and holds sway around the world! *He* is my master! I don't mind telling you. I *want* you to know! Go find him if you want. You have *no fucking chance* against *the FRC*!"

"I get that," said Max dryly. "Do you know where Miller Omen is now?"

"Of course! My master's on his tax haven island, east of Barbados, outside the law. Go to him and die!"

"Soon, soon. Where's Pam's data on tetrodotoxin?"

"Gone, from all her computers. All computers in the

system. I uploaded it to a secure server, and the address was changed as soon as I was finished. I won't know where it is again until Mr. Omen tells me." She strained forward within the light from above. "Ask him while he kills you, you fuck!"

"Okay. That's all we need, then," Max said. He placed his other hand alongside Nancy's head, and abruptly rotated them as if twisting her neck, though neither hand actually touched her. She fell like a rag doll to the floor, and by the time she landed she'd returned to her natural state.

"You didn't—?" Pam asked.

"She's fine. In suspended animation, so she won't alert Omen that we're coming."

"We're going to Barbados?"

"First flight out. Right now, we have to hide your friend here. Do you know this house?"

"Sort of." She thought for a moment, purely as a practical matter. "There's a storage shed out back. I don't think Barry ever uses it."

"That'll do nicely. Grab her feet."

"Can't you, I dunno, make her float?"

"I can, but why should I, when I've got such a willing helper?" He grabbed Nancy under the shoulders, and added, "Using magick all the time can stir up currents none of us needs."

So Pam grabbed Nancy's feet and the two of them carried her slack form out into the night. In the back of the house, away from the party and even streetlights, it was very dark, and the footing was uncertain. But Pam said she knew where the shed was—more or less. They barely avoided walking into a picnic table.

"What do they call you, Max? A magician? A sorcerer?"

"Personally, that stuff makes me think of an old guy in robes and white beard—Dumbledore. I'm an alchemist, but if you can't bring yourself to call me just 'Max,' try 'artist.' Alchemy is an art as well as a science, and 'artist' is a very bland word, suitable for mixed company."

"The artist formerly known as Max," she said, mostly to be saying something. "An alchemist with a gun." But another thought followed hard on that one. "How much power does this Free Range Coalition have? Are they as powerful as she said?"

"Could be. But don't let it worry you. Nan reminded me of a terrier, or one of those wiener dogs—another sign she was just a tool. She yapped. We'll have a better idea what the FRC—" Suddenly a new note, something like excitement, came into his voice in the dark. "Remember what we found in your computer? 'FileRecord-Count'? FRC. And the shooter at your house was from Fort Ross, California."

"What does that mean?"

"I have no idea, unless these guys like to sign their work. And you know . . . maybe they do." Unexpectedly, he laughed.

"What?"

"Our main competitor at Earl's and my radio station was KFRC. They've played the same music they played then for decades, now as oldies, so if they're a front for some cabal they're the lamest front ever. First rule of alchemy: everything means something, but not everything means what you think it does. We should keep an eye open for the initials, but keep an open mind as well."

"Well, my mind and body need to rest," Pam said. "This has been a strenuous night." Max stopped, and they laid Nan's body, none too gently, on the cool grass.

His voice, disembodied in the darkness, might have been coming from a radio now. "I was going to say, when we confront Miller Omen, I expect him to be a lot quieter than Nan . . . the way a shark is quiet. He won't feel any need to impress us with his power; he'll just use it. But from what Nan said, he would still be proud of it, and that might lead him to sign his work in some subtle way."

Pam snorted. " 'He'll just use it.' The guy who put a dart in me. I've got to say, Max, I love your pep talks."

"And *I* love what we're up against, Pam!" Max said, and she could hear his savage grin even though she couldn't see it. "See, I happen to come from a time, not so long ago, where this country was pretty decent. It was never perfect, but I *lived*, actually *lived*, in a time when it was the world's best hope. That hope was as timeless as I am, and as long as I'm here, I intend to help bring it back into style. Things have gone seriously wrong these past few years, and all the wild animals are loose. But I liked being one of the good guys, and I still do. So if you want to know what my art is—*that's* my art."

He took a deep breath. This was something he never talked about. Who was there to listen? But now—

"The guys who fought the British empire to create that hope were artists themselves. Ben Franklin was the premier artist of his age, and he and the other Founding Fathers tried to create a system where freedom could live and thrive, so everyone could be what they wanted to be, including guys like themselves. All men are human; they couldn't foresee everything. But every time America's gone wrong before, it's always gotten back on track. Now it's my turn to help with that. I owe it to Franklin and friends for the freedom they handed us, and I owe it to them because I share their profession."

Pam nodded, then remembered he couldn't see her, either. "You think the Free Range Coalition is political?"

"As much as they have to be, sure. But Nan told us flat out, it's all about the control. Any ideologies are just camouflage. That's why Nan is a tool, in the end— she's still a true believer in whatever fantasy world they spun for her. Omen won't be."

"Well, right now," Pam said, "Nan's a true lump of lead. But we'd better keep going or someone's going to come outside to puke." She bent to grab the body again.

Another twenty steps took them to the shed. Max snapped his fingers and a goblin light flared from their tips, casting his and Pam's shadows in opposite directions. Inside the shed they found a pile of firewood that looked as if it hadn't been disturbed in twenty years, thick with webs. Spider eyes shone red in the crevices. "Lay her down," Max said. "We'll stash her behind that woodpile. Then you go back inside and tell your real friends that she, you, and I are off to someplace mysterious and fun. Which'll be the truth, except for her part."

Pam looked dubiously at the spiderwebs. "But won't Nancy—? I mean, she's awful—horrible—but it gives me the creeps to think of her crawling with spiders."

"Suspended animation protects her from everything. All things being equal, she'll be here until you and I are through with this mess and she won't get a single bite. Anyway, I think I'm protecting the spiders."

"Well, protect *me* if we have to rummage through all this wood."

"Hey, what are you guys doing out there?"

Pam stiffened. "That's Phyllis," she whispered.

"She hasn't seen us," Max answered, extinguishing the light. "Go tell her—"

"Yeah, mysterious and fun."

Pam groped her way out of the shed. Across the yard, Phyllis was standing—leaning—on the back door, in the spill of light from the room.

"Hey, Phyl," Pam called.

"Goodness, girl, you want privacy, that's what this room is for," grinned Phyllis, staring unseeing into the darkness, until Pam entered the light. "It's dark out here."

"I needed some fresh air," Pam said. "I guess I'm still a little under the weather. Nancy and I are taking off."

"What about that guy you brought, that Max?"

"He's going with us."

"Well, if he takes you home and puts you to bed, that leaves the two of them."

"Nancy wouldn't betray me," said Pam.

"Hell, honey, *I'd* betray you with that guy."

"You're a dirty old woman, Phyl."

"You're right," agreed Phyllis happily. "My advice to you is be a dirty *young* woman while you can. You never know when you'll get another chance."

"I'll be sure to keep that in mind," Pam said with a weary smile.

11 WIND

It was late when they reached Fern's house.

The lights in her room were dim, and yet seemed too bright, because the light in Fern had dimmed considerably since Max had seen her just hours before. Cortesia, the nurse, sat quietly beside her bed . . . waiting.

Pam took in the scene at a glance and went to the bedside. Softly, she asked Cortesia, "Where's Dr. Neuberg?"

The response came from Fern, and it was loud against the sound level they'd assumed for the room. "I don't need Neuberg. I knew you'd come, Pam."

"Well, that's more than I did, until just a little while ago," Pam said—and suddenly, for the first time all night, felt herself back in some semblance of normalcy. "How are you feeling, Fern?"

"Old." Fern smiled back, almost contentedly. Then her eyes looked beyond Pam at Max. "Thank you, Barnaby. Cortesia, go away now."

"But Mrs. Jenkins—," said the nurse, pro forma. She knew the old lady was stubborn, and now there was a doctor in the house.

"I'm in good hands, Cortesia. Almost as good as yours."

Cortesia was surprised at the unusual compliment—and then alarmed, suspecting on some nursing level that the old lady did not expect to have another opportunity.

"It's been a pleasure assisting you, ma'am."

Fern nodded, her eyes looking as deep as they still could into the eyes of the last person Fern was ever to know in this life. Where words had failed them, emotion flowed, of friendship, of gratitude, of good-bye. Then the shutters of convention dropped over both pairs of eyes, and Cortesia nodded and went out the door.

Pam sat down beside Fern. She felt her skin and her pulse, then looked around at Max with the smallest of negations. Fern was also looking at Max, and he gave her his own small negation. Fern nodded.

She said, "I'm a lot older than you, Barnaby. I do remember Miriam Hopkins, at the old Chicago Theater on LaSalle. I remember Guy Lombardo at the Avalon Ballroom, while I was dancing with my Earl." Her left hand, bent at the wrist, began to move back and forth just a bit, to the beat in her memory. "But the songs that are running in my head now are from the days you'd come home with Earl for a beer, and you two were so excited about what you were doing. You gave him freedom, Barnaby; it was the most fun he'd had since *The Lone Ranger.*"

Max explained to Pam, "Earl was a great radio engineer. I was just the deejay."

Fern rolled her eyes at Pam. "He was a *great* deejay. That meant something to Earl; radio was his life. So it meant something to me. That's why I paid attention to music for the last time. All I know about Britney Spears is that she doesn't wear underpants." Her gray tongue pushed out through thin lips for a last moment of disdain. "But you sat with Earl and played songs right there in our house, making him marvel at the harmonies and the backup singers and whatever there was that made that particular song stand out. You had a knack right from the start of seeing what made things great. You made them matter. Earl loved that."

"Now you're embarrassing me, Fern. If you don't have a better reason to save your strength, that's a good one."

"No, Barnaby. I might as well use what strength I have."

Pam said, "I take it the reason that you call him Barnaby is that that was his disc jockey name?"

Fern nodded and said, rather proudly, "Barnaby Wilde. It came from a song by Steppenwolf called 'Born to Be Wild,' from . . . 1968."

Max nodded indulgently. "'Sixty-eight was a big year: Bobby Kennedy shot, Martin Luther King, Jr. shot, Nixon elected, first men to orbit the moon, *2001: A Space Odyssey*. We were frisky in sisky-eight."

Fern shook her head. "A long time ago. And I was forty-eight then." She sighed, a sound almost as long as Pam's when she came back from near death. All Fern's air ran out of her. But then she breathed in again. "The other song in my head is that song you couldn't play on the air." Another pause for breath. "'I Feel Like I'm Fixing to Die' Rag."

"Now you're just messing with me," Max said.

"'Give me an *F*!'" said Fern, but fell into a fit of coughing. Her lungs sounded bad.

Max said, "If that's the sort of influence I had on impressionable young minds, maybe they should have switched to robot radio sooner."

"And put you and Earl out of work? Thank God he didn't have to go through that."

"Please, Fern," Pam said. "Rest now."

"Don't worry, honey," answered Fern. "I can live with

dying"—she laughed a very small laugh, which died away as if it had never existed—"so long as a young girl like you isn't facing it, too."

"I'm not a girl and I'm not so young."

"Oh, honey," Fern said, then grew quiet again. When next she spoke, her voice was detectably weaker, and directed at Max. "But dying's still facing down the unknown . . ."

"Not so much, Fern," Max said, and gave her his most reassuring grin. "You see, even now, I know my cue when I hear it, just the way I did with Earl." He came and sat on the edge of her bed, his knees touching Pam's, and took Fern's withered hand in his. His voice was low but had the same ability to make you want to listen that he'd had on KQBU. "I can tell you what will happen next. What happens after death is quite well known, if you hang in the right circles.

"When your soul leaves your body, there's a period of ghostliness, where you see the world but the world does not see you. It's strange and disconcerting, but not scary; it seems perfectly natural, because it is. After a while you start to notice that time seems to be running backward. In fact, the years of your life are being stripped away like the layers of an onion. Think of it like, when you were born you were the pure essence of Fern, and as each day passed after that, you made choices that shaped you into the Fern you are today. Well now, working backward, each choice is *unmade*, so you become more and more like your original, pure self. It's the famous 'life flashing before your eyes.'" He stopped to let her visualize it, and when he was satisfied that she had, he went on.

"You grow younger and younger, and all the people you knew and loved reappear to you. And eventually you become what you were at your very youngest: pure energy. It is universal light, and you are part of it, as it is part of you. You're home."

His voice was growing softer, more restful. "Then you're all one, part and parcel with the Holy Spirit, under whatever name you know it by. You're gone from here, but you're everywhere. And then, somewhere down the line, the Spirit puts out a new burst of energy, that burst finds a place for itself in our world, and nine months later a whole new person is born."

He murmured, "This is not the end, Fern. You're about to begin a whole new adventure. The Celts say this is the *real* beginning of everything."

Fern's eyes were almost closed. "Will you know me when I'm new, Barnaby?"

"I don't know. Let's find out."

Fern's chest rose in a sigh . . . then fell back on its own. This time it did not rise again. The silence lay heavy as they waited to be sure.

When they were, Pam looked at her watch. "I pronounce her at 11:59 P.M., thirty-one October." She looked at Fern again with a great deal of compassion. She'd gotten to know her very well over the years. "She was an exceptional woman."

"And very brave, considering what she went through," Max said.

Pam raised her eyes from Fern, then reached over and took his forearm, almost urgently. "Max, I'll have to call Cortesia back in a minute. But—when you talked about being in a war, earlier, I thought you meant the Gulf War. But Fern's husband Earl died in 1980. If you were playing songs with him before then . . ."

His eyes met hers. "I was in Nam in 'seventy," he said quietly.

"But you can't be older than thirty-five!"

"I was born in 1950, but that doesn't matter anymore. When I mastered alchemy, I stopped aging."

In the depths of the house, midnight struck.

NOVEMBER 1, 2007 – MIDNIGHT PDT
ALL HALLOWS' EVE

11 WIND

As the attending physician, Pam had to call a series of authorities and fill out a series of forms. Max said he'd keep watch from the car to avoid being mentioned in any reports and left her to it, though she was burning with curiosity.

It was still All Hallows' Eve until the sun came up. The night was long. He climbed into the Brera's driver's seat and closed the door. It was quiet inside the vehicle, dark and still. He closed his eyes and began to concentrate. The characteristic furrow in his brow appeared as he summoned the energy he needed. . . .

In the darkness of his mind, he was standing in a stone circle, much like the one in his backyard. He lit the four pumpkins and blinked in their light. He lit the firewood and tossed a handful of nutmeg on the flames; its spicy scent filled his nostrils. He stood looking down at the crystal ball, with the firelight flickering warmly up from below. He saw the shadows in the glass, and was among them, in the same place he'd gone with a real crystal ball.

In the middle distance, he could clearly see Fern. She was standing, her head thrown back, a look of wonder and exaltation on her face. She didn't need him now; his presence would have been an intrusion. She was fine.

In another direction lay San Francisco. Its lights were muted, seen through a veil, but here and there bright bursts showed souls crossing over. He heard the foghorns. The streets between him and the city were *undoing* like Fern, returning to pathways from an earlier day. He walked through their valleys, silent save for the whisper of running water and the hush of bending trees. The valleys became canyons, steep muddy sides rising on both sides of him. He heard the owls. He began to run. . . .

NOVEMBER 1 – 1:30 A.M. PDT
ALL HALLOWS' EVE

11 WIND

Pam rapped tentatively on the passenger-side window. Max opened his eyes. He looked at her impassively, coming back to himself.

After a minute, he popped the door lock for her.

"Asleep?" she asked.

"No," he said.

"Well, then, please—I've been going crazy in there. Tell me about not aging!"

"No," he said quietly.

She drew back. "What?"

He took a deep breath, released it. Looked her in the eye. "Fern was one of the links to my old life, before I was Timeless—when I was just a guy having a good time. I'm somewhere else right now, and you're not a part of it." He turned the Brera's key and brought its engine to purring life. "As for the future—we're not going back to your place, or mine. We're driving to the Airport Hyatt. We'll get a room and you'll get some rest, while I get us two tickets on the next flight to Barbados. Under assumed names, of course."

"I'll pay you back, of course," she said stiffly, smarting from his unexpected rebuff.

"Save your money, Doc. I've invested long term." He put the car in gear.

NOVEMBER 1 - NOON CENTRAL DAYLIGHT TIME
ALL HALLOWS' DAY

12 NIGHT

American 967 left SFO at 6:50 A.M. and was well on its way to Miami for an afternoon connection to Barbados before Pam tried again. Jeremy Theobald and Grace Miller were ostensibly strangers who happened to be seated side-by-side, so she couldn't push it before that. They were finishing their lunch in First Class, and she was covertly studying his face, looking for any sign that he was older than thirty-five. But there were no excess lines around his eyes, no give in the tone of his flesh. His movements, too, were brisk and assured. It was true that he was a little more *thoughtful* than most men in their thirties—maybe a *lot* more thoughtful—but there was nothing that rang false as far as she could see.

And so she was staring at him when he suddenly turned and laid the *USA Today* over her empty dishes.

"There's a K-1 match in Bridgetown tomorrow night. Hakira versus Ortega, both contenders, both coming on, so it says; I'll watch K-1, but I don't follow it, so I couldn't tell you one way or the other."

"I never heard of it. What's K-1?"

"It's one of the new mixed martial arts leagues. UFC is another, IFL is another. K-1 is karate, kickboxing, tae kwon do, and kung fu—a kickass thing, so to speak. Fighters go at it in matches throughout the year, like this one, and the best of them hold a World Grand Prix in Tokyo in December. This is one of the last tune-ups. The paper says that with Barbados the island farthest out in the Atlantic—therefore, farthest away from the tourists—the island's Powers That Be have set up a series of attractive weekends throughout the winter to increase revenues. So we can be sure of a warm welcome."

Throughout all this, Pam's lips were getting tighter and tighter. Now she put her lips to his ear and whispered urgently, "*Please* tell me about not dying!"

He just shook his head, then put his lips to her ear. "I can't discuss my business in public, Pam."

She went back to his ear. "There's no one behind us, and only ten other people in the compartment."

"There's no one behind us because I always take the back row of First Class, to make sure of that. But ten people are ten people."

"But there's no place on a plane that doesn't have people all around. Except the restrooms. . . ." Her eyes lit up. "Want to join the mile-high club?" she asked, and immediately bit her tongue for being a little too light-hearted. "Of conversation?"

"They have microphones in there, in case someone gets locked inside by accident. They go with the smoke and chemical detectors."

She hissed, "But we're on planes almost all day! What about in the Miami airport?"

"The loss of the Fourth Amendment means mikes and cameras everywhere now. If you want privacy you have to make it yourself."

"You're not saying we have to get all the way to Barbados? This isn't because I'm just curious, Max. I'm a doctor who fights death! I'll explode!"

He put his lips back to her ear. "That should be fun to watch." He drew back a foot and said a little louder, "But enough about me. Tell me about *you*, Grace."

She gave him an exceedingly dirty look, then deliberately took another long sip of her Chardonnay before looking out the window at the slowly passing clouds. At long last, she said, "All right, Jeremy. I *am* a doctor . . ."

". . . without a TV or radio show. What a loser."

"I've wanted to be a doctor since I was a very little girl."

"And how long ago was that?"

"I was eight; I'm twenty-eight now; you do the math." But she'd noted and answered his interest. "Now do you want to hear this or not?"

"I do."

"Then—we had a cat named Handlebar, and one day he got very sick. We took him to the vet and the vet said he'd been poisoned—but the vet thought he could help him. I was thrilled to know that someone knew how to fix my cat, and once the crisis had passed and we got Handlebar home, I nursed him every day and as far into the night as I could go before falling asleep. His continuing to live, his getting stronger day by day, seemed like a miracle to me, but a miracle the vet and I could help happen.

"When Handlebar was okay again, I rode my bike

over to the house of the boy I knew had done it. Ricky Holcomb. I knew because he'd told me he would, because Handlebar dug up some flower bulbs in their garden, but the real reason was he was a little creep, mean to animals. I just thought, since I'd been a 'doctor,' I could be a 'policewoman.' I waited till I saw him go out—his parents were both at work during the day—then I crawled in an open window and tried to find the poison."

"Eight's pretty young to be crawling into strange houses tenanted by creepy boys."

"Too young to know better. Anyway, of course, Ricky came home and caught me prowling around. There was nobody there but the two of us, and he was really mad. But all I was thinking about was Handlebar. When Ricky came at me, I put my hands up, like claws, ready to scratch him. I sort of thought that if he'd poisoned my cat, he'd back off if a cat confronted him—something like that. But he kept coming. He grabbed my hands with both of his—and I was still thinking like Handlebar, and remembering how cats fight, where they take their hind legs and *scratch-scratch-scratch*. So while he was holding my hands I kicked my legs up to rake his chest (even though I had shoes on), and by pure accident I kicked him hard in the balls. We fell over and I ran away, and later his parents sent him to military school, so today he's no doubt doing great things in Iraq.

"But I learned something cool about bodies that day." And she punched him lightly on the thigh, close but no cigar, to remind him she hadn't forgiven him. "So watch out."

12 NIGHT

When the phone rang on Pablo Santander's desk, he thought it was the drug deal going down, and he reached for it with languid ease.

"Federal Bureau of Investigation, Special Agent Santander."

"Get out to the airport," Hanrahan said without preamble. "We want a man and a woman who are on their way to Barbados."

"BWIA leaves at two thirty-five," Santander said.

"No. They're coming in from San Francisco, and the earliest they can arrive is three oh five."

"American at five ten, then."

"That's our opinion. They're on American now. Trying to avoid us, so they'll certainly be using false passports, and they *might* take an indirect route through T&T or Georgetown, but we believe they're moving as fast as they can."

"Description?"

"They're probably disguised as well. Starting point, the man is six one, one ninety, Caucasian, blond, green. His name is Max August and he is Code Red. The woman is five seven, one hundred thirty-two, Caucasian, blonde, blue. Her name is Dr. Pamela Blackwell. We want her dead—him, only if you have no choice."

"Code Red."

"Exactly. They're dangerous to kill. You've never had one, have you?"

"Who has? But I know the drill."

"This is no drill. He killed two of our men last night and one of our women is missing."

"I understand." He did. "If you know what flight they're on . . ."

"We don't actually know anything without the missing woman's report, but her disappearance makes it likely they know what she knows. Going to Barbados is the most probable scenario under those circumstances. By the time she failed to check in, it was too late for us to monitor the earliest flight. I've got a passenger list but it doesn't provide descriptions, so you'll have to pick them out from the people coming off the one flight and onto the other. We're pursuing other angles so if you come up empty let me know ASAP."

"I'm on it," he said, and hung up.

Special Agent Santander unlocked his bottom desk drawer and removed his Springfield 1911-A1 pistol in its holster, which he strapped around his chest. Then he bent farther down to fish a small ivory box from the back of the drawer. He took his key ring from his pocket and chose a short ebony tube that looked like an emergency pen. In fact, he could write with it when necessary. But now he inserted the tube into the ivory box and opened it. A small radiant stone was inside. He slid it carefully into the breast pocket of his shirt and closed the disguised Velcro seal to make sure it stayed put.

Then he went out to kill Pamela Blackwell, M.D.

12 NIGHT

Sitting at the Conch Bar in Miami International, Pam suddenly realized that Max could move the conversation away from sensitive points without ever seeming to, and speak at length about himself without ever mentioning specific dates. Things happened when he was "in high school," "in college," "in the war," "after radio," but without any way for an outsider to know when those times occurred. He was smooth, a practiced talker from his deejay days, but the lack of time-stamps must have been carefully cultivated. She remembered last night, how he'd told her his story, or as much of it as he'd had to. And that was key. He'd told her everything she needed to know to hold up her end of the night's adventure, and not a thing more. Max August was a man with many secrets, and he could keep them.

So he surprised her by saying "I grew up here."

"In Miami?"

"Miami Beach." He waved a hand toward the east. "My dad managed several of the bigger hotels over the years. Growing up on the Beach, with all new tourist girls all the time, put me in the mood for a life of fun and frivolity. I could have been a classic beach bum, or at least a classic oldies jock on Majic 102.7." He leaned back in the high, wide bar stool and took a sip of his inferior, overpriced Planter's Punch. "But then there was my uncle Ed, the family hero. He'd traveled all around the world, and not the way we do today; he'd done it at the turn of the century, in the days of McKinley and

Teddy Roosevelt, when Americans could go anywhere, if they were up to it.

"He and I had a little adventure once, and afterward, he gave me a carving of a lion. He said—and I'll never forget it—'Lions are kings, boy. Man likes to think he's somethin' better, 'cause he's got automobiles, and tele-visions, and puts satellites in space like those goddamn Russians, but he still don't know what the hell he's here for. Well, the lions I've met all know what they're here for. They're the kings of nature, and kings by nature, and if you can think like a lion, you'll do all right in this life.' " Max's mouth crooked in an ironic smile. "Of course, I'm a Leo, so that sounded fine to me. Some-times it made for a hell of an ego, but it got me a life I was good with. Thing was, when I started getting in-volved in the *artistic* phase of my life, I found out that the lion carving was a talisman—the fire talisman, a conduit to the magick of light and heat. Uncle Ed was an interesting man, but I never knew how interesting because he was dead by then."

"You still have the lion?"

"I do. It's put away, somewhere safe. I carry the lion inside me now."

"In the hospital room, I saw—"

"Right," he said. "So since then, I've asked myself what exactly that crazy old coot knew from his worldly travels that made him set me on that path."

"It's as if it was all planned from the start," Pam said.

He shrugged, not confirming, not denying.

"But what," she persisted, "if it was planned by some-thing evil?"

"Then it did a piss-poor job, because I've fought the bad guys every step of the way. Like I said, there are no cut-and-dried answers out here, but I judge by the results."

Now it was her turn to cock her head, asking a silent question, and her eyes searched his face. His eyes met hers, and for a long moment there were just the two of them in their world. Then she broke the spell and smiled. "I hope, when this is all over, I share your high opinion of yourself," she said.

"That seems unlikely—"

"*American flight 651 to Bridgetown, Barbados— now boarding at gate C5.*"

Max shrugged again, and let it go. He left the remainder of his drink and headed for C5, scoping the area. Pam nursed her drink and gave him five minutes.

NOVEMBER 1 - 4:45 P.M. EDT
ALL HALLOWS' DAY

12 NIGHT

Pablo Santander sat unobtrusively in the waiting area chair closest to gate C5. He had sat just as unobtrusively as American flight 967 from San Francisco had debarked, and identified six men and seven women as possibles. He had identified himself as an FBI agent to airline security and determined that two of those men and two of the women were booked on flight 651 to Barbados. Among them were Jeremy Theobald and Grace Miller. In the intervening hour he'd run the four names through the Bureau database and those of Homeland Security and the DoD. He had learned their political leanings, banking histories, medical profiles, and sexual predilections, but nothing he saw immediately identified enemies of the state. So he sat and waited for the four to check in, prepared to take all four into custody for further interrogation.

Richard T. Hollingsworth presented his boarding pass, and felt a tap on his shoulder. Santander flashed his FBI credentials and walked the man aside, where he was handed over to airline security and escorted to their station. Three minutes later, Cathy Sullivan underwent the same procedure.

Five minutes later, Jeremy Theobald and Grace Miller had not yet arrived.

Five minutes after that, as the boarding process dwindled to stragglers, Santander went to the attendants and double-checked. There had indeed been no sign of his two other suspects. At his request, the attendant made an announcement:

"Grace Miller, please report to American Airlines gate C5. Grace Miller, please report to gate C5."

Grace Miller did not come, and neither did Jeremy Theobald.

Flight 651 was ready to depart. Agent Santander insisted on eyeballing everyone on board personally. It would delay the takeoff but he was FBI. He loped down the springy jetway, onto the 757, and made his way along the aisle, looking for his prey. They were not there.

He exited the plane and met with airline security, launching a search of the airport.

Richard T. Hollingsworth and Cathy Sullivan sat and waited.

Max and Pam took off.

12 NIGHT

The flight to Grantly Adams International in Bridgetown was nowhere near full. The plan by the island's movers and shakers to entice tourists didn't seem to be working out, though things would undoubtedly pick up as Thanksgiving and Christmas vacationers arrived. The day after Hallowe'en was just too early. First Class had only three other people besides the two sitting in the back row. They were Hank Usher and Betty Reeves, who looked nothing at all like Richard T. and Cathy. They had tickets from Miami to Bridgetown only.

The others consisted of two guys getting quickly sloshed and a woman with a face-lift that had tanned just a little too early. She made a concerted effort to engage one of the guys in conversation, and when that didn't pan out, she turned to the other one. When *that* didn't work, she rose to head aft, into coach, where the semblance of a party had broken out. Screw anybody who said the classes couldn't mix; that was where the action was. It was a pity, she thought, that the big handsome man in the back row of First Class was obviously on his honeymoon—he and his white-blond bimbo had had their heads close together from the moment they boarded the plane. She did wonder why they never kissed, though. They were probably Swedish or some such cold people, and the girl was probably regretting the marriage already.

Five minutes later, the drunker of the two guys decided to head back to coach as well, and that sparked the other guy to go with him. Max and Pam found themselves alone, but just for a moment. The stewardess stuck her head in and looked around brightly.

"Can I get you good people anything else?" she asked.

"We're set," said Max, and that was all the stew needed to join the party in back herself. "Press the attendant call button if you change your mind," she said, vanishing.

Max got up and went to the curtained doorway leading to the party, taking a long look. Then he casually set the curtain so it blocked most of the doorway, in the center of the doorway, with narrow openings on each side. It would hide the First-Class cabin from an accidental viewing and allow him to see anyone coming, if he stood with his back against the bulkhead, which he proceeded to do.

"Join me?" he asked Pam, and she slipped out of her seat and did. The aisle was narrow enough that their arms and shoulders touched, and through the left curtain opening they could see the woman with the orange facial scars chatting avidly at a tall, tanned guy half her age. He had his eye on the stew.

In the quiet of First Class, Pam said softly, "You look just the same to me."

"I thought that'd be a good idea," Max answered. "It wouldn't help to have you wandering about calling my name. Any of my names."

"But to other people, we look different. Different from 'Jeremy' and 'Grace,' different from us. How is that possible?"

"Art," he said.

"Seriously!" she returned fiercely. "Explain it to me, Max."

He looked at her. She looked the same to him as

well, though with a mental shift he could see the face of Betty Reeves as well. Both faces were intent, and not to be trifled with.

"All right. Let me see what I can do here," he said finally. "Somewhere in your science classes, Doctor, they talked about Einstein, relativity, and gravitational lenses, yes?"

"Oh, good," she said. "The simple explanation."

"It's as simple as I can make it. The alternative is to start waving my hands."

"Yeah, okay. Go ahead."

"So Einstein, back in 1916, proposed his general theory of relativity. Doesn't matter what all of it was, but one part involved gravity bending space-time, so one of the tests he proposed for it was to see if light were bent by the gravitation of the sun. During a total solar eclipse in 1919, photos were taken of the stars you could see around the sun when the sun was blocked out—stars you ordinarily couldn't see because the sun's light overpowered theirs. And the photos did indeed show that the stars appeared to be in different places from where we knew them to be—meaning, our image of them was distorted as their light went past the sun. That's the gravitational lens.

"Now, gravity is what holds the universe together, which means it *forms* the space-time continuum. And over in my area of expertise, forces that hold the universe together are even more important than they were to Uncle Al. I talked before about the pure energy at the basis of everything—"

"That's *gravity*?" Pam interrupted.

"Not entirely. *Forming* the space-time continuum doesn't *make* you the space-time continuum, but it's obviously a crucial part of it. So when an alchemist learns to have some minute influence on the energy, he can have some minute influence on gravity. Which gives him some minute influence over light. Which gives him the ability to bend the images flowing from your face and mine to the eyes of other people—and even better, to camera lenses. Meanwhile, light, which is of course a range or spectrum of visible energies, gets some of those energies pushed and others pulled, to change our coloration. So neither humans nor machines can recognize us."

"Damn," Pam said. "Damn damn damn. How long can you keep it up?"

"About six hours," Max answered. "Once again, the universe has a lot more going on than just me, sad to say. Mainly, everything in the universe is moving, changing the way the energy fits together, so the energy I influence dissipates."

"But you can do it again with new energy, right?"

"Yeah. But this will get us through this flight and on to our hotel. At which point I'll be more than ready for a good night's sleep."

"Oh," she said. "I hadn't thought—"

"That I'm human?" he asked, smiling.

As Betty or as Pam, she was a blonde, and she blushed. "It's just that you always seem so . . . in control."

"I have to do my best, with the life I lead. But I'm just a guy with a skill set, like a plumber or an anchorman."

"Sure."

"Really. I can do some stuff, just like everybody can do some stuff. My stuff's out of the ordinary, but it didn't make me something other than human. I get tired, I get hungry, I get—"

"Defensive?"

"Sure. All that."

"Well, you don't have to be defensive, because I'm not attacking. I think what I'm doing is research, trying to grasp this skill set of yours. And when I'm doing research, I forget the human part, too. It's all about the concept. So I forgot you might need sleep." She waved a hand. "It's not as if you haven't been on the go for twenty-four hours."

"You, too."

"No, I caught a nap in the hotel, and on the flight to Miami. Did you?"

"No. I thought I should keep an eye out. Just in case."

"You could have asked me."

"I'm the one who's trained for this. You're the one who had her world turned upside down. You needed the rest. I'll get mine when we're settled."

"The point man."

"Yeah, well." He shrugged. "Anyway, like I've said, I don't talk about myself much, so I'm not very good at it anymore. I'll try to do better."

"You're doing fine," she said. "I'm just an idiot."

"No, you're not. I'm glad to be talking to you." And he was. It struck him that he hadn't felt that way in what was now quite a long time. Simultaneously, as was his way, he was examining that enjoyment, to see if it had any downside. He didn't see any—but if he didn't keep himself on top of things, no one else would. It was what a point man had to do.

But he didn't mention that, and so there was a moment of silence between them. Someone in the main cabin was singing a drunken song, and the convivial hum was growing louder, more uninhibited, leaving First Class that much quieter. They both looked at the half-drawn curtain.

"What happens if somebody tries to come in?" Pam asked at last.

"They won't. They're having a fine time back there."

"But doesn't the stewardess need to keep an eye on the area next to the cockpit?"

"Nevertheless."

"Uh-huh." She turned toward him again. "So when you do your 'stuff'—when you control gravity—"

"I don't control it; I influence it."

"Okay, influence it. Does that have any negative side effects, on, say, airplanes flying over open ocean?"

"Not so's you could notice," he replied. "Which means no. Bending light is not the same as bending big steel machines."

"That's good." But she eyed him intently. "*Could* you bend a big steel machine?"

Max returned her gaze, and said, "I'll tell you as much as I can, Pam. But I can't tell you everything."

"Why not? You have to understand, Max—I *live* to understand. That's what I do. I've got to hear the details."

"No, you don't, and I'll tell you why. Really understanding magick requires changing the way you experience the world; it's not just research. You can hear the words, understand the words the way you've learned to understand them, and miss my meaning by a mile. You can do everything I tell you and it'll seem like one thing, until one day when you see through the masks and find out it's something else altogether. Magick is everywhere, Pam, but it's invisible to untrained eyes."

"So train me. Start me off. I'm in for a penny, with this dart in my side—" And all of a sudden, she remembered that, with all its impact. She hadn't thought about it in quite a while, but now she remembered she was under a sentence of death. It took a moment before she continued. "—I might as well be in for a pound."

"And we might go there, once we're finished with Omen," he said. "You seem like you might be pretty good at it."

"Really?" Now it was her turn to feel pleased.

"Really. But the next couple of days are not the time for lessons. So let's just stick with the basics for now, okay?"

"You Tarzan, me Jane," she said. But there was no arguing it. "All right, Max. Basics. So what's it like being 'Timeless'?"

He craned his neck to get a good view of the stewardess past the curtain. She had moved in on the guy her nip/tucked passenger had started with, and showed no signs of returning to her section. "Being Timeless gives you *time*. You can decide to learn computers, or study Mayan, or work on your backhand, and spend time at it, not worrying that the time's better spent on something else, because you've got all the time you need. You get the ability to delve *deeply* into everything that interests you—and your interests grow. Time makes you huge."

"I would like that. And not just because I'm facing the alternative. I would think most people would."

"It's available."

"Then why don't most people do it? Apart from the little fact that they can't see it."

"That's a big enough reason right there. Society is firm that magick doesn't exist, and it takes a brave soul to even look for it, let alone see it, let alone commit to it, when everything around them says it's false. And let me take that a little farther. Everything around them does *not* say it's false; science says it's true, in its way, as with Einstein, as with quarks. But anything that society says is false is taken as false by people who want to fit in with society without working too hard, which is almost everybody. And that's not by accident. The nature of magick is to create masks so it's not seen; magick on a daily basis works behind the scenes. So when people don't see it and society says 'We all know it's not there,' that's the way the world is set up."

"So maybe we're not supposed to know," Pam said.

"Like Dorothy in Oz? 'Pay no attention to the man behind the curtain'?" Max shook his head. "Didn't work for Dorothy, and it doesn't work for anyone; the thrust of history is clear. Human beings get smarter, over time. We're on a long march to understand our world and our universe, and you can't do that by marking some part of it 'out of bounds,' for the very simple reason that it's all connected—as science says—and if you block off any part, you can't fully know the other parts."

"But if magick—," she said, worrying her lip. "I can't believe I'm saying this; it's just my logical mind at work—"

"That's fine."

"If magick *wants* to stay hidden . . ."

"When society as a whole can handle it," Max said, "sometime farther along the march, it'll be just another aspect of life, like electricity or television are now. People in the Renaissance would have killed to watch some crappy show on the CW, but it wasn't the time for it. And it wasn't that cathode rays wanted to wait for Monday night sitcoms; there just wasn't the structure to handle them. Magick doesn't *want* to stay hidden; it just happens to *be* hidden. Somewhere down the road people will be conjuring up lousy visions with it and never thinking twice."

"That'll be a very different world," said Pam slowly.

"As is ours from the Renaissance."

"And yet here you are, master of the future, today."

Max shrugged.

"So will you finally tell me what happened to you?"

Max took another look at the party in coach. If anything, it was getting wilder. Barbados may not have been bringing in the numbers it wanted, but those that were coming were making up for it in enthusiasm. The stewardess and the guy she'd hit on were having an animated conversation, hands dancing all around, as the lady with the face-lift sulked to one side. Max kept his eye on her as he continued.

"Well, at the end of 1980, three things happened. One, I got a new boss at KQBU, a woman named Madeleine Riggs, and we ended up in bed almost as soon as we met." He smiled a wryly reminiscent smile. "You sure you want to hear this?"

"If it's relevant," Pam said levelly.

"Two, guys with minor magickal powers started attacking me, which of course I didn't understand. But then, three, Valerie Drake—"

"Wait. The singer?"

"Yeah, Val came to QBU for an interview, and brought along her manager, a certain Mr. Cornelius. Turned out, he was actually Cornelius Agrippa, a man born in 1486, and he was Timeless."

Pam gave him a look. He waited calmly. She almost wished he'd seem a little more anxious for her approval, but the logical side of her knew she had to be sure in her own mind that she'd decided what to believe without pressure.

"Keep going."

"Agrippa had arranged to meet me because he was in a war with a man named Wolf Messing, the head of Academgorodok, and that's what I was caught up in. Agrippa thought Wolf's main agent was also keeping an eye on me, in the person of my new boss, Madeleine—but he was wrong. Wolf was *her* agent, and she was unbelievably powerful. She attacked Earl and Fern, by the way, and that's what fried Fern's blood."

"I'm sorry. Though I wish I'd known that professionally."

"Aleksandra—her real name—caught Agrippa by surprise, drove him mad, and thought she'd won the war. But meanwhile, off to the side there was Val and me. Val was nowhere near either of them, magickally, but she'd learned a lot from Agrippa and she taught me as much as she could. Then I took my military skills and my—very limited—magickal skills and went into battle against Aleksandra. And here's the best part about no cut-and-dried answers in magick: even though she massively outclassed me, I managed to do the right thing at the right time, and I beat her. I thought I'd destroyed her.

"That got Agrippa his mind back, but the strain had been too much. He calculated, accurately as it turned out, that he had five years before his time finally ran out, and he devoted those years to making me and Val his successors." Max paused. "Five years later, to the night, he died. And Val died, too."

"The same night?"

"Aleksandra wasn't dead, and she wanted to send a message. She could be here forever, as well."

"Why didn't she kill you?"

"She should have." Deep lines showed suddenly around his mouth, and just as suddenly, Pam understood.

"You were in love with Val."

"We'd been married almost four years."

She put her hand on his arm, gently. "I'm sorry, Max. I didn't know. That's tough."

"Yeah, but it gets worse. Remember what I told Fern, about what happens after death?"

"I was all ears."

"Well . . ."

NOVEMBER 1 - 8:30 P.M. AST
ALL HALLOWS' DAY

12 NIGHT

He told her about his fruitless search for Val, and she listened with great intensity. *A love that strong . . .* , she thought. *Literally beyond death. And then beyond that.* She couldn't have stopped herself from extending her hand toward his for anything in the world. But he, unaware of her intent, raised his arms and arched his back until the muscles of his shoulders popped. She dropped her hand.

She watched him reliving his pain, talking softly about the *Book of the Dead*, and druidic circles, and a demon with lurid red hair. No one else in the world was like this man—and no one was like her now, either. Two days ago she was exactly like them, but not anymore. And all because somewhere deep inside her flesh was a magick dart, stopped but still straining toward her fragile heart. It all came back to her suddenly, and fear flashed through her like lightning. *They really want me dead!* she thought, stunned all over again. *They wanted Agrippa and Valerie Drake dead, and they got them, and they were a hell of a lot stronger than I am!*

Max was her lifeline. He was Timeless and he could save her. She needed him beside her now—and even so, a still small voice said, *Careful, girl . . .*

NOVEMBER 1 - 9:40 P.M. AST
ALL HALLOWS' DAY

12 NIGHT

American 651 kissed the tarmac at BGI as smoothly as a Jamaican bobsled, one minute early. The party was over and everyone was back in their seats, eager to get out on the island.

"Welcome to Barbados," Max said suddenly, cheerfully. "Home of the Bajans." He had shaken off his mood, probably for her. So she answered in kind:

"Not Barbadans? Or Bajorans?"

"There's no Federation yet, Major Kira."

She laughed. But while he was cheering up, the full weight of her situation was toppling back onto her as everyone stood up and began to get their carry-on bags. The lady with the face-lift, the two guys, they were about to begin a holiday. She and Max were about to face down a man Nancy'd said they couldn't beat. Deep within her, another laugh threatened to erupt, but this was a bitter and derisive one, at the complete and utter absurdity of what she'd fallen into.

They went down the mobile stairway and crossed the tarmac to the airport, with Pam regarding the night sky and feeling the isolation of being on a hunk of rock far out in the Atlantic. Even in the late November night, the temperature was in the high seventies and the humidity in the high nineties. Inside, the temperature dropped ten degrees, but not the humidity, which remained especially noticeable to denizens of America's West Coast. This was a New World.

Customs was pretty much a formality. The English-speaking Bajans knew that a crowd coming for a K-1 match would no doubt have items others might frown upon, and welcome to Barbados, friends! Max and Pam were passed along with the line with quick efficiency.

They had no checked luggage, so they walked straight through the lobby, where the crowd from the plane was being met by a variety of hotel drivers and a few relatives or friends. Most of the arrivals were white, most of the greeters black. Most of the greeters wore loose shirts out at the waist, in a subdued variety of colors. It was the "subdued" part that most clearly marked this West Indian island as having a British culture. Only a few men wore anything gaudy.

"I don't like the vibes here," Max said suddenly, softly.

"Why? What's wrong?" Pam asked, snapping her head around toward the crowd. Everything looked normal to her. "Are we in danger, Max?"

"I don't think so," he answered, taking hold of her arm and moving her forward a little more quickly. "But there's something about to break."

Behind them came a sudden scream, then a sudden

shout. Pam tried to turn back but couldn't because Max still had her arm, moving her away. Over her shoulder she saw the woman with the face-lift holding a gun she'd apparently grabbed from a Bajan security guard. The man was gawking at her. *People don't use guns on Barbados,* Pam had time to think, as the guard lunged for his gun and the woman shot him in the stomach and he screamed like a scalded cat. The woman spun toward the stewardess, who was just now coming through the terminal trailing her little bag on wheels. The man they'd both been chatting up in coach was waiting for the stew at the edge of the lobby. He yelled a warning as the older woman let fly with a series of shots. One took him in the arm. One ricocheted through the stunned stew's legs and ripped her bag-cart from her hand. One hit her in the eye.

"You people can't treat me like that!" the woman shouted frantically, watching the stew crumple to the floor. People were running in all directions. The woman pulled the trigger again but her bullets were spent. A second security guard came from out of nowhere and tackled her, rather than use his gun. She ripped at his eyes with her nails and caught something because he shrieked and threw himself away from her, clutching his face. Now two customs officials grabbed her hard by her arms. She kicked out at them, trying to break their shins, trying to stomp their feet.

"Lady, stop!" yelled the customs man clamped on her right arm. Her orange face snapped toward his, trying to bite him, and he reared back, letting go. The other official gave a snort and slammed a heavy fist just behind her left ear. Pam could hear the impact from across the room, as if it echoed in the vast chamber. The woman suddenly sprawled in the official's arms, her

legs splaying crookedly and her head hanging at an odd
angle, like a doll he was dragging home from school.

"Jeez," said the official who'd hit her, staring at what
he held. "I think I killed her."

"You broke her neck," the other one said. "Good on
you, Brian. Stupid cow!"

There was no other sound but the agonized moaning
of the gut-shot guard. The world was frozen. . . .

And then Max was hustling Pam out the door. "Never
get interrogated; that's my motto," he said firmly.

"But I'm a doctor—"

"So's the man taking care of him." She twisted once
more to look, saw a man drop to his knees beside the
guard and apply hard pressure to the wound. Then she
had to look forward again as they pushed their way
through the milling crowd. It seemed to Pam there had
somehow been silence throughout all that, compared to
the cacophony she now heard on all sides. She and Max
were part of one massive organism, with people curs-
ing, crying, babbling, and getting the hell out of Dodge.

"Did we cause that, Max? Did *I* cause it?" Pam
gasped, trying to encompass yet another bolt from the
blue.

"If you had, you'd be the one with the bullet in your
eye," he answered grimly, as they emerged onto the
sidewalk. The row of cabs was all besieged by other passengers, so they kept moving, onto the road that led to
the terminal. "You're having a bad couple of days, but
like they say, it's not all about you. This way—we'll flag
down a cab on the road coming in," he said. "Once we're
well away from here."

12 NIGHT

From the cab, as they drove up the western Caribbean coastline, Pam tried to shut her mind to what she'd just witnessed, so very far from where she'd last experienced violence. No place was safe, even if they weren't gunning for her, but she'd had it in her head that it wouldn't be like that on Barbados. She realized Max had scanned the cabbie with his wiping motion as they'd entered the cab; she was beginning not to notice things like that. Was that good or bad? She forced herself to stare out the windows, forced herself to see the beauty of the island. There was no moon but the stars were bright above the black, rustling palms lining the ghostly white beaches. On the other side of the cab were broad, cultivated fields filled with black, angular shapes in the aftermath of harvesttime. Away in the distance was the mountain that had risen to create this island, so far out to sea. Trees grew up its slopes, but some sort of tall, shaggy tree, not palms, pointed against the sky. There was nothing familiar out there . . . and the images of the guard's stomach and the stew's eye stood in front of everything anyway.

She slumped back against the cracked leather seat.

"You see the excitement?" asked the driver curiously, his eyes watching for wildlife on the road but his mind on the news crackling from his radio.

"No, we were outside already," Max said.

"Bad business. They say some American woman went

crazy. Killed half a dozen people. You must have heard it, hah?"

"Maybe we could talk about something else." Max caught the driver's eyes in the rearview and nodded toward Pam.

"Sure thing," said the driver. But he didn't seem to know what that could be. At last he said, "Americans, hah?"

"That's right," Max replied.

"Mostly, we get the English here."

"Are we that close to England?" Pam asked, trying to remember just where in the Atlantic they were, with a mind that had slowed to a crawl.

"No, ma'am," the driver answered, with his brightest professional smile for the tourist. "But we were an English colony and they don't forget. Plus, you're going to The House, and that's very popular with the English celebrities."

Max also smiled at her, with more sincerity. "The House specializes in privacy. So if we don't stare at the other guests, they won't stare at us—and we won't stare at them because we won't know who they are."

"Didn't Claudette Colbert live on Barbados?" Pam asked, trying to rally and coming up with that from somewhere. "I think I read something. . . ."

"Yes, ma'am, she certainly did," said the driver proudly, with practice. "In Speightstown, a little farther up the coast. She was a very nice old lady, always involved in island life until her strokes. She died at the ripe old age of ninety-two, back in 'ninety-six."

To his surprise, Pam's reaction (in the rearview) was a tightening of her lips and the sharp turn of her head. It had suddenly occurred to her that she was getting really tired of encountering dead women.

"I prefer Stephen Colbert anyway," Max told her.

In ten minutes they arrived at the hotel, rolling up the sweeping drive that overlooked the sea. The main building of The House was an elegantly informal, beautifully landscaped retreat resembling a country house in Devonshire, if Devonshire had palms. As Max and Pam stepped out into the perfumed tropical night, the uniformed help appeared. "No luggage, sir?"

"We'll buy what we need while we're here," he answered.

"Very good, sir. We have excellent shops on the grounds, and we'll find anything beyond that you may require."

"That'll be fine." He slipped the man ten dollars, and soon enough the two of them were in the suite he'd reserved.

The room sat on the edge of a low bluff overlooking two secluded beaches. Its style had changed completely to a tropical motif, but still with an element of British elegance. There were whitewashed wooden ceilings and rattan furnishings, including twin beds. A small fridge purred in the corner, probably fully stocked with gin-and-tonics, and a flat-screen Samsung hung on one wall. There were two complete bathrooms. The veranda led them out to stand as if suspended above the blue-gray sea, which sparkled toward the horizon with all the stars in the universe, blocked here and there by tropical clouds. Occasionally the lights of a fishing boat could be seen, far out to sea. Otherwise they were completely alone with the water and sky.

"It's beautiful, Max," Pam said. "Almost worth the price of admission." She touched his arm. "That sounded ungrateful."

"No, it sounded like a woman with an alchemical

dart in her side." He smiled down at her in the moon-less night. "You should know, I closed off this place like I closed off the room at the party; we're safe here. How are you feeling?"

"Frankly, I'm with you in wanting some sleep. It was a long trip."

"Yes, it was. But what you're feeling is my counter-spell against the dart wearing off."

Fear hit her again. "Wearing off—?"

"Don't worry. I told you it would, and all I have to do is renew it. I'll have to renew it every night until we put an end to Miller Omen, and anyone else who wants you dead."

Pam sat down on the bed closest to the veranda. "Please, do your spell," she said, but the *pain* shot through her all at once. She cried out and rolled sideways onto the bed. Max crossed the room with swift strides. "Lie still," he told her. "You're all right."

This time she fought to keep her eyes open, to see what he did for her—and she did, just as clearly as she'd seen with her eyes closed. The tropical room dis-solved into the Egyptian chamber. Max's hands grew bright as he drew upon the power of Harmakhis, and the lion's mane flickered around his face. And that power flowed into Pam, thick like golden honey, swaddling the pain.

"Oh my God," she muttered at last.

"Sorry. It hit faster than I was expecting, or I would have done it sooner."

"No, I mean . . . what you do! What I saw . . ."

"You'd get used to it, if I did it enough times. Hope-fully, the need for that will be gone soon."

She'd been lying on the bed; he'd been standing over

her. Now their positions came home to both of them. Looking at the other bed in the room, he said, "We can't afford to split up. I don't want you out of my sight. But you can have all the privacy you need."

She looked up at him with her rejuvenated eyes. "I don't need much, Max," she said softly.

He smiled uncomfortably, shook his head. "I hear you, Pam. But . . ."

She understood. "You're still thinking about Val."

He turned over a hand, and said simply, "She's alive somewhere."

Blood suffused Pam's face again. She sat up, got up off the bed, and stood half turned from him. "I'm sorry," she said.

"Don't be," he said. "Nobody else has to deal with this situation. It's hard for me to handle, too." He shrugged. "I will say this, though: it's been a long time since I've had anyone make the offer."

"I can't believe that."

"Pam," he said reasonably, "I can't form long-term relationships."

"Oh," she said stiffly. "Sure."

"I'm sorry, but that's just the way it has to be," he said. "It's not fair to anybody if I do."

"Sure."

"Secondly, I'm your doctor, Doctor. In this case I'm Dr. Feel-Good. It wouldn't be ethical." He turned a palm over. "Third, we're exhausted."

"Not me, anymore," she responded. *But how fucking stupid I am!*

"Pam—"

"It's all right. You're perfectly right." She walked away from him, toward the bathroom. Controlling her voice, if not her face, she put it all behind them. "Tomorrow—how will you find Miller Omen, and his zombis?"

"I think it'll be pretty easy," Max said. Was there a tone of regret in his voice? *Stop being stupid!* she told herself. She went into the bathroom and closed the door, calling "Why easy?"

"Tomorrow's the Day of the Dead."

NOVEMBER 2, 2007 - MIDNIGHT EASTERN DAYLIGHT TIME THE DAY OF THE DEAD

12 NIGHT

Lawrence Breckenridge adjusted his bulk in the dark, cushioned comfort of his Hummer limo and sipped the last of his Century absinthe. Its distinctive alcoholic buzz, the Fée Verte, gave the frosty winter landscape beyond the tinted windows a shimmering spark in the moonlight. *A shimmering spark,* he thought. He smiled, ferally. *His* spark was the Fée Rouge.

His driver exited I-70 at exit 2A, just outside Wheeling, West Virginia. They made two quick rights and came out onto the old National Road, headed back the way they'd come. The limousine plowed through the silent night, turned north on Route 88, passed the Oglebay Resort. Four minutes later they angled onto an uneven gravel road. At the end of it, gates swung wide at his driver's electronic command, and closed smartly behind them as they passed. They drove ahead into a latticed tunnel of trees, most of them witch hazels.

The trees had been at their yellow-orange best three

weeks earlier, the last time Breckenridge had come this way; now they were almost completely barren. Their bark shone gunmetal gray as the limo's headlights picked them out, and swam black above the moon roof in the darker sky.

The Hummer came out of the trees into an extensive area of manicured lawn and ancient shade trees, throwing shadow blossoms on the frost. At the top of the rise ahead of them stood a mansion of the old school—the very old school. Its two tall stories, each some fifteen feet high, stood fronted by great white columns. To each side of the main section sat a section of equal size, all topped by peaked roofs. The mansion was pristine white, and in the early winter haze, atop the glistening hillside, it seemed to hover like a hungry ghost.

The Hummer came to a halt below the high port co-chère. The driver got out, came around smartly, and opened Breckenridge's door. Stepping out of climate control, Breckenridge found the air cold but crisp, smelling of distant smoke. These woods had probably smelled of smoke since the first men had come to them fifty thousand years ago, Breckenridge thought.

He strode to the front door, which opened before him. Inside, a butler stood to receive him, but involuntarily took a step back. Though Breckenridge was not a tall man, there was something about him that carved out more personal space than most people, as if he were twice his size. He had been a chief of staff in the Defense Department, generally unknown to the public at large and completely unknown to them now, but well known among America's power élite as a man who could get things done. Only the people awaiting him inside this mansion, however, knew what he got done *here*.

The chamber around him rose the full two stories, its ceiling lost in shadows thirty feet above them. The room was scaled to match. Portentous paintings decorated the wall, images of stern men in powdered wigs and their uncompromising ladies. Masterfully crafted chairs and tables of witch hazel were arranged on a Portuguese rug extending far beyond the light of several brass floor lamps. This was a home far beyond any true human scale, built long before Toland and Welles even dreamed of *Citizen Kane*. This was a home from the dawn of American history—a home for gods.

The butler, still keeping a distance, bent forward slightly to offer a salver, upon which stood an ebony box. Breckenridge opened the lid and from silver pegs in the black interior removed a necklace formed of nine heavy gold links, much like those seen in the tomb paintings of pharaohs. He slipped it over his head and the weight on his chest was, as ever, satisfying. This mansion was one of the very few places that he could show others more of who and what he really was.

More . . . but not all.

The butler opened the double doors to an inner chamber. Inside, eight people were standing, talking softly, awaiting his entrance. Each of them wore his or her own golden necklace, and as they turned to greet him under recessed lighting, their links sparkled like shimmering sparks. Together, these nine were the *Necklace*. And he was its Gemstone.

They were a group of four men and four women, all but one Caucasian, like Breckenridge. The Caucasian features covered the Caucasian range, from the thick jowls of the avaricious to the thin hair of the ascetic. The African-American woman had that range all to herself. The ages in the room ran from thirty-seven to eighty-two, but the oldest were as sharp and active as the youngest, maybe even more so. The only thing they all had in common was their eyes, somewhere out on the border between *hard* and *fanatic*. In public their eyes showed something else, something normal, but not in this room, where they could be themselves. This was one of the very few places they could show others who and what they really were. Besides Breckenridge, there were:

Richard Hanrahan, in charge of intelligence.

Ruth Glendenning, in charge of training.

Franny Rupp, in charge of ordinance.

Carole van Dusen, in charge of finance.

Michael Salinan, in charge of politics.

Diana Herring, in charge of media.

Porter Allenby, in charge of religion.

Jackson Tower, in charge of magick.

The nine took their places around a circular table made from slabs of witch hazel. Once this area had been part of a forest stretching from Maine to Missouri, but for centuries now the finest of the ancient trees had been part of this room. The people who had sat at this table down through the years were inevitably reminded that appearances change, but strength never does.

Breckenridge strode to his seat but did not sit down. His hands clasping the back of his chair, he began without formality, "There has been a complication, perhaps a significant one, and I thank you all for coming on such short notice. I apologize for being the one to delay us, but *Potus* called a last-minute cabinet meeting."

"Why didn't *Depot* stop him? That's what we put him there for," said Ruth Glendenning contemptuously. She ran the facility for Necklace agents in eastern Pennsylvania; before that she'd been commander of the

Special Operations Division in the D.C. police and had nothing but scorn for every politician down there. The ones she'd covered up for were scum, in her opinion, and the ones who were clean were useless. She was the one black.

"*Depot* doesn't know we're going to war," said Diana Herring reasonably. At thirty-seven, she was the youngest of the group, but her area was media so she had no trouble speaking up if it would make her look better. She always appeared completely sincere and rarely was. "Still less *Potus*. They can lie like nobody's business, but they're better ignorant."

"Exactly," said Breckenridge. "*Depot* and I had to play him carefully—and then he was off into Hillary being a witch. But we handled it. So now listen—Dr. Pamela Blackwell is still alive, which means a zombi antidote is still possible. The spell and artifact we gave Miller Omen to use against her failed. Our agent-in-place at the hospital died, as did the zombi wrangler at her house. The zombis were removed; we weren't compromised. But our agent-in-place at Blackwell's lab vanished."

The others started to murmur, but he held up his hand. "All of that is manageable. It's not the reason I called you here. It's the identity of the man who caused all this havoc." He paused, scanning each of their faces in turn, then pushed a button in the table beside his chair. "Max August," he said.

Each of the room's four walls displayed a 150-inch Panasonic plasma screen, and on each appeared the faces of a man and a woman. The woman was Blackwell in a recent, high-multipixel candid. The man was August, in a posed publicity photo from the late '70s, if the hair and collar were to be believed.

Glendenning sucked air between her teeth. Porter Allenby sat farther back in the shadows. And Jackson Tower spoke for the first time, as if from a great distance. "So," was all he said, but the younger members of the Necklace all turned to him. The Necklace encompassed the range of human endeavor, and that included the occult. It was one thing that set them above other groups that might seek temporal power. Jackson Tower was their sorcerer, and, except for Breckenridge, none of them, despite their expertise in their own fields, could do more than guess at what his field encompassed. Mentally, he dwelt eternally half here and half somewhere else; physically, he'd undergone a complete heart transplant six years before. There was more than a little inhumanity about him. And so, when he spoke, they listened. "The Code Red we've been looking for," he said softly, with infinite satisfaction. "For more than twenty years."

"Sorry. Means nothing to me." That was Michael Salinan, their political guru. He was forty-one, his head shaved bald, his ears out wide and pointed. It made him easy to caricature, a useful trait in a politician; he was the Bat-Boy. "I know what a Code Red is, but who's Max August?"

"He caused us to sever ties with Northcliff," said Herring. "And ACC, I think. That's what the reports say. He went after them with some sophistication, and it was best to cut them loose. He's—"

Tower impaled her with his thousand-yard stare. "A student of Cornelius Agrippa."

It was clear from the looks on all their faces that they understood that, too well. Most had not overlapped Agrippa's time, but they all knew the history of the Necklace. Agrippa had been a determined enemy for over two centuries.

"August has been Timeless since 1985," Tower continued. "It happened just three months before Agrippa passed. So August barely made it to that level before he was on his own. On the one hand, he appears to have a natural aptitude for the art, to have progressed as fast as we now know he has, and to have hidden from us all these years. On the other, he's been on his own all these years. A lot of what he knows is self-taught."

"Which makes him even more dangerous, in my opinion," said Breckenridge. "Knowledge gained through personal work is more *reliable*, if you follow me. Agrippa got him off the ground but he continued to fly through personal strength."

Salinan asked, "How do you know it's him? If he's hidden that long . . ."

Breckenridge turned a hand toward Richard Hanrahan, their intelligence chief. Now seventy-eight, he had joined the FRC during Korea, when he was running COMINT, and had moved up to the Necklace during Vietnam. As the longest-serving member, this was his mansion until he died, and despite his age he showed no signs of passing it on. "AT&T, BellSouth, and Verizon funnel every phone call in their systems to NSA, whose supercomputers sift them for keywords," he said in a clear, concise voice. "Naturally, listening for 'August,' or 'Max,' is all but useless; the words have too many other uses. But August once used the stage name of 'Barnaby Wilde.' Even that is problematic, since 'Barnaby Wilde' was very popular and still has fan clubs. It wouldn't surprise me if August encouraged them to create the noise. He's very good."

"Yes," said Tower sepulchrally. "Not a single sighting."

"But," said Breckenridge, "everyone makes a slip

sooner or later. His came when an old friend called him up. Her name was Fern and she said, 'Barnaby, I need to see you.' The computers knew Barnaby Wilde knew a Fern, knew she was talking *to* him, not *about* him. That was all it needed. Unfortunately, by then our people were dying; it took twelve hours for the result to kick out. We tried running a backtrace on the call, but the number the old lady called wasn't a working number and the routing disappeared into some very strange pathways. Dick's people are trying to decipher it now, but they're not optimistic. The man is a Code Red."

"Get the old lady to talk," Salinan said.

"She died in the interim."

"So did we lose him completely?" demanded Herring.

"Not exactly. We must assume that August forced the agent who's gone missing to talk. Her job at the lab was run entirely through Miller Omen, and he knows better than to tell her about the FRC. But she knows Omen, and she knows where he is."

"Then August's gone to Barbados?"

"August *and* Blackwell," said Hanrahan. "He's keeping her with him, undoubtedly to deal with the dart spell. We dispatched an FBI man in Miami to intercept them as they came through last evening, and he came up empty, which isn't surprising considering who we're dealing with. So I'm sending two full teams to Bridgetown."

"Omen won't like that," answered Herring. "He's got an ego the size of a house."

"What do we care? He works for us," growled Franny Rupp, hunched forward in her chair. She manufactured farm equipment in Fort Wayne, Indiana, and was still reserving judgment on the "pretty girl from the teevee," as she privately considered her. There was no question that Diana filled her link in the Necklace admirably, but something about her got Franny's back hair up.

"He wants to join the Necklace when an opening appears," offered Salinan. "And we might well want him."

"So let him learn to work for the group," Rupp snapped.

Carole van Dusen, their banker, leaned forward. She was old but she'd been beautiful once, and the exquisite bone structure was fully intact. "Are we certain they didn't charter a private plane, or pursue some other such avenue?"

Hanrahan answered that one. "Satellites show no sign of anything like that."

"Couldn't a Code Red fool satellites?"

"No. Satellites watch from multiple viewpoints; bending light for one wouldn't fool the others. On a flight direct from San Francisco to Barbados, we'd have picked him up at some point, if only for a moment—but there was nothing. If they went to Barbados they went on a scheduled route and we have them all covered."

"Couldn't he fly to, say, London, then Barbados?" asked Salinan.

"He could but it would take too long," Hanrahan replied.

"But it's *possible* they could have gone elsewhere. After us, perhaps."

"He doesn't know about us."

"August is a Code Red," Salinan reminded him.

"We would know if he made the slightest move toward us, and he never has. Never. We are *absolutely* certain of that."

"That's good enough for me," Glendenning interjected quietly. "But if—I say *if*—he were to reach Barbados and take out Omen, what would be our liability?"

"Very limited," Breckenridge responded. "He'd have to get Omen to talk, which would not be easy, due to that ego Diana mentioned. Omen knows we can get him a pardon if he's brought to justice; he has no reason to talk and every reason not to. And August would have to know that there was something to talk about. Since we gave Omen the dart spell, the trail ends with him, not us. Therefore, the odds of the operation being dismantled are minute. But they are certainly higher than they were."

Glendenning said, "Then, in addition to the two extra teams in Barbados, I suggest we find our missing agent in San Francisco and ask her what she said, assuming she's still alive."

Hanrahan smiled. "Already under way."

Herring spun her pen on the witch hazel table. "Why has August taken Blackwell under his wing?" she asked suspiciously.

"She's pretty," said Hanrahan. "A damsel in distress."

"Had she been involved with magick previously?"

"No, but she grew up in New Mexico," Tower said. "New Mexico is White Sands and Roswell, and Jicarilla Apache. It's in the air down there."

Breckenridge looked around the table. "We'll continue to monitor events, and if there's any hint of danger we'll alert you immediately. I say again, we are certain August doesn't know about us, but that could change in the days ahead, so monitor your own areas. This is no time to make a slip of our own. We'll reassemble as originally scheduled in three days."

• • •

Outside in the thirty-foot antechamber, the members of the Necklace eddied and flowed into individual consultations, but soon began to leave. It was late and the farthest journey home, Tower's, was over seven hundred miles. Before he left, however, he took Franny Rupp aside.

"Miss Rupp," he said while staring into the wall behind her, "I believe we have items once owned by Max August."

"I think so," she answered, annoyed as usual by his manner. "I'd have to dig 'em out."

"Do," he replied.

Breckenridge and Hanrahan stood talking in low tones, watching them all go. Watching particularly Michael Salinan and Diana Herring. The master of politics and the mistress of media spoke to others separately, lingering, laughing. Then Diana was out the door. Michael had a last few words for Allenby, then he bid the two old men good night.

That was the last of the group. Hanrahan lit a Coyolar Puro, his first cigar since they had started to arrive; the young ones objected to secondhand smoke. Then he and Breckenridge, who had shared his smoke for decades, retired to the interior of the mansion.

They paused at a door that opened only to the touch of Hanrahan's hand. In the event of his demise, Breckenridge had the ability to activate the door, but any unauthorized activation while Hanrahan was alive would lead to swift retaliation. Hanrahan was not the past master of intelligence for nothing.

They stepped into a hall with three rooms. Hanrahan led the way into the farthest one, his electronic nerve center. The actual business of spycraft was conducted at a farm in Moundsville, fifteen miles south. An underground jet-train connected the two; the tunnel had been built under the guise of sanitation when US 250 was widened. But spycraft, particularly data analysis, does not benefit from micromanagement, so Hanrahan spent a good part of his time alone in this room, correlating his people's input.

Now, however, he fiddled with a remote and brought up one of the four plasma screens on the south wall. It showed two blobs of light, one slightly more red-orange than the other, which revealed themselves as human forms.

"Heat signatures," Hanrahan said. "The limo is bugged as well." He brought up the sound.

It was an unmistakable heavy breathing, gasping cries, and the sweaty pound of flesh. The rhythmic pulse of the light-forms was hypnotic.

"Won't one of them—Diana, probably—find the mikes?" Breckenridge asked curiously.

"No mikes in the passenger compartment. It operates by the vibration of the glass between them and the driver."

"I'm amazed that they think we don't know," Breckenridge said, shaking his head sorrowfully. "They know who we are."

"I don't think they do, Renzo," Hanrahan countered. "They're the youngest members. They know they're damn good at what they do, they know they were good enough in the FRC to get promoted to the Necklace. They've always been the best, so they can't quite grasp that we're better."

"And they're young and licentious."

"That, too," Hanrahan answered indulgently. "Meanwhile, I've made certain no one else will know. You have to admit, Renzo, we've done things we regret on our way up, too."

"I regret nothing," said Breckenridge, suddenly cold. Meeting-room disagreements were one thing, but he never accepted real criticism from anyone. "Everything I've done, I've done with one clear purpose in mind."

His old friend regarded him equably. "Renzo, we have mutually assured destruction. Either one of us talks, we both go away. But I'm not worried about me; keeping secrets is what I do. And I'm not worried about you."

Lawrence Breckenridge slowly thawed. "Fine. But we don't need any distractions when we're three days from the Foreign Resource Collection."

"Diana and Michael are professionals. She has Senator Pluscher on 'Press the Meat' and *Hardball*, and Fox will go full bore. Monday morning, we've got Limbaugh, Hannity, *Good Morning America*, an AP piece, and a WaPo editorial. The Senate will be staging an immigration debate."

"I don't need to know how it happens, Dick. I just need to know it does."

"And what you also need to know is, worldly power becomes a more potent aphrodisiac and pure lust fades. They'll learn."

"I'm sure you're right." Breckenridge sighed again, lost in thought for a moment. Then he said, "We were chosen for the Necklace by men who believed we could drive it onward, and we turned out all right. These two do in fact carry their weight quite well. They are the future of the Necklace." He flipped a hand toward the plasma screen. "But how long is that going to go on?"

"You let me know," Hanrahan replied. "I've got to call Omen and take his shit."

"It's his plan, Dick. As he keeps telling us. But it's a good plan, worthy of our goals. So we take his shit and then see what he delivers. He could be part of the future

as well—once we take the shit out of him." Breckenridge turned toward the door. "Well, I'm afraid I don't
have time to watch love in bloom." He tapped his old
friend's shoulder in farewell. "We have work to do."

NOVEMBER 2 - 1:45 A.M. ATLANTIC STANDARD TIME
THE DAY OF THE DEAD

12 NIGHT

The midnight-blue phone awakened Miller Omen from
a particularly satisfying dream. It had something to do
with testing a new compound of his own devising on
black bucks—but the details slipped away as he woke.
Not that he tried to hold on to them; when the blue
phone rang his entire attention focused on what it had
to say. They were just three days from launch.

"Omen."

It was Hanrahan, his liaison. "I have an alert, Mr.
Omen. We haven't found Blackwell and August, so we
are now operating on the assumption that they've arrived in Barbados."

"You're supposed to take care of this, Hanrahan,"
said Omen shortly, his displeasure unambiguous.

"Yes, sir," the old man answered tonelessly.

"So what might you be doing about it?"

"Four men will arrive around ten A.M. as backup.
I can provide more if you want—"

"Just send me August's description, please. I'll take
care of it."

"He's Code Red."

"Yes, you said so."

Omen hung up the blue phone and lay thinking. He was tall and thin, with a prominent Adam's apple and bony shoulders. His face was in keeping with that: an equine face, exposing huge teeth when he laughed. He didn't look like he laughed much. His eyes were gray and calculating beneath a mop of toned hair. But for all he lacked in physical power and good looks, he made up for it with worldly power. Nancy had leapt into his bed once she realized what he had to offer.

Thinking of Nancy reminded him that he'd been indiscreet with his pillow talk. She'd had to know that he had everything he needed to do everything he wanted, but now he hoped she'd taken that secret to her grave; the FRC might have a beef there. Still, any Code Red worth his salt would have killed her. The dread Code Red . . .

He pressed a button on the control box beside his phone. As always, the result made him feel slightly vertiginous, even nauseous; it was a sound pitched so high he couldn't hear it so much as feel it in his back teeth, like a dog whistle. But the rapid appearance of Tilit showed that, as always, his all-but-deaf security chief could hear it perfectly. Tilit was also mute, but his shortcomings were irrelevant to the position he held; the man was crafty and freakishly ripped.

"Tilit," Omen said, "we've probably got a sorcerer on the island, guarding the woman who was supposed to be killed in San Francisco. She should be weakened by the dart I ordered up, but this guy's supposed to be good, so maybe not. Your best bet's to find couples who arrived on the evening planes and come anywhere close to the descriptions I'll have in a minute, then stay with those people. We don't want *indiscriminate* killing so close to the deadline, but if we get any sense *at all* that we've found our quarry . . ."

Tilit dragged a finger across his throat.

"Absolutely," Omen said. "Take a *stone* and take them out."

Tilit nodded and left. Omen went behind him, but headed for his office. The room, lit only by a low quarter moon, had an expansive view of that moon, across a patio and edgeless pool to the sea below. He had never worried about anyone watching him in his office; they'd have to hover somewhere in that view, and he had all the sensors and alarms a man could buy. But now he was facing a Code Red—whatever that really was.

As his calling card to the FRC, he had approached the shadowy cartel with his drugs and troops and allowed them to pick the war. They had welcomed him as an ally, as he'd planned, but along the way they'd informed him that he might face sorcerers before it was all over. They'd claimed sorcerers existed.

Using his secure line, standing in the shadows, he called his captain of the guards on Omen Key. "Report, Giles."

"No problems, Squire," the man said. "Everything's proceeding smoothly."

"Good. Now, you remember that *stone* I gave you?"

"Yes, sir."

"Is it where I left it?"

"Of course. My men never go near it."

"All right. Make certain they don't, and put them on high alert. You might have unwanted visitors who can threaten the zombis."

"What's the stone got to do with it?"

"Just do your job, Giles."

"Yes, sir."

Omen hung up. He took one of the other *stones* the FRC had given him from a desk drawer, and walked it out to the edge of the patio, underneath the stars. He set the *stone* carefully on the patio, then stood and looked out at the world beyond, from on high. *Sorcerers*, he thought. *What a world*.

NOVEMBER 2 - 2:15 A.M. EASTERN DAYLIGHT TIME
THE DAY OF THE DEAD

12 NIGHT

Lawrence Breckenridge's Sikorsky S-92 helicopter left Pittsburgh International Airport, headed for JFK. Though the chopper could land on the mansion's lawn, its appearance over Wheeling, which had no airport of its own, would never go unnoticed, even in the middle of the night. So he always flew to PIT and drove the sixty miles. Part of being the Gemstone in the Necklace was staying off other people's radar. In many ways, Breckenridge was as elusive as the Code Red he wanted dead.

His driver was his pilot and he trusted the man as much as he could trust anyone. Even so, Breckenridge closed and locked the door between the cockpit and the cabin. The ceiling in the cabin was three inches above his five foot nine and there were just four expansive, heavily padded chairs in a space whose standard configuration held ten, so he felt perfectly at home and at ease as he churned through the night. The last-quarter Leo moon was visible out the left windows. In the windows themselves was his reflection: middle-aged, moon-faced, with stony black eyes. Eyes that saw what no one else on Earth saw.

He settled into his ergonomic chair, straightened his spine, placed his hands on his thighs, and relaxed the muscles in his neck. Then he consciously worked his way down his body in the manner he'd mastered some fifty years before. He drained the tension from each muscle, and then he drained it from his mind. He sat, eyes closed, feeling the space around his body, around his helicopter, feeling high and alone in the sky.

Jackson Tower was supposed to be the sorcerer of the Necklace. Jackson Tower thought he was, and so did the rest of them—even including Dick Hanrahan. But they had no idea who they were dealing with. That was the point.

First there were the words:

Coraxo cahisa coremo, od belanu azodiazodore . . .
Das Daox cocasu ol Eanio vohima . . .

They echoed as from a far distance in the far distance of his open and expanded mind . . .

Ohyo! Ohyo! Noibu Ohyo! Casaganu!

She was coming in response. He felt her presence, her power, her glorious starlight growing brilliance . . .

NIISO! Carupe up nidali! NIISO I A I D A!

She was standing before him, naked, splendid, aflame in her aura! La Fée Rouge!

ALEKSANDRA!

Why?

"Diabola," he cried, "I have news of Max August."

The starlight pulsed. *What?*

"He has surfaced, with a woman, as you predicted. We are stalking him."

He is extremely dangerous, Lawrence! She stepped

forward, her aura brushing his. He stepped forward as well. He was not her equal but he would take his respect from her, and meet her halfway.

"You have never told me why Max August is important."

He is an alchemist—his own master! And his luck is good! They stood in the midst of a mindscape, auras joined at the breast, their faces just inches apart. Aleksandra was so exquisitely beautiful it all but tore him apart. *A part of me loves him, Lawrence!* Her lust, her guilt, his pain. *All of me knows he must die!* Her chill, his stabbing joy.

"The FRC will kill him. You've given us all we need."

Who is the woman? She stepped forward once more, now her blazing endless eyes filled his vision. No time for pain or joy. "Dr. Pamela Blackwell, blond, blue, five seven, one hundred thirty-two, intelligent," he relayed in one thought. The passport photo, the lab badge, candids from surveillance for the past year: they were in his mind, they were in her mind. He felt the catlike spite and he held that feeling unacknowledged, deep, not for her to have. He was not her equal but he would take what he could get.

She dies, too!

"Yes!"

She stepped inside him, merging with him, melding with him, and he exploded in ecstasy!

·····································

13 CORN SEED

Cambridge, Cambridgeshire:

Eva Delia stood, slightly knock-kneed, twisting a Kleenex in her thin, trembling hands. Her head darted from side to side like a frightened bird's, and in truth, she was little more than that. Her mind was carefully, heavily swaddled in meds. It kept her from bolting, or dissolving, by making sure she understood as little as possible of what was happening to her.

The lady with the drowning hair carved her face. "Hello, Eva Delia. I'm Mrs. Westbury. How was your journey?"

"Uh?" said Eva Delia fretfully, tearing her Kleenex in two. Her green-black eyes were huge, the whites showing all around.

"She'll be fine," said the black white man.

"Of course she will," said the lady with the drowning hair. "Eva Delia, this is your new home. You'll have your own room. It's very pretty, just like you."

Eva Delia's eyes filled with fears and she let out a burble of sound.

The lady's face straightened, and she spoke to the white black man, which Eva Delia wasn't supposed to hear, so she didn't. The man said she was afraid of being thought pretty, but Eva Delia didn't hear that. The man said there was no history of sexual assault as far as they could determine, but the words meant nothing to Eva Delia. The man said Eva Delia's parents were dead, she'd been institutionalized since she was six, she'd turned sixteen on thirty-one October and had to be moved to a halfway house what with the budget cuts, but that was gibberish. Gibberibberibberibberrrrrrrrrrrrrr.

The lady looked back at Eva Delia and the sudden sound nearly drove Eva Delia to her knees.

"You're going to get better here, honey. You won't have to be locked up anymore. Tomorrow we'll dial back your meds and it'll all be better."

Eva Delia Kerr kissed the lady's hair. It smelled like *hope*!

NOVEMBER 2 - 8:45 A.M. ATLANTIC STANDARD TIME
THE DAY OF THE DEAD

13 CORN SEED

The Bajan sun had been warming the day for nearly three hours when Pam began dancing on the sweeping lawn behind The House. She felt as if she needed another three hours' sleep, and three hours beyond that, but she was up, she was ambulatory, more or less. She and Max had hit the resort's salons as soon as they opened at 8:30, and she was testing her new footwear. She'd wanted sandals but Max had insisted on running shoes—a reminder that this was no holiday.

They were both wearing straw hats and sunglasses, shorts and bright shirts in honor of the tropics. They were people enjoying their vacation. And, truth to tell, except for the jet lag (and the heat, and humidity), Pam felt pretty good. She didn't know what life was all about anymore, but each new day felt very much like another lease on it. Right at the moment she appreciated that more than she could have imagined.

Max, leaning against a huge baobab tree, watching her, asked, "Shoes fit all right?"

"Fine."

"You like to dance?"

"Salsa. I told you."

"So you did." He pushed up off the baobab. "Ready to go?"

"Sure. Let's do this thing!" Her embarrassment of the night before was best left well behind her, she figured. Today was for keeping busy. And maybe that was the best way for the living to pass the Day of the Dead.

They walked to the hotel pool, where Max looked around for a moment, and then led her to a stool at the bar. The bartender at nine in the morning was a girl who hardly looked old enough to drink herself, but was blessed with a decent body that she showed to its best advantage in a red Brazilian bikini.

"Where would I find tickets for the fight tonight?" Max asked her, sliding onto his own stool.

"They're sold out, I believe, sir."

"Oh, officially," said Max offhandedly. "But I'll bet there's someone around who could help me get some." He slid a twenty-dollar bill across the mahogany bar.

"That would be Henry," she answered cheerfully, sliding the bill into her bikini bottom. "Right over there." She waved a carmined fingernail toward a beefy, mahogany-colored man in his thirties, standing beside the towel rack. He caught the move and drifted their way, his oiled, wavy hair catching the sun.

"Yes, Amanda?" he asked politely, eyeing Max and Pam.

"Gentleman looking for tickets for tonight, Henry."

Max already had a fifty between his fingers. "In the front row," he added.

"I'm sorry, sir," said Henry, and looked it. "That I can't do. But third row, square in the center—"

Max sucked air between his teeth. "Third row—how depressing. Maybe you can point me toward someone holding first-row tickets, and I could speak with him." He slipped the fifty into Henry's shirt pocket. Henry regarded it with even greater sadness.

"There are a number of gentlemen in this hotel, sir, of course. But I would not expect any joy there. They've come a long distance, you see." He began to pull the money from his pocket but Max forestalled him.

"Let me worry about that. Who has the best tickets you know of?" He put a second fifty beside the first one.

"That would almost certainly be Mr. Rideau, an American broker. His seats are right beside Mr. Omen's."

Max felt rather than saw Pam react to the name, and he was already turning back to the bartender, sliding another twenty over to her. Everyone's eyes followed the money now. "Two mimosas, Amanda," he said. "Something for you, Henry?"

"Just a Diet Coca-Cola."

Max waited until everyone was served, then asked, "Who's this Mr. Omen, to have such good seats? And where can I find him?"

"Mr. Omen, sir, is a major American industrialist. He has an estate here on the island, but it is difficult to reach him."

"Then what about Mr. Rideau?"

"Mr. G. Wilson Rideau is stopping at the Sandy Lane." Henry spread his hands. "But I believe he's quite enthusiastic about this contest. If I were you, I'd approach Miss Sandalwood, here in the hotel. She was given her tickets—"

"You may be right, Henry," Max said. "But it's early, so I'll try Mr. Rideau first. If that fails, I'll look you up again. You'll be around for a while?"

"I'm on duty until four, sir. Amanda will know where to find me."

"Good. Well, then, to luck!" He downed the mimosa.

"To luck," Pam echoed, and downed her own.

They crossed the grounds to the beach, where they removed their new shoes and began to stroll along the sand. The ocean to their left was amazingly calm beneath a sky of Caribbean blue.

"The Sandy Lane's the most exclusive resort on the island," Max said. "I didn't want to stay there because I figured guys like Rideau would be there."

"We can walk to it?"

"Sure. It's all one beach. You can scope the other resorts as we go by, tell me where you'd rather have stayed."

"I like our place just fine," she said, and took his hand. All of a sudden she had nothing further to say— nothing worth saying. She let the breeze blow through her hair, the sun warm her skin, the ocean slide around her ankles, and she was content.

13 CORN SEED

"Mr. Rideau is the gentleman swimming laps just now," said the lifeguard, pointing discreetly toward a barrel-chested man surging up and down the pool with a ferocious butterfly stroke.

Max and Pam wandered over to a table and chairs beneath a canopy and watched Rideau swim. Pam started to ask a question, then decided Max would be busy and should operate unimpeded. So she went to the Sandy Lane's bar and got them another round of mimosas. She was thirsty and they were good.

After five minutes, Rideau took a final lap, all out, and came up out of the pool, sweeping water over the bystanders in front of him. He took no notice of their mild complaints as he grabbed his towel and began to dry off.

Max became very still, his eyes focused on the man across the way.

Suddenly, Rideau took an uncertain step to the side. Then another. He seemed to be trying to maintain his balance, as if the pool tiles were tilting under his feet. He lurched toward a chaise longue and sat down on it hard, almost overbalancing it. But he stayed seated, slumped, his head hanging forward. One of the pool boys noticed and came to see what was wrong.

"Are you feeling all right, sir?" the boy asked.

Rideau threw up all over his legs.

A doctor was called. He examined Rideau, seemed satisfied, and then he and the pool boy, who'd returned after washing off somewhere beyond the guests' view, supported the man as they made their way into the hotel. Rideau was staggering.

"What did you do?" Pam asked.

"Labyrinthitis," smiled Max. "As I'm sure you're aware, Doc, it's a strange little ailment of the inner ear— the part that controls balance. It has the same effects as seasickness—dizziness, vomiting. I'm afraid Rideau won't be able to make it to the fight tonight."

"And you did it with gravity," Pam said, not so much a question as statement of fact. She knew she'd never be able to present a dissertation on this but she was writing it avidly in her head. "You changed the pressure in his ear."

Max finished his second mimosa. "Let's go get the tickets."

• • •

Ten minutes later, Max stationed Pam near a palm tree, easy for him to see but difficult for anyone in the doorway of G. Wilson Rideau's bungalow. Then he knocked.

She watched him turn on the charm as a young man, probably Rideau's assistant or butler or lover or son, answered the knock. Max's smile was wide, his gestures expansive, as he explained how he'd heard of Mr. Rideau's illness. He had no wish to be a vulture, but he very much wanted to see the K-1, and if Mr. Rideau had decided not to go, Max was prepared to buy Mr. Rideau's tickets.

The young man disappeared into the suite, then returned.

Colored cardboard and colored bank notes changed hands.

13 CORN SEED

The four agents from Federal Response Control could not have been welcomed more effusively when they arrived at Miller Omen's tropical home. He came bustling in as soon as they'd put their bags down in the breezeway.

"The FRC is always Johnny-on-the-spot," he said. "And I can really use you boys. I have my personal security scouring the city, but that leaves the rest of the island, and with resorts scattered all around the coast . . ."

"Excuse me, sir," said the team leader, a man named Kelvin. "But you're the nexus of August's interest. I would expect him to be near rather than far."

"Of course," Omen answered, spreading his hands expansively. "As we draw closer to the go-date. But August just arrived last night, if Hanrahan's to be believed"—he enjoyed their reaction to that—"so he'll need time to get his bearings and figure out his plan. If it were me, I'd hole up well off the beaten track while I did that. So if you guys split into two teams and work your way up the east and west coasts, meeting in the north— then come back down the center of the island—"

"If I may, sir—"

"You may not." Abruptly, their genial host was gone, replaced by their local commander. "I live here, and I know what to do. So go do it."

"Yes, sir," said Kelvin.

"Now."

"Yes, sir."

"My butler will give you maps and directions on your way out."

"Yes, sir."

The four men filed from the room, and when they'd gone, Omen broke into his rare horsey smile. *Fucking FRC wants to horn in on my operation, now that they've compromised it. Of course the sorcerer's nearby, but Tilit can handle that. If I need these guys, I'll know where to find them.*

NOVEMBER 2 - 10:30 A.M. AST
THE DAY OF THE DEAD

13 CORN SEED

"Where to, sir?" the cabbie asked.

"Westbury Cemetery."

"Meeting someone?"

"Yes, we are."

"I'd keep my eyes open there—with the lady and all, sir."

Max looked back at Pam. "We're going to the bad part of town."

"Wonderful," she said sweetly. "I could have done that in Oakland."

The cabbie said, "Things'd be pretty slow this time of the day, but even so, the Orleans is not a good place to be."

"Thanks, but we've got to commune with my ancestors."

"Just be sure you don't meet them," said the cabbie, and then decided he'd said too much. If the Americans were determined to be cowboys, that was up to them.

The inside of the cab was decorated with picture post-cards of the island, each with a price in American and Barbados dollars to get to the pictured place. The radio was playing something Pam classified as "Caribbean," bouncy and bright. Max leaned forward.

"What's good in music down here now?"

"Good, sir?" the cabbie asked. "Good like what?"

"Good like good."

"Well, sir, I like Rihanna. She's all over MTV now, but she's a good Bajan girl. You might ask the fellows at Branscombe's, on Broad Street. They're our biggest music store; they could advise you."

"I know it, thanks."

"I have a great price on an all-day tour, with lunch and island stories included," the cabbie continued. "We can swing by Branscombe's and play your purchases on my player." He tapped the dash.

"Not today, Chauncy," said Max, looking at the cab-bie's license. "Is that really your name, 'Chauncy'?"

In the rearview mirror, Pam saw the driver's eyes smile. "It really is, sir. You know we were a British is-land."

"I do know, but Chauncy's an unusual name in *England*. You don't often hear it these days."

"We like our ways slow down here, sir."

"Well, don't think it's not appreciated."

They were coming into the city, suddenly running on a long road beside a longer harbor. The sun was brilliant on the turquoise water, and this was November, not July. Tropical paradise, exhibit A. But Bridgetown belied the stereotype, looking every bit of its British heritage. Instead of the exotic tropical structures of Caribbean travelogues and pirate movies, this city boasted precise, concise, civil servant architecture. *Low, squat, square—white—almost no balconies,* Pam realized. *In the tropics!* Rather, casement windows no different from London's or New York's marched stiffly across the white-cream walls. This had been an outpost of empire; whatever dwelt here was to be ignored.

They turned on President Kennedy Drive and entered a more residential part of town. Almost at once, the residences started going downhill, architecturally speaking.

The cabbie pulled to a stop in the cab zone outside their destination. Like the rest of Bridgetown, the cemetery looked as if it belonged in England, or rather, that it once had. Now it was slovenly around the edges, the statues over the graves sometimes headless. A lonely crypt with shattered windows bore the legend TEMPUS FUGIT. "Shall I wait, sir?" Chauncy asked.

"No, thank you, Chauncy. Enjoy the day."

"Always."

The taxi spurted away. "Not leaving a back trail?" Pam asked knowingly.

"Exactly." Max nodded. "They must assume we're on the island so they have to be looking for us. They might pick us up on one leg of our excursions but not the whole thing."

They walked into the surrounding neighborhood. They could have been in any small American town circa 1920, or any American ghetto circa 1960, if the remaining paint on the boxy old buildings had peeled under tropical skies. The streets were wide and empty—amazingly empty considering the rest of Bridgetown had shown a reasonable amount of traffic. It was so quiet they could hear the songbirds chittering in distant trees. Max's eyes were watchful, ready, and Pam took comfort therein. There was nothing she could see that threatened them.

"This is the bad part of town?" Pam asked, instinctively keeping her voice conspiratorial. "Where is everybody?"

"Asleep, hungover, drugged out."

"But we're meeting someone here?"

"An old friend."

Max suddenly took her elbow and steered her into a shadowed alleyway, before turning to scan the street behind them. A cat lurked across the open concrete, stalking something invisible; if it had been anywhere but in the cat's mind, Max would have seen it. There was nothing else. He took Pam down the next alley into a thicket of hanging laundry. The sopping shirts and trousers and dresses hung in a solid canopy, so that they had to push things aside to make their way through, only to find another laundry line right before them. They pushed through that one, too, getting damp now, and then a third. Finally they emerged from the alley into a riot of backyards, festooned with garbage and bottles and used condoms. The doctor in Pam approved of the condoms. "Don't say I never take you anywhere," Max murmured in her ear.

He led the way unerringly through the maze, but Pam was soon lost. A dog barked savagely from inside a shuttered house. A sour yell told it to shut up. A woman shrieked. A gun went off. Pam stayed close to Max.

A man appeared from a side path and walked past them, taking no notice.

"We're invisible?" Pam demanded.

"Mmm," agreed Max, looking innocent.

"You forgot to tell me that," Pam said.

"Did I? My bad," he said. "It happened in the middle of that laundry gauntlet, so no one looking into the alley would see it."

"More gravitational lenses?" she asked.

"I didn't do this one. My friend did. She's mambo—a priestess of vodou—and she has her own ways."

They went through a rough hole in a six-foot fence and entered sudden open space—a muddy field thirty yards across marked everywhere with hoofprints, surrounded on three sides by the fence. On the far side stood a purple building, apparently a stable; they continued toward it. Max slid the wide door aside so that Pam could enter and bowed her in. She didn't hesitate, but stepped out of the bright light into a large room that smelled of animals, sweat, and incense. As her eyes adjusted she came to see the haze of the incense hanging motionless in the air, but there was no sign of human life.

"Stand still," Max said, taking her elbow, but gently. She stopped and stood beside him, peering into the gloom. Then she heard the sound of someone (something?) approaching, crunching the straw that covered the dirt floor. Max wiped his hand in its familiar arc. An old woman, little more than skin and bones, wearing a red-and-green patterned dress that hung on her, slowly appeared. She stopped when she recognized him. "Max!" She looked delighted.

"Mama Locha!" he answered, and went forward to hug and kiss her. The hug was fervent but gentle, since she looked as if she could all too easily snap in two. The kiss was less restrained, and Pam wondered what the relationship was between the two. Though Mama Locha was much younger than Fern Jenkins, the image of Max and Fern together came back. If the women aged and he didn't . . .

"Say hello to my *friend* Pam, Mama."

"Welcome, *friend* Pam." The old woman's eyes, large and dark in her shrunken face, drank Pam in. Pam could almost hear the shutter click, and then Mama Locha indicated a place on the straw for them to sit. She and Max sat facing each other and Pam sat to the side, knowing she was watching two artists at work. Suddenly, Pam caught a glimpse of something moving on the edge of the shadows, flittering above the straw, and she hunched in closer to the others.

Max said, "You're looking well, Mama."

She grinned impishly, showing perfect teeth. "And you learned to be too slick in the show business, boy."

"Slick but true. I embellish but I never lie. And I've seen you looking worse."

"But feeling better, Max. Feeling better." Mama Locha threw a glance at Pam. "I met this boy in 1988, in India. I hate to leave my island but Max was very good to me, especially after I underestimated the man I followed there, the first time." Then back to Max. "So why have you come to see me now, boy?"

"I need a lot of help, Mama. And I need it fast. Five things—first, a boat, to visit Miller Omen's island."

"Oh," Mama Locha said with a sneer. "*Squire* Omen, if you please. On Omen Key."

"And where is Omen Key?"

"Thirteen kilometers out to the east. It's this little hunk of rock and dirt, maybe five kilometers by four. Nothing there but jungle and bird shit, but seems like he made it his official residence, and all of a sudden his companies owe no taxes, to America, where it matters to some, or here, where it wouldn't, except he has Omen

Export in Bridgetown and it does some business. Seems like legitimate business." She cocked her narrow head. "What's *your* business with him?"

"Zombis."

"You're stereotyping our Caribbean, Max."

"Nope, speaking from personal experience—Pam's and mine together. Can you get us a boat?"

"I can get you a boat, of course I can. But visiting Omen Key is dangerous, boy. He's ringed his island with security. I've been curious myself, you know."

"I can handle it," he said flatly.

Pam saw the thing move again, in the shadows like a hummingbird. But it was too fast and it wasn't a hummingbird. Pam thought, *I should tell them—but surely they know. If I can see it—*

"Well, all right, boy," Mama Locha said, growing businesslike. "I can get you your boat. You'll want a pilot."

"I'd rather not," Max said.

"You'll want a pilot," Mama Locha repeated. "There's nothing else out there but Atlantic Ocean, and you have to find not only the island but the right spot on the island."

"You know the right spot?"

"I told you, I've never gotten on since he bought it. But I've been there, as a girl. I'll think about it today. What time will you want it tonight?"

"There's a big fight tonight, at Wildey—but of course, this neighborhood knows that better than anyone. That'll focus attention on this side of the island, far away from Omen Key. I figure the time to go is ten."

"All right. And you'll be wanting weapons?"

"Two pistols and a rifle, with plenty of ammo. Pam likes a 7.65-millimeter automatic, preferably a CZ-83.

I'd go for any of the good 9-millimeters, and an AR-15 or one of its clones. Night-vision goggles, too."

"I can get the guns, boy. We'll have to see about the goggles; that's a bit dodgier. I'll do what I can and make delivery this afternoon."

"We're at The House."

"Fancy."

"I also need the following ingredients," he said, and handed her a list.

"What are these?" Mama asked.

"The makings of a powder that will destroy zombis. Pam invented it."

Mama looked at Pam again, maybe seeking something she didn't see the first time—and found it. "What's that in your side, *friend* Pam?"

Max said, "A dart," but Mama waved him off.

"Let the girl tell me," she said.

"A dart," Pam echoed, spreading her hands helplessly. "Max says it's magick, and headed for my heart, but he has it under control."

"What does this boy know?" Mama said. "Let me see."

Pam slid across the straw to sit beside the old priestess, and raised her top. She started to point out the spot but Mama was already homed in on it.

"Maggie!" she called.

A young woman, very fit inside a plain white dress that clung to every curve, stepped from the shadows at the back of the stable, swirling the incense.

"Bring me a pink candle and a cat's brain."

Pam sat very still after that.

Maggie returned with the two requested items, and a box of kitchen matches, a small metal pot, and a stand on six-inch legs on which the pot was clearly built to sit.

The woman laid them beside Mama Locha, kissed the old woman's hand. The old woman patted her head, and Maggie returned to the shadows. Pam looked at the very tiny feline cerebrum, the size of a walnut.

Mama Locha lit the pink candle and set it beneath the stand, then put the pot on top. She picked up the cat brain in her right hand, her skinny, knobby fingers encompassing it. She looked directly at Pam a third time, but this time she was looking through her.

She began to speak in what was some form of English, but not any Pam could comprehend. The words rose and fell, settling into an insistent chant, rising in volume. Pam looked at Max. He raised his palms: *It's cool.*

Then Mama Locha's speech changed, grew less distinct and more like a series of hisses. Max knew she was going deep into vodou, speaking the langage beyond English or French, the words of Danbhalah-Wedo, the Grand Serpent, father of the *loas*.

As her chant reached its throbbing crescendo, Mama Locha held her right hand above the little pot and squeezed. Gray matter dripped from her hand into the pot, where it immediately began to steam, then sizzle. The smell hit Pam's nose like a blow, but oddly, after a career in infectious disease research, she welcomed the blow.

Mama Locha waited till the sizzling reached a certain point, then leaned down to blow out the candle. As everyone's eyes adjusted to the returning gloom, she snatched up a bottle from somewhere nearby and poured its contents into the pot. Steam exploded with a new smell, of rum. A moment passed, then Mama stabbed her thin fingers into the pot and withdrew them covered in gray paste. She clasped them to Pam's side.

Pam felt as if she'd been kicked by a horse. For one thing, it was scorching. She cried out and twisted away, but Mama's hand remained attached to her side as if glued there. And gradually the burning and the pain subsided, to be replaced with white warmth and a sense of well-being, almost love.

"Don't get her high, Mama," Max said. "She's got serious work to do."

"She'll be all right," Mama replied. "And better than you had her."

"I stopped the dart," Max said with some asperity.

"Yes, you did, but it was still trying to reach her heart. I used the pink candle to burn the cat's brain with love and contentment. Now the dart's striving and sense of direction are both grown blurry; this cat would rather drowse in the sun." She looked at Pam one more time. "Neither of us can stop it forever. You must find the one who did you."

"I know," Pam said.

"But *now* you're doing as well as you can do."

"Thank you, Mama," Pam blurted.

The old woman inclined her head and raised her hand, for Pam to kiss. Pam did not hesitate.

Mama smiled, and looked down at the list. "I can get these ingredients. Easy. And perhaps," she said, looking back at Pam, "I could have that recipe later."

"If it works, Mama, you bet," Max said, and Pam nodded.

"What's the talcum powder for?" Mama asked her.

Pam said, "Ordinarily, I'd make this as a liquid, for injection, or possibly as a cream. But if we meet zombis again, I don't expect I'll have time to ready a syringe, and I don't expect to want to get close enough to apply it topically. If I infuse the powder, I can blanket them like a fog. So long as it enters through their scratches, it'll work."

"Smart," Mama said, nodding approvingly. "Now, you said five things, and that's four, Max."

"Right. I also want some ringside tickets for the K-1 match tonight—sections B or D."

Pam sat forward. "We have those, don't we?"

"Ones next to Miller Omen, yes. But listen, Young Wild West, Miller Omen's looking everywhere for us, and a couple, no matter how well disguised, that enters his life now—he's bound to at least suspect, and at most kill us in our seats."

"I did wonder . . . ," Pam began.

"He will hear that his good friend Rideau took sick and sold his tickets to a couple. He'll be waiting for that couple. So we're going to sit where we can watch what happens. Wearing new faces, of course."

"And we need to get these tickets through Mama," Pam said slowly, "because getting them the same way you got Rideau's might turn him right back to us."

Mama Locha smiled, showing her perfect teeth, and turned to Max. "All right, the boy knows *something*. We would hate to lose you, Max." She leaned forward and touched Max's hand. "So what is Squire Omen doing with zombis? I don't like zombis anywhere near me."

"I'm not altogether sure yet, Mama, but once Pam found a way to free zombis from their spell, Squire Omen tried to kill her with the dart. When that failed, he sent zombis after her. Clearly, he's got something going with the walking dead. As you say, this is not zombi country, which makes for a real good place to hide zombis, but hide them why? That's the question."

"And I'll be happy to hear your answer, boy."

Pam said sharply, "Max!"

"What, Pam?"

"Over there—" She stabbed a finger at the thing, now hovering boldly in the light, but somehow still in shadow. It had the silhouette of a woman but was no more than six inches high—attenuated, with limbs of slim muscle almost horselike, and whispering wings. It quivered like a taut spring, and its long hair bobbed at its ends. But in the next instant, it was not a woman but a cloud.

"That's just Cocorik," drawled Mama Locha. "She lives here."

Max said, "It's a sylph, an elemental of the air. What do you call them, Mama?"

"Flitters."

Max said to Pam, "Elementals are manifestations of nature. People sometimes glimpse them from the corners of their eyes—you did, that first night—but they're more visible around power; it makes them manifest. Even then it's hard to see them clearly. They do what they do but they're not evil. In fact, approached the right way, they're an artist's best allies, because they're everywhere."

Mama Locha said, "This is her home, too." The cloud soared upward into the high shadows, leaving tendrils of mist behind. "If Max weren't here, you wouldn't see that," the old woman added.

"Thank you, Mama. We'll wait to hear from you," Max said, getting to his feet. Pam followed suit.

"Thank you for coming, boy. Nice to meet you, girl."

Pam smiled, "Nice to meet *you*, Mama." She hadn't forgotten the danger around her, or the danger inside her, but more and more, she was liking this secret world she'd fallen into.

13 CORN SEED

Miller Omen, wearing flip-flops, shorts, and a ragged Meridian Pharmaceuticals T-shirt, entered his office. No alarm had sounded since last night; nothing physical or metaphysical to indicate that the Code Red had come around. Omen could have moved all his preparations to another room but he liked this one, and so long as it was safe he would stay with it. They had only eighteen hours to go.

The walls were covered with maps. Covering each map was a clear plastic sheet, so that black Magic-Markered lines, arrows, and numbers could be written over the topography. Wind directions and water currents were inscribed in yellow and blue respectively. Political divisions were in orange. Omen examined the maps, even though he knew them by heart. Was there anything the inclusion of a sorcerer would affect? Of course, a wild card could have an effect anywhere, but in terms of command operations, there was nothing to be gained by making changes at this late date. That was something he'd learned from practical experience in his twenty-five years of climbing ladders. Be sure you're right, then go ahead.

He checked his inbox for reports from the front. The preparations for the police and military were perfectly on track. That was what bothered him about the Code Red. That was chance in its most virulent form, and it required him to rely on the FRC's *rocks* for protection. None of that appealed to him.

Using his secure line, he called Giles. "Report."

"No problems, Squire," the captain of the guards replied. "The canisters are coming out ahead of schedule. We can have them loaded a good two hours early tonight if the ship's prepared."

"I'll make certain that it is. What about visitors?"

"No sign of anything."

"The *stone* has an individual alarm. You're aware of what it sounds like."

"I am. Hasn't sounded." Giles clearly had something he wanted to add.

"What is it?" Omen asked quietly.

"Squire, the men were already pushing to beat your schedule. Now they've been on full alert for nearly twelve hours."

"And so?"

"They're tired," Giles said. "Tired men make mistakes."

"Not men I employ," said Omen.

"Squire, it would be a good idea to let some of them stand down. We can still respond to anything."

"You don't know what could happen."

"No, Squire, I don't—"

"So don't presume to know what it takes to respond. Keep everyone on high alert. There's only eighteen hours to go. Are these ballerinas I've got working for me?"

"No, Squire."

"Are you a ballerina?"

"No, Squire."

"Then do what I tell you." Omen hung up.

Nobody was slacking off now, or any time before the operation was complete. His genius and the FRC's connections would change the world. And then he'd know if he wanted to, or could, work with them in the future. They played their cards close to the vest—there was an inner circle from which he was carefully excluded so far—but they'd have to open up after this.

After he gave them a country.

13 CORN SEED

Max and Pam went back out in the noonday sun, passing through the horse corral out back. *I don't remember seeing or hearing any horses in the stable,* Pam thought. *Just Cocorik.* They went through the hole in the fence and back into the hodgepodge of backyards.

There were more people up and about now, washing sheets and flimsy teddies, lounging in the sun. Between shifts in the sex trade. More than one voice was raised in anger, more than one in crowlike complaint.

Pam looked around—raised her arm and looked back and forth between it and the half-naked girl scrubbing last night's stains from her linen ten feet beyond. The arm and the girl looked equally visible to Pam, but the girl looked up to rub sweat from her forehead and didn't seem to see her. From the corner of her own eye, Pam caught a glimpse of something small darting on the path ahead, and rather smugly thought *sylph.*

Max said, "You notice how Mama never asked about you directly."

"Well, yeah, now that you mention it."

"She accepted you for being with me, a *friend,* but it

was up to me to tell her about you if I wanted to. That's the etiquette of our art."

"It all seems very civilized, except for the fresh-squeezed cat brain and the flying elemental."

"Every artist has his own way of approaching magick; it's bigger than any one of us. But anyone who approaches deserves respect."

"Even the bad guys."

"Even the bad guys. A master is a master even if you're going up against him."

"So do you want to tell me about Mama Locha in 1988?"

"No. That's her story."

"But you apparently got involved. In India."

"Nice weather we're having, isn't it?"

"Would she have helped you out here if she didn't know you?"

"Maybe, once she was satisfied with me. That would have taken some time, though." They came back to the alley with the hanging wash. "Let's find another cab."

NOVEMBER 2 - 12:15 P.M. AST
THE DAY OF THE DEAD

13 CORN SEED

Tilit and his sergeant caught up with Chauncy as he was about to pull away from the Fairchild bus station. They slid into his backseat; he turned to ask "Where to?" and had a 9mm Glock shoved in his face.

"We checked the company records, so don't lie to us," the sergeant, whose name was Ballantine, said. He was a foot shorter than Tilit, burned by the sun, wearing a sweater vest despite the heat, to hide the heat he was packing. "You picked up a couple this morning at ten twenty-eight."

"Y-yes."

"What did they look like?"

"They—had dark hair—"

"Lie again and you're dead."

"I'm not lying! Why would I lie?"

Tilit whistled sharply, the one sound he could make, and waved a hand dismissively: a matching description was not to be expected.

"You picked them up at the Buccaneer Bay?"

"As you must know."

"There's no one who could possibly be those people at the Buccaneer Bay."

"They could have been visiting. They could have walked from somewhere else. I just picked them up!"

"Records say you took them to Westbury Cemetery. Where did they go from there?"

"I didn't notice."

The Glock slammed against Chauncy's mouth. He felt a tooth break, felt blood pour over his lips.

"Where?"

"In—into the Orleans. I don't know any more than that!"

"Two white people, walking into the Orleans."

"I warned them."

"What else did they say? Clues as to where they were headed."

"Nothing." Chauncy cringed. "Honestly. Nothing."

Tilit pointed his Glock at Chauncy's forehead. From an oversized pocket of his pants he pulled a bright orange and yellow rectangle. Chauncy was astounded to recognize a remnant of his own childhood: a Super Speak & Spell. The Glock never wavered as Tilit typed with his free hand, and the Speak & Spell must have been modified because it repeated what he wrote in its grotesque mechanical voice. **GIVE ME SOMETHING OR U DIE.**

"Oakland!" Chauncy said frantically. "She said she knew Oakland!"

"It's them," said Ballantine, and looked at Tilit. The mute nodded, and tilted his head sideways. They were leaving.

They left.

Chauncy sat in a pool of piss and listened to his heart pound.

He'd liked his passengers. The man had seemed like an old friend from the moment they'd met. He was glad the two men had gone away . . . and he was glad he hadn't mentioned Branscombe's.

NOVEMBER 2 - 12:30 P.M. AST
THE DAY OF THE DEAD

13 CORN SEED

Max and Pam disembarked at National Heroes' Square fifteen minutes later, just two long blocks from the bus station, and turned into Broad Street.

Max said, "It's five miles back to the hotel. A good part of it's through interesting old streets, the rest is along the beach again, and it's all flat. We've got plenty of time; would you like to walk it?"

"Sure. I feel fine today. And we can avoid a taxi."

"Then let's make the most of it."

They strolled slowly into the narrowing passageway of a pedestrian mall—three-story white buildings whose windowed ground floors promised the glories of shopping. It was Brighton gone west, Santa Monica gone small. But for all that, the mood was cheerful, bright as the sun that bounced off the tiles beneath their feet. There were twenty, thirty people in the block ahead of them, doing a lot of chatting, a lot of laughing. Everywhere Pam looked there were bright candles, chrysanthemums and marigolds, and skulls spun from sugar. She saw meats simmering in spicy sauces, distinctive bread loaves, fish cakes, and bubbling chocolate drinks. She saw religious amulets adorned with cigarettes and tiny bottles of rum.

"Day of the Dead," she said.

"Yep," Max answered. "After All Hallows' Day, we celebrate all the *normal* people who died. So today's more of a party."

"You said Hallowe'en was a party, too."

"It is. The Celts were looking forward into the darkness, the Catholics look back, glad it's going away."

"Doesn't seem very dark right now. It's gorgeous, and fun." She admired the small sculpture of a dancing skeleton, wearing a rakish serape and holding two maracas. "And there's a meaning behind each day. All Hallows' Eve, All Hallows' Day, Day of the Dead . . ."

"Sure there's a meaning behind each day. They don't all have names like this, but they all mean something. Every sunrise is a new beginning. The Mayans based everything on that one fact."

"And you're into Mayans," Pam said. "But hold that thought, if you please. I want to go back to paying attention to the world. I keep forgetting and coming back to it, but I do it, and I've seen things. You can start with Cocorik. But I see that bird's nest in the corner of the roof on the green-trimmed building—the sun shining into it makes a perfect Yin/Yáng symbol. I see the woman on the balcony of the hotel at the far, far end of the street—she's the single scarlet thing, a scarlet woman, framed by all the white buildings. I see that the sun is a part of almost everybody's logo down here."

"Okay. Good. You're looking."

"But what am I looking *for*? I know, 'I'll know it when I see it' or something—"

"No, that's right."

"But what then? If you're not teaching me anything, what good does it do me? I mean, I'm sure it's a good thing, a mind exercise if nothing else—"

"Even a nonalchemist would tell you to keep your eyes open right now." He leaned closer in the midst of the moving throng. "Look, Pam, let's be clear. I am going to do everything I can to keep you alive, and that includes making you a more effective person, but you are not my disciple, because I don't do disciples."

"Why not?"

"I *was* a disciple. I found my master, a man I considered almost superhuman, reduced to a gibbering idiot. I saw his other disciple—my wife—die."

Pam's mouth tightened stubbornly. She was not to be put off. "Okay, then let's come at it from another way. Answer a simple question. You tell me what happens after death, you *think*. But you've never actually been dead. That's the part I want to understand. When does *thinking* become *knowing* in alchemy?"

"It's a good point. You do have to examine your reality on a continuous basis. Make sure what you think you know holds water."

"Ahhh!" she said disgustedly.

"Oh, no. When you first get into magick, it's easy to fly right into the cosmos. So treat magick like medical research, or your first trip to Barbados. Explore but verify. Anyway," he said, "I'd say thinking becomes knowing when alternative scenarios keep falling apart. The great Sherlock 'Olmes said, 'When you have eliminated the impossible, whatever remains, however improbable, must be the truth.'" He pointed down the street. "And the truth is, there's our CD store."

It was indeed Branscombe's, the place Chauncy had recommended. They went into its air-conditioned interior and found a store much like any other, at the front. But farther in, beyond the first assault of the international music machine, Max found what he was looking for: local music, and an atmosphere that welcomed interest. Unlike a Virgin, Branscombe's had not been remodeled as a condition of existence. It lived in two worlds, just like Max. He launched into a conversation with the clerk behind the counter, one enthusiast to another, and soon they were moving from Soca to Ragga Soca to Rapso to Chutney. They played samples and the discussion got lively. Max liked Rihanna's "Umbrella" as much as the next guy, but he wanted the stuff he couldn't get outside the island.

Pam stood at the end of the counter and marveled at Max's enthusiasm. Even with everything else on his plate, he really did love music. This real interest and affinity for music probably ten people in America knew about was fun to watch.

Later, carrying a bag with seven CDs in it, he escorted her back to Broad Street, whistling. They strolled along, people-watching, window-shopping, until they came to Temple Street, running away on their left toward the water. It ran past Temple Yard, where wall-to-wall Rastas sold everything, literally, under the sun, though the emphasis was on leather goods. Reggae, ganja, red-gold-and-green filled the expanse. Pam spotted a back-pack she liked and bought it on the spot.

"To carry the antidote powder in," she explained. "It has a Velcro seal underneath the snap-down flap."

"It ought to," Max said. "Dope couriers use those. It'll be perfect." For his own part, while she'd been get-ting her bag, he'd been buying some of the savory mutton sandwiches and chocolate drinks being offered. Pam realized she was hungry, and that she hadn't had time to think about that.

They strolled along in companionable silence, enjoy-ing the food. Only once she'd swallowed the last of hers did Pam speak again. "Since you know so much about so much, Max, how are you on advice to the lovelorn?"

"I have a perfect record with advice. No one ever takes it."

"Well, here's the deal. I'm twenty-eight years old. My little clock's got a lot of ticking to do yet, but it's a little louder than it used to be. I haven't stopped time like some people. So a guy—that guy I told you about, that I might have called about the Hallowe'en party—he's a doctor, too. He works in pediatrics at Kaiser. He's a good guy, a sweet guy. I think he really loves me. He better, because he asked me to marry him. And I said no." Pam looked away. "Because he says that he wants to have kids, too, and it wouldn't be safe if I kept work-ing in disease control. Something could affect the child in the womb, or afterward I could bring something home."

Max took an ostentatious step back from her. "You *do* disinfect, don't you?"

She scowled at him. "Idiot. Of course. We're kept completely isolated from the germs. And yet I can't help thinking that something *could* happen; I *could* hurt my kids. So I tend to agree with him. But what it means is, I would have to quit my job. I could still be a doctor, just not an epidemiologist. And I *like* being an epidemiologist." She spread her hands. "I feel it's important. So I said no. How crazy is that?"

"It's not crazy at all. You like your work better than you like this guy."

"Evidently."

"Then you made the right choice."

"But that could mean I'd never have kids!"

"It could, but that's not what I meant." His tone changed, a deejay talking in parentheses. "And notice how when I say you did the right thing, you disagreed with me. My record remains unbroken." Then back to normal: "What I meant was, you like your work better than you like *this guy*. Someday, you might meet a guy who adds up differently."

She pulled a face. "Someday my prince will come."

"It's been known to happen."

Silence returned.

When they came to the library, they went inside and used the Internet to find a photo of Miller Omen.

"That's the man who caused the dart in my side," Pam said wonderingly, her finger tracing Omen's horsey face. "The man who sent zombis and hit men after me."

"Probably. The downside to Nancy's being out of the loop is, we don't know much about the fabled Free Range Coalition. There could be others involved."

"But you said we needed to find the man who caused the dart. If it's not Omen—"

"Then we'll keep going. Don't worry."

"Why should I worry?" she asked, rolling her eyes.

They used Google Earth for a photo of Omen Key. As a small, obscure island it got a high view from the satellite, so that it pixeled out quickly, but it clearly showed an island covered with palm trees and a cleared area in the upper center. A straight road ran from that point to a large dock on the coast. Interestingly, it was the coast that did not face Barbados.

They went back out into the brilliance, and ambled on until they reached Princess Alice Highway, at the shore. They waited a moment for two cars to go by, then ran across the hot asphalt and onto the beach beyond. The mid-afternoon sun was spread across the water like lemon jam, and a fresh breeze blew in over the breakers as they walked once again up the sand.

After a time, the shore began to drop below the highway, until eventually they had it all to themselves. Around the sweep of a cove far ahead they could see other people, moving from their cars to the surf, but the only way to this spot was by walking and they were the only ones doing it. They came to a cove of their own, sheltered by palms.

"Want to go for a swim?" Max asked.

"Big time," she answered. "But I don't have a suit."

"Forget the suit. No one can see us."

"*You* can see me."

He burst out laughing.

"What?" she asked.

He had to choke down laughter to answer her. "Hoist on my own petard," he said at last, and in the instant, she saw the whole picture. She couldn't get naked because he hadn't wanted her to get naked the night before. So he couldn't say "It's okay now," because why would it be? And she couldn't say "What the hell," because of his dead wife. So neither one of them could say anything, and they just stood there on the sand.

And yet . . . he was laughing. Pretty soon, she was laughing, too.

13 CORN SEED

The harsh voice of Tilit's modified Speak & Spell explained his instructions to Ballantine and the six men from Omen's security force who had joined them. Then the eight of them fanned out and made their way into the Orleans.

The people on the sun-drenched streets were more numerous now, and they looked carefully at these eight men . . . and they decided they didn't need to challenge them. The eight worked their way along, asking if anyone had seen a white couple at eleven o'clock. They were not happy, but neither were they surprised, when all the answers were negative.

So then Ballantine got on the phone to check for cabs leaving the Orleans before noon.

....

13 CORN SEED

The two men in the unmarked Camry waited to be certain Barry Leander wouldn't suddenly reappear in search of something he'd forgotten. The driver's name was Cullins, and his partner was Dominick. When they got a heads-up that Leander had entered the lab, they entered his house.

Dominick kept an eye out while Cullins jimmied the lock. The warning for the house alarm began. They entered and passed a *stone* over the alarm keypad. The sound stopped.

The two men proceeded to search the house, methodically seeking any place a grown woman could be hidden. Though there was no reason to believe Leander's house had secret rooms, they took that into account anyway, tapping their way along the walls, the floors, the ceilings. It took them over an hour to decide Nancy Reinking was not inside.

Then they went to the backyard.

13 CORN SEED

Nancy dreamed.

She was the mistress of a vast castle, with menservants—strong, tall, and heartbreakingly handsome—who attended upon her every wish. Her wishes ran toward sex, and they were only too glad to drive her through the most glorious and inventive positions, pounding away at her selfish body, satisfying her utterly yet leaving her always ready for more. Sometimes, though, she preferred taking a break and dealing with the ladies' maids. Them she would order into the most degrading positions, sprawled on their bellies, cleaning the marble floors with tiny brushes and little water. Then, when they failed to provide perfect results, she could order her menservants to whip them, to reduce them to sobbing little waifs and then fuck them at her command. But fucking at one remove gave Nancy little pleasure, so she took up the whip herself and beat them till they died. It was hard to compare against sex, but being their harsh mistress, wielding the rod of power herself, gave her a thrill that might have been even more intense. The power, the blood, it spoke to something deep within her, and in her dreams she knew that that was what she had to have. It was why she'd accepted Miller Omen's offer, why she'd joined the FRC. Power wasn't just for men anymore. She was one of the new breed of women, soft and hard at the same time, and that was why she owned this castle and all these slaves, and why she'd do anything to keep them.

Miller Omen came into her dream castle. He was tall and thin to start with, and in his bristling armor he towered above her. She slung her whip languidly toward him, its bloody tip embracing him. She pulled him toward her, pulling herself toward him, too, and they met in the center of the vast slate hall. Her soft flesh pressed against the spikes in his armor but she was unscathed. His power radiated from his eyes inside his open helmet, and her own power radiated back. She began to pull pieces of his armor from him. She ordered her menservants to help and they stepped forward smartly. But they pulled her away from Omen. She ordered them to stop. But they waved at her with a glowing *stone* . . .

She woke up.

To find two men dressed in common clothes leaning over her holding that same *stone*. For a moment she was more than ready to lie back and enjoy it, use them as foreplay before taking Miller Omen . . . then she realized she was covered in spiders. She shrieked, even as the men began sweeping the spiders off her. But there were webs on her, in her hair. She jerked upward convulsively. One man seized her, pulled her free, and she felt like a little girl in the arms of her father.

"It's okay, Nancy," Cullins said. "You're safe now."

13 CORN SEED

When Max and Pam got back to their room at The House, Max broke into a wide grin.

"What?"

"My defenses have been breached—by Maggie."

"Breached?"

"No one can get in if I don't allow it. I allowed for Mama and her ladies, and they took advantage."

He opened the door. Sitting in the center of their room was a stack of small boxes and a bundle wrapped in a colorful cloth.

Pam went and opened the nearest box. "It's my ingredients," she said.

Max opened the bundle. "And the rest of it." He handed her a smoothly polished CZ-83, then took out a Glock 25 and an AR-15. "And there's a rifle case to keep them all dry when we swim to the island. But no night goggles. Well, we'll get by."

"Mama got most of this from the mainland—Mexico, Panama—since this morning," Pam said, checking off the packets and tins. "Because she's not just a priestess, is she, Max? She's something higher. The way Maggie kissed her hand."

"As did you," said Max. "But I was mostly struck by the nice weather we're having." He pulled out two sheets of paper. "Here's a map of where we'll find the boat tonight. And a note: people are looking for us. They were in the Orleans by two o'clock."

"That was fast."

"They're good; we knew that. But before we give them the chance to find us, cowgirl, I've got to do some meditation, for want of a better word. And you've got to put that antidote together."

"It won't take long to mix my batch—my witch's brew—" her eyes twinkled, "and I can do that quietly enough. Then I plan to infuse it into the talc, which'll be even quieter."

"Just keep your fancy new Czech toy handy, just in case."

"You think there'll be trouble?"

"No, but I've heard that I don't know everything."

"You can count on me." But she was troubled by a sudden thought, as she stared moodily at the gun. "Don't you ever wonder, Max, if *I'm* all I seem? I could have been put out there as a decoy, you know, to catch you with your guard down—the way Aleksandra could have done with Val." Her face grew resolute. "I could *be* Aleksandra."

"No, I checked you, that night in the hospital room. Satisfying myself that you were who you were supposed to be was the first thing I did."

"But she fooled you before. She fooled Agrippa. She's not human."

"And I'm not who I was when all that happened. I'm sure you're Pam Blackwell. I saw who you were the first night, and I've seen a lot more of you since then. Trust me: I trust you."

She blushed. She *wished* she wouldn't do that. "Okay."

"Then that's settled."

She stretched, releasing all her tension, twisting her shoulders back and forth. "I had to say it."

"Yes, you did. Explore but verify. You're not the

damsel in distress anymore. You're part of this little caper."

She ducked her head, even more embarrassed. She *had* to stop that. "Then I'll keep alert while you get cosmic," she told the floor.

"Thanks." Max nodded and sat down in another chair. If he had any trepidation about her being a menace, he showed no sign of it. He sat up straight, put his feet flat on the floor, and laid his hands comfortably on his thighs. He closed his eyes.

That was it.

Pam sat and watched him, listening to the world all around.

Then she went to work.

NOVEMBER 2 - 4:45 P.M. AST
THE DAY OF THE DEAD

13 CORN SEED

As the western sky prepared for another in a series of spectacular sunsets, Tilit and Ballantine found the cabbie who'd taken Max and Pam into the heart of Bridgetown. They'd had to wait all afternoon since learning the man had taken other passengers on his special tour around the island. All he could tell them was that he'd delivered the couple they were interested in to National Heroes' Square, from which they could have gone anywhere. Tilit and Ballantine made sure he told them everything he knew. Then Ballantine shot him dead because it had been a long, hard day.

13 CORN SEED

Out on his patio, his feet in the pool, Miller Omen was just tucking into his last high tea in Barbados when he took a call on the midnight-blue phone. The sky to the west was purple clouds split by stabs of setting sunlight, and he squinted as he took in the report.

"We've found Nancy Reinking," Hanrahan told him.

"Dead?"

"No, alive."

Omen took a sip of Darjeeling as he considered. "What did she tell the Code Red?"

"She told him about you. Nothing else, she says."

"You believe her?"

"When we found her, she was in a trance. A sorcerer we use probed her mind working long distance, telling the agents in place what to do. It's not as satisfactory as him doing it himself, he says, but she seems clear enough."

I'll bet she is, Omen thought grimly. *She knows what'll happen if she tells them too much. But that means I still don't know.* "Send her down to me," he told Hanrahan. "I'll keep her close for the duration."

"Not to Barbados," said the old man up north.

"No, you're right. No time for that now. Send her to the staging area."

"Yes, sir. What about August and Blackwell?"

"We have a good idea who they're pretending to be, and we're close behind them, but we don't have them in hand. Of course, neither do your guys."

"You sent my guys to the farthest edges of the island," the old man said flatly.

"No place is that far on Barbados, Hanrahan. There was no reason to assume August and Blackwell would be here in town. But my men are doing fine on their own, and our friend Wilson Rideau leads me to believe that I should be seeing them in just a few hours. Don't worry about it; the net is drawing tight." As if on cue, Tilit and Ballantine appeared in his doorway; the deaf man held up a finger to show they had their own report. "I've got to go," Omen said.

NOVEMBER 2 - 5:15 P.M. EASTERN DAYLIGHT TIME
THE DAY OF THE DEAD

13 CORN SEED

Dick Hanrahan hung up his blue phone. When he had been young—a time he recalled more and more often these days—he would have cut Omen's heart out for the way the man treated him. But with age came wisdom, and all that really mattered was what actually happened in the world. If Omen pulled off his grand scheme, they would meet more directly, and Omen would learn his true place in the scheme of things. If he didn't pull it off, he'd learn his true place that way, but the place would be very different.

"Join or die," Ben Franklin told the colonists, and those were still the only options with the colonists' oldest enemies.

13 CORN SEED

Max's meditation was long since finished. Pam's powdered antidote filled her backpack, which was securely locked in their room (physically, magickally). The two of them were off to The House's shops to buy some clothes for their night at the K-1 match, and some food they hoped they could eat on the clifftop while watching the ocean. Peaceful walkways meandered through the trees, which threw sharp sunset shadows far across the emerald lawn. Birds sang strange songs in the baobabs. Max and Pam were in no hurry at all.

They came to a magnificent sundial, mounted on a thick pedestal. Its western edge was rosy in the dying light, and its ornate marker's shadow fell just past the copper V of five in the evening.

8 JAGUAR

Max and Val stood facing each other, completely nude, in the intersection of the Queen's Chamber Passage and the Grand Gallery, the center of the Great Pyramid of Giza. The harsh, upturned light of their propane lantern threw their shadows high on the looming walls. All else was darkness. They had known each other four months and they were head-over-heels in love.

Val's long hair, freed at last from the scarf she'd worn earlier, caught the light in waves as it spilled across her shoulders. Her flat stomach tensed as she took a deep breath, then she released a single high note with the most beautiful voice in the world. The note exploded into the space, echoed high above, and came back again and again.

"Now we know where they got the idea for cathedrals," Val said impishly. "It sounds amazing in here."

"I used to do that in tunnels," Max said, "with a simple *boop!* And I can tell you, this sounds better than a tunnel, and you sound better than a boop."

"Better than Betty Boop. Better than a boob, too."

"Or a boob tube. But why settle for *a* boob when you can have *two*?"

"*Phthhh*," she answered disdainfully. Then she whirled around, arms wide, hair floating. "I'm stoked that we did this, Max!"

"Me, too. It's one thing to see the pyramid on a tour. But this is how the pyramid really is, in the dead of night, with no one else at all."

"You're really into the magick now, aren't you?"

"Yes, ma'am, I am. It's a whole new Unknown for me to explore, and I know now that that's what I do in my life. Explore the Unknown, whether it's a jungle or a way of entertaining people. *You* know."

"I do. Entertaining people is what brought us together, but pushing the limits is what keeps us together. And Corny, of course." His name seemed to echo more strongly than her other words. They listened to it die away.

"Do you think he'll teach us everything we need to know before . . . he passes?" Max asked. "It seems like we've done a lot in four months, but he says we've only scratched the surface."

"He told me that, too, in the beginning. The thing is, you take in many, many things, so it seems like they could go on forever—but then they start to hang together and you see it's really simple."

"So you understand it."

"Not me! I'm getting there, but no, I wouldn't say I understand it *all*." She followed that by letting out another crystalline note for the echo. "Besides, he's Corny. I'm still betting he won't pass at all."

"You've known him longer than I have."

"You don't think so?"

"I'm not qualified to say one way or the other. But I guess I give him credit for knowing his business."

"He prides himself on his *realism*. I call it *cynicism*, and I kick his butt when he gets too far into it. He'll work it out. Or the three of us will work it out together."

From far away came a slight metallic sound—the only sound beyond their voices they'd heard in twenty minutes. Val tensed.

"Relax," Max told her. "It's a guard checking the gate, and finding it secure."

"You're sure," she said skeptically. "What if it's a rat or something?"

"It's not a rat."

"And you know this because you're a point man."

He shrugged. "Evidently. But I know what a rat sounds like. I know what a gate sounds like." He grinned. "I know what the most beautiful voice in the world sounds like—"

"Would you cut that out?"

"—and I know what the most beautiful woman in the world looks like."

"Ahh, Max . . ." She came across the cold stone into his arms. "I love you."

"I love you, too," he said. It echoed from the stones of time. One of his hands went to the back of her neck, underneath her hair, and the other slid gently down her back to her hip. Her hands were equally busy, sliding down his sides, along the ribs, to his central point. His hand on her hip brushed lightly up her side to cup her breast. His warm breath flowed across her neck as his teeth settled lightly on her shoulder. Her body molded itself to his. By mutual unspoken assent, they were done with standing. They stepped apart, Val lay on their Egyptian carpet, and Max lay beside her. He reached out and snapped off the lantern.

All else was darkness.

APRIL 23, 1981 - 5:30 A.M. EET

9 EAGLE

They slipped out of the pyramid just before dawn and walked quickly to their rented Oldsmobile, parked a quarter mile beyond the gate. They both had their clothes on, Val's hair was hidden inside a scarf again, and large sunglasses masked her eyes, even though the light was only gray. No one saw them go.

Driving back to their hotel, they turned into the rising sun's brilliance. "Harmakhis," Val said, shading her eyes even behind her specs.

He laughed easily. "I think we can both testify that Egyptian gods are damn powerful," he said.

"And you've got a gift for reaching them," she said. "Speaking as someone who's not that far ahead of you."

"But I can already see places where Egyptians didn't go, that I want to go. The Mayans went to the very nature of Time. Each new sunrise for them was less a god than an entirely new *reality*. Here and now *is* reality."

"What we just did was perfectly real," she said comfortably. "Good old sex magick."

"Sure. But I want to know everything, Val. I want it all."

He slowed the Olds as they reached their destination, the venerable Mena House, and the sun in their eyes blinded them long enough for paparazzi to bolt from behind the date palms and explode their flashes through the windows. "Goddammit!" Max snarled.

"Miss Drake!" the photog on her side pleaded, banging on the window. "Miss Drake. Please! One picture!"

The one on Max's side joined the chorus. "Miss Drake! Miss Drake! One picture! Miss Drake!"

Max floored the Olds and surged onto the hotel grounds, spewing rocks and sand behind. He was damn sure he hadn't injured the men, and damn sure he'd come as close to it as possible. The car fishtailed slightly, he caught it, and they braked to a stop behind the former hunting lodge of royalty. *Now,* Max thought, *they're hunting royalty here.*

He and Val got out of the car. She was less shaken by it than he was. She was well used to it.

"How do you suppose they knew you were here?" he asked her.

"Someone in the hotel tipped them, probably," she said.

"And they sat out there all night."

"It's what they do. They're just trying to make a living."

"Then why don't you go back and give them their picture?"

"Because I'm trying to have a good time with my sweetie."

They walked toward the Mena's Moorish grandeur, the sharp dark triangle of the pyramid rising in the background, through palms that threw sharp sunrise shadows far across the emerald lawn. Birds sang strange songs. Max and Val were in no hurry at all.

"I still have to pinch myself sometimes," Max said. "Valerie Drake."

"I'm just me," she responded.

"Yeah. Valerie Drake," he said, laughing.

"Too much for you?"

"Not at all. But—Valerie Drake."

"You want me to hit you?"

"I'm just saying."

"But you're *not* saying you're a star-fucker, are you?"

"That I am not."

"So then you're not fucking the star. You're fucking a flesh-and-blood woman, who's fucking you back. I'm not a poster. I'm right here."

"Yeah, sure, but, if we hadn't met, I'd be somewhere else now, with someone else. You'd be somewhere else now, with someone else. But I got the best and most desired woman in the world—and you got a deejay. Life is amazing."

"Pretty sure of yourself, aren't you? If we hadn't met, I see you in Times Square with a raincoat," she said. "And anyway, here you are, with me, and I'm here with you, and that's what matters. Love the one you're with."

"You owe Stephen Stills a nickel."

"I'm serious. Whatever *might* have happened, here and now's reality, pal."

They came to a magnificent sundial, mounted on a thick pedestal. Its eastern edge was rosy in the brightening light, and its ornate marker's shadow fell just past the copper V of five in the morning.

NOVEMBER 2, 2007 – 5:20 P.M. ATLANTIC STANDARD TIME THE DAY OF THE DEAD

13 CORN SEED

"Max?"

He realized Pam was talking to him. "Sorry?"

"Where'd you go?"

But he just shook his head.

NOVEMBER 2 – 5:30 P.M. AST THE DAY OF THE DEAD

13 CORN SEED

Finishing his high tea, surrounded now by falling darkness, Miller Omen called Carole van Dusen, his money manager in Boston. She answered on the second ring: "Hello, Miller."

"Hello, Carole. How did my portfolio adjustment go?"

"Very, very smoothly."

"You didn't attract any attention?"

"Not a bit of it. I worked through four of my established fronts, and the stocks you wanted moved have no profile on the street."

Omen made one of his rare sounds of satisfaction. "If this turns out the way I plan, Carole, I'll quadruple your fee."

"That's kind of you, Miller, but there's no need. Our arrangement is adequate," she replied, her dry brahman tone indicating the inconsequence of money. She was an old woman, somewhere in her eighties, and a legend in her field. Omen had been lucky to get a referral from Chester Regie; she had her clientele and rarely took on a new account these days. But he'd known she was the one he needed to maximize his profit from the coup, and had gone after her with his usual persistence.

"I'll send you a gift, then. If I may," he said.

She didn't answer directly, but said, "You're sounding very chipper tonight."

"My life is good right now."

"How pleasant for you. That portfolio you chose was rather an odd mixture," she continued. "Zheng Tai Investment Company of Hong Kong, Tamiku Oil of Japan, and the Amalgamated Suriname Trading Company ring no bells for anyone, including myself. The rest of the lot was even more obscure. What is it that you know, Miller?"

"I'm sorry, Carole, but I can't say."

"My discretion is, I believe, well accepted at this point," she said mildly.

"Sorry. I'm just part of a process. It may come to you, though."

"All right, Miller. Fair enough. But you also asked me to buy one hundred thousand shares of Meridian Pharmaceuticals—your own firm." She had no need to point out that he could have acquired them himself with his options, if the acquisition could stand the light of day.

"I just wanted to introduce you to the company," he said, and for the first time in their acquaintance, she laughed—a more delighted sound than his bare chuckle.

"Well, then," she said, "the market's closed for the weekend, so we shall see what we shall see on Monday."

"Yes, Monday will be very interesting," he said. "Thanks again, Carole. Have a nice evening."

NOVEMBER 2 - 5:40 P.M. EASTERN DAYLIGHT TIME
THE DAY OF THE DEAD

13 CORN SEED

"You, too, Miller."

Carole van Dusen hung up her phone. In her precise, birdlike way, she wrote a series of symbols on her yellow scratch pad without pause or reflection. It was a code she had developed for herself in 1942, based on the Dow and other factors, including the noontime temperature in the randomly chosen Wichita, Kansas, and no one but herself had ever been able to decipher it. Dick Hanrahan's people had tried in 1994 and gotten nowhere, and if they couldn't do it, no one could.

Anyone the Necklace was interested in had to be vetted by two of the nine, and at least one of the two had to do it without the subject suspecting. So far, Miller Omen was passing all of her tests but one. He should have expected her to see the link in his portfolio. Even if she hadn't known already, she'd have dug to find that all the companies had business ties to the same obscure country. He played it low-key but was cocky.

She'd always liked cocky, but he had to back it up. If he delivered, cocky was fine.

She wondered what Dick would have to say. Like her code, the schemes of the Necklace involved many moving parts.

NOVEMBER 2 - 5:45 P.M. ATLANTIC STANDARD TIME
THE DAY OF THE DEAD

13 CORN SEED

Tilit lay flat on the bench in his exercise room pressing 665 pounds, looking up past the weights, past the bar, through the glass ceiling at the first night star. The world unassisted record was 715; he doubted he would ever match that. But 665 was plenty good enough for any man, and in any event, it was just a means to an end. His massively developed form was a by-product of what he heard when he exercised—the only time he heard anything at all.

It was a symphony of musculature, singing under the strain of the lifts. As he, who had never heard real music, interpreted the nerve messages surging through his inner self, each of his pectoralis majors made a deep humming undertone. The anterior deltoids were darker, the triceps brighter, and his hands had a high, grating keen, warning of the danger if the bar slipped. But he was never going to let it slip, so the grace note was the triumphant bugle call in his brain.

....

13 CORN SEED

Dominick, Cullins, and Nancy sat and watched Nancy's apartment for ten minutes before Cullins went inside. By all accounts, the Code Red and the doctor were far away from Oakland, but the FRC didn't operate sloppily. When Cullins was sure no one else was watching the place, he opened the back door for Nancy and his partner.

"I can't say I never doubted you guys would find me," Nancy said, slightly breathless, as they went inside, "since I didn't have time to think about things one way or the other before August attacked me, but I knew the group would have my back. Not that I expected to need you, since I was just supposed to be a watcher, but you know what I mean."

"We do," said Cullins. "And now you're not a virgin anymore."

"Uh, thanks?"

"You're more than a watcher now."

"Oh, right."

"Because of which," said Dominick, "we've got to move you out of here before any of August's friends come looking."

"He has friends?" Nancy asked, a bit taken aback.

"Actually, we don't know," the man answered. "So better to be safe than sorry."

"I hear that," she said.

"Gather everything that's personal," Cullins said.

"Anything you don't mind leaving, or anything that doesn't give a clue to your identity or your past, stays here. You'll get clothes and everything else you need in Barbados, courtesy of Mr. Omen. What we're concerned with here is anything that can lead August to you."

"Okay," said Nancy. "I'll have to think a little."

"No problem," said Dominick. "If you don't mind, since Alan and I have been at this a little longer, we'll go through the apartment as well, and pull out anything that looks like something you need to consider."

"Um. Okay. There's some stuff that's private, you know."

"Fine. We're not looking to find your vibrator." He chuckled knowingly.

"Speak for yourself," Cullins said, and joined the general laughter.

"I'll be sorry to leave the Bay Area," Nancy said moments later. "I've lived here a long time. But I don't think I'll mind Barbados, somehow, and I love having guys like you on my side."

"I wish we were going with you," said Dominick. He chuckled again.

"I'll send you a postcard," she said. "Through channels, of course." *Man!* she thought. *The FRC really has its act together.*

···

13 CORN SEED

Lawrence Breckenridge and Ryan Montclief enjoyed a delicious meal in a private room in Midtown Manhattan. It resembled an elegant Knickerbocker dining room, with intricate décor and cozy lighting above the small dining table. The lighting came from lamps resembling gas lamps; there were no windows; because the room was constructed in the center of a steel vault filled with soundproofing material and alarms. The vault existed in the center of a building that appeared to be occupied by a high-end art dealer, looking out on West Forty-seventh Street. But behind its showroom floor, visible through front windows, the building was completely hollowed out, and the four-story space around the vault was laced with more alarms. The Knickerbocker room could only be reached through its two doorways (that Montclief knew about); Breckenridge and the person he wished to meet entered different buildings blocks away and walked long, clean tunnels to reach their rendezvous. In Midtown Manhattan, they were as insulated from the world as it was possible to be.

Ryan Montclief was the chairman of the Joint Chiefs of Staff.

"Let me propose two hypotheticals," said Lawrence Breckenridge. He took a sip of his Bartolo Mascarello 1989 Barolo while waiting, pro forma, for assent. Montclief inclined his head.

"One. Suppose, for argument's sake, that about a

month before the next election, a terrorist bombing took place in Lòs Angeles—a big one. Killed, oh, thirty thousand people this time, including the Republican presidential candidate who happened to be campaigning there. There would be chaos, of course. Fear and madness. Now suppose the president went on national television and announced that the Justice Department and Homeland Security both believed it was too dangerous to change leadership in the middle of the war, and so the elections were postponed till a more peaceful time."

"Uh-huh."

"What would be the Joint Chiefs' position?"

"I think the Navy would be reluctant," said Montclief. "But we would stand and salute. Your larger problem would be the Democrats."

"What could they say? 'Have an election because we would win'? It's weak—wouldn't prevail against presidential leadership in a crisis. That's why it's the Republican who would die."

"Do you know who these people will be, Larry?"

"Doesn't matter to the scenario," said Breckenridge, though he had a pretty good idea.

"Well," said Montclief, leaning back in his chair, "it's an interesting hypothesis."

"I'm just examining it. I'd be curious as to how well it flies among your friends."

"I'll let you know." The general lifted his wineglass, then finished his own Barolo. "And the other hypothetical?"

"Suppose elections went ahead, but six months into his term, the new president was assassinated."

"By terrorists, or a lone gunman?"

"Doesn't matter."

"Well, who's the vice president?"

"Doesn't matter."

"It doesn't?"

"The real question is, would the people be able to live with it and move on? Would they stay in line for it?"

"That, I'll have to think on. The military would back the new man, I'm certain of that. Against all enemies, foreign and domestic." Montclief picked up the bottle, studied it, and poured the last of it into his glass. "Now I have a question for you, Larry."

"Certainly," said Breckenridge.

"Why do you live in this godforsaken town, instead of the District? That's where your kind of action is."

Breckenridge smiled, nodded, and gave Montclief his standard answer. "I wanted to see the world outside the Village."

They both laughed. The Village was the inbred collection of movers and shakers who ran the business of Washington—politicians, lobbyists, journalists. Washington was their city, and they could be counted upon to keep power where it belonged, among themselves. Montclief was laughing because he understood its complete artificiality, as all of them in the Village did. Breckenridge was laughing because it wasn't the complete answer. He also lived in Manhattan because the Gemstone in the Necklace had always lived in Manhattan. Lawrence Breckenridge didn't like New York's compression, but he was willing to sacrifice anything to be the Gemstone, including himself. The world outside the Village could be a dangerous place if left to its own devices, so it had to be shaped. He meant to be the one man who shaped it.

That was why he, who lived to rule, subjected himself to Aleksandra. Not, like so many powerful men, because he secretly wished to surrender his power. He subjected himself to Aleksandra because she *gave* him power, so he could run the Necklace, and everything the Necklace ran. That was a whale of a lot more than a Village.

NOVEMBER 2 - 8:15 P.M. ATLANTIC STANDARD TIME THE DAY OF THE DEAD

13 CORN SEED

Wildey Auditorium was hot and sweaty, but packed with stylish people, including Max and Pam. Their trip to The House's fashion shops had dressed them to the nines. He wore a light white jacket over an open shirt and light slacks. Beneath the jacket was a flat holster with his Glock 25. Pam had had the hotel salon put some highlights in her blond hair, and the clothier had provided a mid-length dress, with high neck and scooped back—a swirl of orange mesh over a form-fitting cream lining. Down the slow curve of her back, at the very bottom of the scoop, Max saw for the first time the multicolored image of a fish.

He asked, "Puffer fish?" and she nodded her blond head. "Beautiful," he said, with the obligatory, "Nice tat, too."

"I got it when I got my doctorate. You should get one, Max. Not a fish—"

"Can't do it. No tattoo, no earring, no anything that leaves permanent marks on the body. Somewhere down the line they're bound to be out of style."

"What if you get drunk in Tijuana?"

"I'll let the donkey drive."

Pam was feeling great physically, and mentally she was more than ready to meet the man who'd tried to kill her. She felt a *frisson* of fear, of course she did, but that just added to the glitter of the night. Miller Omen was somewhere in this crowd, and she was searching for his face when Max put his arm around her shoulders and turned her aside, saying softly, "I'll be damned."

"What?"

"Let's see what." He looked casually over his shoulder. "It's okay. I'll introduce you to some *friends*."

Pam shifted her shoulders. "Is there anybody on this island you *don't* know?"

She turned to find a striking couple making their way toward them. They both appeared to be in their late teens or early twenties, until she looked more closely and saw very *adult* eyes. It was jarring to her because Max didn't have eyes anywhere near that old. The eyes of the girl, if that's what she was, were dark and deep, framed by striking red hair curling to the shoulders of a lithe dancer's body. Her features were slightly Slavic, with a sensuous mouth, high cheekbones, and a strong, straight nose. The guy, if that's what *he* was, had the sun-bronzed skin and features of an Amerindian—wide mouth, wide nose, wide cheekbones—but his eyes were pale, sun-bleached. The flat brow above them gave that Indian look of stern nobility, though the eyes themselves were laughing. His light brown hair was sunstreaked, tousled, and gelled to the minute. Pam had thought Max moved with an animal's grace, but this guy moved as if he truly were an animal; even in his immaculate tuxedo he seemed to be prowling the hall.

"Pam, this is Sly and Rosa," said Max. "Sly and Rosa, this is Pam. She's a *friend*."

"De-lighted!" said Sly, smiling deep into her eyes as if he and Pam were sharing a great joke.

"Hello," said Rosa, also smiling, but watchful in the depths of those eyes. Her accent was indefinable—something European, maybe French.

"Any *friend* of Max's," said Pam, at a loss for what else to say. These had to be *artists*. She suddenly felt completely out of place.

Max shook Sly's hand, and bent to kiss Rosa's, which caused her to pull it back with an ironic smile. They all three laughed at the joke. Max said, "We're here for Miller Omen. That a problem?"

"Not at all," answered Sly. "We're here for Dmitri Sprüm. That a problem for you?"

"Not at all," Max responded. "I remember when Russians were the awfulest thing in the world, but those days are long gone. You should know, though, that Omen's scouring the island for a man and a woman. *That* could be a problem for you."

"Thank you, Max," Rosa said. "We'll keep it in mind. But we can take care of ourselves."

"I hope they do mistake us," said Sly enthusiastically. "Life's been too damn quiet down here. I need some action."

"Anything short of an atomic bomb," Max explained to Pam.

"We need to move along, Sly. I want popcorn. All these years and it's still my favorite," said Rosa, consulting her tickets. "Let us know how it comes out, Max. Pleasure to have met you, Pam."

"You two kids be in by midnight." Max grinned.

"Into *something*, I can only pray!" Sly answered.

Rosa leaned in to Max and said something in a voice too low for Pam to hear. But she thought she could read Rosa's lips: *Good for you.*

"Bye, guys," Max said. "Give my regards to the buffalo gnomes."

Sly and Rosa both laughed, he easily, she a bit more reservedly. The couples parted and the teens were swallowed by the throng.

"What?" Pam asked.

"What what?"

" 'The buffalo gnomes'? What does that mean? Or can't you tell me?"

"I can tell you. He knows buffaloes, and she knows gnomes, and one night when we were all drunk together my deejay mind kept trying to make something out of 'Where the buffalo *roam.*' But I couldn't make it work so I said 'Where the buffalo gnomes?' It's . . . you had to be there."

"Are you *sure* you were popular once?" Pam asked.

"So they tell me. Too often."

"So now explain 'he knows buffaloes, and she knows gnomes'?"

"That I can't do."

"Argh!" She clenched her fists, and he backed his thigh away.

So then she asked, "What was the deal with the hand-kissing?"

"Rosa's anything but a grand lady. The hand-kissing makes her laugh, and she doesn't laugh all that much. But Sly, on the other hand—eh. Suffice it to say that we each have our different styles."

"As artists."

"Uh-huh."

"And I'm a *friend*," Pam said.

"Exactly."

"So how many artists like you are there in the world?"

"*This* world?"

"Yes, this world."

"Not enough."

They went up a ramp, then down again into the cavernous auditorium. This was Barbados's premier sports facility, and the promoters had decorated it handsomely, with colorful banners above the colorful crowd and colorful spotlights sweeping the floor. The seats faced the square arena, very much like a common boxing ring, in which a nearly nude girl in high heels and three postage stamps strutted and exhorted the hot, sweaty, and altogether rowdy crowd. In the center of the ring a Rapso band rocked out.

G. Wilson Rideau's erstwhile seats were almost in the middle of section C's front row. In the *exact* middle sat three men, and beyond them were a man and a woman who couldn't keep their hands off each other. In Max's quick appraisal, he decided ecstasy. But those two only served to set off the calm power of the three quiet men. The three *waiting* men.

The man closest to the center was Miller Omen, easily recognizable from his photo. Beside him were a man just as tall as he and a man a foot shorter.

Max and Pam settled into their seats thirty feet away, at an angle to the men. The view was perfect. "I could just shoot them and be done with it," Pam said. In the flashing lights and surging sounds of the arena, it was hard to tell how ironic she was being, if ironic at all.

"Whoa, cowgirl. We need Mr. Omen alive. I'll let you know when you can blast away." Surreptitiously, he did his hand-wipe as he appraised them.

Omen turned toward the tall man and spoke. It was inaudible from where Max was sitting, but Max read it as *Tell it!* or maybe *Tilit!* The tall man stood, and began looking at the faces of the crowd behind them, silently. So it was *Tilit*. Probably his name. Max looked away.

So did everyone else as the bout finally began. K-1 set fighters against each other using any martial art from kung fu to kickboxing (the "K"), until one emerged as the best in the world (the "1"). Like boxing, K-1 was staged in rounds of three minutes each, but unlike boxing, almost anything was legal. Small wonder it, and the rest of the mixed martial arts variants, were eating boxing's lunch.

Hakira and Ortega were everything the paper had said they'd be. It was hard for Pam to tear her eyes away as they kicked and spun and leapt around the ring. Even though the violence bothered her, as a woman and as a doctor, the speed and grace and sheer strangeness of the moves fascinated her. Still, when she did look over at Omen, the man showed her something equally strange. He was straining forward in his seat, eyes locked on the ring, his mouth half open in something close to exaltation—and he didn't seem to care who saw him. No, he really didn't care. He was a man above caring. Each blow a fighter took seemed to run through him like an electric current, so that he was rocking back and forth, bobbing and weaving. If anyone had come to claim the seat next to him, that person would have gotten his own workout dealing with Omen's enthusiasm.

Max, however, was seeing something altogether different. His gaze, slightly oblique, showed him an aura around Miller Omen—an aura emanating from his right front pants pocket. It was a *stone*.

Nancy's words came back to him: "We have magick, too!"

Stones were meteorites, gathered from the very few that fell all the way to earth without burning up. Sorcerers through the ages had poured their power into these missiles—these missives—from God. *Stones* functioned as occult weapons for those without sorcery themselves, so Miller Omen was not an artist, but he did know people who were. He was like a child with a howitzer . . . but he was no child.

Max said, "I've got to get closer. Wait here. I'll protect you while I'm gone."

"Why can't I go with you?"

"It's not couples night where I'm going."

He made his way to the aisle and headed toward the back of the auditorium. Then he walked with long-legged strides to the concessions area. Nearby, men and women were coming and going from a central vending area, laden with food and drink. He followed a beer vendor as he started off to work, and blacked him out as soon as he was out of sight on the ramp between the public area and auditorium. Then he made them both invisible as he shucked both their clothes and donned the vendor's.

Two minutes later, a man no one, including Pam, had seen before, wearing a vendor's uniform and carrying a vendor's beer, came to the front row of seats. "Beer! Getcher beer here!" he called, and did a brisk business as he worked his way along. When he came to the three men in the middle he slowed a little, to give them a chance to make an order, but they evidently weren't going to miss Max August by getting drunk. So Max had to stumble and fall.

He went down apparently hard, hard enough to make

even Omen gasp, but at the last second he used his control of gravity to lessen the impact. He came to a halt half an inch off the floor, but grunted *"Shit!"* in apparent pain. His drinks splattered out across the floor.

Tilit, watchful, had one hand inside his coat. The smaller man, more annoyed than concerned, leaned forward to help Max to his feet. Max took his hand and, as with Pam's friends at their party, *read* him quickly. Name, Ballantine; occupation, thug. But Max let him go abruptly, apparently too angry at his own clumsiness to want any help. Sadly, his ankle wouldn't take the weight and he toppled onto Miller Omen's knees. Omen had to support him, and—

Omen's center was race. His great-great-grandfather had commanded troops for the Confederacy. His grandfather had been a Grand Cyclops in the Ku Klux Klan when the Klan ran Indiana.

Just then, Ortega danced past a spinning tae kwon do kick and snapped the side of his arm into Hakira's raised leg. The sound of bones shattering was sharp above the crowd roar. Hakira was thrown off balance, and tried to recover, but that involved his broken leg, which gave way beneath him before he was able to balance, and he fell awkwardly onto the canvas. Where he lay still. Ortega backed off in triumph and concern . . .

. . . but Omen leapt to his feet, his face flushed, roaring full-throated approval, nearly throwing the vendor down again. Maybe the crowd didn't need a leader to follow, but follow they did. All around other men and women were on their feet, pumping their fists, screaming for more. Max limped the rest of the aisle and headed up the ramp. As he passed Pam, he caught her eye, knowing she hadn't missed the interaction with Omen, knowing she knew who he was even if she couldn't recognize him. She got up and followed him from the arena. As they went up the aisle fifteen feet apart, the word "dead" began to sweep through the crowd, with growing horror and growing excitement.

Outside Wildey Auditorium, the city was rocking with street parties capping the Day of the Dead. Invitations to join this party or that came from all sides as they hurried into the surrounding streets. With all the drunks and all the confusion, it was simple as could be to find a car to boost.

NOVEMBER 2 - 6:45 P.M. PACIFIC DAYLIGHT TIME
THE DAY OF THE DEAD

13 CORN SEED

Night had fallen sharply over the Pacific horizon as Nancy arrived at the Mountain View airstrip. As a Bay Area native who'd gone to school just up 101 at Stanford, she knew that Air Force spy planes used to take off from there and soar out over the Pacific for flights of many hours' duration, seeking enemy planes and ships. Now there was just the one aircraft, a private aircraft, but it might have been just as big as the old ones.

"A Boeing Business Jet," Cullins said in answer to her study of it. "Same as any cross-country jet but without all the cramped rows of seats. You'll have the whole cabin to relax in."

"And you won't have to pony up five bucks for a sandwich," Dominick added cheerfully.

"Listen," she said, turning toward them both. "Thanks a lot, you guys. If it hadn't been for you, I might still be lying among the spiders. I don't know if I'll see you again, but I hope I do, and I won't forget what you did for me."

"Just part of the job, Nancy," said Cullins.

Impulsively, she leaned forward and gave each of them a hug. Dominick returned it with pleasure, and a look passed between them. Maybe, she thought, when this was over . . .

But she turned and ascended the stairs to the jet. She was a young pro, but she was determined to be a real pro. The job lay ahead.

Then the steward came forward to greet her, and suddenly she was thinking about the long flight that lay ahead. He was stunningly handsome. "Welcome aboard, Miss Reinking," he said in a warm baritone.

"Nancy, please," she answered.

"Nancy it is. My name is Chad. Please follow me."

He led her to a comfortable area very much like a living room, with roomy leather chairs, a seven-foot couch, and wide tables. Fixed lamps suspended from the ceiling broke the area into sections of light, turning the cabin into several personal spaces. Nancy continued to think about the long flight as she looked at the couch.

"When you're ready," Chad said, "I'll serve your evening meal. We have a selection so study the menu"—he handed her a printed sheet listing steak, chicken, and scallops among a half-dozen entrees, she saw—"and in the meantime, what can I get you to drink?"

"Viognier," Nancy answered. "And why don't you join me? It's been a tough day."

"So I understand," Chad said with a conspiratorial look. "I'll be happy to join you after takeoff, Nancy, but right now we both have to buckle up. You can take any seat you like. Once we're airborne I'll bring us both a bottle of Condrieu, the best Viognier in the world."

She chose a chair by a window as the engines began to rev. Outside, the black sky was forever. With her plane jundling down the runway, passing the ground lights, she thought about her life so far. *If only Mom and Dad could see me now*, she thought. *They thought a behavioral science degree from Stanford was a complete waste of my time and their money. Too little money to be made in research. But it doesn't matter where you are; the Free Range Coalition will find the people it needs. They needed me, and now I'm flying first class.* She thought of calling them and telling them she was on a Boeing Business Jet on its way to . . . well, she'd say Cape Cod. There was a phone set into the table beside her seat. It was still early enough; they'd be eating dinner in front of the TV. And they'd worry if she just vanished without telling them anything, or saying good-bye.

But she shook her head. Mr. Omen hadn't told her what the Coalition had planned, but she'd known from various communications over the past ten months that it should be happening soon, and the urgency with which Cullins and Dominick had cleaned her up and moved her out indicated the same thing. She wasn't going to upset the apple cart now, and if moving up in the FRC meant she had to cut her parents off, disappear completely from their lives, then so be it. She was, indeed, one of the people the FRC needed, and she knew she needed them as well.

Her life was just taking off, like her jet.

··

13 CORN SEED

It took Max and Pam forty-five minutes to drive to the southeast coast of the island, through Marchfield and Six Cross Roads and down toward The Crane resort, but cutting off on a dirt road just as the water came into view. At once they were swallowed by the palm trees on either side, so that they might as well have been motoring through a high, narrow canyon. There was no moon, and Max flicked off the lights, leaving only pale starlight half obscured by clots of clouds to guide their way. Pam had no idea what they'd do if they encountered an oncoming vehicle. But there was no one. They rumbled along in almost total darkness, parallel to the coast, for a good ten minutes.

At a crossroads, a palm trunk to the right of their road showed a ghostly yellow smear. Max took the even narrower road there and they soon came out from among the palms onto a wide, flat beach, deserted save for a small boat floating black on the tide. There were no lights on the sand, no lights in the water beyond. Max pulled to a stop on the sand, and figures stood up from beside the boat, raising their left hands. Each showed a pale yellow smear.

"It's okay," Max told Pam. They got out of the car. The salt breeze was strong in their nostrils, and gulls called down the wind. One of the figures approached them, and when it was close enough, Pam recognized Mama Locha.

"You couldn't find anybody competent to be our pilot?" Max asked the old woman in a low tone.

"Nobody I'm prepared to lose to this foolishness, boy," she responded tartly.

"You just can't keep away from me, Mama," he said.

"Who says it's not Pamela I came for? We only *use* men in *my* vodou."

Pam saw something moving at the corner of her vision, and spun toward it. It was gone in the same instant she remembered that it would be. Another elemental, over the wide sand beach; if it was a sylph it would be in air-spirit heaven here.

But she asked, dubiously, "Max, if I start to ignore things I barely see—what if it's not an elemental? What if it's a . . . a wildcat, or whatever they have down here? Something *real*?"

"Then you'd better hope Mama or I see it. But you'll get used to the elementals pretty quickly, and then you won't even notice them."

"You're in the *worrying* stage," Mama Locha told her. "You know things aren't what you thought they were, so you worry about what else you don't know. Only solution is time and experience."

"Intern's syndrome," Pam said. "All interns have all diseases. I didn't like it in med school, but it's *kind* of exciting now."

She and Max retreated to the shadows of the palms to change their clothes, switching from their fancy public duds to black tees and black jeans. They were separated by ten feet, which might have been ten miles in the deep black shadows. Out of habit Pam folded her dress and laid it in the shore grass, but she had the feeling she would never wear it again. When they came out of the shadows, each had his pistol, and Max had his rifle case slung over his shoulder. He thought she looked better in the tee than in the fancy dress.

They walked down the wide beach to the boat bobbing in the surf as the wind whispered down the sands. The other figures waiting there were eight younger women; they had to be Mama's priestesses. Maggie was among them, but she, like the others, was wearing a black shift now.

Now that the newcomers could make out the boat, it was revealed as what New Englanders call a whaler—a twenty-foot glorified rowboat with a small mast. The young women climbed in first and took the oars, four to a side. Max, Pam, and Mama Locha pushed them out into the surf, then scrambled in behind as the rowers pulled.

They set off into the Atlantic, moving swiftly to the rhythm of the oars. Around them was only the sound of the ocean and the dwindling cries of shorebirds; the oarlocks were well oiled and the priestesses rocked their paddles as one. Max had known boats since earliest childhood, and he admired their facility.

As the bird cries faded, Mama Locha raised a sail, which took the wind at once. The priestesses shipped their oars.

"We'll sail until we're within sight of Omen Key, then go back to rowing," Mama said, taking the sheet and rudder. She kept her voice down, even on the open sea.

"You know where to land now?" Max asked her.

"I think so."

"You *think* so."

"I told you I'd think about it and I've thought about it," Mama said with some asperity. "I can't do any more than that, boy."

"And what has your thinking gotten you?"

"There's a small beach on the south side of the key, with a path that leads up to the jungle. The guards use it for smoking and swimming, so if any of them feel restless tonight, they might well be there. Then we'll try somewhere else. But if no one's there, it's the easiest way in. Any security has got to be simple, so even the dumbest guard can turn it off to come or go. And some of those boys are dumb." Several priestesses giggled. They were speeding over the swells now, sending spray flying.

"From the photo we saw, it's about two miles—three kilometers—to a clearing in the jungle from the south," Max said. "That's most likely the control center. It'd be quicker to come in from the north."

"There's no way in from the north, boy."

"How thoroughly have you scouted this island, Mama?" Max asked.

"I knew that island before Squire Omen moved in, but I haven't been over since they started shooting at me," she replied. "I left them well alone after that."

"How long before we get there?" Pam asked, and she was dismayed to hear a beat of weariness in her voice. She shouldn't be tired so soon after renewing her energy with Max—or was the power of the dart overcoming his alchemy?

"Less than an hour," Mama Locha answered her. "Plenty of time to let my poultice *sit* this time." She reached across the boat, pulled up Pam's tee, and smeared the cat brain on Pam's side again. Almost at once Pam felt relief, and that spaciness Max had warned her about.

"Why are you taking this girl along with you, boy?" Mama asked.

"I want to go, Mama," Pam said, her voice stronger. "I want to hit back at the bastard who tried to kill me. I want to destroy his zombis with my potion."

"That's the cat talking," said the vodou queen. "I'm asking you, Max."

"Because I don't know what's on Omen Key," he said soberly. "Something could happen to set off the dart, and I need to be with her to counter that."

"My girls and I could watch her."

"With all respect, Mama, you couldn't. The dart is alchemical, not vodou; you can make her feel better but that's all. The people we're up against, the people backing Omen, are my kind of bad guys."

"Besides, I want to go," Pam said. "Cat or no cat. I can take care of myself. Ask Max."

"She can," he said, smiling. "She's a cowgirl."

In the darkness, among the priestesses, Pam saw the white gleams of several grins. She laughed. "Don't worry, Mama," she said.

"Still, take this, girl." She handed Pam a small bundle. "It's *paquets congo*—protection. Keep it in your pocket, for when the vodou comes."

It's funny, Pam thought. *She says French words with a British/Caribbean accent.* And she wondered how vodou had mutated as it made its way south through the polyglot islands. But the *paquets congo* felt warm to the touch, and comforting. In the dark, Pam couldn't see what it consisted of, but she appreciated having it. She slid it into the pocket of her jeans below the dart, and lay back against the curved side of the boat. She let all the night's vodou wash over her.

Above them was the full black sky, around them the ocean, both sweeping from horizon to horizon. The only difference between the two was stars above, no stars below. Otherwise it was as if they were in a huge dark sphere. But the stars above were bright, there were patterns in them; it was easy to understand how people had navigated by them over all the dark waters of the world. . . .

"There's Mars," Max said, pointing at a red dot just above the water, almost straight ahead. "And there"—he pointed high upward, behind them—"that very pale yellow thing is Uranus. Right overhead is Eris, the planet they found just three years ago, but it's invisible to the naked eye."

"But you know it's there," Pam said.

"Me and any astronomer."

"I thought Uranus was invisible, too."

"Not when it's at its brightest, in a clear sky like tonight."

Pam looked up and found it, pale yellow as advertised. Pale yellow like the girls' hands. She switched her gaze to Mars. "In the world of *artistry*," she said, the italics audible, " 'Mars' means 'war,' doesn't it?"

"Energy, yeah," Max answered. "War comes from that; so does your feeling better."

"But it's straight ahead of us; right where we're going. Does that mean we'll have an energetic evening?"

"Probably it does, cowgirl."

"But you can't say definitely."

"Nope. The universe influences, it doesn't dictate. If it were cut-and-dried, mechanical, it would make science happy but it wouldn't be very lifelike. Life, as noted, is made of probabilities, not particles. Explore but verify."

Pam laid her head back and looked again at the

starry sweep above. The only sounds were the wind, the water, and the creaking of the boat. "So astrology's true, too?"

"Sure."

"Sure," she echoed ironically. "Why not?"

"Sir Isaac Newton believed in it, and when challenged by Edmund Halley, the comet discoverer, Newton said, 'I have studied these things—you have not.' I've studied 'em, too. I find, like Newton, that they work, so I believe." His smile was visible in the dark. "Why not?"

"Well, Mars and Uranus and all the planets are extremely far away."

"Uh-huh. There's a force that connects them and us, though."

"Gravity?"

"Right the first time. Ask Newton; it holds *everything* together, even at low, shall we say 'subliminal' levels. The universe is completely interconnected, no matter how big it may be. It's a matrix."

"Completely interconnected at very low levels," Pam said.

"If they were high levels, planets would be crashing into each other and we'd all be one black hole. As it is, they're far enough way that they just *influence*."

"But why should Mars influence me?"

"Gravitational theory says you and Mars want *nothing* more than to close the distance between you. Science claims that's just an impersonal 'gravitational force' . . . but then, science doesn't understand gravity. It's the great unsolved mystery of physics, defeating even Einstein. When science decided not to look for consciousness in the universe, it condemned itself to unsolved mysteries." He lay back in the boat, resting on his elbows, relaxing in the night. "Whatever."

"No you don't!" she said sharply. "Not 'whatever.' I want to follow this." Pam looked back at him, a pale gray shape in the dark. "Are you working with everything in the universe?"

"Hardly. I stick with the planets in this solar system. That's plenty, when you remember the minor planets—the asteroids, between Mars and Jupiter, and the so-called TransNeptunian Objects out beyond Neptune. The TNOs include Eris, and now Pluto, and hundreds of others."

"How many minor planets are there?"

"Astronomers find more in both groups all the time. We know hundreds of thousands of asteroids, but I work with the first two hundred and sixty—"

"Two hundred and sixty!"

"Not too many compared to hundreds of thousands. It's not hard to learn two hundred and sixty concepts when you see the structure involved, and they show subtle facets in the structure that individual planets can't. It's like buying a high-def TV. That's one of my particular areas of exploration and expertise, since nobody else knows that stuff, as far as I know."

"But if you're the only one who knows . . . ," she said, immediately thinking of the life he led.

"I've written it all down, for just that reason. I call it the *Codex*. Whenever I go where no one else has, I keep a record, as clear and straightforward as I can. I'm sharpening what's in there all the time, as I see things more and more clearly. It's for my reference, too. And yes," he said, "you never know."

"Would you ever publish it?"

"You know I don't advertise my knowledge. I'd only show it to someone who really wanted to learn."

"That would be me!" she responded.

"Yeah, well, we'll see."

"Really? That's not what you said yesterday."

"Energy changes."

"Go, energy!" said Pam, too loud for the empty ocean.

Mama Locha spoke for the first time in quite a while. "The boy doesn't know vodou for shit, though. He can *call* and that's about it."

"Hell, anybody can *call*," said Max. "I would never claim to be a houngan. Someday I'll get you to *really* teach me."

"Well, you might want to hurry up. You may be Timeless but I'm not."

"You've got a long way yet to go, Mama."

"Pfui!" Mama let out the sail as the wind shifted, and turned toward Pam. "Vodou works that same energy he's talking about, but vodou uses the energy inside the body and sends it *along* that energy to do its work. Like a radio wave. Vodou *lives* in the Darkness, and we don't give a shit about *asteroids*."

"But Darkness," said Pam, "is traditionally considered *bad* . . ."

"Tradition is overrated," said Max. "It's only in the past two years that my pals the astronomers proved the existence of Dark Matter—so called because it's invisible to every instrument they have. But it turns out that Dark Matter is ninety percent of all matter in the universe. What we see is just ten percent—the same percentage my pals the neurologists say we use of our brains."

"If they can't detect it, how did they prove it exists?"

Max's broad grin split his head's silhouette. "My pals the gravitational lenses. When light from a visible galaxy travels near or through clumps of Dark Matter, the light bends. So the bottom line is, the universe is disguised the same way we're disguised." Max laughed. "Almost all the universe is invisible to us, and if it were *bad*, we'd be in serious trouble. But it's not bad. It's just energy. *Lots* of energy."

"Which we can *use*," Mama Locha said.

"By the way," Max added, "the guys who found Dark Matter would call Newton the premier scientist of his time, but artists call him the premier *artist* of his time. The tradition *The DaVinci Code* was based on puts him in charge of the Holy Grail back then."

"Okay," said Pam, "that's enough. My ten-percent brain is officially overloading now."

NOVEMBER 2 - 11:00 P.M. AST
THE DAY OF THE DEAD

13 CORN SEED

Mama Locha turned the whaler into the wind and let the sail sag, then lowered it. "Any closer and they'd see it on the horizon," she murmured. The priestesses began to row again, with only occasional yellow hand signals from their queen to correct the course.

Soon a mass of darkness began to grow to the east. It showed only warning lights, to keep stray craft from running aground on it; there was no sign of human habitation. But there were the cries of the wheeling gulls.

The boat turned a little to the north and began to slide past the island, parallel to its shore.

They pulled to at a distance of one hundred yards from a sheltered cove. All aboard stared at the beach there, seeking any sign of life. Night-vision goggles would have come in handy, but their own senses would do. Those senses included more than sight.

Across the dark water came a sullen mutter, now louder and now softer as the winds changed. It was the low throb of drums.

"D'you think there'll be zombis in the jungle?" Pam asked softly, leaning forward against his shoulder. She still wasn't afraid but she was definitely keyed up. She'd seen zombis.

"Doubt it," said Max, spreading black camouflage across his face and hands. "They're too slow to catch infiltrators. Here." He handed her the can.

"Animals?"

"Maybe a wild boar or two. No wildcats, if that's what you're thinking."

"What about sharks in the ocean?"

"I can set up a vibe around us to keep them at bay."

"What about some trick to help us see?"

"There you got me. I can bend light, but I can't improve it."

Meanwhile, the vodou priestesses and their queen were continuing to *feel* for life in the darkness, and judging from their unchanged demeanor, still coming up empty. But Pam saw things riding on the swells—small, shadowy things.

"Are there water elementals, Max?"

"Naiads. Yes, they're out there," he said. "And to answer your next question, fire elementals are called salamanders."

"Am I asking too many questions?"

"Ummm."

More grins from around the boat.

After five minutes, when they were all as certain as they could be that the coast was clear of human beings, Max and Pam were ready to go in.

"The security is seven steps up the path from the beach," Mama whispered. "The moon comes up an hour after midnight."

"Come back for us at three, but stay way out," Max replied. "I'll signal if it's safe to come in."

"Fine by me, boy. My girls and I have to catch some certain fish for our work, and it might well take that long. You'll have a stinking boat ride home."

"Looking forward to it."

Max slid his rifle case across his back, tightened the strap to hold it. He turned to Pam. "We had a saying in 'Nam, before any engagement: 'Well, good luck.' It was both banal and meaningless, which is what made it perfect for that war. And any war since."

"You're saying this is banal and meaningless?"

"Just being superstitious."

"You?"

"A soldier will take anything he can get."

"Well, then," she said, " 'good luck' from Pam in 'Nam."

He was smiling as they slipped over the side of the boat. "Baron Samedi be with you," Mama Locha called.

They swam slowly, letting the swells carry them shoreward. Eight miles from Barbados, the water was cold but not too cold, and faintly phosphorescent. Shore-birds soared overhead, calling down the wind. The swimmers' eyes stayed locked on the cove. Soon the swells began to grow larger, and the swimmers came to a halt just beyond the surf line. Max touched Pam's shoulder. She squeezed his hand. Then they separated and swam forward with the waves. Max had bodysurfed around the world and tonight, in the dark off Omen Key, he had one of his best rides ever. The wave swept over him as he stuck his arms out ahead to point his course and rode it as it surged and thundered. At the end he was sliding up along the wet sand, slowing to an easy stop. He scrambled to his feet, watching Pam ride in to his right, but focusing on the world around him.

There was nothing nearby. The larger night was filled with the hollow chirping of frogs and insects. And from above, inland, came the rumble of the eerie drums, their rhythm slower than the natural sounds, emphasizing their strangeness, their lack of harmony with life.

Pam got up off the sand, widened her eyes at him. He shook his head, knelt and opened the rifle case, took out the weapons. He handed her the CZ-83, stuck his Glock in his pocket, and slung the AR-15 over his shoulder. Then he reached out to touch her hand, and together they ran across the open sand to the cliff-shadows. The path upward was a pale ribbon through tumbled gray rocks.

He gestured for her to stay where she was, then took five steps up the path and looked carefully for the security ahead. It was concealed in a patch of St. John's wort, but not too well; the guards indeed were complacent. He took one more step, knelt, and went to work on it. In less than a minute he had bypassed it. He motioned for Pam to come on up.

At the top of the cliff they entered a deep forest of palms and ferns. The sounds of the frogs, the bugs, the drums, though still distant, grew louder, echoing among the tree trunks, filling what little emptiness remained in this jungle. But there were still no sounds of humans—or zombis—nearby. The pale light that fell from the stars above was blocked, shadowed, and the path the guards used ran on ahead, toward the north, before disappearing in darkness.

It wasn't Hallowe'en but it felt exactly like the night Ichabod Crane rode through the forest of the Headless Horseman, Pam thought. Anything could be hidden in that forest.

Max put his lips to her ear. "Stay two steps behind me," he whispered, and touched her shoulder. They started along the path.

Twenty feet in, the jungle canopy grew so thick he could no longer see the path. He stopped, snapped his fingers softly, and goblin light played on his fingertips. Its flickering showed their route turning left. Looking that way he saw a patch of starlight thirty yards along. He extinguished the light on his fingers, waited for his eyes to readjust to the darkness, then moved on, with Pam close behind. On the one hand, it was dangerous to follow the trail, since the guards used it, too, but on the other hand, he and Pam could move much faster on it. And it was dangerous to use any light. But the so-familiar jungle was Max August's element, and he knew how to work it. All the old sensations sparked all the old pleasures—a strange word for adrenaline and hyperawareness, things normally found on the edge of extinction, but the danger only sweetened the moment. Before he'd gotten into alchemy, point was where he'd felt most alive. And *dangerous*.

Around him now, beneath the fern fronds, among the palm trunks, the elementals of earth and air were following him, curious as to his intentions. Unlike his time in Vietnam, he knew them, heard them, saw them. If it came to it, he could use them to warn of danger, but he wouldn't go there unless absolutely necessary. For one thing, they would then be *his* point men. But more important, it was too easy for a magick man to start relying on his magick all the time. His magick, in the end, depended on his ability to use it. If he let his personal edge dull, not all the magick in the universe would save him. So, paradoxically, facing danger was the best way to maintain his safety. And Pam's.

She, too, was riding on adrenaline—really beginning to feel at home with it, in this strange new world she'd been dragged into. The world was still amorphous, with sudden connections and insights popping up out of nowhere at any time, but she was getting a sense of the shape of it. She had a lot of faith in Max—probably too much, she had to remind herself. He himself said he wasn't omnipotent. But she hadn't seen any reason to lose faith. And beyond that, she had faith in herself. Growing up, she'd been exactly what he called her— Young Wild West, Cowgirl Pam—but she'd put that behind her to go to med school and work in her painstakingly disciplined field. Now, though, in just two nights, she'd done more things requiring physical courage than she might have expected to do in the rest of her life, even if she lived to be a hundred. She'd shot a man, knifed a zombi, dodged a sylph, seen a sky full of energy. She still had a magick dart in her side but that seemed like a ding you'd pick up playing sports: shake it off, rub some dirt on it. She was playing on the right team. She knew that.

And she was feeling *dangerous*.

As they padded along, the surrounding sounds of the frogs and the bugs stayed constant, but the sound of the drums grew louder. It was a steady, monotonous beat, too slow to emulate a heartbeat, but somehow thrilling just the same. It got into your head. It had gotten in the frogs' and insects' heads; their steady rhythms broke now and again, unable to compete.

All at once an unearthly whistle broke them completely, leaving only the drums. After a long interval, the chirpers began again, tentatively. After a longer interval, Pam's heart slowed down. She felt a little less dangerous, but even more aware.

"What was that?"

He leaned in. "I dunno, but it's not a wildcat. And it's not close, either. Don't worry yet."

"Nicely put," she whispered sarcastically.

They went on, picking their way from light patch to light patch. Despite the jerky nature of the trek, they were making good time. They'd gone maybe three-quarters of a mile when Max heard footsteps coming the other way on the trail, and the clink of metal on metal. He reached back for Pam; she'd heard it too, and took his hand. He led her off the path, into the jungle, moving carefully so as not to betray their presence, moving deliberately to be out of sight before the guards arrived. He was pleased but not at all surprised that she aped his movements so completely that only one branch broke beneath their feet. If Max had been the opposition, he'd have heard that and prepared, but the guards were talking among themselves, and the drums covered a lot. The drums were probably why the men were talking louder than they ordinarily would. Max stopped, pushed Pam to crouch down, turned back and crouched himself.

Judging from the voices, two men were approaching. They ambled along, hashing over last Sunday's Dolphins game. One had had the under and was cruelly disappointed, even now. But he was sure he could make it up on the Bills. They had no idea any hostile was within eight miles of them.

As they passed him by, Max rose silently, stepped out behind them like a ghost. He chopped the butt of his AR-15 into the back of the right man's head, then swung it again into the turning, surprised face of the left man—careful not to break the man's night-vision goggles. Both went down without a cry.

Max pulled black plastic straps from his jeans pocket, knelt, and with quick efficiency bound the men's limp hands, then their feet. He grabbed handfuls of dead fronds and stuffed them in the men's mouths, then slit one man's shirt, cut it to rags, and used the strips to tie the fronds tightly in place. After that he relieved them of their ammo carriers, knives, grenades, and finally, their goggles. Only then did he drag them, one after the other, deep into the jungle, sit them up against massive palm trunks, and use the final cloth strips to secure them there.

Then he remained in his crouch and listened for a full two minutes.

When he was satisfied, he stood, went back, and handed Pam one set of goggles. She put them on, came close, put her lips to his ear.

"Pardon my sense of caution, but . . . no killing?"

He shook his head, whispered back, "Not unless we have to."

"You killed that guy in the hospital, without a second thought."

"I had no choice then. If I have a choice, I believe in life."

"Young Wild East," she said. But she really had expected no less. A point man who chose not to kill. An alchemist who took on the real world. And, of course, a thirty-five-year-old who was born when Truman was president. Maybe he wasn't omnipotent, but he was omni-something. Omnivorous, maybe. Omnivorous for life.

If there was any question of her *not* falling for him, it was answered right then. She felt it, saw it, accepted it, went with it.

He waved at her and made a face, enjoying the benefits of their newly won night vision. They turned and moved on, able to see the world around them for the first time. The palms were extraordinarily close and thick, their fronds sweeping together overhead. The path was four feet wide. The drums grew louder.

And all at once they turned a corner and the jungle ended. They halted on a dime, then scrambled back into concealment. Thirty yards away, a looming fortress squatted massively in the starlight.

"But that's supposed to be a mile farther on!" Pam whispered.

Max was nodding slowly, seemingly happily. "They altered the Google shot," he whispered back.

"How could they do that?"

"It wouldn't be hard. One little intern, someone like your Nancy—"

"She's not *my* Nancy!"

"—replacing the real satellite photo at Google HQ with a Photoshopped one, changing the program code to block any newer photo. Who's gonna know? No outsider's supposed to get on this island. The air routes to Europe run north of here. It's just another level of control and disinformation from the FRC."

"You seem pretty cheerful about it."

"They're a worthy opponent."

"An opponent that can reach almost anywhere!"

"Google's not Fort Knox. And why figure 'almost'? Give 'em full credit, then you won't underestimate 'em. But remember, we can go 'almost' anywhere ourselves." Max smiled. "But I did wonder why the guards' beach would be so far from the command post . . ."

The building ahead of them was stark and simple. It was triangular, pointed to the right like a wedge, facing the road that led to the dock on the eastern coast (assuming that part of the photo was true). In profile, then, it was like a slice of birthday cake, three stories tall, divided into three horizontal sections by two indentations. Tubing ran from a portal in the side and gathered at the rear of the flat roof, which was undoubtedly a helipad. There were no lights around the building but dim light showed in the lowest of the two indentations—light from inside. And the sound of the drumming was finally identifiable as coming from there.

Max turned and looked Pam over. "I don't feel any electronics, which isn't a hundred percent, but there have to be more guards. We'll wait."

They stood for another five minutes, the now-thundering drums beginning to have an effect on them as well. The beat was so monotonous that they began to develop an active aversion to each new blow. Pam wondered how Max liked *this* music. But they stood among the palms and waited.

Two new guards came around the front point of the building. They were more watchful than the first two, clearly making their regular rounds.

They stopped at a point closer to the front than the rear. Through the night goggles, Max and Pam watched as one guard punched a keypad on the wall—one, two, three times. Pam squeezed Max's hand in excitement. Then the guard removed his own goggles and leaned his head against the box. Retinal scan.

A hidden door slid back with a whooshing sound as its airtight rubber seals parted. The guard went inside, down unseen steps, while his buddy waited. A new man came up and out to join the buddy. Those two spoke briefly with the now-unseen first guard inside the building. The door slid shut with another *pffnt*. The new guard and the old one went on about their patrol, around the back end of the building.

"Very nice," said Max. "The overlap makes sure there's always one with knowledge of what's been happening and one with fresh eyes. Now, other than my devastating charm, why the hand-squeeze?"

"I caught the key code," Pam whispered.

"Yeah?" he said with interest. "It was too dark for me."

"This afternoon while you were meditating, I was thinking about what you said, about the FRC liking to sign their work. I wondered what 'FRC' would be on a telephone, and it's 'three-seven-two.' That's what he punched."

"You saw the numbers?"

"No, I saw where his finger went on the pad. Upper right, lower left, back up."

"That's assuming the pad's a three-by-three like a phone."

"Oh," she said, suddenly deflated. "Right."

"No, no," he said. "If you know the movements it shouldn't matter. That's great, Pam."

"Well," she said, deflecting the praise but still glad to get it, "we still have to fake a retinal scan. You can't do that with gravity lenses, since you don't know what retina to fake."

"Exactly. But I know where a real retina can be found."

"Oh, yeah . . ."

They turned and ran back the eighth of a mile to the spot where Max had left the first guards tied. Pam had time to wonder if they'd recognize it out of all the jungle they'd passed, but she took it for granted Max would, and in fact, she did as well. The first place they'd been able to see the jungle was very clear in her mind.

They found the men conscious and squirming to get free of their bonds, with no success thus far. Max turned his rifle around and clocked each of the men once more.

"You're not going to remove the eyeball, are you?" Pam asked, suddenly wary.

"Hell, no. What kind of guy do you think I am?"

He untied the smaller of the two guards from the tree and hoisted him onto his shoulders. They went back the eighth of a mile to their watching post.

In a few minutes, the two building guards reappeared on their rounds. They moved along the side of the building and disappeared around the back edge.

Max looked at Pam. "Ready?"

"I was *born* ready!" Pam chuckled, throwing back her shoulders, sticking out her chest, all macho (and not macho at all). "Let's do it," she said huskily. "So to speak." He nodded, saying nothing.

He stashed his rifle case among the ferns, leaving each of them with one pistol. Then they ran across the open space toward the hidden door. Once again, no alarm sounded.

"Look," she said, "it *is* like a telephone pad." She took a deep breath and punched 3-7-2.

A light began to glow above the pad.

Max took his unconscious captive, pried open the right eyelid, and pushed the eye against the glow.

The door slid open, *pffnt*.

They were met with the overpowering stench of dead flesh.

NOVEMBER 3, 2007 – MIDNIGHT AST

13 CORN SEED

Max ran his unconscious captive back to the edge of the clearing and hid him well off the trail. It was a gamble; the door might close again after a certain amount of time. But carrying the guard inside meant concealing him there, and there might not be any good place for that. In any event, the door did not close before he came running back. He and Pam hustled inside. There, she spotted a button beside the door, pressed it, and the door slid shut with a hollow thunk, shutting them in.

At the bottom of the steps, a ten-foot-tall corridor ran ahead of them. The drums were now even louder, echoing off the concrete from speakers recessed in the walls. On the right loomed a solid-looking door labeled GUARDS. The infiltrators jogged past it, down the hall, and came to a larger, intersecting corridor. The stench of flesh came most strongly from the left. Without hesitation, they both turned that way.

At the end of the main corridor, they came to an area that reminded Max—for a moment—of a public aquarium. Like many such, there was a circular central section surrounded by a viewing section where onlookers could stand and peer through huge glass windows at what lurked within. But here the windows were mesh-reinforced, and what lurked within was only dimly visible.

Around the right side of the curve, outside the central section, Max and Pam spotted metronomic movement, heard shuffling footsteps. Shifting their position, they saw maybe fifty zombis moving like clockwork toward curved wooden benches. Some zombis were already sitting there quietly, and the others joined them. Now all of them were seated, their heads and arms continuing to jerk slightly with each new beat of the drums. They looked neither right nor left, clearly oblivious to the invaders' stares. Instead, on the beat, each flopped his mouth open and took a breath. Then, mouths still open, they just sat.

They had come from the direction of an air lock in the outside wall of the central section. Max and Pam moved back beyond the seated zombis' view and closer to the windows in the central section. Peering intently through the gloom inside, they finally made out the occupants of the round room.

More zombis.

The inner chamber was filled with a green humid mist, in which the hulking, hazy figures stood before long tables, in long rows, like statues. Only their arms stirred, in an unbroken rhythm.

"That's what the drums are for," Pam whispered, the light breaking at last. "They regulate the zombis' movements! Wherever they go on this island, they always hear them. Because their hearts are barely beating, they don't have the internal rhythm we take for granted. Without the drums they'd lose their focus."

"They give them focus," Max agreed, "*and* they keep

their minds from working at all. Everything is bound up in the beat."

They were *making* something to the beat. Pam remembered Max's description of their making the talisman—the endless hours of patient work. By getting right up against the glass, she managed to see what they were making now.

"Holy shit," she whispered, her own heart going into her throat.

Now Max saw it, too. Canisters in the center of the circle, also in neat rows, labeled with one word: SARIN.

The zombis were manufacturing the world's most deadly nerve agent, best known from the 1995 Aum Shinrikyo attack on the Tokyo subway. And all at once the brilliance of it flashed like lightning in Pam's mind: the zombis could stand in their sealed-off room and patiently create a gas that would kill any normal human being. They breathed once an hour, Max had said, so they had to be rotated in and out. She and Max had just missed the changing of the guard, the previous shift coming out to breathe, and the next shift taking over. Together, the two shifts could make, en masse, twenty-four hours a day, what normal labs would need weeks or months of painstaking mechanical effort to achieve.

Which, of course, was why her antidote to zombi status had to be suppressed. Miller Omen and the FRC were preparing for something massive and horrendous, and she was in their way. The stolen data, the talisman, the dart, and if all else failed, the three zombis—it wasn't even close to overkill, from their point of view, if it suppressed her knowledge completely.

But it hadn't.

She was standing on the other side of the glass from

the zombis, and she had her antidote in her newly pur-
chased Bajan backpack. She was so close . . . and yet so
far. Because if she used the antidote on those zombis,
they would all die as they began to breathe the sarin
that surrounded them. Assuming she or Max could find
a way to introduce the antidote into that hermetically
sealed chamber in the first place.

"There's got to be a way to flush the chamber," Max
said softly, reading her thoughts.

"The sarin has to go someplace contained and safe,"
she agreed. "They wouldn't release it into the open,
even on this little island. But that means they'll still
have it available."

"I might be able to do something about that," he said.
"Let's scout this place."

They started their circle to the left, leaving the sitting zombis for last. A quarter of the way around, they
came to a doorway. Pam tried it and it swung open.
She went inside and found a storage area. "Max!" she
hissed.

"What?"

She was examining the neatly labeled boxes stacked
inside. "It's Omen's ingredients for his zombi potion.
Pharmaceutically pure tetrodotoxin. And this is an ex-
tract of pomme cajou. Jesus Christ!" She was angry
now. "I work my ass off in an underfunded government lab to save people, and he's using his state-of-
the-art pharmaceutical empire to turn them into living
corpses!"

"Come on," Max said, more excited about the future
than the past.

They walked the rest of the loop, finding nothing
until they came to the seated zombis. It was eerie to
step out in front of their slack-jawed gaze, but the zom-

bis did not move beyond their jerks to the beat of the drums. They stank of putrefaction.

Across from them, on the inner wall, was the airlock between the two areas. Beside that were three levers on the wall, the first labeled helpfully LAB AIR LOCK, the second LAB EMERGENCY VENT, and the third OBSERVATION ROOM SEAL. Farther still to the left, along the curved wall, six enviro-suits hung from hangers, in neat precision on a steel rod, with six helmets on a rack above.

"Get one of these on," Pam said. There had been a time for the point man; this was the doctor at work. "We'll flush the room, then go inside and release the antidote. How functional will the people be once they've been treated?"

"Beats me," Max replied. "I've never even heard of its being done before. But I'd lay odds the answer is 'not very.' Are you thinking of evacuating them?"

"Aren't you?"

"If we can, but I wouldn't bank on it. Herding cats would be easier. Herding *slugs* would be easier."

"Well, first things first." She took one of the enviro-suits from its hanger and sat on the bench to slide her feet into its legs. Max did the same.

All at once they heard voices, jumbled and confused, from the corridor outside the viewing room, the corridor they had come down. It sounded like a sudden argument among several people—and it sounded close.

Moving with common purpose, Max and Pam finished sealing themselves into their suits. Pam moved quickly to grab two helmets, handed one to Max. They donned them and sealed them, and as soon as Pam was ready, with her backpack in her gloved hands, she turned and flipped the AIR LOCK lever. There was the faint sound of air being evacuated from within the lock, then the door to the corridor slid open. She and Max went inside. With an interior lever, she closed the door behind them and looked at Max. It was dim inside his helmet but she saw him nod.

She opened the interior air lock door.

The room revealed before them was large, but seemed cramped by its many inhabitants and the green gas that hung like a grim parody of an aurora borealis. They moved forward slowly, among the monsters, and in their bulky suits they moved like monsters themselves. Pam, for all her *esprit de combat*, could not help but remember the fear she'd felt when the three original zombis had battered their way into her home. Now there were fifty of the brutes surrounding her in the claustrophobic room. For the moment, they seemed engrossed in their brain-dead occupations, unaware or uncaring that others had entered their domain. But would that last?

Outside the window, Miller Omen, Tilit, Ballantine, and a group of uniformed men entered the observation room.

Omen was continuing to argue with the man who was probably the captain of his guards, judging by the filigree. There were a total of seven of them, now standing not ten feet away from their unseen nemeses.

Max and Pam drifted slowly backward, into the center of the chamber, the center of the concealing monsters and mist—beside the sarin cans. Both of them were thanking whatever gods they honored that the lighting was so dim.

Omen gestured emphatically and the three regular guards began to search the observation room; one went left, one right, and the third stood ready to take on anyone flushed by the others. Each held a .45 automatic in his hand. Their captain watched with ill-concealed displeasure; it was obvious that Omen believed, or at least suspected, that security had been breached, while the captain was certain his men had done their job. Omen's two personal guards had their backs to the outer wall, bracketing the doorway from the hall, weapons at the ready.

Max and Pam watched as the uniforms made their way around the enclosing circle. The men were tense, alert—scouring the hallway with their eyes. But they never looked inside the zombi chamber. And the one who passed the four suits and helmets missed it, too focused on finding human beings.

When the men finished their rounds and returned to the starting point, the captain surveyed the result with cold satisfaction, then turned to Omen. He said something, apparently mild, and Omen gestured to Tilit. Tilit blew the captain's brains out, spattering gore across the meshed window.

Omen turned to the guard who'd been stationary during the search and jabbed his finger at him; he was now in charge. The guard saluted. Omen, Tilit, and Ballantine stalked out. The new captain ordered his mates to gather up the corpse of his predecessor and carry it away.

Max and Pam, inside their suits, breathed sighs of relief.

And so at last they could take a long look at the creatures surrounding them. Pam, in particular, turned to look directly into the face of the nearest zombi.

He was big, heavy, with the unhealthy weight of a pumpkin gone rotten, or a neutered animal. It seemed to pull his skin down; his face looked as if it were melting.

His lips were pendulous, his eyes almost lost in the folds. The eyes were absolutely lifeless, doll's eyes; they did not blink. But he stood at his table and methodically mixed the chemicals he'd been given. To Pam's practiced eyes, the tips of his fingers, of his ears, were decaying, dying from a lack of circulation. Hence the smell of dead flesh that would be overpowering in this enclosed chamber if she weren't wearing a closed suit.

This thing before her had been a living man and, according to Max, still was. According to Max, he could shed all these trappings and go back to his old life, albeit horribly damaged by his ordeal. Maybe he had a wife, a family.

Maybe they were in here with him.

Pam felt that she'd run through all her emotions in these last few days. She was disgusted and sickened and angry. She looked around for Max. He was at the red-smeared window, peering down the corridor. He looked back and gave her a thumbs-up.

She went back toward the air lock and found the evacuation lever inside the room. It was deep between two iron flanges, to keep a zombi from accidentally activating it. But there was room for her gloved hand to reach in and take hold. She looked back at Max. He again gave her the go-ahead sign.

She flipped the lever and the gas in the room at once began to swirl up through a vent in the roof. The gas was thick enough to form visible green currents as it went.

Max turned, and made his wiping motion, but this time he continued the arc, rounding it off, bringing his hand down and back underneath, as if he were scooping up a handful of the gas. In the gas above his hand a sphere of emptiness appeared, while the rest of it continued to visibly flow past him.

When the room was clear, Pam flipped the lever back to its closed position. *Well,* she thought, *here goes nothing.* She opened her backpack, scooped out her own handful of the antidote, and started sowing it around the room, like seed.

No sooner did the powder settle on the stoic forms than the zombis began to move in ways foreign to the beat of the drums—first making short involuntary movements, then twitches, then quickly spasms. The people rocked and shuddered, and Pam looked on with the great fear that she'd just killed every one of them. They fell to their knees, their chests, and writhed like beads of water on a skillet.

But then their spasms began to slow. All the tension seemed to drain out of their bodies. And it was clear that lying on the floor of the chamber were, once more, human beings. Exhausted, drained, and damaged, but alive and out from under the zombi curse. There was a definite difference in everything about them.

Max took her arm, pulled her toward the door. She resisted at first, then acquiesced. They went in to the air lock and closed the door after them. A mist of disinfectant blasted over them, like a car wash, hosing down their suits. A blast of air struck them, again like a car wash. When it ended he opened the outside door and they went through.

Once they had their helmets off, he said, "Assuming they recover enough strength to walk, they'll see how to open and close the door. But we can't wait to watch it."

"I cured them, Max!" Pam said excitedly. "I saved them!"

"I think you did." He smiled. "But now we have to find out what the sarin was made for. And we still have to end Omen's curse on you."

She wholeheartedly agreed with both those statements. Within a minute she was out of her suit and ready to move on. But first she sowed the rest of her antidote over the quiescent second shift, and watched with a now-practiced eye in better light as they began to shake and topple. "I saved them," she said again, with delicious satisfaction. "Goddammit, I did!" Then, pistol in hand, she moved toward the corridor she and Max had come in by.

"How are you going to handle Omen and his men?" she asked.

"Quite probably I'll have to kill Omen. The others . . . up to them. I don't want to kill anybody, but killing Omen is the surest way to end his curse on you, and 'sure' is a very good way to handle things that nasty."

He started to enter the corridor, but she held his arm. "What did you do with the sarin—when you did that hand motion?"

"Scooped a handful into another dimension. Call it the subconscious."

"The subconscious is a *place*?"

"We're standing in it, all the time. But we don't see it. And since we don't, it's a great place to hide shit."

They made their way cautiously on down the main corridor, ready for whatever might come. Omen could well have stationed guards along the way if he'd remained suspicious of intruders. But there was no sign of anyone.

They came to the intersection. The door to the guard room was still closed, but Max couldn't leave that potential threat to come up behind them. He moved toward the door, waving Pam back, but she came after him. He turned around and gestured forcefully: *Stay there!* She shook her head, but he was implacable, so with an angry moue she stood where she was. He raised a finger, whirled it around: *Keep an eye out.* She nodded shortly.

Max ran to the far side of the door, the side with the push pad. He turned to face the door through which they'd entered the corridor and did his wiping thing. No one would be coming in that way. Then he flattened himself against the wall beside the guards' door, reached sideways . . . pushed it open.

There appeared to be no reaction.

He spun into and through the doorway, keeping low, AR-15 at the ready.

The room was empty.

He gave it a quick once-over to make sure. No one would come up behind them from this direction.

He came back into the corridor, gesturing for Pam to hurry. They went back into the main corridor and headed to the right.

The short corridor led to a counterpart of the sarin area, but this rounded room had no central tank; rather, it was outfitted with comfortable leather chairs and couches. To one side stood a low stage surmounted by a sleek dais, both made of dark mahogany. Everything spoke of power and money . . .

"Stand very still."

The voice came from behind them. They stood very still.

"Put your weapons on the floor." Pam looked at Max and he nodded, his eyes serious. They complied.

"Now turn around, and kick them over here." They turned, and found themselves facing Miller Omen and his entire crew. All had their weapons pointed toward them. Max and Pam kicked their weapons over and two of the uniforms scooped them up.

Omen took a step forward, eyeing Pam up and down, and said coolly, "I assume you're Dr. Pamela Blackwell." When Pam did not reply, he said, "What did Nancy tell you about me?"

Pam kept her head up, defiantly. "Nothing."

"And yet you're here," Omen answered. He stepped forward briskly and hit her hard in the face. She turned at the last second or he'd have broken her jaw. As it was, she went down sprawling among the comfortable chairs, sending one sliding across the smooth floor. Max stirred. Ballantine held a gun on him and said, "Nuh-uh."

Omen stood over Pam and said, "I'm glad to wrap this up, Dr. Blackwell. You've led me a merry chase but it's worked out perfectly in the end." He gave her a sharp kick and she rolled over, but when he saw she wouldn't respond, he turned his attention to Max. "I have everything I need, so I was leaving my little island anyway."

Pam got shakily to her feet. Max helped her up but kept his eyes on Omen. "Where are you off to, big guy?"

"Why do you care? You're not leaving this room—little guy."

• • •

Miller Omen held his pistol steady. It felt good in his hand—the weight of it, the steel, the coiled power. The death of the captain of the guards was still warm in his hand. A Code Red had come after him, and that Code Red was now his. The two intruders were under his complete control on a small, lost island in the Atlantic, and they knew it.

Certainly Dr. Blackwell did. There was fear in her,

as all her dreams of the Code Red's mystical invincibility met stark truth. But there was also a passion, as if she were on some roller coaster ride. Taking that out of her would be his pleasure. He almost shot her right then, eager to look down on his handiwork—down on the flesh and the blood found in all human bodies. But there was more to be gotten from the sorcerer.

"Who sent you here, August?" Omen demanded.

"Nobody."

"You expect me to believe that?"

"Of course not. It's the truth."

He was putting up a brass front, showing no worries about what Omen might do. Once again, Omen felt the driving urge to gun him down right now and see the shock in everybody's eyes. You weren't supposed to kill a Code Red without a *stone*; supposedly, the death of a magician released a shitload of power, and the FRC wanted it sucked into their rock. Omen had a rock on him, but he had a gun in his hand, and he liked the gun a lot better.

Which wasn't to say the *stone* didn't have its uses. He reached into his pant pocket with his free hand and grasped it, then used the *mind-push* the FRC had taught him to start Pam's dart once more toward her heart. Her wince caught Max's attention at once, and at once Max stopped the dart. But they all knew it was only temporary, now.

"You can't take it out," Omen told him flatly. "I know that. All you can do is fight it. But if I kill you, the fight's over, and she follows you to hell. So spare yourselves the pain and tell me, what do you know about my plan?"

"Only whatever you choose to tell us. Don't you want to flaunt your superiority a little more?"

Omen feinted at Pam, and smiled as she flinched. The battle for control of the dart was really not doing her any good. He took her arm. "I might flaunt it the way I like best."

Pam snarled, "Let go of me."

"Everyone says that at first." He jerked her and she gasped in pain. "You know what I do in my 'normal' life, don't you, Doctor? I run a pharmaceutical company. People think of my drugs as helping people live, but I think of them as helping people die. The ability to afford one's life-care is the primary dividing line between those who deserve life and those who don't. You will agree, Doctor, that ridding society of the unfit strengthens the society—makes the fit even fitter by removing potential pathogens."

"Like hell," Pam said, holding tight to her side.

"What do you say, Code Red? I can rid society of her right this instant unless you tell me who else knows about my operation. Try me."

August, seemingly unmoved, considered for a moment before answering, "The black man."

"Is that a title?"

"No."

"Then who's the black man?"

"He's the man you turned into a zombi."

"Which one?"

"Hard to say. They look so much alike to start with, and then the zombi paste takes their individuality. Of course, Pam gave that back to them."

The girl was looking at him incredulously. What was he saying?

Omen signaled Ballantine, who nodded and went to check.

"What good will it do even if you have turned those

niggers back?" Omen said harshly. "They're still niggers. You said it yourself: they're nothing to me."

"Except for the black man," said August coolly.

"Is he another Code Red?"

"Red, black, what's the difference?"

"Where is he now?"

But before August could answer, there were sudden
shots from the direction of the chamber. One, two—
three—

Then a growing sort of howl—

Forty of the men and women who'd been held in the
chamber burst into the room on rubbery but churning
legs. The smaller bodyguard and two of the uniforms
went down in the first mad rush. One especially dark-
skinned man lunged toward Omen, who delightedly put
a bullet between his eyes. "I bet you wish you were a
zombi now!" he snarled. Then, to Max: "Is that him?"

But Max had seized the moment and grabbed Pam,
driving her behind the mahogany dais. Omen's next shot
snapped past them, just as Tilit and the guards opened
fire on the mob. Max braced himself against the back of
the podium, eyes closed and brow furrowed. The tendons in his neck bulged as sweat sparkled on his face.
Pam's eyes grew wide.

"None of them is the black man, Omen!" Max shouted
over the gunfire, cutting through the clamor with his
trained radio voice. His eyes were still closed.

Omen held his fire. "Where is he, then?"

"He's behind you."

Omen snapped his head around. Something *was*
there!

Only now he caught *another* movement from the
corner of his eye.

"Shut him down, August!" Omen shouted.

"He doesn't answer to me! He's got his own power!"

Omen's eyes darted sideways, down. There was definitely something moving just at the edge of his awareness, something quick and sly. He looked at Tilit to see if he'd caught it, but his security chief was only looking at him, strangely. Was he blind as well as mute? Couldn't he see it? *There it was again!*

Or—*no!* There were flashes from *two separate places!* There were *two* of them!

Omen clutched the *stone.* He didn't understand it, he'd never had to use it for protection, but he'd been through the FRC course. He tried to focus his will. He tried to focus his *thoughts.* But something black lunged at him as soon as he committed to it, and as he reeled backward, something else grabbed his leg. He knew in his bones that the gun was useless now. He needed the FRC's *stone*—

Then there was *another* flash! And *another and another!* All at once, the flashes on the fringes were exploding in numbers! There were five of them, ten, twenty, a hundred, two hundred! Black men all around him, above him, below him. He knew he couldn't forget about Max but when he tried to turn his eyes to him, all he saw were other shapes, *black* shapes, clustering between them, coming his way. They filled his vision, filling every crevice of the world, black men with yellow eyes and lolling lips and drool. He tried to run but they were everywhere, closing on him. Omen screamed. They were diving from the heavens. They were crushing him. He died.

13 CORN SEED

Pam watched it all, saw it all, as if it were a dream. She saw the elementals just as Omen did, but she understood what they were. She felt no rising wave of urgency as they increased their visibility. Then, when other shapes appeared, to her they seemed flecks of starlight. Certainly they weren't humanoid, nor were they black. It was as if the walls had rolled back and showed them all the surrounding, star-spangled heavens she'd peered up into as they sailed across the sea. As if all the things in it, and particularly the asteroids in their belt, were crashing inward, spiraling toward Miller Omen. But they were lights in the darkness, and the lights grew brighter, filling more of the darkness, and it was not frightening. It was fascinating, inspiring, supremely glorious . . .

• • •

And the pain in her side stopped.

"What—?" she gasped, unconsciously twisting toward the side where the pain had been, the side she'd been favoring for two and a half days.

"The dart is gone," Max said, his slow but certain voice showing sudden immense fatigue. "It was born from Omen's will; it ended with his death."

And Omen was definitely dead. The star was gone, the sky was gone, leaving only the circular room filled with bodies. One of the bodies was Omen's, twisted and motionless. Their other captors, Tilit and the guards, were lying beside him, but moving, albeit slowly. And the surviving former zombis were also making feeble gestures. "You didn't kill anyone else," Pam said, mostly to reassure herself that what she was seeing was real now.

Max might not have heard her. He drew his fingers across his closed eyes, wiped the sweat down his face. "I broke down the masks in this room," he said, still speaking as if it cost him a great effort. "I showed him his subconscious. The masks keep the world small enough and familiar enough for us to be comfortable in. To be aware of everything is more than untrained flesh and blood can stand. Omen wasn't trained, and when I began to break down his illusion, he became aware of the elementals close around him, and then the asteroids in the wider universe, the two hundred and sixty essential asteroids, each with its own energy, its own power, its own existence, around and above and below him."

"I saw them, too," Pam said. "But they didn't kill me. They didn't kill the guards. It was too *big* for him"

"I focused it all on Omen's special fear. I read his mind at the fight when I touched him; he hated blacks because he feared them. So I gave him the idea that his nemesis was a black man. It drew his attention better than anything else would have, and he didn't associate it with me because it was *his* special fear. His mind took it from there, straight to overload." Max sighed. "You don't share his fears, and if the guards do, there was still no need to kill them."

Pam looked at the men on the floor. "What will happen to them?"

"They'll be ambulatory about six hours from now—it takes that long for their neural systems to reset. We'll be long gone."

"Not yet," Pam said. She took his arm, pulled him

around with her own neural system not quite under control, and kissed him hard. "Thank you, Max," she said, her voice so choked she could barely speak. "You did everything you said you'd do, that first night in the hospital. Everything you told me was true, just like you said. Thank God I believed you!"

To her surprise, he kissed her right back. Something had changed since last night. But just as she began to go with that, he took her shoulders and moved her gently away, saying, "We've got to get everybody who's alive out of this place, Pam. As quickly as possible."

He crouched beside Omen's body and took the *stone* from his dead hand. "Here," he said, handing it to her. "It's chock-full of power, even if you're not trained to use it. Just remember, it's not bad power or good power, and it can't hurt you, so you might as well see what it's like."

She took it from him gingerly and felt a slight tingling, but no cosmic amazingness. She slipped it into the pocket of her jeans, and the tingling went to her thigh. That was okay. Particularly after that kiss.

The two of them set about clearing the compound. Pam led the ones who could walk, while Max carried out a quick but thorough search of Omen's control center. He found printed data on the zombi "experiments," but nothing indicating what the larger plan might be. Omen had not been a sloppy man. There might be something on the two computers in the room, but they were encrypted with passwords, and he knew as well as anyone how many man-hours it might take to crack them. All he could do was take their hard drives, with the idea of sending them to Dave, his computer Jedi. But even Dave couldn't crack them in time to make a difference, probably. Everything pointed to Omen's plan bearing fruit very soon.

He wrapped the drives carefully in a dead man's shirt, stuffed the package inside his own shirt, then started carrying the comatose guards outside. There he searched them for hidden weapons, taking extra care with Tilit, before binding each to a tree. Finally, he went back inside to help Pam with any stragglers who couldn't walk without help. He left Ballantine's body where it lay, bruised and twisted; the man had gone down in the first wave of the captives' assault, and though they'd lacked the strength to overpower him, their sheer weight had suffocated him.

The Leo moon had risen, a waning crescent like the Cheshire cat's smile, barely visible through the trees, when Max and Pam were certain the sarin manufacturing area was clear. Red Mars was high overhead as Max stood in the clearing, snapped his fingers, and formed the witch-light on their tips. This time, however, he snapped the fingers of his left hand as well, then held his hands together as if cradling an invisible ball. In that configuration, the witchfire grew to fill the space until his hands glowed, the bones showing through his skin. Max turned his wrists upward, elegantly, causing the ball to rise in front of his face . . . then snapped them forward, like tossing a beach ball. The fireball flew to strike the side of the compound with an audible *smack*, and instantly, the building burst into eye-blinding flame. Less than five minutes later, the lab was reduced to ash and slag steel. And the drums finally stopped.

"Fire cleanses everything," Max said. "Even poison gas."

Behind them rose a murmur of awe and fear. It was the men and women who had been zombis, now aware of their surroundings and certainly aware that they'd seen more magick. Pam stepped toward them, raising her hands in a gesture of peace. "It's all right," she said, and was grateful that Bajans spoke English so they would understand her, though there was no telling—*no empirical data, Dr. Blackwell!*—as to how well their minds were working just yet. "You're safe and you're free. There'll be no more zombis. He destroyed the prison. He killed the boss. We'll take you home." Her words and her manner had the desired effect; the people's agitation grew visibly less.

But Max said, "We can't take them with us on Mama's little boat. We'll have her send people back to pick them up."

"I should stay and see to them, then," she said.

"We can give them water, but they need food and hospital care," Max answered. "And we have to find out what Omen's plan is. We'll tell Mama and she can *call* her people right away, with vodou. There'll be boats heading out from Barbados before we even get back. This island will be cleared in three hours tops."

"Can't you *call* the people yourself? Or *call* Mama? There's a lot of gangrene here. There'll be lots of amputations."

"I don't know who her people are. And whatever she and the ladies are doing until three, they don't want interruptions. Will a couple of hours make that much of a difference?"

"I suppose not," Pam said. "I just want them healed." She turned and spoke softly to the people again. "Others will come very soon. All of you must stay together, here. You are in no danger." She shivered, turned again to Max. "As soon as I said that, I felt a chill."

"Intern's syndrome," he said, in the process of retrieving his waterproof rifle case. He laid the wrapped hard drives inside and locked it tight. "You see all the possibilities without the experience to judge. I like our odds."

They left the people hobbling around the clearing, like people waking after a long sleep, rediscovering the world. Many were in pain, but the common expression was gratitude.

NOVEMBER 3 - 1:30 A.M. AST

13 CORN SEED

As Max and Pam, wearing their night goggles, double-timed their way back along the jungle trail toward the beach where they'd started, Pam couldn't help smiling. She had saved those people! In the past, she'd worked on studies that ended up saving people—a whole lot more people than she'd saved tonight—but never before had she saved people with her own hands. Everyone she'd helped to cure was important, but this felt a whole lot better.

And she felt better. Better than she had for three days. When Max had first treated her—which was how she, as a doctor, now saw it—and they'd run along the hospital's hall, she'd felt strong and powerful, but looking back she could see that it was the magick overriding her weakness. Now she'd lost the weakness. She probably felt less powerful, but her feeling of well-being was one hundred percent natural, and natural was better.

They were coming toward the spot on the trail where Max had attacked the first two guards. She had no trouble recognizing it. What she had trouble with was the entrails spread across the dirt in the muddy moonlight.

"Holy Christ!" she said, stumbling to a halt in a moment of strong dissociation. Max had said there were no wild animals, said there was no danger, and Max was never wrong. If Max were wrong, then everything she'd just finished working into her reality was unreal. "Max . . ."

He motioned her to be quiet. His head was cocked, listening.

From a distance—but not a great distance now—that strange whistle they'd heard before sounded again.

"I wonder what that is," he muttered.

"It sounds . . . weird. Like something up your alley."

"It does. But—"

With no warning whatsoever, a shape leapt onto the trail ahead.

Its hips were wide, womanish, over massive meaty thighs, tapering to thin reptilian legs, feet, claws. With thin, wiry arms and three-clawed fingers, it could have been a five-foot tyrannosaurus, but it was covered in matted gray fur, spotted with black. Its eyes were large, slanted, and *cold*. Below them were small holes where a nose might be, small holes where ears might be, and a thin lipless mouth, showing the tips of fangs.

In the instant, it attacked, its clawed feet hurling dirt behind it. Max had no time to grab the rifle, but he emptied his Glock at the thing. It was like shooting a redwood. Though it began to bleed, in a color that looked *wrong* through green goggles, the dino never slowed. Max dropped to one side, hurling the pistol aside, taking the fall on both hands, kicking back at the lunging shape. He drove his boot into the thing's hip, adding his anti-grav thrust. It was like kicking a redwood.

The thing barely stumbled as it went past, then turned on a dime. It was focused solely on Max, not Pam, and Pam knew that was part of Max's plan. She pointed her CZ-83 at the creature and pumped four shots into it, but it never gave her a second look. It knew what it wanted.

"Save your ammo!" Max snapped, not looking at her, either. He had his knife out, crouched against the next charge, focused. "Reload now! If it gets past me—"

The creature exploded forward, a gray blur in the night. It grabbed Max's free arm, claws digging deep in his flesh, but he shoved his blade up and under the breastbone. The knife went in, but only partway; the strong flesh was backed by strong musculature. Everything except the flat head and claws seemed ribbed with it. Still, the thing skipped backward, whistling softly; round two was a draw.

Max went after it. He ducked a swipe of the wiry arm but walked right into a knee to the face powered by those swift, strong thighs. The thing fought like a human! He reeled sideways, feeling blood surge down his face, and a great weight landed on his shoulders, driving him to the ground as the claws of hands and feet ripped his flesh. Snorting breath with the scent of man and blood burned his neck. Max arched and twisted from hips to feet, hurling the bottom-heavy monster over his head.

It rolled over and up, natural athletic ability compensating for its ungainly build. Max came up off the ground himself and drove his knife once more beneath the breastbone, trying for the same spot. It couldn't be a perfect match but it came close enough that some of the previous resistance wasn't there now. This time it cut in to the hilt.

The creature gave its weird, full-throated whistle, and there was a thread of pain in it, but it staggered only slightly as it swiped at Max. He ducked the claws and made damn sure to avoid the kick this time. The knife was deep in its chest.

"Gun!" Max yelled.

Pam flipped him his reloaded Glock. She'd been waiting.

He caught the pistol broadside, flipped it himself and grabbed it with a proper grip. Then he ran straight toward the creature. It grabbed him, snapped at his neck, missed by no more than an inch, and now had Max tightly in its grasp. But in the same moment, Max took ahold of his knife and yanked it free, stuck the muzzle of the semiautomatic against the open wound, and emptied the clip. Under the breastbone, through undefended flesh, he pumped a full seventeen rounds.

Nothing's innards could withstand that. The monster staggered sharply backward, fell backward, rolled to its side and went slack. Its bladder emptied with stinking suddenness, a completely alien smell.

Pam walked toward it, her CZ-83 at the ready.

"Get back!" Max snapped.

She continued onward, grim. "We need to be sure it's dead," she said, and raised her pistol. Standing behind the dino's head, gingerly but determined, she leaned forward, aimed the gun at its staring eyeball, and emptied her clip.

The heavy head rocked slightly under the impact but the monster was already gone. "Sorry," she said. "I had to be sure. Too many slasher films." She looked up at Max, who was bleeding from a dozen places. "This is why you keep a doctor on hand, huh?"

"I'm off the grid," he said solemnly. "I can't get

medical." But all of a sudden, he slumped back against a tree.

"Max?" Pam cried, rushing toward him.

"That . . . was close," he said, leaning on the bark. "I like to think I'm a tough guy, the great and powerful Oz . . . but that was close."

"You were great!" She took his arms.

"I was lucky—lucky to have you right there. If I'd been on my own . . ." He doggedly slid down the tree trunk, lowering himself to sit with his back against it. "I can lose, you know. *I* sure know."

There was a lot of blood, but Pam couldn't see anything significant. The danger was infection from those unfamiliar claws. "Well, you didn't lose this time. I'll cleanse the wounds and apply some Bactroban. Get you something better when we get back . . ." *Oh. Yeah . . .*

"Can't go to the CVS. *Can* go to Mama's. You and she can work it out."

"I could just whip out my cell, call my supplier, give 'em our address." Her palms went up. "Joke!"

"I'll joke you," he said, mock-tough. His moment of weakness was already receding. For a man with all the time in the world, there was never any time for moments like that.

"Hold still," she said, the doctor and the woman. She started applying antibiotic cream and square bandages.

"You brought medical supplies?" he asked incredulously. "I thought that was part of the joke."

"Invite a doctor to a revolution, she's gonna come prepared," Pam responded. "For you and me, at least. Not forty recovering zombis. Turn around."

As she worked on his other arm, she asked the million-dollar question. "What was that *thing*, Max?"

"I don't know for sure."

"*You* don't?"

"No, smart-ass. But I'm guessing chupacabra."

"No!"

"You've heard of chupacabra?"

"I get cable. Also my tetradotoxin research was in the tropics. But mostly, I get cable."

"So you know 'chupacabra' means 'goat-sucker.' They bite the neck and suck the blood like a vampire. First reported in Puerto Rico in 1992, but they've been spotted all up and down the hemisphere, from Chile to Maine." He regarded the body before them. "That's what they're said to look like. Though I heard something about multicolored spines along the backbone."

"Like Cylons."

"You *do* get cable."

"Is it wild? You said there weren't any wild animals."

"It's not wild. It didn't get that hefty on this little island," Max answered. "It was put here as a guard dog."

"Roaming loose? It was in the woods when we came through here?"

"We heard it."

"Then why doesn't it kill the guards?"

"Aversion training would be my guess. Conditioned not to attack anyone in the uniform. But an unconscious guard, helpless, was just too tempting."

"If we had left without facing it, killing it . . . with those poor people back there in the clearing . . ." Suddenly she blurted, "You said they were in no danger!"

"I was wrong," Max said. "I fucked up. You're getting the benefit of a high-grade alchemist here, but at the end of the day I'm human, and I'm sorry. At least it's dead now."

She shook her head, lips tight; there was no answer to that. So she asked, "Why did you use a human gun and knife instead of your alchemy in the fight?"

"I used it right at the beginning, but once a fight gets going there's never any time. It takes a little mental *oomph* to work magick, and by the time you're *oomphing*, you're getting hammered."

"Well, the fighting was spectacular. What style was it?"

"I don't have a style. It's kinda sorta the UFC I told you about—*mixed* martial arts—which means 'whatever works.'"

"Kinda sorta whatever works—but not *exactly*."

"Pre-cisely." He was his old self again.

NOVEMBER 3 - 2:15 A.M. AST

13 CORN SEED

They made it back to the cliff above the guards' beach, but then held up and took a long look around. It was probable that Omen had summoned his entire force to the compound when he suspected intruders, but no one in his right mind would station himself in a boxed area beneath an overlook, and Mama wasn't due back for forty-five minutes. Instead, they settled in among the palms, not on the edge of the cliff but back a little, in the star shadows, where they still commanded a good view of the ocean and of the path down to it. If any security remained on Omen Key, they might check the beach. So they sat quietly and talked in soft voices, with pauses for shared listening.

"Goat-sucker," Pam said. "A new-world vampire."

"Maybe," Max said. "They're still on the fringes, of my knowledge at least. Chupacabras kind of look like gargoyles, so one theory is, medieval gargoyle carvings are based on them, which would mean they came here from Europe like rats and syphilis. But another is that they're the result of a secret American genetics experiment on Puerto Rico, just like some people think AIDS was. And of course, they could always be aliens."

He stopped to listen. Pam listened, too. The jungle in the dead of night, without the drums, was the most primeval sound in the world. . . .

After a time he picked up the thread. "Having seen a chupacabra now, my theory would be it's a link to dinosaurs, like the Loch Ness monster. There was one strain called *saurornithoides*, which stood upright like we do. It weighed a hundred and ten pounds, had a large brain, wide-set eyes for good stereoscopic vision, and opposable thumbs. It was fast. Wherever I first read about it, it had the great line that *saurornithoides* were 'separated from other dinosaurs as men are separated from cows.' If an asteroid hadn't crushed Chik'xulub in the Yucatan just then and decimated the dinosaurs, *saurornithoides* might have taken the niche humans hold today. You and I might look just like that chupacabra."

"It *was* hard telling you two apart," Pam said sweetly. "Probably the light." Then she turned her head to listen again.

In a little while, when she was satisfied they were still alone, she said, "Did you—?" But she hesitated, seemingly changing her mind, before adding, "—learn anything from Squire Omen about the FRC?"

"Not much. But something. I didn't have a great deal

of time before his mind went, but I got the very clear image of a Golden Necklace."

"Necklace? What's that mean?"

"No idea. Just another brick in the wall at this point."

In the jungle distance a tree branch cracked loose and tumbled noisily to the ground. The night life grew silent for a time, then gradually picked up the pace. Over time, they decided it was just happenstance.

Pam said, "I'm back among the living, Max."

"You were never gone."

"I was pretty close, that first day."

"But no cigar."

"No. But now that the dart is gone, and we saved the zombis . . . I'm here with you. Still here with you."

"I get third billing?"

"You're lucky it's not fourth. I'm just sitting here enjoying the pleasures of being alive. The salty breeze, the sound of the surf, the stars, the grass . . ."

Again she seemed to change her train of thought. "What's today known for, Max? We've had All Hallows' Eve, All Hallows' Day, the Day of the Dead. What's November third?"

"A reminder that you don't stay at a high point forever," Max answered. "November three has nothing associated with it in any major calendar. But we're still here, even on days that aren't special and amazing. There are no holes in Time."

She looked out over the ocean and for a moment the sensation of the endlessness surrounding them, behind the masks, came back to her.

"We should split up," Max said unexpectedly.

Pam stiffened. "What the *hell* are you talking about?"

"The dart's gone. The reason for keeping you nearby is gone. I think you should go to a safe house."

"While you do what?"

"Screw with whatever the FRC's got planned—"

"With their zombis, you mean. So you still need me."

"I can make up the antidote."

"You don't know the recipe."

"Actually, I do. I watched you make your second batch."

"Nevertheless," she said firmly, "I'm sticking right by your side." She emphasized her point by poking him in the ribs, none too gently. But she avoided his wounds.

"It's dangerous, Pam," he told her.

"No shit, Max."

"No shit. We've done just fine so far, but neither one of us gets a pass if 'close' gets *too* close. We both nearly got there tonight."

"So why are you going ahead?"

"It's what I do."

"Well, it's what I *want* to do. Look," she said, "this is all dangerous, but it's also exciting. Physically, mentally, spiritually. I want to know what you know about the world. About the *universe*. And goddammit, I want to be with you!"

"I don't do disciples," he said.

"I'm not asking to be a disciple," she responded emphatically. "I'm not *asking* for *anything*. I'm a part of this; you said so. I can handle my cowgirl end, and, if you're a point man, I'm . . . a search-and-destroy woman. That's what I do with diseases, and what we're up against is a disease in its own way. I've proved that I can help you. I want to do it, Max."

"Okay."

"Huh?" She drew back, regarding him narrowly. "Now what?"

"Now nothing. You made your point. I've pushed

you hard to get you to bail. I had to push you, so you'd decide for yourself what you really wanted. You want in, I get it." He leaned toward her. "And to tell you the truth, I want you in."

"You do?" she said. He looked at her, she looked at him, every molecule of air between them suddenly charged, every calculation in their lives recalibrating. It was really no surprise and yet it was, the way it always is.

"What about Val?" Pam asked softly. She had to ask, though she dreaded the answer.

He said, "This is our time, Pam."

Lust and adrenaline and maybe even gravity, under a tropical moon through softly waving palms. So long delayed, it was overwhelming, and it was beautiful.

NOVEMBER 3 - 2:50 A.M. EASTERN DAYLIGHT TIME

13 CORN SEED

Nancy's jet came in low, with the moon above and moonshine below, sparkling on the black water. Barbados was a black solid in the midst of that water, marked only at one end by the bright pearls of runway lights. Nancy sat back in her cushy seat, the seat belt low and tight across her lap, and felt a deep tingle of anticipation.

Would Miller Omen be here? She honestly didn't know. The FRC was going out of its way to provide her with first-class treatment, and she'd served Omen in particular very well, but his big plan, whatever it was, might be taking up his time. She hoped it wouldn't be

Tilit; he gave her the creeps and that would be a huge comedown. But oh well.

The plane's wheels touched the tarmac, bounced once, and settled onto solid ground. She checked her watch. They'd been in the air just over five hours. That's what regular jets took to fly to the East Coast, and here they were much farther south in the Atlantic. This was one fast airplane.

As they taxied toward the terminal, marked by bright lights she could only partially see beyond the wing, Chad, as immaculate as she herself, came back from up front and steadied himself against the top of her chair, smiling down at her.

"Will you be staying on the island?" she asked him. She still wanted Miller Omen but there was no denying Chad was hot.

"I'm afraid I can't," he said. "I go where the plane goes, and we'll be wheels up before dawn."

She wanted to ask how they could stay in touch, but she knew full well that that would break FRC rules. Need to know, baby. "Well, I'm sure this isn't the last time I'll take a flight like this," was all she said.

He smiled again, then went to unlatch the door in the side of the plane. She undid her seat belt and stood up, stretching hugely.

Her wrists were grabbed from behind.

"What—?"

Chad had her wrists in an unyielding grip. Two other men were surging onto the plane.

"Let me go!" she demanded sharply, but the new men flanked her, each grabbing a shoulder, pressing some nerve that caused her to cry out and stop resisting. "Chad!" The three men hustled her out the door, down the steps, onto the tarmac. Ahead of her was a sign emblazoned by spotlights.

CAMP DELTA
JTF GUANTANAMO
"HONOR BOUND TO DEFEND FREEDOM"

NOVEMBER 3 - 3:00 A.M. ATLANTIC STANDARD TIME

13 CORN SEED

By three o'clock, the Leo moon was bathing the ocean below them in its pale gray light—pale and gray enough that a small boat on the water in the distance would be difficult if not impossible to make out, but not so pale and gray as to hide two swimmers near the shore. Still, Max was very sure they could make it. Pam had lost herself in their urgent lovemaking; he had not been that lucky, because he'd never for a second lost track of what was around them—but he'd been lucky enough.

At three on the dot, Max sparked the witchfire on his fingertips, cupping his hand to shield the light from any nearby observer. But it was visible from the offshore gloom, and he got an immediate response; Mama Locha and her girls were back. He and Pam returned to the path to the beach, bypassed the alarm, and descended. Then they ran across the sand, continued through the surf, dove into the waves, and swam back out to the boat. Nobody shot at them. Piece of cake.

Maggie was covered in fish scales, but Pam didn't ask.

13 CORN SEED

It was still an hour to dawn when the first of Mama Locha's contacts made it back to the compound on Omen Key. As Max had predicted, as soon as they'd explained what had happened Mama sent out a *call* on the vodou vibe, and rescue boats were setting out before the smaller boat reached Barbados. Three fishing smacks with room for all the former zombis made the crossing easily, circling the small island to dock at the main port. The crews who came were wary even though they'd been told the danger was past. Omen Key was already a dark legend.

Still, they encountered no living human being (or chupacabra, though Mama had refrained from mentioning that) as they made their way along the wide road from the dock. The thing was, when they reached the site of the razed compound, they still encountered no living human being.

All of the former zombis were dead, having evidently been herded together before being gunned down at close range.

The uniformed guards, still woozy, remained tied to their trees—but there was no sign of Tilit.

And when the fishermen made it back to the dock, one of their boats was missing.

13 CORN SEED

Max and Pam were sitting in Mama Locha's stable, eating food prepared by Maggie personally and waiting for the sun to rise. Pam had had no idea she was so hungry until the first bit of food entered her mouth; then she couldn't wolf it down fast enough. Max politely refrained from laughing; for one thing, he was just as hungry. The two of them had showered and changed into fresh clothing they'd left in their car, and now it was simply a question of waiting to see what the FRC would do in response to the death of Miller Omen.

But then the atmosphere changed. Max sat up straight, and Pam felt as if a storm front had blown in. The air grew heavy, and the hairs on her arms stood up. Looking around, she saw nothing but concerned faces, and waited to hear what was up. It was the vodou telegraph, its effects as clear as a fire alarm.

Mama Locha broke the news. "All the people on the island are dead."

"Oh my God!" Pam blurted. And then: "Did I kill them?"

"No, girl. It wasn't your antidote. They were shot," Mama said. "And the man with no uniform was gone."

"Tilit," Max muttered, staggered. "He must have had some immunity to my alchemy. Even then, to free himself—"

Pam said, "I thought—"

"So did I! And I was wrong!" He stood up abruptly, and began to pace savagely around the room. He knew better than anyone else how omniscient he wasn't, but he'd tried to use the expansion of his mind to encompass every variable and make decisions worthy of a Timeless man. Worthy of Agrippa. He knew it was a pipe dream, that Agrippa had made mistakes, that anyone would, but two in one night, getting a lot of people killed? Over time he'd get better, he'd know more, have more experience, but still, he was here *now*, people depended on him *now*!

He should have known! Pam's intuition—dismissed as Intern's Syndrome. The chupacabra! But he still hadn't felt the energy. He'd missed the wave, because he was thinking of love.

"Tilit must have used a *stone* in his work," he snapped. "He didn't have one on him, I would have found it, but he must have had contact with one often enough to give him residual energy."

"You couldn't know, Max," Pam said, getting to her feet as well. And wondering about her own *stone*.

"The hell I couldn't!" Max snapped. "I could have *read* him when I *read* Omen and Ballantine at the arena, and I *would* have known!" But there was nothing to do but fix it. "Tilit got off Omen Key?"

"Yes," Mama said. "One of the fishing boats was taken."

"Then he's here, on Barbados. It's a hundred miles to either St. Lucia or St. Vincent, and he'd be visible on the open water once the sun came up. Even if he wanted to hide out on one of those islands, he wouldn't risk the journey now. He's come back here."

"Probably a lot of weaponry at Omen's estate," Pam ventured.

"Sure . . ." But Max was thinking furiously. "Mama, Omen was planning to use the sarin, and maybe the zombis. He wouldn't use them here; why would he? So he'd have transport. You said he has an export business here. Who do you know who'd know about that?"

"There's a boy, Sportie. He works in customs at the airport. And he has the morning shift—starts at six."

"Let's get down there."

NOVEMBER 3 - 6:20 A.M. AST

1 SERPENT

Mama Locha, Max, and Pam walked out of the rising sun into the risen darkness of the customs shed. It was a huge shelter, a remnant of colonial days when anything and everything might be brought to this edge of the British empire. It smelled of old paper and spices.

"There's Sportie," Mama said, and pointed toward a heavyset man in his twenties wearing the uniform of a customs inspector. As they made their way across the vast floor, the other occupants gave them a long once-over, though most stepped back out of respect for Mama Locha. Those that didn't were moved back by their more savvy friends.

A TV beside the Pepsi machine was tuned to CNN. The orotund tones of a Wise Old Man of Washington, who had been wrong about every aspect of the fake Iraqi war, was echoing through the shelter, making it very clear that he saw even greater danger coming from the Middle East and everyone should keep his eyes focused on that spot for signs of renewed trouble. He thundered, "Freedom requires consistency!" and Pam did a double take, only to spy the news crawl at the bottom of the screen reporting that G. Wilson Rideau had been nominated to become the Federal Reserve Chairman.

"Max—?"

"Uh-huh." He nodded cynically. He'd seen it, too.

"FRC!" she said.

"Probably."

"It's like we're all being set up!"

"Not while we're alive," he said, and took her hand.

Mama came to a halt in front of Sportie. Everyone was staring at her and talking in low tones. "Hello," Sportie said, looking nervously at Mama and her unknown friends.

"Hello, Sportie," she said equably. "These people have some questions for you, boy."

"Anything for you, Mama. You know that."

She turned a hand, passing him on to Max, who said without preamble, "Miller Omen's exports. Where do they go?"

"Ah," said Sportie, lighting up, and they knew they'd struck pay dirt. "I thought . . . Well, actually, this is the kind of thing that makes my job here interesting."

"Go on."

"Officially, maybe seventy percent of his shipping goes to the United States, and the rest goes to Mexico. Everything always in perfect order. Routine, by now."

"Except that it isn't, right?" Max said.

"I had a call, maybe three weeks back. A cargo plane had arrived in a place that was not Mexico, with papers for Mexico. But the place was Suriname. Once the error was discovered, the pilot produced papers showing a destination of . . . Suriname."

"Where's Suriname?" Pam asked.

"On the north coast of South America," said Sportie, who had been looking for a reason to turn his attention on her. "There are three little countries between Vene-zuela and Brazil—Guyana, Suriname, and French Gui-ana. Suriname's in the middle."

"It was a British colony once," Max said. "They traded it to the Dutch for a colony called Manhattan."

"Very astute of the Dutch," Pam said.

"But it's independent now," Sportie offered.

"How long a flight to Suriname?" Max asked.

"In a transport plane, under two hours. It's less than a thousand kilometers." For the Americans' benefit he added, "Six hundred miles."

"These papers the pilot had," Max said. "They looked official, did they?"

"Oh, absolutely. Surinamese customs accepted them without question, especially since flights had come from Barbados fairly regularly for months. But it was the first we'd heard about it."

"What did you do about it?" Mama asked.

Sportie smiled happily, a man of the world. "Looked the other way, of course. Who's going to bother a man rich enough to own his own island? Surinamese cus-toms have the same attitude. I only know about it be-cause one of their men vacationed here two years ago and we swapped a few stories, being in the same line of work and all."

"Any Omen exports going out today? To Mexico?"

"Oh, yes. There was a flight that left just twenty min-utes before you arrived."

His visitors gave him the looks he expected. He was enjoying himself.

"And it was supposed to be carrying fifteen large crates of pharmaceuticals, but they were never delivered. It left with just one passenger—that mute who works for Mr. Omen."

"Sportie," said Max, "how would I go about renting a plane without leaving a paper trail of my own?"

Sportie looked at Mama and saw it was down with her. "Come with me," he said.

NOVEMBER 3 - 6:30 A.M. AST

1 SERPENT

Humming above the Atlantic, Tilit sat at the computer fastened to the front wall of the hold in his C-130J Hercules and typed in a code. There was no need to send it; the contact was continuous, through a network of worldwide satellites with 512-bit symmetric encryption, twice the U.S. government's Top Secret standard. Soon enough, words appeared on his screen. Their primary question was why the sender wasn't using voice contact, but Tilit proceeded to explain. Soon his fingers were explaining everything else that had happened to Miller Omen's plan.

NOVEMBER 3 - 6:45 A.M. AST

1 SERPENT

Max taxied his rented Cessna Caravan 675 along BGI runway 2-L, looking up at the fleecy clouds in the tropical sky with real pleasure. He had learned flying 1983, in Germany, during a sojourn there with Agrippa, and before that year was over the them had logged over one hundred thousand miles, mostly over the North Atlantic. That was another story in another life, but taking off into this new Atlantic morning brought the old feelings back—the feelings for flight but not the feelings for Val. She was just part of the memory. It comforted him and it bothered him at the same time. How much of Val could he put aside? How much could he keep?

The day outside his windshield was beautiful, perfect for flying; the forecast showed no tropical storms to the south, which was unusual for this late in the year. His official flight plan showed an aerial tour of the island and its neighbors, but the air traffic controllers would turn a blind eye when he diverted from it. That had taken spot cash, which never seemed a problem for Max, and with Sportie's help the process had gone smoothly. He and Pam should be able to make the flight in a little over three hours; the Cessna flew half as fast as a transport plane, at 210 mph, but it was top of the line for small private prop-craft and Max felt lucky to have rented it on the spur of the moment. He could have had its tarted-up big sister, the Grand Caravan, but that baby flew at the same speed with less maneuverability and range due to its extended length and weight. Not that range should be a problem; either Cessna could do one thousand miles easily, and they were only going six hundred. But although Max enjoyed the good things in life, he didn't need filigree. The 675 was a solid little beast and he liked her flexibility.

Pam occupied the copilot's seat. She was used to small aircraft from various excursions to disease-ridden parts of the world, but she'd always sat back in the passenger section. Sitting right up front, watching the ground speed by and then drop away with a 180-degree view, was a new sensation. As they quickly left solid ground behind them, she was very aware that below her padded seat was nothing but thin air and ocean. One screwup and the puffer fish on her coccyx would be back in the drink.

Max slipped a CD into the player. There was engine noise but the sound system was built for that. As they soared up into the fluffy white clouds and vast blue sky, they had Soca music all around.

NOVEMBER 3 - 6:45 A.M. EASTERN DAYLIGHT TIME

13 CORN SEED

Lawrence Breckenridge was bench-pressing 205 pounds in his brownstone on East Thirty-fifth Street. He had four widescreens high on the wall before him, showing Bloomberg, CNN, MSNBC, and C-SPAN; the Bluetooth on his ear allowed him to listen to whichever one took his interest. It also allowed him to take the voice-only call from Dick Hanrahan. They avoided video to minimize the signal, and that kept Breckenridge from any concern about working out in the nude. From where he stood, he could look below the screens at the Manhattan traffic, through windows that did not allow the traffic to look back. If it had, they would have noticed some real tone to his sixty-seven-year-old form.

At his age most men have lost more than 25 percent of their muscle mass, but he was committed to his good health. The things the Necklace could do with medicine were astounding, really, and Aleksandra had given him vitality in exchange for service, but at the end of the day—or the beginning, actually—he was responsible for his own life. He had no intention of leaving his power and his Diabola a moment sooner than he had to.

He generally arose at six to receive the morning briefing from the CIA, but this morning he'd been up since five, awaiting the call that would tell him that Max August was dead. He had been looking forward with great anticipation to conveying the news to Aleksandra, and there was no pretending he wasn't. But as soon as he'd awakened, he'd *felt* for a vibe that would tell him of success, and hadn't found it. As time went by, he'd grown more and more certain that their plan had gone awry, and he'd funneled his certainty into his lifts. So he was streaming with sweat and not at all surprised when he heard what Hanrahan had to tell him.

"I've already ordered the teams on Barbados to leave no stone unturned," Hanrahan said. "But we've got to worry about offense more than defense, Renzo. With Omen dead, we need a new commander on site in Suriname. I would like to volunteer—"

"No," said Breckenridge decisively. "You have been and will continue to be our central command, Dick. You take care of the world; I'll get someone else in country."

"I thought you'd say that," Hanrahan replied dryly. "So let me suggest Rita Diamante. She's used to running an army in a danger zone."

"That's a good choice." Breckenridge nodded, though Hanrahan couldn't see him. "She's more accustomed to war than Omen ever was, even if she's a little free with her products. And of course, she's in Miami, which puts her closest to the action. Get her and her people down there ASAP."

"Using her own jet, she can be there in about four hours."

"Get her up and moving. But send Jackson as well. The way August is progressing, we need a sorcerer on site."

"Tilit says there was no discussion of Omen's end game, Renzo. How would August know about Suriname?"

"How would he know about anything? The man is dangerous. Extremely dangerous."

"I can route Jackson through Miami. He and Diamante can continue together. But they won't get there till the middle of the afternoon."

"That's fine. There's time. But they need to be on the same page, since August combines both their skills."

"You know," Hanrahan said, "he and Blackwell have to fly as well, if they're headed south. I'll task the satellites, and alert our friends in the Surinamese Air Force."

"The Luchtmacht is a joke. They've got, what, five planes?"

"It'll do. And it's all we have at the moment."

"Yes, at the moment. Well, if they are in the air, they'll be in a private plane, and we won't miss them this time."

NOVEMBER 3 - 5:50 A.M. CENTRAL DAYLIGHT TIME

13 CORN SEED

Jackson Tower sprinted through the Minnesota forest on a trail he ran every night he could. Both the Leo moon and Virgo Venus cast their light through the overhead branches, illuminating his path through strange clusterings of darkness. He preferred nights when the moon was down, because he knew this path perfectly, but any night was a good night.

He ran with almost overflowing energy, tirelessly mile after mile, marking little clouds of exhalation in the cold. He ran to the beat of his heart. It was mechanical, the product of Necklace science after his human heart had begun to fail—and he was not too spiritual to relish the idea that he was so important to the Necklace that they didn't want him to die. Moreover, he liked his new heart. It was keyed to him just like the old one, so it speeded up when he ran or grew excited, and slowed when he sat in meditation. But whatever it did, it never missed a beat. It was as reliable and unending as any device could be, freeing him to concentrate on more esoteric things.

Tonight he was concentrating on Max August, student of Cornelius Agrippa. He had to admit that it galled him, a disc jockey stumbling across the old wizard and learning the secret of Timelessness, when his own studies had not yet succeeded. But it's always easier when someone tells you the answer.

Strong men find their own answers, and are all the stronger for it. That was the voice of Yellow Beaver.

"Exactly," Tower answered.

When you kill him, the power you take will be immense, added Goodwife Brandwynne with her characteristic simper. *You'll grow so much stronger, Jackson.*

"I won't kill him. I won't be there."

She laughed at him. At once, he realized that he *would* be there. He would bring the Code Red down.

Jackson Tower, sorcerer to the all-powerful Necklace, maintained his center of being in the world of darkness, which was populated by ghosts. The howls of long-dead wolves echoed through the living trees, and the screams of slaughtered settlers. Phantom flames crackled in the wood. But dead Dakota shamans, English witches, and one American spiritualist were the shades he spent the nights with. They had each, in their time, crossed into the shadow-land, and when they'd died they'd stayed there while their bodies turned to dust. Tower had crossed in his time, and he, like they, stayed as long as he could, because they saw things he couldn't see on his own, and they told him.

Jackson Tower was a natural-born sorcerer. Ever since he'd been a boy, he'd known about the black world. First he'd found the elementals, then the totems, then the shades. Over time they'd led him to the matrix that lies beneath all the worlds, and the arts of power. Then he'd turned to the forbidden books of antiquity, and it had all come easy to him, so that now there was no man he knew of who could challenge his supremacy in the mystic arts.

He ran out of the forest into the relative brilliance of the shores of Lake Superior, facing infinite sky and water. The crystalline moon, twinkling Venus, and sparkling stars shone clearly in both venues. "As above, so below," said the ancients, and when the world was reduced to two starscapes mirroring each other, he had the sensation of running on the edge of eternity. A drowned sailor called to him from offshore but Tower paid no attention to that. Now the sorcerer was waiting.

His secure cell rang.

"Sir," said Hanrahan, "Miller Omen is dead. We're tasking Rita Diamante to replace him, but she'll need your more experienced hand to face the Code Red. Please leave at once and pick her up in Miami."

"Of course," replied Tower, his distant voice betraying nothing of his satisfaction.

"Bon voyage."

"Wait," said Tower. "What was the resolution with that Nancy Reinking?"

"Not yet resolved. But we're following your recommendation," said Hanrahan.

NOVEMBER 3 - 7:00 A.M. EASTERN DAYLIGHT TIME

13 CORN SEED

Rita Diamante lay sprawled on a chaise longue at the far end of her private pier, listening idly to water and murder.

She was forty-three years old, and she dressed like twenty-three, in silk tops and low-rise designer jeans, but as rosy dawn began to creep over the Atlantic, her face betrayed her. When up and around, she availed herself of plastic surgery and Botox and exquisitely applied makeup. She had a doctor on staff for the first two, and a cosmetologist for the third. When up and around, she was a spectacular presence, with amazing cheekbones and eyes of crystalline black. But her lips, however often injected, were always tight and mean, and when the nightlife was over, when the coke ran down, her face grew slack and showed the touch of time. In those moments, she preferred to be alone, even if the shreds of her silk top and her flushed breasts proved she'd had company not too long before.

Mérides could make her scream, and he was making Jesús scream, but for vastly different reasons.

Jesús had been caught stealing. It was an old story: when you ran a criminal empire, you were surrounded by criminals. People had always stolen from her and always would, but there were fewer every year because of Mérides. When a thief was uncovered, when a traitor was revealed, Rita had Mérides deal with it. He was in the mansion now, her taste on his lips and the blood of Jesús on his hands.

She liked it when Mérides came back and put those hands on her. She'd been that way from the jump.

Now she got up and pulled a University of Miami sweatshirt over her nakedness, before strolling back along the pier to her house. Inside was a spectacular display of Miami deco, but she passed through that to a heavy door in an inner wall. Inside was a room perhaps twelve by twelve, covered floor to ceiling with white tile. The tile at the moment was splattered with blood. It was good to have a room like that; rumors that she had it circulated among her men and made some of them think twice. Cleanup was a breeze, as the blood washed straight out into the bay.

"Jesús quiere hacer restitución, Rita," Mérides told her.

"Si me gustas, puede vivir," she answered, looking deep into the captive's rheumy eyes, demanding his attention. *"Si me gustas."*

"Sí, sí," babbled Jesús, and started to explain. She didn't care, and was glad when her private line rang. Then she read the lighted caller ID: FLORIDA RECLAMATION COUNCIL. She straightened, turned, walked out the door and closed it firmly behind her.

"Diamante," she said crisply, watching the sun climb from the sea. Pelicans sailed along the shoreline, black on orange.

"Miss Diamante, this is Hanrahan." He knew better than to call her "ma'am." In some places it would have denoted respect, but no one who thought she was twenty-three wanted to hear it. Instead, he came straight to the point.

The fact of the matter was, running drugs through Miami almost inevitably led to using drugs, but you only survived if you used the drugs and didn't let them use you. Rita Diamante had crafted her own empire before the FRC ever came calling, continued to run it exceptionally well, and it made her attractive to larger syndicates. She was more than prepared to take on Hanrahan's mission.

Frankly, she thought it was about damn time.

NOVEMBER 3 - 7:00 A.M. EDT

1 SERPENT

Nancy lay sprawled on concrete. Cold and alone and drained by her fear, she had finally fallen asleep at 6:45. They gave her fifteen minutes, then rousted her.

"Welcome to Camp X-Ray, Nancy," said the first man. His eyes were locked on her, unwavering, as if they could see her soul. *Technique,* she thought. *I know that one.*

"We're your tour guides," said the second man. They were not dressed like soldiers, which gave her some hope, but their bearing and their haircuts said otherwise. The first one's forearm showed the tattoo of an eagle snapping an olive branch in two.

They were in a small room, barely six feet long and

four wide, painted white. The floor was concrete. A narrow window, some six inches wide, let in bright Cuban sunlight and morning heat. A flat bunk covered in green rubber ran along one wall, and a stainless steel toilet was attached to the opposite wall. The two men took most of the remaining space.

She still found it hard to believe she was in Guantánamo, in Cuba—hard to believe Chad had helped put her here, after they'd fucked twice. With no sleep, she had to wonder if she were hallucinating. But she was a strong-willed person by nature, and she'd had some basic training in being stronger. This was not a hallucination. This had to be dealt with.

They must know I'm in the Free Range Coalition, she considered. *They set it all up—the rescue, the cleaning out of my apartment, the plane. All to get me to talk about the FRC. But that's not what people like me do!* She was scared, there was no denying it, but she was also proud of herself as she deliberately faced her visitors down. "What do you mean, Camp X-Ray? Your sign said Camp Delta," she said dismissively.

"Oh, well, Camp Delta's for long-term terrorists, and visiting inspectors, but Camp X-Ray is officially abandoned. We like the quiet over here," said the first man.

"And the lack of oversight," said the second.

"It's kind of primitive, but it's home."

"There's no place like it."

"That's for damn sure."

"Well," said Nancy, "I want a lawyer. You have no right to hold me."

"Sure we do," said the first man.

"It's completely legal," said the second.

"Completely," said the first. "You could look it up, except you can't."

"What's the Free Range Coalition?" asked the second.

She crossed her arms over her chest. "I'm not talking till I see my lawyer."

"Well, of course you're talking," said the first man.

"That's what people do in Camp X-Ray," said the second.

"People talk all the time. Yak yak yak. It's enough to drive you crazy," said the first.

"I think it drove *me* crazy," said the second, and as he said it, a look passed through his eyes that said it was all true. Nancy had a sudden epiphany that they carried on their witty banter because they didn't like their work, didn't like what their work did to *them*. But she also knew they did their work.

"Look," Nancy said, trying to head them off, "enough of this bullshit. I'm an American citizen and I want a lawyer."

"What's your point?" asked the first man.

"What do you mean? You can't hold an American citizen without a lawyer! And you can't hold an American citizen *here* at *all*!"

"I believe the media *did* say that, when the law was passed," said the second man judiciously, "but you know the media these days. Or you should, considering who you're working for. The House version of the law said it applied to everyone, while the Senate version said not to citizens. But two weeks later, before they even tried to find a compromise, the Senate version was changed to read just like the House version. It was all very mysterious. And the media had lost interest so they never ran an update. So yes, despite what you think you know, Nancy, you're here perfectly legally."

"And you don't get a lawyer," added the first man. "There are no lawyers."

"It's the law," said the second.

"I'm not an 'enemy combatant,'" Nancy said.

"Sure you are."

"That's ridiculous. I can't be—"

"See, you should have read the law yourself, since it applies to everyone in the world. The president can declare you an enemy combatant, the secretary of defense can declare you an enemy combatant, or 'another competent tribunal established under the authority' of those guys can declare you an enemy combatant."

"We went with the 'other competent tribunal.'"

"Who? Why? I've done nothing to the government."

"How would you know? We're everywhere."

"I work in a disease control lab. I help people!"

"You were put there by the FRC."

"What?"

"The FRC. They put you there. So you're not just some little lab rat. You're a spy."

"I don't know anything about any FRC," Nancy said. "Is that like KFC? Fried chicken?"

"Bada bing! You'll be here all week, try the veal," said the first man.

"Or the rat," said the second.

"I honestly don't know anything about the FRC," Nancy said as sincerely as she knew how.

"Now that's good. That's what you're supposed to say."

Nancy stared at the man.

"The thing is, we're not sure if that's what you've always said."

"And we want to be sure."

"Wait, wait," she said, confused. "You want to be sure . . . that I *didn't* talk about this 'FRC' . . . ?"

"Right."

"I thought you *wanted* me to talk about it. Even though I don't know what it is."

"You're not the first to make that mistake."

"So you're saying that *you're* in the FRC? Here in Guantánamo." Nancy shook her head ruefully. "Now I really am confused."

"Why?" asked the first man.

"If you don't know what the FRC is, why should you be surprised to find it in Guantánamo?" asked the second. Both men stared levelly at her, waiting for her answer.

She would not give in to this. "What I am is confused. Like I said. I thought you thought *I* was in this group, then it sounded like *you* were."

"We are," said the first.

"So you can talk to us," said the second.

"I can't, because I don't know anything. What is the FRC?"

"You know what the FRC is," said the first. "I'm not talking about the FRC."

"Why not?"

"Because we don't talk about it."

"Well then, you can hardly expect me to talk about it."

"But some people think you *did*," said the second man.

A cold wave of fear rushed over her then, but she felt she hid it well. "What do you mean?"

"Well, after you got out from under the spiders, you were debriefed, and people were just not convinced that you'd kept quiet."

"You were dealing with a Code Red, Nancy. They can be very persuasive."

"It's a real puzzler, isn't it? You won't admit you know about the FRC so you can't tell us what you told Max August about the FRC. How can we resolve that?"

"Oh yeah," said the second man, brightening. "We can torture you."

"Legally."

"I don't know anything! And nothing you can do to me can change that!"

"Well," said the first man, "let's see."

NOVEMBER 3 - 9:05 A.M. SURINAME TIME

1 SERPENT

The C-130J Hercules rumbled to a halt right at the far end of the runway that crossed an open field on the eastern edge of Suriname, some hundred miles south-west of the capital of Paramaribo. Officially there were only two airports large enough to handle a C-130J, the international one at Zanderij and the combination domestic carrier and military base at Zorg en Hoop. Tellingly, the civilian airport was an hour south of the capital, while the military base was right outside, just two miles away. But most people in this steaming country avoided officialdom whenever and wherever possible. There were four other airports with hard-surfaced runways to handle a cargo plane, and thirty-five more for travelers in smaller craft. This landing strip was not at all fancy but it was free.

The cargo door in the rear of the behemoth opened

and Tilit walked down onto the surprisingly well-maintained tarmac. The heat hit him like a hammer, even after Barbados, but he shrugged it off. A short man, dressed like a civilian but with an unmistakably military air, came forward smartly to greet him.

"My name is Calderón," he said in functional English. "I work for the ambassador. I know you cannot speak. Come with me."

Tilit knew him by reputation and photo. He pulled out his speaking box.

ALL OK? it croaked.

"All is fine," said Calderón. "I'm sorry for Mr. Omen but everything is proceeding on schedule. You'll be staying with me until we get further orders."

Tilit nodded. The two men walked to the side of the runway where a beat-up, dust-covered RAV4 was parked. They got in and drove away into the surrounding jungle. A flock of white birds shot up from the trees to mark their passage, and then life was back to normal.

NOVEMBER 3 - 8:15 A.M. EASTERN DAYLIGHT TIME

1 SERPENT

Carole van Dusen received the report on Miller Omen's death and Rita Diamante's ascension as part of her morning briefing from the Necklace. There was nothing to be done on the financial front since Miller's plan was still in play, but she did regret his passing. She had really thought that he could become a solid link in the chain, in the not-too-distant future. And she definitely preferred men to women in leadership roles.

She gazed sourly at Christopher Columbus among the bushy bare trees of Louisburg Square, and wondered if that was her age, her generation, or her sex.

NOVEMBER 3 - 8:30 A.M. ATLANTIC STANDARD TIME

1 SERPENT

Max and Pam were flying smoothly over open water, which sparkled at the edge of every wave below as far as the eye could see. After a long period of simply enjoying the sights and the Soca, Pam brought up what was on her mind. "Why two hundred and sixty asteroids?"

"Why not?" Max asked, looking her way with an ironic smile.

"That's kind of an unusual number, isn't it? Why not two hundred and fifty? Or three hundred, or a thousand?"

Max stretched his shoulders, rolling the kinks out. "Okay, Pam, here's the deal," he said as he leaned forward to snap off the CD player. Then he put the Cessna on autopilot and turned so he could look at her while keeping an eye on the sky ahead. "I told you I've written down what I've learned. I learned it by putting my nose to the grindstone and determining what was actually true, as opposed to what's been handed down to us. A lot of what's been handed down is extremely valuable; a lot more is pure crap, corrupted by minds less enlightened than the ones that first worked it through. Without personal work, you can't tell which is which. So I do the work, and have, now, for years. If you go down this road, you'll have to do it, too. And that means—"

"Explore but verify," she said.

"Exactly. Does the picture you're getting hold up for you? But here's why I say two hundred and sixty.

"As you might imagine, I'm very interested in Time. The people most interested in Time, that we know of, were the Mayans. Our knowledge of the Mayans is severely limited because when the Spanish conquered them, they deliberately burned every Mayan document they could get their hands on. But some of it survives, and the people of northern Guatemala, the descendents of the Mayans, still practice what they remember, so there's more evidence there.

"The Mayans based everything on Time, which they said was just the unfolding of Reality. They had three major calendars counting different rhythms within it. The human calendar charted their human interactions, the earth calendar charted the world in general, and the divine calendar charted their daily life, because they considered daily life the manifestation of the divine, no more and no less. The divine calendar had two hundred and sixty days, and as you say, that's an unusual number. No other system uses it. Meaning the divine calendar was something they alone knew."

Pam's eyes shifted once more to the vast panorama outside the Cessna's windows. The wide world of the tropics, as a set piece spread below her—and the people who lived down there, under the hot, hot sun . . .

"The divine calendar of the Mayans was made of two interlocking cycles," Max went on. He raised his hands with the fingers splayed and interspersed like the cogs of two wheels, and he rotated them like cogs. "One went around every thirteen days, the other every twenty. By the time both sides got back to their starting point, thirteen times twenty days had gone by, or two hundred and sixty.

"In our calendar, of course, we count November one, then November two, then November three—only the day number changes as long as we're in the period called November. But the Mayan divine calendar was different, so their days went, say, Eleven Wind, then Twelve Night, then Thirteen Corn Seed—both sides changing every day, as both cycles turned. And since thirteen was as high as the one cycle went, the day after Thirteen Corn Seed is One Serpent. With me so far?"

"Yeah, so far." Pam had sat through med school lectures; this was no problem—yet.

"Now," Max continued, "all that, despite its sexy antiquity and hints of mystic secrets, would be worth absolutely nothing if it weren't for one thing. It works. If you know the meanings of the days of the Mayan divine calendar, you can absolutely see the shape of each day—which begins at dawn, by the way; not midnight."

"Harmakhis," said Pam. "The sun on the horizon." But she immediately thought, *No, that's Egyptian.*

"Same idea, though," Max said. She looked at him sharply, and he, waiting for that look, added easily, "I didn't read your mind; I read your face. Both the Egyptians and the Mayans worshipped the sun, so they both paid close attention to the beginning of each day." He reached forward and made a slight adjustment to their course before continuing.

"So—every dawn, a new day began. For example, those days I mentioned a minute ago are the days we've been living through.

"Eleven Wind means Owning Possibilities. That was the day we met, when you were attacked by Omen's spell and got introduced to magick. And before the dawn, you owned your situation and decided to fight back.

"Twelve Night means Fulfilling a Private World. That was the day we flew disguised to Barbados, with people looking everywhere for us, but not finding us. The night . . . I turned you down.

"Thirteen Corn Seed means Managing the Public World. That was yesterday, when we went to visit Mama, went shopping, went to the fights, took a boat to Omen Key, killed Miller Omen—"

Pam said, "Made love, out in the open."

"I haven't forgotten," he answered, and leaned over to prove it. After a while, he continued, "Came the dawn and we moved into One Serpent, which means Establishing Yáng—Establishing Internal Power. That's what we're doing today."

Pam frowned. "I like the sound of it, so long as it's *us* and not the FRC. But how does One Serpent meaning something to the Mayans square with November three meaning nothing to the Celts?"

"Different systems, different attempts to quantify the universe. The Mayans watched the days, the Celts watched the seasons. *But it's the same universe.* It's like listening to music, with me concentrating on the backbeat and you on the lyrics. Same song, different experiences—but both experiences are real. And if someone asked me what I heard and asked you what you heard, they'd have a better idea of the song than either of us. That's the whole secret of my success. I compare and contrast systems. Theoretically, they're systematizing the same universe, so I explore and I verify."

Pam said, "Okay. Keep going. Let's establish some internal power."

"All right. I knew about the two hundred and sixty days of the Mayan calendar. And I knew about asteroids. They were two separate systems until a new Mayan year got started, and I happened to notice that the first day of the calendar, One Nipple . . ." He took a professional beat, so she could echo, "One Nipple?"

"Others translate it as One Crocodile or One Waterlily. It means Establishing Reality."

"I can live with 'nipple,' thanks. And so 'one' means 'establishing'?"

"Yep. It's exactly that straightforward." He was really pleased with the way this conversation was going. "Now we turn our attention to Ceres, the number one asteroid to be discovered, on January 1, 1801."

"All ones. Got it. But isn't it a dwarf planet now?" Pam asked.

"Both dwarf planet *and* asteroid, by official designation. But either way, it's the asteroid leader. In astrology, the asteroids are the people in the world around you—the many 'others' in your story. You relate to some of them, because once you Establish your Reality on this planet Earth, you're *bound* to relate to other people, and they to you." The capital letters were clearly marked in his delivery. "Ceres, as the leader of the others, stands for the pure concept of Relationship, the *need* for Relationship in your life, just as Mars stands for the pure concept of Energy. The rest of the asteroids establish *specific* relationships, but Ceres is Relationship as a basic function. When you enter this world, on your first day in your new Reality, the One Nipple is your *most* basic relationship, and you *need* it. So then, we have One Nipple, Establishing Reality, and we have Ceres, Basic Relationship. One looks at the situation one way, one looks at it another, but they're describing the same situation, the same universe. They're describing our human condition."

"I'll have to think about that," she said.

"Exactly," he said. "Decide for yourself."

"But when you say, 'Establishing *Reality*,' you're talking metaphorically, right?"

"Could be," he said, causing her to give him a long, hard look. He ignored that look, refusing to be drawn out. So she let it go. "Well, okay, it also sounds like we're back to gravity, pulling things together."

"And so we are. But not right now." He made a few new adjustments to the autopilot's course, and they tilted gently to the west. "*Any*-way, once I saw that the meaning of the first Mayan day and the first asteroid were different images of the same situation, I started looking at the following days and asteroids, and saw that they matched up as well, right down the line. The first two hundred and sixty asteroids to be found match the Mayan divine calendar, meaning for meaning. That can be cross-checked, just like science. So in the end, you have two hundred and sixty concepts that play out predictably, in two separate systems, right in front of your eyes—and seeing them both in action, you can understand those two hundred and sixty concepts better than with either system alone. You can see the whole circle of life with two hundred and sixty facets, and therefore, you see a whole hell of a lot more going on in the world." Suddenly, his face split in an uncontrollable grin; she thought it was utterly adorable. "What can I tell you,

Pam? It's *fun* to see the matrix beneath the masks. It is for me, anyway." He sat back in his seat, stretched his legs. "And *that* is why I pay attention to two hundred and sixty asteroids."

"So if I were to learn those two hundred and sixty concepts, I'd see more going on in the world around me?"

"Absolutely. But since you're not going to be learning those concepts in the midst of our war with the FRC, you can start with simply looking for their effects. Look for changes in the way life plays out—where things take a demonstrable turn from day to day."

"Okay—and then what? How does seeing more in the world help me become Timeless?"

"One step at a time, cowgirl."

"But—"

"One step at a time."

Pam snorted derisively. But she turned her head and looked out the Cessna's window, at the endless blue sky and sea. She'd seen almost nothing of this two days ago, flying at night, but now it was everywhere, one huge empty space, consisting of clouds, sky, sun, and sea. Four things—five if you counted the plane. Six if you threw in some birds far below. Could there really be 260 things contributing to this view? She tried to make it so, but failed.

"Fine," she said at last. "I have to learn for myself. But since I can't see asteroids, what's the one that's tied to today's Mayan day? To Establishing Internal Power?"

"It's called *Artemis*. She's the Greek goddess of the empty spaces—the wilderness, where you have to establish your own internal power. She's all about self-sufficiency."

"A point woman," Pam ventured, and Max nodded

agreement, but she continued, "How is self-sufficiency a relationship?"

"Oh, I can guarantee you that being on point keeps you related to everything around you. There may not be any people there—you *hope* there aren't any people there—but you're more attuned to other people than ever."

"Well, what else can you tell me?" she asked. "What else do you see for today?"

Without hesitation, he replied, "Based on everything I know, we get *odds*, not *certainties*—that we'll fight at least twice, that we'll meet several strange people, that you'll get to know Artemis, that we'll have a fantastic dinner, and that I'll talk with the elementals. Loose women are in there somewhere. Omen will be replaced, and our enemies will come from the south and above." His hand cupped the chin of her rather nonplussed face. "Any carny fortune-teller would sound just the same. So—"

"Verify. Keep my eyes open. You can stop reminding me," she said. Then she kissed him, getting started on establishing some power.

NOVEMBER 3 - 9:00 A.M. EASTERN DAYLIGHT TIME

1 SERPENT

Jackson Tower flew south, seated in the cabin of his Citation X private jet. He rarely used the aircraft, since most of his work was accomplished in his mind. When he did use it, it was almost always to fly to Pittsburgh, on his way to Wheeling, a trip of about an hour and a half; a jet for that always felt like a cannon shooting a fly. He could interrogate women in California from Duluth. He could calculate Dr. Blackwell's horoscope and predict the influences she'd be under from Duluth. He had no need to meet people in the flesh to know all about them. But the Suriname project was so important, and so wrong-footed by now, that it made all the sense in the world for him to go. He could expect—and the charts of the next few days absolutely backed him up—that Rita Diamante would do an expert job on the ground, but she had no magick whatsoever, so the Necklace needed him to deal with that in real time. Especially since the Moon had just moved from Leo to Virgo. It was time to go to work.

He had never gone up against a Code Red, and he was looking forward to it. He had Max August's horoscope for July 31, 1950, 11:56 A.M., Miami, courtesy of the FRC; apparently someone had encountered the man back in the '80s and had gotten it then. There was a complete dossier on him, bolstered by memoranda on the few encounters they'd had with him over the years. Tower did a chart for New Year's Eve 1980, when the first encounter with August climaxed, and New Year's Eve 1985, when his mentor and his wife both died, and October 31, 1991, when they'd tried to recruit him. After he'd said no, he'd gone completely off the grid as far as the FRC was concerned—until this Hallowe'en, the anniversary of his disappearance. The charts began to paint a picture of this Max August—what caused him pride, what caused him stress, what caused him pain. And the recurrence of the last day of the month throughout was extremely significant.

Tower knew that witches held cross-quarter sabbats on the last day of the month because that's the Day

Before, the Day Out of Time, the Zero Day, when the old reality dissolved so a new reality could congeal. Max August hadn't chosen his birth date, and he hadn't chosen the night of his mystic breakthrough, and he hadn't chosen the night the two people he loved most had died, and he hadn't chosen the night he understood how far underground he'd have to go to survive. In one sense, those last three had been chosen by his enemies. But their prominence in his life was undeniable. Max August, born on the Zero Day of August, was a man far outside everyday reality.

Specifically, as Tower read the chart of his birth, in the way of astrologers for four thousand years, he thought: *This is a man accustomed to being known in the world. The world has been good to him and he feels a bond with it. He takes things that could be nothing, like soldiering or disc jockeying, and makes them not only something, but something unique and special, because he feels that the world deserves some excellence. There's the Leo in him! He's a powerful, persuasive speaker, speaking to and for the world. He loves to be out on the edge; if he can't go there physically, he'll go mentally. But he is strong physically as well as mentally, and particularly so in the face of danger and tragedy. That means, however, that his life is linked to danger and tragedy.*

The women he attracts—there's surely more than one—are sensible, successful, intelligent, unusual, and very female. They'll go out on the edge with him, share his adventure. But the duality brings moments of harsh confrontation. The women must be strong and resolute. But he fights to the last breath, not to let them down.

As for his enemies, the cause of his danger—they're a primal force. An institutional conspiracy of enlight-

*ened beings, shaping government and religion to their
own ends, infinite in possibility.*

Jackson Tower might have been reading that last
with more enthusiasm than it deserved, but he finished
his preliminary examination both fascinated and em-
powered by what the universe had revealed to him, as
he always did. There was plenty more, but this was
enough to start his mind working. The better he understood an adversary the more control he had over him.
He left his padded seat to sit in the scarlet circle marked
permanently on the floor of his jet, and at 38,000 feet
he sent his mind soaring even higher.

NOVEMBER 3 - 9:00 A.M. EDT

1 SERPENT

Inside her private hangar at Homestead, Rita Diamante,
with Mérides at her side, surveyed the preparations of
her own Citation X. They had to get their shit all in order and do it before Tower arrived from Duluth, in no
more than an hour.

"There's a hell of a lot riding on this," she told Mérides in Miami Spanish. "A chance to show some people
I know what we can do on short notice, and a chance
to get to know one of those people personally."

"You gonna fuck him?"

"With pleasure if it comes to that." Rita and Mérides
shared her bed many nights but both knew better than
to become attached. "Keep workin' it, Alberto. I've got
my own shit to do." She went up the steps and into the
main cabin, closing the hatch behind her.

The Citation X was the world's fastest business jet; it would take only about three and a half hours to cover the 2,200 miles to Suriname. In her trade she had many occasions to fly south, but usually, if she went as far as she was going today, she was headed for Panama or Colombia. She had never set foot in Suriname, nor had she ever wanted to, so she was studying up, with limited time to do it. She took a hit of her private coke and a toke of her private weed. The two balanced her, charging her brain but taking the edge off, as she read through the CIA *Factbook* on her seventeen-inch MacBook Pro.

"First explored by the Spaniards in the sixteenth century and then settled by the English in the mid-seventeenth century, Suriname became a Dutch colony in 1667. With the abolition of slavery in 1863, workers were brought in from India and Java. Independence from the Netherlands was granted in 1975. Five years later the civilian government was replaced by a military regime that soon declared a socialist republic. It continued to exert control through a succession of nominally civilian administrations until 1987, when international pressure finally forced a democratic election. In 1990, the military overthrew the civilian leadership, but a democratically elected government—a four-party New Front coalition—returned to power in 1991 and has ruled since."

Funny how socialist republics always face international pressure, she thought. *And their own military. But leave it to fucking Castro to stick it out.*

"Area: 163,270 sq. km. Slightly larger than Georgia."
Sherman marched right through Georgia, didn't he?

"Climate: tropical; moderated by trade winds. Smallest independent country on South American continent; mostly tropical rain forest. Great diversity of flora and fauna that, for the most part, is increasingly threatened by new development. Relatively small population, mostly along the coast."

"Threatened by new development." Yeah, that sounds about right.

NOVEMBER 3 - 9:06 A.M. EDT

1 SERPENT

"Sir, I think we've got 'em."

Hanrahan moved quickly despite his age. He pushed his way past the seated techs at the Moundsville farm and squatted beside the speaker, searching his computer screen. It showed a satellite image of open water, from so high up the waves were just swatches of color, but the colors were reds and oranges, an infrared shot. There was one single blemish.

"Can't see them in visible light. Pretty much where we'd expect to find them if they left soon after Tilit. And—"

"Just shoot 'em down."

NOVEMBER 3 - 9:15 A.M. ATLANTIC STANDARD TIME

1 SERPENT

Max and Pam flew south. From their vantage point at 23,000 feet above the southern Caribbean, they could see the barest hint of land on the horizon. And then they saw the Surinamese Air Force rising up from it.

There were two C-212-400 Aviocars, dirty white gleams in the morning sun coming straight for them. The underside of their wings and fuselage were painted a crisp blue, and orange stripes circled the aircraft at the cockpit and tail, making them look like twin Christmas presents. The presents opened fire.

"How can they see us?" Pam demanded, her voice lost in the roar of Max slipping their Cessna sideways, away from the bullet stream. Even to Pam it was clear that their plane was much more maneuverable. But their plane had no weapons, and they were headed toward the Aviocars' home base. They might make a run for Guyana or French Guiana, however far away they were to east or west, but what would those countries think of two unannounced Americans under fire? They might be about to find out.

"Get your life jacket from under your seat and put it on, right now," Max said, as calmly as he'd explained the asteroids. "Then look in the cabinet behind you. There are two parachutes. Put one here beside me, put the other one on over your jacket."

"I don't know how," Pam said, trying to match his tone.

"You'll see it. I've gotta dive so brace yourself, and . . . Go!"

At his word, the Cessna rocketed down an invisible roller coaster, but she was prepared, bending down and pulling out the life jacket. It was surprisingly easy to get it around her and pull the straps tight, and as she did so, she repeated her earlier question. "How can they see us?"

"I was blocking visibility from the satellites, not from humans," Max answered. "Now I've switched to these guys."

Indeed, the Aviocars weren't following them any longer; evidently, their prey had completely vanished. But Max, speeding low over the waves, knew it was just a matter of time, and not much of that, before they turned on them again. And now they did.

"Once I stop hiding from the satellites, the satellites can tell them where we are," he said. "So let's try Plan C."

Pam couldn't delay to see what that was; she was getting her feet under her and standing, even as he called "Left!" and matched word with deed. Holding tight to her seat with her left hand, she fumbled with the cabinet behind her, got it open. Two white packs were right there.

"Coming around," he said, and the smaller craft leaned back the other way. She swung herself back to her seat and began to scan the chute. As advertised, it wasn't hard to see what to do with it. But what she saw out the window was more intriguing. The Aviocar on the left was diving toward the ocean just as they had done—but he didn't pull up and he didn't slow down. The plane struck the water with a tremendous splash and one blue wing went spinning high in the air.

She looked at Max, saw the familiar strain and sweat. Without being told, she knew the other pilot had succumbed to the subconscious.

"Strap that chute on tight," Max said grimly.

"What about you?" Pam asked.

"If I need it I'll get everything on."

"Will you need it?"

"We've got a shot at not," Max said, his eyes locked on their remaining assailant. Again, he focused his energy . . . but then the Aviocar started firing straight at them. Max had to break off and bank.

"Satellites again," he muttered. "What a world we live in!" They rose swiftly, gracefully, and Pam saw the land ahead, now closer but still too damn far away. Max said, "The Aviocar's clumsier than we are, but at top speed it's our equal. The American Air Force used its predecessor, the 300, for secret missions during the first Iraq war. That's a 400 and it's learned some lessons. Get your harness back on."

"Can I hold the wheel while you do your thing?" Pam gasped.

He laughed. "Nice idea, but this is more than holding the wheel. Unfortunately."

Max dived back toward the sparkling water, holding the angle so the Aviocar could follow, line up on them. He waited until he knew he would fire if he were the pursuer and abruptly pulled upward, just as the bullets flew by. Pam felt the blood draining from her head to her feet, felt light-headed, but fought to stay conscious and keep from throwing up. Looking back and down, she saw their attacker trying to follow them, but he was forced to take a much longer curve, lunging upward. When it finally curved enough to point at the Cessna, heeling over on its back, it let loose again, and the bullets rattled hard against the Cessna's left wing. Max looked out, saw daylight streaming through ragged holes, but felt the little plane maintaining structural integrity. He soared sideways, now closer to the distant land than the Aviocar, and he meant to keep it that way. Of course, he still had to land in a country that apparently had declared war on him.

But only "apparently." He knew this for an attack by the FRC, using Luchtmacht pilots in their control. Didn't change the lethality of it, but at least the bad guys weren't fighting for God and country. Just a payoff, though that might be worse. The FRC could certainly pay.

He put more space between himself and the Aviocar as he darted straight ahead and the Air Force plane slewed back onto his track. It was a race to the land, with the Aviocar barreling after them like Indiana Jones's boulder. There was a moment when he tried to resume his mind control, but then the bullets were flying again. Max pulled back on the stick and shot upward into a barrel roll. The Aviocar instantly saw what he was trying to do and dodged to the right, but Max still came down behind the plane, where it could not fire at them. They sat facing its tail section, daring the pilot to try to turn on them with his less agile craft.

Instead, the Aviocar abruptly powered down. It began a slow descent, its tail dropping, its nose pointing up, as the Cessna swerved to avoid passing directly over it and surged into a sharp ascent. But there was one moment when the lower plane had a shot at the higher, and it took it. Max felt the slamming impact of shells in his right wing. Instantly he compensated, sliding sideways away from the metal stream. But the Cessna hung, sluggish. He knew its structural integrity was gone. But he wasn't finished yet.

He let the Cessna pull him down. He came abreast of the Aviocar, came right up on the bastard, pointed his Glock at his own side window, fired once to blow a hole in the glass, let the crush of air press his hand against the metal frame to steady it. He aimed as best he could and emptied his clip. The right windows of the Aviocar's cockpit exploded inward. But the pilot over there held steady, unscathed. He pointed its nose landward and went away.

The Cessna wasn't going anywhere but down. Its single engine coughed, gave up, and the whole plane began shuddering with irregular rhythm. It began a long spiral toward the water.

"We're getting out of here," Max said, as calm as ever. But Pam was getting her first rush of fear. Jumping out of an airplane, into open ocean? She bit her lip and told herself she'd been through worse now; it had to be doable. Her brain flashed, *What would Artemis do?*

Max disengaged his harness, and she followed suit. Max pulled back hard, to straighten the plane out as best he could. Pam tried to move with calm deliberation, but the Cessna was shuddering and still angled downward, so she had to scramble upward in the aisle to reach the exit door. "Hold the red handle, jump, count to three, pull the handle," Max said finally through gritted teeth as he tried to keep the plane steady. "Look directly at the handle while you do it so there's no slipup. Piece of cake."

Pam didn't waste time. It was very clear that the longer she took, the longer it would be before Max could follow her. The longer she'd have to think about what lay ahead. "Well, good luck!" she shouted, popped the door, and went straight out into nothingness. Nothingness that hit her with hard winds. Resisting the urge to look up, she looked at the red handle, counted "one— two—three!" and yanked it.

The canopy spread and caught the air; she absorbed the harsh jerk of her harness. And then she began the long, angled descent into the wet blue nowhere.

1 SERPENT

Lawrence Breckenridge's jet made an uneventful landing in Indianapolis. The governor's limo, its seal covered and plate changed, was waiting for him and his pilot/driver at the airport. They drove onto I-465 and turned north, following the ring road around the capital city until they reached Fishers. The in-car navigation system led them through the recently burgeoning town to a large limestone campus set well back from the street. The driver, now serving as his bodyguard, accompanied Breckenridge to the front door.

The visitor was expected, and immediately ushered into the office of Taylor Crawford, the senior vice president of Meridian Pharmaceuticals, while the driver stood outside.

"Mr. Breckenridge," said Crawford, rising with the appropriate mix of welcome and reserve; it wouldn't do to appear too anxious. "This is a pleasure."

"The pleasure's all mine, Mr. Crawford."

"Please have a seat. Can I get you anything?"

"I'm fine."

"Good, then. What brings you here?"

"Your boss is dead."

Crawford stared at him, then blinked, recovering. "Miller Omen is dead?"

"Since about one o'clock this morning, Barbados time. Which means you're now in charge of Meridian, and primed to take his place in our First Response Council, if you're so inclined."

"Yes, yes, absolutely," Crawford blurted. Truth to

tell, he had suspected something like this ever since Breckenridge's man had called him at home to make the appointment this morning, but it was still a shock. Omen had been secretive about the Council but he'd prepped his someday-successor enough to give him an idea of what it could mean. Now Crawford was going to find out everything, and he couldn't help but believe it was going to do him a world of good.

But he needed to demonstrate his command, or so he thought. "I can leave for Barbados right away," he said.

"No. We've sent another to pick up that assignment. We just need you to take charge here at Meridian, deal with the coming media inquiries, shareholder concerns, all of that."

"Oh."

"Don't worry." Breckenridge smiled. "There'll be more once things have stabilized."

"Not a problem. I will—"

"Excuse me," said Breckenridge. His cell phone was humming Rachmaninoff's "Isle of the Dead." He enjoyed seeing whether new acquaintances knew it, and was gratified to spot recognition in Crawford's head tilt. That was a plus. "Yes?"

It was Hanrahan. "Code Red eliminated. Our flying friends."

"Very good. Provide for them."

"Done."

Breckenridge carefully returned his cell to his pocket. "Things are going well," he told Crawford. "You now have your chance to be on board."

"I am, sir," Crawford said. "Whatever you need."

"My people will contact you, provide you with the larger picture, but for now, keep Meridian stable, and welcome to the Council." He stood up. The meeting was over. He shook Crawford's hand and went straight out the door.

Back in the limo, he instructed his driver to take him to Geist Reservoir. They drove east on 116th Street, dropped to 113th at Olio, and looked for a place to park beside the water, where Breckenridge would not be disturbed. The driver got out and walked off to stand at a distance, where he could be on call if needed, and make certain no one approached the vehicle. He never knew what his boss did in times like these, but he didn't need to know.

Inside, safe from prying eyes, Lawrence Breckenridge reported to Aleksandra.

She was greatly pleased, and then, so was he. They showed each other how much.

NOVEMBER 3 - 10:00 A.M. EDT

1 SERPENT

Rita's stiletto heel was rapping on the tarmac when Tower's jet hit the runway. She was ready to rumble and wearing a Bluetooth. The jet taxied to a stop, opened its passenger door, and disgorged a tall, thin man who came down the stairs in a dynamic stride, carrying a single suitcase.

"Rita Diamante," he said. A statement, not a query, in a distinctly sepulchral voice. The skin across the bones of his face was tight. "Jackson Tower."

"Sure, Mr. Tower," she replied with a confident grin. "Wheels up as soon as you're on board."

"My pilot will bring across my equipment." He started

up the stairs, to be interrupted by his secure cell. He stopped, answered it. "Tower."

He listened, and then he nodded. "Thank you. I will tell Diamante." He turned to look down at Rita. "That was Hanrahan," he told her. "The Code Red is ended."

"That guy Max August?"

"Yes. And the doctor, Blackwell."

"Max August is dead?" she asked.

"Yes." Her questions were already growing annoying.

"He sounded tougher than that when Hanrahan described him to me," Rita said matter-of-factly. "I'd've thought he'd've lasted longer. I guess I just have a lot of respect for magick."

"Umm," Tower said, his face disapproving. He saw women's wiles all too clearly. "It doesn't change our primary job, though, so we're still on our way as soon as my equipment is brought over." He turned back and almost bounded up the stairs. Next to his own jet, his man was unloading a large wooden shipping container, perhaps five by five by five. He wrestled it onto a baggage cart single-handedly, then rolled the cart toward Rita's jet, where Mérides jumped up to help him load it.

The interior of Diamante's jet was as sleek as an eel, Tower saw. Jet-black and scarlet were the colors that slid along the walls, over the furniture, in random patterns. There were two padded chairs, black with a single red pinstripe rising from the floor, driving along the right arm and up and over the top. Between them was a shining black table set with a ruby crystal decanter and one ashtray, sparkling in a baby spot.

Tower strapped himself into the right-hand chair as Rita took her place on the left. *It looks like raw decadence,* he mused. *It looks like Hell. And its message is clear. 'I can love you, I can kill you, and you don't know which I will choose.' But I know you perfectly, Diamante. I did your chart when I vetted you for this job.* The woman was wearing a tight tank top, tangerine, that ended just above her diamond-studded navel and low-rise, skintight cerulean jeans. *And here you are,* he thought. *You've not only maintained your drug empire twice as long as the average, you've expanded it. You've exceeded even my expectations. But now we shall see you firsthand.*

She spoke to her Bluetooth. *"Andamos, Córdobes."* The jet jerked slightly as its brakes relaxed, and began to roll forward. No one blocked the runway; once it started it drove half the length of the former air base and surged into the Florida sky.

As soon as they were airborne, Rita unbuckled her belt. "What can I get you, Mr. Tower? The cocaine you would expect to be primo, but I also have some single-malt, Laphroaig Private Reserve, forty-five years old, made only for me, and beautiful Cuban Cohibas, again just for me."

"I'll have the Laphroaig," Tower replied tonelessly. "I was unaware that they made a forty-five-year-old."

"Forty's the highest they admit to," Rita said, smoothly producing two ruby crystal goblets from a hidden drawer in the table and setting them down in circular depressions on top. "Rocks? Soda? Water?"

"Not on first acquaintance," Tower said.

"A man after my own heart," Rita said, lifting the decanter from its depression and pouring three fingers into his goblet. Then she did the same for herself. Tower smelled the Scotch with his full attention, drawing its essence fully into himself, before he took his first sip. He considered it, his cheeks showing the slightest of tongue-tasting movements. He swallowed. There were benefits to the world outside the forest. "You will have to give me the name of your contact," he said.

"Of course, but I'll also send you a case to get you started, once we come back from this little adventure." As she settled back in her chair, she added, "This will make everyone's job easier, won't it? The death of the Code Red."

Tower sucked back one side of his mouth, making a clicking sound. "Perhaps. Max August wasn't the only one. There could still be others."

"Yeah? I don't know much about that part."

"My colleagues and I on the Council look for them on a regular basis and we believe there are no more than six, but they're like fish in the sea. We catch their movement but not them, so we can't be certain. Whatever their reasons, they all have the ability to live off the grid. I see nothing, and I've heard nothing, to make me believe there are any more Code Reds in this operation, but we've had one potential setback in Miller Omen's death. In the best scenario, I will be completely superfluous to your work, but one mistake is more than we allow ourselves."

"Makes sense. I didn't get where I am by being sloppy, either."

She was not obviously brownnosing, her tone as matter-of-fact as his, but she *was* brownnosing and it annoyed her that he showed no reaction to it. Nevertheless, it had happened twice now and that was enough. *Maybe that's the difference between him and me,* she thought. *He stops at one mistake, I go for two.* She resolved then and there to follow his example.

"So," Tower said, "here is the plan. I'm certain you'll have no trouble taking it on." He gave her a succinct overview of Omen's work so far, then, "It was his intent to run the Suriname end of it from a ranch he bought in the hills of the rain forest, far from the capital. I now believe we should have a person closer to the scene. Since these are zombis, they should do exactly as they're told, but having you nearby to deal with any problems tightens things down."

"Where will you be?"

"At the ranch. My work, if there is any, won't require personal contact."

Why doesn't that surprise me? Rita thought. "I hope my men and I will be upwind of the sarin."

"Of course," he said, his tone clearly adding *stupid*. "The trade winds blow steadily to the west. You will be to the south, outside the danger zone. The spot is already under our control so it's ready and waiting for you. And, there are mercenaries in place, hired by Omen, who can be your forward guard if you wish."

"Canaries in a coal mine, huh?" Rita said, unfazed by his tone. "Then fine. We'll get it done."

For one deep moment, Jackson Tower felt so strongly attracted to her that his mechanical heart picked up its pace in response. But he shook his head shortly, realizing the new Scotch had more kick than he'd thought. He believed that a mystic should be pure. He had never had a woman, or anything else, including his own hand. It was why he lived where few could, and how he lived there. It was why he looked upon the "real" world from a great distance. It was why he was the sorcerer of the most powerful group on Earth.

And still, she was just the kind of woman he would have if he had one—dark and brutal and impure as all hell.

1 SERPENT

Max came down faster than he liked. The Cessna had been too low when he'd jumped and the chute hadn't had enough time to do all its magic. He'd lived too long in San Francisco back in the day not to know that the best way to hit the water was completely vertical. If he took an angle it probably wouldn't kill him—probably—but it wouldn't be fun. So he took one last look to judge the distance to where Pam was already in the water and spread his alchemical shark-repellent energy field wide enough to encompass her as he went in as straight as he could.

The warm blue water surged over his head and his momentum took him thirty feet below the waves before he could stop himself. He fought to make sure the chute didn't entangle him, got his eyes open, and saw something large darting away in the turquoise shadows. Away was good. He bobbed to the surface just as he slipped out of the chute, and tried to regain his bearings. All he could see was sparkling water, everywhere he looked, but the swells carried him up for better views, and he knew he hadn't turned much, if at all, from his original orientation. That meant Pam would be at ten o'clock . . . and the third time he went up, the sea cooperated and lowered itself between them enough for him to see her blond head and orange life jacket some fifty yards away.

"Pam!" he called, and the sound carried over the warm water, on the wind. He saw her turn. He began to swim.

The water was definitely warm this close to the equator, seventy-five or eighty degrees. It was the proverbial bathwater, except that there was a hell of a lot of it. But it took him only a little more than five minutes to reach her because she was swimming to meet him as well.

"All right?" he asked, winded.

"Sure," she said, even more winded. "Parachuting's a piece of cake, like you said. But I'm not wild about where we ended up."

"Think of it as a large Jacuzzi."

"You've got the shark protection going, yes?"

"Absolutely."

"But we're still way the hell offshore. I saw land before we went down, and it's got to be three, four miles. A long way to dog paddle. Can you conjure up a raft for us?"

"Too dangerous. We were evidently visible to satellites when there was only our plane and open water. It'd be the same with a raft."

"They can see something that small, really?"

"Yes, but if we ride the waves, they can't pick us out. And we'll be rescued soon enough."

"What do you mean?" she asked, galvanized.

"Mama's got friends all around the Caribbean. As soon as the Luchtmacht plane came at us, I sent her a vodou *call* on the ether. Assuming I did it right, she'll have been in touch with her friends down here. Some-one will come with a boat."

"How will they find us in open ocean? Oh. Same way, huh?"

"If I do it right, I'm a human beacon. You can practi-cally see my head spin around. So you might as well lie back, float, and work on your tan."

"Won't the satellite see the boat?"

"Lots of boats come out from the coast. Be hard to pinpoint the one that picks us up."

"And you didn't think to tell me this?"

"I was kind of busy there at the end."

"All right, I'll give you that." She splashed some water at him. "Am I ever in real danger when I'm with you, Max?"

He gave her a serious look, made a little difficult by their riding the swells. "Absolutely," he said soberly. "I like to avoid danger whenever possible, but don't ever start thinking we win just by showing up. We have real enemies with real weapons of their own, like Luchtmacht planes that make us jump out of ours. Not a whole lot I could do for you there. I just happen to know a few things they—most of them—don't know. Things their weapons don't quite cover." He took her hand. "C'mon. Turn off your mind and gently float downstream."

"You know, Max," she answered dubiously, "I'm good with asteroids crashing out of space now, but floating in the middle of the ocean still makes me just a little nervous."

"*I* think it's awful damn peaceful out here."

"*You* would," Pam answered. *Lie back and enjoy it,* she thought, but there was no way she'd say that out loud.

NOVEMBER 3 – 2:30 P.M. GREENWICH MEAN TIME

1 SERPENT

Cambridge, Cambridgeshire:

Eva Delia Kerr had been at the halfway house for a day and a half, and she was definitely settling in. The meds she'd been given before transport had been dialed back, and as she gradually emerged from her mental fog, gradually grew more aware of the world around her, Eva Delia began to find little things that made a house a home. She knew where her room was, and it was very pretty, on the second floor but not ever barred, just like Mrs. West had said. Eva Delia couldn't really remember Mrs. West's full name yet, it was a funny one, but it was okay to call her Mrs. West so she called her Mrs. West. But her room was pretty and she liked to walk around it. Around and around and around, in the world around.

Cambridge was a real city, so she could see little things and she could see big things. Outside this house were Cambridgeshire streets and Cambridgeshire houses and Cambridgeshire cars and Cambridgeshire cats. There were also lorries from other places because their stickers had strange secret codes. Eva Delia couldn't go outside and walk in the street yet, but that was part of the hope that was growing inside her, that she could walk around the whole city, and maybe the whole world, and find the secret codes. Then maybe she'd know where she fit in.

Down the hall the radio began to play a song, and Eva Delia threw back her head and SCREE*EEEEEEEE-AMED!!!*

The floor nurse came running. She found Eva Delia in a fetal position on the floor, her legs churning, turning her body round and round. Her slim hands were wrapped around her throat—not tightly, as the nurse at first feared, but simply holding it, cradling it. Her lips were so tight shut as to be white lines. The nurse tried to gentle her out of it, tried to get her to tell why she was so afraid, but Eva Delia would not be gentle, not be not afraid, not open her mouth and use her throat. So the nurse, rather sadly, rather disappointed, gave her an injection. Soon Eva Delia drifted away from the fear and the codes and even the lorries. Her hands dropped away from her throat, and her mouth slid open, and she began to snore. But now and again she whimpered, some sort of high-pitched sound.

Mrs. Westbury arrived in time to help the nurse lift Eva Delia into her bed.

"What's happened, Brenda?"

"I've no idea, ma'am. She was fine when I looked in on her fifteen minutes before, walking in circles but cheerful. I wasn't expecting anything like this."

Mrs. Westbury made a sympathetic clucking sound. "Poor girl. Let's keep her sedated for six hours, then re-evaluate. I believe we'll decrease her medication more slowly."

Down the hall, BBC2's Steve Wright finished playing "Love Has No Pride" by Valerie Drake and segued into Tears for Fears.

NOVEMBER 3 - 11:00 A.M. EASTERN DAYLIGHT TIME

1 SERPENT

The interrogators dragged Nancy across the dusty ground. Her head hanging, she could see the dust stirred up by her feet, blowing behind her in the fitful tropical wind. It was brutally hot, even in November. The clouds promised rain later but it was dry as death now. She wanted to ask for water but she didn't want to talk with them at all anymore.

She had told them almost everything they wanted to hear. She'd had to. But she'd come to feel deep down

that it was death to admit she'd told Max and Pam
about the FRC, and so she'd held out on that. She admitted she'd been caught by surprise, especially after
ten months of anonymity, especially after she thought
the dart had killed Pam. She hadn't known about the
zombis but she'd been confident that the FRC would
make certain Pam was dead, so it was a hell of a shock
to see her walk in that door. But she'd covered as best
she could, just as she'd been taught. It wasn't her fault
that the sorcerer had seen through her. He was a Code
Red, for God's sake. But she'd told him she didn't know
who she was working for, that she'd been contacted
(she was thinking it through as best she could as they
twisted her arms tighter and tighter behind her back, so
that she thought for sure they'd rip from her shoulders),
contacted by an unknown man, offered a monthly pay-
ment to watch. She'd sent the package with the dart
but she had never known who was behind it. That's
what she'd told the sorcerer. She swore.

It didn't seem to matter.

Below her, embedded in the dirt, was an arrow. Her
dragging feet scraped across it.

"That's the way to Mecca," the first man said. "We
installed it for our guests."

"Sorry we've got nothing for the way to the country
club," said the second.

The men dragged her into a small hut with a corru-
gated tin roof. The temperature inside was like an oven,
far more stifling than the noon heat outside. Her feet
slid across the tiled floor, which showed no dust at all;
it was scuffed but appeared to have been washed. Her
toes began to blister.

They came to a halt. It was easiest to let her head
hang but she worried it would make her look guilty.

She lifted her head and saw a wooden box, about seven feet long, four feet wide, and two feet deep. There were legs at the corners; at one end they elevated the box six inches and at the other end two feet, so the box was slanted. At both ends there were manacles.

"You hot, Nancy?" asked one man. "I know I am. It's brutal in here, isn't it?"

"'Tain't the heat, it's the humanity," said the other.

"You need to cool off, hot girl," said the first man. He let go of her arm, while the second man continued to hold her tightly, and began to unbutton her blouse.

"Oh my God," she whispered.

"Relax, baby. We're not going to rape you," the man said, opening her blouse and slipping it over her free arm.

"I don't believe you," she said.

"No reason you should," he said, reaching back to unsnap her bra. "But it's the truth."

Very quickly, her jeans and panties went off as well, leaving her completely naked. Trembling. Both men took hold of her and moved her toward the box. She struggled as they forced her down onto it, onto her back, and manacled her hands and feet so that she lay spread-eagled on the hot wooden surface.

"See, Nancy," one man said, "you have a great body, but you're not in the best of shape just now. Not really sexy, you know."

"Sweaty, dirty, beginning to bruise," said the other.

"I've told you everything!" she yelled.

"Well, we have to be sure," said one man.

He picked up a heavy woolen blanket and attached it to a hook on one side of the box, at the level of her head. Then he stretched it over her upturned face and attached it on the other side. She could hardly breathe.

Then he dumped water on the blanket.

For a very brief moment it felt good, cool, but disorienting. Then the volume of water increased. It soaked the blanket, filling all the space around her head. Her sinuses filled. She couldn't breathe. There was no air. Sudden, overpowering panic hit her as she struggled against her bonds, tried to turn her head, but her limbs were held fast and the blanket, heavy with the water, clung to her face. She couldn't breathe at all! She gasped, sputtered—finally took a breath of dirty water. She spasmed, choking, but the water kept coming! Her body fought and fought but she was drowning! She sucked in water again, felt herself fading . . . fading into death . . .

She went limp. The men watched her for a moment, knowing she couldn't fake it any longer than that, then whipped the sodden blanket from her head. One began giving her artificial respiration, stiff-arming her chest. She gagged. Water splurted from her mouth. She coughed, came to. Gradually awareness came back into her eyes.

"Waterboarding," said one man.

"Perfectly legal," said the other.

"Not torture at all."

"What did you say about the FRC?"

Her eyes darted around the room. There was no escape. But if she told them, they'd kill her. She had to lie.

"Noth . . ." she said.

They dropped the thick wet wool back over her face.

1 SERPENT

Max and Pam were floating, watching the clouds drift by above.

Pam thought, *It was so good last night . . . because nobody mentioned Val. But she's the six-hundred-pound elephant in the room. If Max and I do this thing, there's no guarantee that she won't come back someday—and until that day, he'll stay obsessed with her. That's a terrible recipe for success. I must be crazy.*

Max thought, *Someday I'll find Val. I love Val. But I love the Val I knew twenty-two years ago. She won't be the same when I find her. She can't be. I will find her, but I have no idea what will happen then. And meanwhile, I live in this world, and I'm in the prime of my life . . . and Pam is smart and brave and beautiful.*

Pam thought, *What am I to him? I'm not like him in any way. I was scared, jumping out of that plane. I did it, but I didn't like it. And I don't like being in the middle of all this empty ocean . . . if I let myself think about it. So think about the future. He likes me because I've kept up with him, but what if I start to shy away? It won't last if I can't keep up.*

Max thought, *Pam had it, right from the start. She listened, she thought, she acted. She's not some space cadet. There's a let-down now that the dart is gone; all that extra adrenaline has died away, and she's bound to be feeling shaky. But she jumped without any fuss. She can live this life.*

Pam thought, *How can I compete with his wife?*

Max thought, *Wanting her doesn't mean quitting on Val.*

The sound of an inboard motor broke the ocean stillness. Pam surged quickly upright, treading water, looking hard until she picked out a small boat racing straight for them. It was only another three minutes before it powered down and surged to a halt right alongside, rocking them on its waves. The pilot was a tall black woman, as were her two crew members; the three were pretty obviously sisters. They all had crisp black hair helmeting their heads, wore one-piece bathing suits, and had a peculiar tattoo on their left calves.

"We come from Mama Locha," said the pilot as the nearest sister dropped a ladder over the side.

"Fast," added the middle woman, the heaviest of the three. "She likes you a lot."

"We like her a whole lot more," said Pam, climbing up and over with no wasted effort. "Fast is good. Fast is real good." Max floated patiently, waiting until she was in, then followed hard on her heels. As soon as he was aboard, the pilot said, "Please take hold of something," and put it in gear. The boat had been stationary for no more than forty seconds. In another forty they were making over twenty-five knots across the waves.

"I am Amba," said the pilot, above the sound of the wind, water, and motor. "These are my sisters, Kwasiba and Adyuba." Her accent was a delightful mixture of sounds Pam had never heard blended before, but it seemed familiar to Max. "Amba, Kwasiba, and Adyuba," he echoed. "Saturday, Sunday, and Monday."

"Well," Amba smiled shyly, but her eyes were curious at the same time, "these are our names in the world. Do you speak Sranan Tongo, Mr. . . . August, is it?"

Now it was his turn to laugh. "Actually, my name *is* August . . . Saturday. But I spend all *my* time denying it. And yes, I speak a little Sranan. I passed a summer down here in 1996."

Now Adyuba spoke again. "I am sorry to hear that."

Max laughed again. "Hot," he agreed, nodding.

"But more," said Kwasiba. She was the shortest of the three. "We did not know you were here. We would have helped you then as well, and we would be old friends."

"You ladies would have been, maybe, ten?"

"We are shaman from birth," said Amba, with such dignity that Max spread his hands.

"I apologize. I was ignorant then, and I'm ignorant now."

"That's all right," said Kwasiba cheerfully. "We'll be old friends starting today."

Max worked his way forward to confer with Amba at the wheel, while Pam stayed back with Kwasiba and Adyuba. But she didn't fail to notice Max taking Amba's hand the way he'd taken Nancy's and the others' at the party, the way he'd taken Miller Omen's.

To the two sisters she said, "Nice boat."

"It's an old smuggling boat. We bought it last year at auction," Kwasiba told her.

"Boats are like cars in Suriname. Better than cars. The rivers and ocean never wash out," Adyuba added. The sun on the waves and the girls' dark skins was brilliant, beautiful.

"You live by the water?"

"We are Ndyuka, a tribe of the Maroons," Adyuba told her proudly. "Our village is far away on the Tapanahoni River. But we live in Para. That's Paramaribo, the capital city."

"And you call *yourselves* 'Maroons'?" Pam asked

noncommittally. It didn't sound like a politically correct term.

But Adyuba laughed. " 'Maroon' comes from the Spanish *cimarrón*, meaning 'cattle that run away,' " she said. "When the Dutch settlers needed a workforce for their plantations, they did what everybody else did in the 1700s, and stole it from Africa. And though all masters are masters, the Dutch were particular bastards; *eighty percent* of my people died from their treatment. The *first* resort for Dutch discipline was amputation. So finally my people fled into the rain forest, familiar countryside for them, and created villages like those they'd known at home. The Dutch tried to recapture them but the runaway cattle were comfortable in the jungle and the Dutch were not, so finally they had to sign a peace treaty. We Maroons have been one of the spices in Surinamese life ever since."

"How many spices are there?" Pam asked.

"In Suriname?" Kwasiba laughed again. In addition to being the shortest, she seemed to be the heartiest of the three, but Adyuba laughed as well. Kwasiba said, "There are the Maroons, the Hindustanis—"

"Hindustanis?"

"They were brought to work the fields when the Maroons had gone. And the Dutch had learned from their experience with us so they were not slaughtered so freely."

"So there are Maroons, Hindustanis," said Adyuba, "Javanese, Indios, Creoles, Chinese, Dutch, and English."

Max came back to join them then. "It's pretty much what I expected," he told Pam. "The ladies got an actual phone call from Mama Locha." Kwasiba and Adyuba nodded as he continued. "They've known each other since the ladies were nine. They've never been part of Mama's priestesses-in-training—different traditions—but they accompanied their mother to a general gathering in Caracas one Midsummer and fell under Mama's spell, socially speaking. Their mother and Mama exchanged recipes." Of course he wasn't talking soup. "Their mother's dead now but the two worlds have kept in touch in several ways, one of which is the vodou *call*. Once there was no way to telephone across the Caribbean, and now that there is, the phones are tapped. Vodou used to be the only way to communicate, and the best way, really. If you could see the vodou energy, it would form a matrix over all the islands, all of Central and South America."

"Why did Mama use the phone, then?"

"Because magick is never one hundred percent, and she didn't want any slipups. She likes us. But they spoke to each other in a dialect Homeland Security isn't concerned with." Max rubbed his lower lip. He must have hit it somewhere in the scramble out of the plane, and it was bleeding. "But the bad guys are paying attention here since they're planning something here. Anything they don't expect to see will catch their attention."

"Does Amba know what their plan is?"

"No. Most of Suriname is jungle, of course, and most of the peoples who lived there have gravitated toward Para or the other cities, like everywhere else. And Suriname's not heavily populated to start with—only four hundred thousand in the whole country. So the number of people who know what's going on in any part of the jungle is pretty small. And—four of the ones who would know have turned up dead in the past year." Kwasiba and Adyuba nodded.

"Didn't that spark some sort of investigation?"

"Who's going to investigate? I remind you, it was the Luchtmacht that shot us down."

"Did these four hang around one particular area?"

Kwasiba shook her head. "They were bushmen; all the forest was their home. If they had any particular spot they all liked, we don't know about it."

Now the coast of Suriname was rising up before them, and by unspoken agreement they let go of what they didn't know, to just sit back and watch it come. The temperature in the November afternoon was nearly one hundred, though the constant trade winds made things close to bearable. Max and Pam, completely dry though salt-encrusted, moved up to the prow.

Driving into the mouth of the wide Suriname River, they could soon see smoke from the chimneys of Paramaribo on a peninsula far ahead. The sisters started chattering among themselves and slowed the boat as they began to meet oncoming traffic, but not too much; Amba delighted in maneuvering around the slower craft. Mosquitos appeared, drifting hungrily but still unable to keep up. The water around them turned from turquoise to brown from swamp runoff and sewage.

"Weird women," Pam said to Max. "That's one prediction down."

"Yep."

"What language are they speaking?"

"Sranan Tongo," he said.

"That's what she said before. I never heard of it."

"It means, precisely, 'Suriname tongue,' and it's a mix of all the languages that have come through here—a sort of pidgin. It's the only way all the peoples of Suriname could communicate back in the day, and they all still speak it. You can pick up everything you'll need in a day. It's fun."

"I believe you. But all I speak is English. How far is that going to get me?"

"Pretty far in town. But just about nowhere in the jungle."

"And we're headed for the jungle, aren't we?"

"That would be my guess."

The river split into two channels now. The one to the right turned south, with Paramaribo on the western bank. The other ran east, with Nieuw Amsterdam and Marienburg on the north. At the fork lay Geertruidenberg, and beyond that were the suburbs of Boom Jachtlust, Meerzorg, and Speeringhoek. The boat's motor changed tone, throttled down, and they drifted in a dying wake to a halt at an old pier on an undistinguished waterfront. Small boats bobbed cheek-by-jowl as far as the eye could see, some new, some very old, with the occasional fisherman's shack breaking the parade. Along the shore slumped a series of weathered warehouses, some used for their original purpose, a few converted to down-home diners, many abandoned. Most everything had been painted white at one time; the roofs were what remained of the original brown shingles. Fluffy white clouds in the sky above had grown thicker where sea met land and formed a solid bank to the north. Amba said, "This is Geertruidenberg—Gberg, we call it. We have a house two blocks from here, and it is protected."

Pam asked, "What are *we* going to do, Max?"

"If you get lucky," he said, "we're taking a shower together, and then catching up on our sleep. I wouldn't want to predict when we'll have the chance to do any of that again."

1 SERPENT

Jackson Tower and Rita Diamante's long day's journey into Suriname ended at Johan Adolf Pengel International Airport, universally known by its location in Zanderij, thirty miles south of the capital. They descended the jet's steps onto the tarmac beneath heavy white clouds. It was weather she was used to, living in Miami, but it brought sweat pouring from the Minnesotan. It didn't affect his vitality, however, as he left her behind on the walk to the long, nearly modern terminal. Every brisk step of the way he was looking in all directions, considering the palms in the distance, the strong shafts of sunlight slanting through the clouds, and finally the terminal, just as a small, sharp-featured man whose easy smile could not mask the predatory glint in his eye stepped forward to greet them. It was the American ambassador, Carlton E. Hughes.

"Welcome, welcome, welcome," Hughes said warmly. "How was your trip?"

"It's not over yet," Rita answered shortly. She hadn't had to gawk like the sorcerer, but she'd taken in the terrain as they'd come over land and was anxious to get the complete lay of the land. She had just a day and a half to change anything about the plan she didn't like and she was anxious to get going.

On the other hand, the ambassador was a trained professional who could be counted upon to schmooze anyone he met, so he evinced no notice of her tone as he escorted his visitors to his mystic green Hummer H1 Alpha. The driver, wearing khaki pants and a button-down white shirt open at the neck, carried their luggage behind them. Mérides rolled Tower's large crate. "No, Ms. Diamante. Your trip's not over," Hughes answered Rita equably. "But it's not too bad. Just another three hours to the plantation, and four to the staging ground."

"It's Miss Diamante, and *señorita* is better, Mr. Ambassador. And why so long, especially when I have to get all the way back up here tomorrow, and then play dress-up at a state dinner?"

"We're at the tail end of the dry season. The dirt roads are fine, and so are the paved highways, though we won't be traveling on them. But the so-called middle roads, unpaved but topped with bauxite, are very dusty and consequently difficult to negotiate. My driver is excellent but we'll still be slowed from time to time simply because we won't be able to see." He reached for her elbow, then decided against it. "You're very good, taking up the reins on such short notice, *señorita*. We were all prepared for Mr. Omen."

"I'm happy to get my shot." She took *his* elbow. "I imagine you know what that's like, Mr. Ambassador."

"Oh yes," he responded in measured tones. "I've been with State since 1975, under Gerald Ford."

"And you thought you'd be somewhere beyond Suriname by now."

"Not at all. I was ambassador to Saudi under Reagan," Hughes said. "I helped Usama channel his money, and ours, into the Afghan-Russian war. But the FRC had long-range plans for me—these plans, as it turns out—so I was moved off the fast track. Life has nonetheless been very interesting, and there was always the promise of what we're doing now."

"Well, if we pull this off, everybody'll do all right, Mr. Hughes."

For the first time, Tower spoke. Even Hughes, the consummate professional, blinked at the sound of his distant voice. "I need you to do two things for me, Mr. Ambassador."

"Certainly, sir."

"One, use your contacts in the Surinamese government to have certain substances completely interdicted. No one is to buy or sell them under any circumstances, nor are they to be imported. I have a list for you, direct from the list-maker's computer."

"No problem."

"Two, I assume you're in contact with Omen's man Tilit."

"He's with my man Calderón."

"Then I will provide you with *stones* for them both— *stones* worthy of this assignment. I want them to start a search for August and Blackwell."

Rita shot Tower a sharp glance. Was he kidding? "You said they were dead."

Tower stared into the far distance, his eyes narrowing. "Humor me."

"But what's changed?"

"Nothing. That's the point."

NOVEMBER 3 - 3:15 P.M. ST

1 SERPENT

Tilit sat in his room at Calderón's house and felt the vibrations of his Super Speak & Spell in his hands. He couldn't hear it with his ears, and he couldn't hear it within his muscles; the only option open to him was the slight vibration caused by its speaker. He typed in a phrase and let it play back for him. Then he typed in another.

U R SUCH A MAN, the box said. **U R SUCH A MAN. I LUV U.** As always in these moments, Tilit thought of Lilian, the social worker who touched him at the shelter in Fountain Square. She was the only woman he had never paid for, and when she had abandoned him to marry some insurance salesman, Tilit had hunted them down on their honeymoon on Hilton Head, to kill them both. But when he saw her through the window of their rental house, he had simply turned and walked away without a single second thought. He didn't understand it at the time, but later he realized it was his gift of love, to the only woman who would ever love him.

Calderón, coming down the hall to alert him to their new assignment, heard the harsh voice ahead. **I LUV U. BETTER I STAY WITH U.** *Poor dumb bastard,* Calderón thought. He knocked before he remembered that his guest wouldn't hear that, either. So he opened the door slowly, and let it swing slowly wide as he stood with his hands in plain sight. Tilit was holding a gun on him as the door revealed him, but lowered it when he saw who it was. Calderón said clearly, "For some reason, they think the man who killed Omen may still be alive. And the woman, too. They want us to search."

Tilit stood up quickly. Was there still a chance to avenge Master Omen? He heard the song of triumph in his brain once more as he put the Speak & Spell away.

1 SERPENT

Nancy moaned inside her hood. It was the only thing that offered any sort of relief, moaning, even if her breath made the inside of the hood even hotter and staler. She thought she was going to pass out. She wished with all her heart that she would. She thought about fighting them the next time they came for her, but she had no spirit left for it. She thought about her mom and dad, how they would never get to be proud of her, would never even know what happened to her. She'd be a hole in their lives forever.

The temperature in her room was unbearable. She was slick with sweat, and the stench of sweat and fear permeated the hood. She'd also peed herself, lying there hour after hour, and that was in the air as well. Since they'd dragged her back to her tiny white room she'd been lying naked on the concrete floor, lying in her pee, with a tight black hood over her head and her arms and legs tied too tightly together. If she relaxed at all it felt like some part of her would pull loose, but to ease the strain took more strength than she had, so she rocked back and forth in greater or lesser pain, and wished she could die. All she had to do was admit she'd told the Code Red about them. But in her heart of hearts she could not bring herself to do that. It might be a relief to die, but she could not choose that.

This wasn't how it was supposed to be! She had joined the FRC because they were ruthless and she'd thought she was. They were never supposed to turn on her. She was supposed to be on the winning side! But they must know how junior she was, how powerful the Code Red was. Why would they hold her responsible for something she couldn't help? That was too ruthless by far.

The door to her room clicked open.

"Damn, Nancy!" said the first man. "This place is rank!"

A jolt of ice-cold water struck her naked flesh. She spasmed, and felt her left arm jerk from its socket. She screamed into her hood, but the water kept spraying her, hosing her down. She lay quietly, whimpering.

Finally they turned the water off. Hands took her shoulders and lifted her, causing her to scream again. They set her up on her bunk, and removed her bonds. Her arms and legs lay like hunks of dead meat—dead meat infested with maggots that itched and scurried deep within. That was all she could feel. Then they removed her hood.

In the white room she almost went blind. She slumped backward, eyes closed, panting breathlessly against the white wall. The men did not touch her again.

After a while she felt she could open her eyes. She did. The men were simply standing, waiting.

"Are you satisfied . . . now . . . ?" she whispered.

"Not really," said the first man.

"We still think you talked about the FRC," said the second.

"After all this?" she asked.

"All what?" answered the first man.

"This is just the tip of the iceberg," said the second.

"You remember the zombis you told us about?" asked the first man.

Nancy didn't say anything. What was there to say?

"You remember we said we didn't find you attractive?" asked the second man.

"But we know someone who would," said the first.

"If he knew what 'attractive' was," said the second.

"Party on, Nancy," said the first.

They backed out of the room, and for a moment Nancy saw the door was open and thought she could do something about that, if she could just make her legs work. But in the next instant, a hulking figure filled the doorway, and drums began to beat.

It was a zombi.

NOVEMBER 3 - 5:00 P.M. SURINAME TIME

1 SERPENT

Max and Pam lay sound asleep in each other's arms. A lizard scampered up their window frame, did seven push-ups, and skittered away.

NOVEMBER 3 - 5:30 P.M. ST

1 SERPENT

Elsewhere in Gberg, Tilit was prowling. Calderón had given him an old and well-used jeep so he could drive through the neighborhoods, but he preferred to park it and wander on foot.

He missed Ballantine; he and Calderón had divided the Paramaribo area between them, and Tilit had the suburbs. Ballantine would have given him the city, where there were more people. Tilit could move his huge body through crowds with little physical contact, probably due to his inability to fully engage with the people there, and he liked that. It made him feel special. And there was another reason.

Squire Omen had once said that the top guy in the FRC was like that, too.

NOVEMBER 3 - 6:00 P.M. ST

1 SERPENT

The crimson sun was settling lightly on the forested peaks of Suriname as the mystic green Hummer carrying Jackson Tower, Rita Diamante, Mérides, and Carlton E. Hughes motored over the narrowest mountain road Tower had ever seen or wished to see. As the sun fell the Hummer rose, until at last they pulled to a halt on a small shelf beside the road.

"Take a look before it gets dark," said Hughes. The three got out on the inward side and went carefully to the precipitous edge.

They looked down into a narrow valley, closed at the far end. The land there was mostly cultivated, with rows of fruit trees both below and above an ornate villa. Marking out the villa's grounds was a low hedge covered in bright flowers, probably honeysuckle. Flower beds of yellow and orange ran alongside the main house, bordering a brick patio with umbrella tables leading to a blue swimming pool. Farther back was a gazebo, a barn, a corral with seven horses, and several zombis standing statuelike. Against the opposite hills, an airstrip, a hangar, and accompanying sheds swam in the growing shadows. A herd of cattle grazed peacefully in the far reaches of the valley.

"It was built in 1888 for Juup Vanderdecken, a Dutch sailor retiring from the sea. He called it Katrina, after his ship, not the hurricane. Vanderdecken became the leading citizen down here for his time, but nothing lasts in Suriname. Vanderdecken left after seven years and the plantation went through a series of owners. It was abandoned when Miller Omen picked it up and conducted extensive renovations. He intended it to be the palace from which he'd rule."

"Isn't it ridiculously far from the action?" Rita demanded.

"Well now, the action is where the ruler wants it to be. And Paramaribo will be much less action-oriented for a while. But the main thing for our purposes is its location in the valley. You'll note that the far end of the valley is closed off, with just the one opening at this end. And if you look closely at the hills forming the valley . . ."

Just at that moment, a final shaft of sunlight caught the far ridge, and the watchers saw a distinctive line, slightly curved, running along the ridgeline.

"That," said Hughes, pointing, "is one half of a retractable roof. With the other half on this side and a front panel, the valley can be completely enclosed, like a football stadium. Couple that with its location to the south while the trade winds blow west, and you'll understand."

Rita nodded, smiling for the first time since long before she'd landed.

"A country of the living—opening for the dead," said Jackson Tower from the outer depths.

The sun went down.

1 SERPENT

The crimson sun was setting lightly over Paramaribo as Max and Pam, rejuvenated, clean, and wearing fresh clothes courtesy of the sisters and some unknown boy-friends, strolled in the garden behind the sisters' house. They were unabashedly holding hands. The garden was a small tropical paradise, with orange and banana trees offering fruit ripe for the picking, and a pond where two armored catfish held motionless vigil in the shad-ows. On the far side of the yard, catching the last red rays of light, stood a sort of sculpture, made of wheels and wires, resembling a robot. Pam decided it must have come with the house; none of the sisters, even Kwasiba, seemed like the kind to make it. But then, she barely knew them.

"Max," she said, her voice as quiet as the world, "you said Establishing Reality and Basic Relationship and gravity and love and sex all came from the same place."

"Uh-huh."

"Tell me more about that."

The scent of warm oranges drifted past. Birds began to sing the onset of night. Finally, he said, "This one I'll take to the Torah—a.k.a. the Old Testament Bible. I am aware that 'Bible' is a loaded concept for many people, pro and con, but I'm just quoting what's there."

"Okay."

"Well, the guy who started writing it, Moses, says he was an artist, and he wrote it as an artist, which proves it. And the first thing he wrote was, 'In the beginning Elohim created the heavens and the earth.'"

"All right, Scoob, I'll play," Pam said. "What's 'Elohim'? As opposed to 'God,' which is the way I heard it."

"You heard it the way it was turned into English. But when it was written down, in the first line of the first book of the holy scripture of two major religions, it was 'Elohim.' 'Elohim' as a word is a female singular concept with a male plural ending. The real English equivalent is 'Goddess-ers.' That doesn't make sense in everyday English, let alone monotheistic religions, so we made it 'God.' But the original Aramaic is right there on display."

"I'm with you so far."

"It's Elohim who creates everything. The seven days of creation, from 'heaven and earth' to 'rested on the seventh day'—that's all Elohim. Then, abruptly, the story starts up all over again: 'This is the account of the heavens and the earth when they were created, in the day that *Jehovah-Elohim* made earth and heaven.' First time we've seen that name. And what's the first thing Jehovah-Elohim does? He forms the adam out of dust from the ground. Problem is, back on day six, 'Elohim created the adam in Their own image, in the image of Elohim they created him; male and female They created them.'"

Pam grabbed his arm. "Are you telling me there's Basic Relationship because there are *two Gods*?"

Max said, "No."

"Oh."

"It's more subtle than that. When Moses—the artist, remember, who's been to the mountaintop and come back with the Ten Commandments by the time he's writing all this down—tells about encountering the burning bush, he writes, 'When Jehovah saw that he turned aside to look, Elohim called to him from the midst of

the bush.' Two entities; the distinction's always made.
But not because there are two Gods. There's only one
Deity—but it is plural.

"That's very hard to grasp, at first. What is Moses
trying to say when he calls it 'Goddess-ers'—a femi-
nine singular with a male plural? Or when he says 'Elohim created the adam in Their own image . . . male and
female They created them.' Somehow the adam, the
human being, is a 'him' and then a 'them'—a male and
female 'them.' "

"So if there's not two Gods, then *'God'* is *Goddess*,"
breathed Pam, her eyes alight. "*Goddess* created the
plural human—all the males and females in the world!
And it's right in plain sight! This makes *The Da Vinci
Code*—"

"Nope. You're still not there," Max said gently. He
remembered coming to the same conclusion, brimming
with the same epiphany, striding forcefully around
Agrippa's deck. "Because all the males and females in
the world are made in the image of Elohim. Since generation is a hallmark of women, the closest you can
come to putting the whole concept of Elohim into a
word would be a female singular with a male plural.
'Goddess-ers' is trying to describe something that is
male *and* female, singular *and* plural. It's God *and* Goddess *and* you *and* me, all at once. Everything in all its
aspects.

"When Moses met the burning bush, he thought he
met God. But by the time he'd been to the top of Mount
Sinai, he knew he'd met Elohim. And so he wrote,
'When Jehovah saw that he turned aside to look, Elohim called to him from the midst of the bush.' But later,
'Moses went up to Elohim, and *Jehovah* called to him
from the mountain.' He's very clear about it. Moses'

religion had just one God—nobody disputes that—but he gives his God two names, in the same situation. And one of those names is a plural. So Moses' God is One and Two at the same time.

"Now, that's all good for somebody like him, but how can we *puny humans* get any sort of handle on that? We can, of course, take the traditional route and say, 'God moves in mysterious ways. We can never understand it.' But you know what? We *can* understand it, because others have understood, because we're all created by Elohim, because there isn't anything else. So—what is the *reality* of The One That Is Two? What have we seen with our own eyes right here on Earth?"

"Hermaphrodites . . . ," Pam ventured.

"No, no, no. Way too literal. We're talking about something cosmic here."

"When you talk about cosmic," Pam said with a touch of impatience, "I've seen golden energy, I've seen asteroids come crashing down out of space. . . ."

"And you've seen metal filings show that there's an energy between the two poles of a magnet—a single magnet," Max said. "You've seen lightbulbs show that there's an energy between two ends of an electrical circuit—a single circuit. It is perfectly possible in this world to conceive of a single energy that connects the two ends of a single thing. And that is what Elohim is, ultimately. Goddess-ers is one thing that's two things that's one thing—that's neither female nor male, but both at the same time. It's all of humanity. It's the energy that connects all of humanity. It's the energy that *makes* all of humanity. It's Jehovah and it's us, and it's all the same. It's. All. The. Same. That's why anyone can utilize that power, *if they know it's there*. That's why magick works."

"You said that energy was gravity, or sex—not elec-tromagnetism or electricity."

"All one thing; that's what you have to wrap your mind around. Gravity, electromagnetism, love, sex, Elo-him, vodou—one thing that holds us together, seen by different observers. You'll have to admit, holding to-gether is the absolute minimum for Reality. You don't hold together, you got nothin'. But if you're of a religious persuasion, the absolute minimum for Reality is the Deity. So let's propose the radical idea that the Deity, far beyond the comfortable concept of an old man with a beard, is simply energy—a single omnipotent energy that creates two poles within itself, so it can flow. The flow holds the two poles together. The flow creates prog-ress, and Time. The flow creates Life, and all the indi-vidual lives, and it creates Jehovah. All within the single, eternal Elohim. All within the Universe, spreading out-ward from the Big Bang.

"So now we come to the answer to your question. Why does Establishing Reality mean Basic Relationship? Be-cause the very nature of *everything* is a relationship. Like a magnet, or a circuit, or heaven and earth: two halves equals one whole. And we can run with that a little. If it's your nature to be dual, but you're only one person, then it's your nature—human nature—to want to be part of a couple. By the time the energy gets all the way down to the human level, we're not built to be two things at once. We lock into one pole or the other, male or female. We take one of the two available options; there aren't any more; just two. And we end up feeling incomplete, walk-ing around as a single pole in search of another pole so we can get some energy flowing. That's how the world *actually works*."

"But it doesn't have to be just love, does it? Or sex?"

"Not at all. Love's a very satisfying version of it, but there's some sort of energy exchange in any relationship. That's why we have so many relationships—why there are so many asteroids. We like relating to other people; other people like relating to us. Only one or two of our many relationships might qualify as love, but that just makes love the prize."

"It sounds so very simple."

"It *is* simple. Agrippa kept saying it was simple; real artists have always said it's simple. I tried many ways of getting to it over the years, and they were mostly useful one way or another, but the ultimate reality really is simple. Everything comes from the single Elohim, which contains the multitudes. Unity is not male *or* female, heaven *or* earth. Unity is everything, and everything *in* Unity is connected. How else could it be Unity? So all magick is, really, is using the connections that already exist behind the masks, and the energy that we're a part of."

The garden was completely dark now, but for just one moment, Pam felt as if she saw all the connections, between her and everything else in the universe, as brilliant streams of light. She was radiating like the sun, and so was everything else. Incredible!

And then, inevitably, it all faded away. . . .

1 SERPENT

The crimson sun was floating low and heavy over New Jersey, in a sky threatening rain or even snow. On Manhattan's East Thirty-fifth Street, the light raked the roofs while the street below was gray and gloomy.

In his brownstone, Lawrence Breckenridge was striding past his solarium when a horrible pain exploded in his chest. Clutching at his breast he stumbled and fell to the tiles with a brutal crash. It occurred to him that this was a heart attack. It occurred to him that this was not supposed to happen to him. . . .

But then the pain grew warm, loosening its hold on him. He felt pleasure, raw body *pleasure*, and he thought that must be the way death feels, to get you to go with it. The orgasm to end all orgasms. And Aleksandra was standing over him—her mesmerizing face contorted in fury.

Max August is alive!

Breckenridge lay on the tiles, gasping like a fish out of water. She had never forced herself upon him this way before, and as good as it felt to have her near, her rage was unendurable. This was not the relationship he expected to have with her, Diabola or no.

"How?" he ground out, but a flash of impatient scarlet was her only answer. He focused on her. "You can destroy him!"

He lives in your world. You destroy him! Do not fail me!

The next moment she was gone. It took him ten minutes to get to his feet, feeling every one of his sixty-seven years. But as soon as he was ambulatory, he started making calls.

NOVEMBER 3 - 7:00 P.M. SURINAME TIME

1 SERPENT

Jackson Tower ran along an ancient track that circled the base of the valley. Finally free of other people, he was dressed now in a loose-fitting, pure white robe, marked with crimson symbols, and the golden chain symbolizing his membership in the Necklace swung side to side around his neck. It was much warmer here than it had been in Minnesota, but his heartbeat was slower to keep his body's temperature cooler.

As he ran, he immersed himself in the world of spirits that filled his new location. Some of the animal screams were familiar, some infinitely exotic. Flames leapt luridly along the western hills, while a swollen river roared down the valley floor. He had come upon three different native shamans, one of whom was far older than Yellow Beaver. The man must have roamed this valley when men first came to it; his calls were almost birdlike, completely unintelligible even for Tower, who registered intent rather than language. Tower would come back to him in the nights ahead. There was also a black man, a healer among the slaves, and something Tower could not define—the *idea* of a white man, but not the man himself—as if the man had lived in the spirit world but held himself apart from it. That, too, would be a fascinating subject in the future. But tonight, Tower ran to find a living man. The spirits were telling him he would find one.

And there he was. A middle-aged man, one of the locals, probably come for a look-see at the new foreign tenant. Standing to one side of the path, he raised a hand in greeting, though his face was so unexpressive that he could not reveal what he thought of this white man in a white robe. Jackson Tower raised his own hand in the evil-eye gesture. Midnight-blue power snapped like a jagged snake from between his outstretched fingers to the man's forehead. The man recoiled, dove twisting to the dirt. He came up in a roll clutching a knife, digging for his tormentor. Tower's face was eager, inhuman, his eyes staring the whole thousand yards straight through his attacker. He barely moved as the man lunged at him, screaming pain and hatred, the word for "witch" cut suddenly silent as the man's head exploded. Chunks of bone and brain burned blue arcs through the night as the body left its feet and somersaulted onto its back.

The chunks lay sizzling in the dirt, extinguishing one by one like stars at the end of days. Tower stared down at the headless corpse. The power had been so entrancing, the result so swift, that he remained motionless another two minutes, just drinking it in. The three shamans danced madly around and around the two of them, shrieking shock and awe. The ghostly river sent a stream of ghostly water to surge through the corpse. Tower watched.

Then he pointed his hand at the corpse, jerked the hand and jerked the corpse. It rose a few inches from the dirt, enough to get its hands underneath, and climbed slowly back to its feet. Tower turned peremptorily back toward the plantation house, and the dead man followed behind.

1 SERPENT

Max left Amba's car on the eastern side of the Suriname River and took the ferry across to Para. He had disguised himself again so even if the military, or anyone else, had his description, he wouldn't be spotted.

Since Amba, Kwasiba, and Adyuba, friendly and helpful as they were, had simply not known enough to pinpoint the FRC's base of operations in-country, Max had to find it on his own. Even with all the magickal tricks at his disposal, he couldn't do anything without some starting point—some "sourdough starter." But he had been to Para in '96, so he had a good idea of where to find what he needed. He seriously doubted that the city had changed much—not, at least, the parts he intended to visit.

As he walked up the Knuffeld from the ferry landing, he enjoyed the sight of the elegant white riverfront mansions built for the colonial Dutch, but he preferred the humid smells of food and flowers, sewage and human beings. Motorized vehicles drove on the British side of the road, but most of the traffic he encountered in the early evening was on foot. The middle class strolled along shopping—Amerindians, barefoot, carried huge baskets on their heads—vendors pushed their carts wherever they had room. Dogs ran among them all; back in the day there'd been three dogs for every person in Paramaribo and there was nothing to show that had changed. Workers in dusty trucks were coming in late from the fields, each man carrying a small cage holding a bird. The birds kept the men company during the day, Max knew. He gave himself a moment to wish he could adopt a pet sometime—but he knew that was impossible.

There was clearly no such thing as zoning. Thatched huts sat alongside one-story shacks on stilts and two-story wooden houses that wouldn't look out of place in Europe. Very few buildings were taller than three stories, so the skyline was less the buildings than the raggedy palm trees towering above them. Most houses had balconies on each floor; everything was painted white. It reminded Max a little of Savannah, Georgia: islands of colonial stability set against the tropical heat and lushness. But what made it very different from Savannah was the presence of pastel mosques among the churches, cathedrals, and temples.

Even as he registered the idea, the 'Isha call to prayer echoed over the crowd. It was 23 Shawwal for the followers of Abu al-Qasim Muhammad ibn 'Abd Allah ibn 'Abd al-Muttalib ibn Hashim. Yet another way to count time, and so, another reality.

Max stayed on the side streets, just outside the town center, drifting in and out of bars, of whorehouses, of sidewalk checkers games. The streets were wide and straight; the sidewalks were mostly covered, to provide shelter from the rains when they came. He would smile, and buy himself a drink (which he toyed with rather than end up dead drunk in the street), and listen. He never initiated any conversation on the subject that interested him, but now and again someone would say he had run into trouble in the jungle and Max would listen, slowly drawing out the story. People liked to talk with him. Soon the crowd they were in was laughing, gesticulating, having the best conversation of the night. It was Saturday night and the crowd was loose. Max lied when he had to. He was a tourist, he was a honey-mooner, he was an executive from a bauxite company. Little by little he put together a picture.

There appeared to be an area three hours southwest of the city that had been blocked off from the world. Roads were closed, traffic diverted; some people had met Surinamese guards and others had met foreigners, but everyone agreed the men at the roads were tough, no-nonsense pros. Max knew three firms in suburban Virginia alone where you could hire guys like that by the dozen, and he wondered who the FRC had used.

It reminded the old-timers of the coups they'd lived through, starting in 1980. They had no desire to go back to the days of the generals, but what could anyone do?

NOVEMBER 3 - 7:30 P.M. ST

1 SERPENT

Jackson Tower, sweating only slightly, led the headless man into his newly secured sanctum sanctorum, in the library of his mansion. It was a high-ceilinged, circular room, with books lining the walls on all sides. Two rolling ladders reached to the shadowy top shelves. Above them was a circular skylight, but the room's main illumination came from a curiously modeled oil lamp, strung from the skylight by a silver chain. Beside the wall farthest from the lamp stood the contents of his packing crate, now revealed as a large ceremonial drum, carved in an African style. The library floor had previously been covered with a priceless oriental rug, but the zombis stationed here for Omen, and now Tower, had moved all the furniture to another room, and taken the rug along with it. In its place, Tower had carefully drawn a magick circle on the polished hardwood. Unlike the conceptual circle Max had made of white stones in his San Francisco yard, this one followed the template laid down over centuries by those who sought congress with demons. Tower made certain not to touch its markings as he stepped across them into its confines, and orchestrated the dead man's steps to do the same.

The circle was nine feet in diameter, and specifically nine *feet* rather than three meters or any such. The ancient system of feet was based on the human foot; the metric system was purely scientific and had no place in human magick. Inside was a second circle eight feet in diameter, and in the space between the two were written the names of the gods Tower worshipped. At the north end of the circle was an altar, prepared with his magickal paraphernalia. Outside the circle to the west was a triangle, seven feet per side.

Tower moved to a spot before his altar and pointed at the floor. The corpse lay down on its back, its ragged neck oriented toward the circle's center. From the altar, Tower took a sword with precise Qabalistic markings etched the length of its steel blade. He wrapped both hands around its crystal handle and pointed it downward, suspending it over the dead man's breastbone. He spoke a short prayer in his sepulchral voice. He speared.

The body writhed in agony, thick red blood draining slowly from the wounds, as Tower carefully broke through the rib cage, opening the chest cavity. He was careful not to damage the heart because that was his prize. As soon as he could, he bent and cut the heart from its moorings. It was still beating, and more blood spilled across his hands as he reverently lifted it free. Some blood fell upon the floor, where it seemed to evaporate. Tower laid the heart on the altar. He licked the blood from his hands.

Tower let his own heartbeat slow to normal, and then at last he spoke in a sonorous drone, resonating with perfect, rigorous pitch, as he imposed his will on this world:

"Hear ye, and be ye ready, in whatever part of the Universe ye may be, to obey the Voice of Mighty Names! By these hidden Names shall ye discover the brightest magicks of this terrestrial realm and render the knowledge of them unto me!"

On all sides of the circle, shapeless, unhealthy forms began to cluster. A sound like the wind, but made of breathy mutterings, rose in volume. It was death or worse to step outside the circle now. The forms grew simultaneously more distinct and more united, melting into each other to form a lambent film of energy around the circle—which all at once exploded outward, away from the circle, to pass through the library walls. Tower looked upward through the skylight and saw the pale fire receding against the night sky. Then he bowed his head and dismissed the spirits he had summoned, as men had dictated for twelve millennia.

Now he waited.

1 SERPENT

Pam straightened her shoulders, then wandered into the kitchen of the sisters' house. A mélange of scents filled the air, with pots bubbling on the stove, fresh tropical fruit heaped in bowls. A wide-bladed fan in the ceiling whirled slowly but effectively, keeping the room from becoming too warm. "Hi, Adyuba," she said. "Can I help?"

"You can keep me company," said the youngest of the three sisters. "We will eat in fifteen minutes. Where's Max?"

"He's skipping dinner. And that's saying something because he predicted a great one. But he was anxious to get busy, and we slept a long time. He borrowed Amba's car to go to Paramaribo."

"You didn't go with him?"

"He's doing one of his listening tours, to see if he can pick up any information of what's coming, and women aren't allowed in some places he wants to go. He's been here before, of course, so he knows."

"And you approve of that?"

"Of course not."

The women nodded at each other. "Well, he's foolish on two levels, then," said Adyuba equably. "We're having a fantastic dinner that he will have never tasted before. In this kitchen, we mix all the cultures together to create new delights."

"Is that why you came up from your village? To create something new?"

"Surely. Most of us still live in the rain forest, but

more and more of us are coming to Para. Amba, Kwa-siba, and I come here because we know the old ways, and we want to go to 'university.'"

"In magick."

"Every culture has its own skills and knowledge. We learn from all. Since there are so many Hindustanis in Para, we call it 'Hindu Vodou.'"

"Then I hope to learn from you as well. I'm learning something new—a lot of something news—every day now." Pam took it upon herself to taste the contents of a bubbling pot. "Mmmm," she said, delighted. "It smells heavenly, but tastes even better than that."

Adyuba nodded. "It's *moksi meti*—rice and black beans stewed with chicken and Madame Janet, a hot, hot, hot yellow pepper. *Gember limonade* to drink. Ginger lemonade."

"Yum! And you're sure I can't do anything."

"Not a thing."

Pam turned her head to watch as a red-and-green parrot came to roost in the light from the window on the robot outside. He started preening his feathers.

"I hope you and Max have a chance to work together," Pam said to Adyuba. "He's very good, I think."

"Oh, yes. He and Lorelei fought a forest demon in Belize that no one else had survived. That was in . . . 2002."

"Who's Lorelei?"

"Another at his level."

"Like Sly and Rosa?"

"I don't know them."

Pam was remembering that Max had said he'd never found anyone else he could talk to the way he talked with her. "So," she asked, "are you learning everything in Para that you came for?"

"Oh, yes. But we still want to go to Holland—Europe. We want to experience medieval European magick; I am fascinated by gargoyles and alchemy. I wish I could have known Agrippa. We have a long way to go, but working with Max and you will be good for us."

"Not me," Pam said. "I'm just a *friend*. Adyuba, do you need to be special to be a . . ."

"Shaman. Healer. Medicine woman," the girl said.

"Not witch?"

"No, no!" Adyuba was shocked. "Witches are evil. I know some people don't think so but they're wrong."

Politics, Pam thought. *Even in magick.*

"Well, do you need to be special to be a shaman?"

"Yes, if by 'special' you mean that not everyone can do it. But there are still many people." Adyuba bent to taste the *moksi meti* for herself. She rolled it around in her mouth, then reached for some ketchup.

"How many people at Max's level are there in the world?" Pam asked.

"Not many," Adyuba answered. "Alchemy is the ulti-mate. It comes all the way from ancient Egypt."

"Does it now?"

"To become a master alchemist requires time."

"Max has Time."

"Max had *enough* time to get *more* time. That's what I want," said Adyuba, adding a pinch of lemongrass and lowering the heat.

"So do we all," Pam said. "How many are at *your* level?"

"In Suriname, you'll meet all we know tomorrow night. About thirty. We've invited everyone who can come to join in preparing the antidote. Your antidote, I believe."

"I guess so."

"Kwasiba checked while you slept. The ingredients you need have been marked not for sale, as Max expected. Mama Locha is rounding up more ingredients, from Central America, and tomorrow night—"

Her brains exploded against the bright wall.

NOVEMBER 3 - 7:45 P.M. ST

1 SERPENT

Max doubled over, a headache exploding.

NOVEMBER 3 - 8:40 P.M. ST

1 SERPENT

In the Sipalawini Valley, a black helicopter settled onto the landing pad one hundred yards from the mansion house. The blades slowly spun down, then Tilit climbed from the pilot's chair. He whistled, and from the big house, two zombis began to shamble his way. Usually he despised their slow pace, but when landing a helicopter it gave the blades time to stop so the creatures wouldn't get their heads cut off. Not that they'd notice right away.

When they arrived, he led them around to the passenger side and opened the door. Dr. Blackwell lay strapped in her seat, slack, unconscious. Tilit opened her seat belt and gestured descriptively to the nearest zombi; the creature picked her up as if she weighed nothing. Then Tilit led the way back across the lawn to the house.

He knew this house intimately, having been at Miller Omen's side while it was being remodeled, in preparation for Omen's reign as warlord and viceroy of the FRC. The interior was pure South American, with high ceilings and great fans to keep the air flowing—but the fans would shut off and Filtration Reuse Canisters would maintain safe air when the valley closed down. The floors and ceilings were exquisitely matched hardwoods. Rugs were woven in native fashion and never smaller than twenty by twenty. The walls were adobe, but adobe crafted by artisans; flat, with intricate filigree, and none of the semi-shapeless contours seen in poorer dwellings. Native art graced those walls but each piece was subtly spotlit. It was the home of someone who took the native culture and ran it through a great man's sensibilities. It was still hard on Tilit to think that Omen was dead, that someone else was occupying this house. But at least he had one of the killers.

Jackson Tower hurried forward, peering intently at Pamela Blackwell. His eyes were slits. "Finally," he said from far, far away.

Tilit typed briskly on his modified Super Speak & Spell, and the grotesque mechanical voice echoed his words. **NO AUGUST. DRUGGED GIRL. SHE HAD MASTER OMEN STONE**.

"Where is it?" Tower inquired.

Tilit pointed to himself. Tower said, "Give it to me," and Tilit readily complied. Having previously carried such a *stone* had saved him on Omen Key. Carrying another had gotten him past the witches' defenses. But he had never liked them. They had their uses but he was like his master in his preference for a good pistol.

His old master. He reached for the second *stone* in his jeans pocket but Tower said, "Keep it for now. The night is young."

The sorcerer gave Omen's *stone* a predatory glance before sliding it into a square pocket on his blood-stained white robe. "Do you have any idea where August is now?"

Tilit shook his head.

Tower nodded his. "Secure *her* in the slave chamber," he said, and started to turn away.

Tilit typed, **KILL HER. AVENGE MASTER OMEN**.

Tower turned back, his eyes deep and black. "No. She has value."

BAIT?

"And information. One way or the other, she'll connect me to August."

R U BETTER THAN HIM?

Tower placed his hand on Tilit's shoulder, and looked him straight in the eye. Tilit found it hard to return that gaze; it felt like sticking his hand into an open power line. Tower said, "Magick is said to have no cut-and-dried answers, but . . . yes, I am."

Tilit nodded, satisfied. He did not like another man in Master Omen's house, but as a warrior he had to admire Tower's strength of purpose. He could serve this man with confidence. He whistled to the zombis, watched their heads turn slowly around, and led them as they carried the woman into the back of the mansion.

With real satisfaction, Tower watched them leave. Tilit had the burden of enforced silence, but in all other respects he was a perfect servant. The man's skills in the real world balanced Tower's mystical skills. He had been wasted working for Omen, a man who only had power from a *stone*. But Tilit and Tower were a perfect Yin and Yáng, and the sorcerer looked forward to a long, fruitful, and *quiet* association.

He turned with his characteristic energy and hurried back to his sanctum sanctorum. He reentered the circle, lifted his bloody sword above the body, and intoned:

"Hear ye, and be ye ready, in whatever part of the Universe ye may be, to obey the Voice of Mighty Names! By these hidden Names shall ye protect this dwelling, reducing any search from without to nothingness and chaos!"

As before, a lambent film of energy formed like a bubble around the circle, then expanded with shapes swirling in it like oil on water. This time it filled the room and clung subtly to the ceiling, walls, and floor, even as he *saw* it spread throughout the mansion, until it had attached itself to every inch of it like a second skin. Any attempt to seek out Dr. Blackwell by the Code Red now would fail, and fail with no notice of failure. She would simply be unreachable for him.

Something stirred in Tower's mind—a hint of an idea that he'd heard of something similar in August's past. But he couldn't pin it down, and let it go. He dismissed the spirits and stepped carefully out of the circle, then strode to his bedroom and retrieved his secure satellite phone. He called Hanrahan to report his progress.

1 SERPENT

Rita Diamante walked among zombis, accompanied by Miller Omen's head merc, and thought, *Thank God the moon's not up.* She considered herself fearless, normally, but these creatures standing in silent rows reeked of death and decay, and she was a Caribbean girl even if she had lived her whole life in Miami. It had nothing to do with the coke and the weed in her system; she'd lived long enough to know what was true in that state and what wasn't. It was just part of her soul, which she didn't often consult.

She had finally arrived at their camp just ninety minutes before, after traveling westward from Omen's mansion. When she went back up to Paramaribo, the journey north would take about the same time as the journey south to his quarters, but right now it was the end of a long, long day, and she was only beginning her work. Omen had set this operation in motion, hired the mercs, and everything she saw told her he had done a good job of it. They said he was an egomaniac but she dealt with them all the time. She knew he knew his shit.

What she had to do now was acquaint herself with her new army in time to lead it, and acquaint herself with the facts on the ground. It was one thing to read a document on a plane, another to calculate exactly how it would all play out in real-time Suriname. Fortunately, she had all the drugs she needed to stay awake all night and all the following day, and the knowledge to use them. She wondered briefly what Omen had known about her kind of pharmaceuticals.

Knowledge of her troops was key to any strategy. The mercs Omen had hired for this job didn't concern her at all; you knew what you were getting there. But all these living dead people would make or break the war. They were just normal-sized people, and that concerned her; she'd expected hulks. And they stood at attention without the slightest movement, like statues.

"Make that one dance," she said to the head merc, whose name was Fontaine, and pointed at a bald man with a green head scarf.

"It doesn't work that way, *señorita*. I'm sorry. They have enough to do just walking."

That made her feel even more uneasy; it made the zombis even less like human beings. Rita pulled a crystal vial from her cleavage, unscrewed the top, and poured a little blow in her palm, sheltering it from the breeze. She stuck her hand up under the bald man's nose, held it there. The bastards were supposed to breathe every fifteen to twenty minutes. What would coke do to him?

But she got tired of that after ninety seconds and snorted the load herself.

Everywhere around her, the jungle valley she and the living dead inhabited rose to jungle mountains, and stars burned from the dead black sky above. Any animals of the night were far enough removed in the hills that their noises were lost, and the zombis were silent, so the only sound on this entire desolate parade ground was the sigh of the wind. The way it moved her hair at the edge of her vision was the only movement.

The satellite phone on her hip vibrated.

It was Hanrahan with an update, calling from the real world.

She very much liked the feel of that vibration.

1 SERPENT

Max yanked Amba's car sharply to the side of the road, a block from the sisters' house in Gberg, and went the rest of the way on foot, moving as fast as he could but alert for any trap. There was no sign of disturbance, but he was here because he knew there'd been one. There'd been no mistaking the *call*. He came to the house, calm and peaceful in the sporadic streetlights, and stepped through a mystical veil to disaster.

The area inside the illusion was a crime scene, with torn sod and blood the obvious marks of a battle. A parrot on the roof cried in unearthly distress. Max ran into the house and found Amba and Kwasiba sobbing over the body of Adyuba. Above them the bright wall was sprayed with gray brain and dark blood. They both looked up darkly when he entered but, seeing him, dissolved back into tears. Max did not see Pam but he couldn't go there first. He approached the sisters slowly, waited for Kwasiba to look at him again.

"What happened?" he asked gently but intently.

"A man," she said haltingly. "Very big. Completely silent. He came for your woman and Adyuba caught him. He cut her down."

"I think I know him. His name is Tilit. I'm very sorry, Kwasiba."

"Tilit will be the sorry one."

"Yes, he will." Max looked at the brains on the wall. "And Pam?" he asked.

"He took her. By the time Amba and I got here, he was tumbling her into his car. She was unconscious.

We tried to hex him but it did no good. He must have had a *stone*."

"He is a *witch*!" Kwasiba said venomously.

"Yes, he is, and he works for bigger witches who gave him his *stone*. Pam had one, too, but she doesn't know how to use it."

"How do you think the witch knew where to come?"

"The people he works for have strong magick. If they did sorcery to find our magick, they would have found you"—it was suddenly very clear—"and not me, because the three of you and Pam's *stone* would have registered as more intriguing than just me."

"We will find the man, and those who sent him."

"You and me both, Kwasiba. I assume you have contacts throughout the country."

"From Brasil to Venezuela. All the north coast. All will help find those who murdered Adyuba!"

"And I'll use everything I know as well. We will avenge her." He thought for a moment. "Who can you put me in contact with for a good rifle with a long-range scope, and supplies for a jungle trek? Including topo maps."

She thought, the idea of hitting back at Adyuba's killers percolating in her. "On this side of the river?"

"If possible."

"My friend Gert." She looked at her sister, and Amba nodded. "Gert."

"I need directions," Max said. "Now, when the ingredients for Pam's antidote arrive tomorrow, we can't work with them here. Where can we go?"

The answer to that one came more quickly. "Our people own a warehouse, down at the water."

Max said, "Give me those directions, too. I'm sorry, but you'll have to take Adyuba and go there now."

"We'll call our friends for tonight instead of tomorrow. They'll help us protect it."

"I'll be back by tomorrow evening. If I'm not, you know what to do."

"Where are you going, Max?"

"Out on point."

NOVEMBER 3 - 9:30 P.M. ST

1 SERPENT

The first thing Max did once he'd connected with Gert was drive south toward Zanderij, but he turned off the Kennedy Highway as soon as he saw the savanna. Hiding himself from satellite view, he drove onward, his headlights sweeping the deep darkness, until he spotted a grove of trees that felt right to him. Alchemical intuition. He pulled off the road and parked, then went and sat down in a spot that felt right, in among the trees.

He didn't need the rituals other magicians depended on; Agrippa had been adamant that what the magus needed was between his ears, and drawing circles was impractical for a man of action. Theoretically, Max could have done this work in the middle of Paramaribo, or Tokyo if he had to, but it was simpler to go with the flow as much as possible. Tonight, that meant immersing himself in the natural world of Suriname.

He sat calmly and let his mind expand to fill the area. He had no idea what was actually beyond the limits of his vision, which were nearby in a forest under a moonless sky, but it wasn't the actual forest he was interested in. He opened his mind and his heart to the spirits of the jungle, the ancient jungle that had stood on this land for so long that his own claim to Timelessness seemed laughable. People had hacked away at it over the centuries but it was essentially untouched, and there was no question about its having an identity all its own. It was that identity Max sought, and soon found.

In the infinite varieties of trees, ferns, orchids, herbs, mosses, algae, he could feel the fertile earth. He could hear the squeaks, the squawks, the snorts, the screams of the night prowlers. Closer to hand, he could hear the whine of the mosquitos, but the same energy that had protected him from sharks protected him from them. Something shifted in the underbrush and gave out a short hoot but kept its distance.

He sent his mind beyond those things. His consciousness expanded and expanded, merging with all before it—seeking to know it intimately, and announcing his presence to those who could feel it. It was not long at all before he was answered. From the corners of his eyes, even in the dark, he saw the elementals.

They came closer, curious, and it became possible for him to see them almost straight on. It would have been futile to look directly at them, but he could look just past them and keep them toward the front of his view. His mind encompassed them, and their collective mind encompassed him. In that meeting of the minds he asked them two things. First was Pam's whereabouts, as he radiated her image and her spirit for them. The elementals hadn't seen her, but in response to his desire they agreed to look for her. So then he asked them where the zombis were, and radiated everything he knew about them. This time the answer was immediate and definite; images of the hidden valley and the way there flooded his brain. The directions were for elementals, not men—shapes of energy flowing across the terrain, not roads. But he was used to deciphering their communications; he would be able to work it out. The elementals were certain that Pam was not to be found there, but it was his best hope while they spread their search across the land.

He thanked the little creatures and let his mind pull back. Then he stood up, got back in his car, and drove south.

NOVEMBER 3 - 10:00 P.M. ST

1 SERPENT

The moon had not yet risen, but away from the trees, in the savanna, the brilliant stars made the night dark gray instead of pitch black. Once he passed the airport at Zanderij he left the pavement for the dirt, but the roads, reddish in the starlight from their bauxite covering, were generally straight and there was only an occasional pickup headed the other way. The land was gently rolling, with occasional clusters of small trees, mostly the gnarled savanna cashew. If it had been daytime it would have been brutal out here, with no cover from the equatorial sun, but it was pleasant now and he had his window open. Air-conditioning was fine when needed, but he preferred his reality unfiltered. He'd had the radio tuned to Magic FM—yes, that was its name, 88.1 on your dial—but then he turned it off, to drive onward through the night in the silence of his thoughts.

Words came unbidden: *"Richard Kimble ponders his fate as he looks at the world for the last time. And sees only darkness. But in that darkness, fate moves its huge hand."* He knew those words because he, like much of 1960s America, had been glued to ABC on Tuesday nights at ten when *The Fugitive* had played out its 120 episodes. He'd been alive and sentient in 1963. No other thirty-five-year-old could say that.

That was the other thing he had never settled, internally—the other thing besides Val. He was very good at deflecting any specific references to dates. He could *be* a thirty-five-year-old with no trouble at all. But the cost was the inability to talk about life in the '50s, '60s, and much of the '70s. He knew so many cool things that he couldn't share. People who looked like him didn't know them; people who knew them didn't look like him. Oh, he could pretend he was a fan of old TV or whatever; it wasn't impossible to talk about David Janssen and the one-armed man. But he had to pretend, to act as if he'd caught a few episodes on late-night TV in the '80s or seen a random VHS tape (amazingly, the DVD collection of what had once been the highest-rated show of all time had only just come out). Seventy-two percent of America had watched the final episode in 1967. Any of those people who were still alive could relate—well, that was the word, wasn't it? *Relate.* He couldn't relate; he could only stand at one remove. Because of course if he got drunk or stoned or just said to hell with it, and told the truth about himself, he was screwed. Sure, he could move somewhere else, start over with new acquaintances. That's what he was going to be doing for the next centuries anyway. But he couldn't be careless with this gift he'd been given. It would be, on the one hand, dangerous, and on the other disrespectful. If that was the price of being Timeless, it was a small price to pay, but it *was* a price.

"Hey, aren't you Max August?" How he hated that question.

1 SERPENT

Pam came around slowly. At the very first edges of
consciousness, she thought she was back in Alta Bates
hospital, with a dart in her side, dying. But that was just
sense-association. Coming back further into this world,
she saw that she was laid out on a low, rude bed, in a
low, rude room with barred windows. Sitting across
from her in a straight-backed chair was a man in his
fifties fairly radiating energy—pretty much the exact
opposite of herself in every way.

She wanted to ask where she was, what had happened
to her, but she decided the man was going to tell her. So
she rubbed her eyes once, just once, and turned them
toward the man, quietly waiting. She didn't have to wait
long.

"Dr. Blackwell, my name is Jackson Tower," the
man said, in a voice unlike any she had ever heard.
"You are in a slave chamber. Masters in previous eras
kept their unwilling concubines here, to do with as
they wished, so it was built to be escape-proof, and
Miller Omen made improvements. Hope is an illusion
in this room." He turned a hand over. "But you needn't
fear for your virtue. I do not waste magickal power on
women."

Her eyes and her mouth grew small. What was this?

"I am the sorcerer of the . . . FRC, far superior to
your friend Max August," Tower assured her.

"Like hell you are!" she responded.

"Your scientific skepticism is useless here."

"It's *magickal* skepticism. I know Max August, and

he's been rolling up your Fucking Ridiculous Claptrap with ease."

Nothing disturbed Tower's inhuman gaze. "You also know of his plans for the future. But you know nothing of magick. You will tell me how August intends to deploy your zombi antidote."

"Well, I hope you're sorcerer enough to recognize the truth when you hear it," Pam said forcefully, "because I don't know. Max handled all that."

"I don't have to recognize truth. I have Tilit." He couldn't miss her reaction. "Ah, you remember Tilit."

"He killed over twenty helpless people," Pam said coldly.

"He'd have killed you if it weren't for me. And he *will* kill you if he doesn't like your answers. He needs me to ask the questions, but he's fully competent to hear your eager responses." Tower smiled, and watching his eyes her blood ran cold. "Tell me, Doctor—have you heard of waterboarding?"

1 SERPENT

Nancy lay sprawled on her cot, unable to move. She was bruised and bleeding. All she could do was cry, but each tear running along her temples bludgeoned her with memories of water. She couldn't even make her eyes focus when the door opened and the two men came in again.

They took her by the arms and got her upright. She could not stand so they dragged her just as they had before. They dragged her out of her cell, out of the building, and back to the dirt area. It was cool now, by Cuban standards. More waterboarding? But . . .

"Yes, Nancy, you told us everything," said the first man, close beside her left ear.

"It's really a testament that you held out as long as you did," said the second man, on her right.

"If things had gone differently, you might have gone far in the FRC."

"We salute you. Really."

They laid her down against a wire mesh wall. Her head lolled back as the mesh gave a little and she saw the sky, a spectacular Caribbean sky, star-spangled. Satellites moved swiftly across her vision. Mars was bright red.

The first man shot her through the temple.

"Perfectly legal," the second man said, with a sort of sob.

NOVEMBER 4, 2007 - MIDNIGHT SURINAME TIME

1 SERPENT

Jackson Tower strode from the slave chamber. The woman appeared to be telling the truth about her ignorance of the Code Red's plans, but Tilit had little else to do with his time, so he might as well continue her treatment while Tower pursued his special line of research. Making Tilit happy was a good bonding move.

The sorcerer returned to his sanctum, but this time he walked around the circle, to the large African drum. According to Franny Rupp's records in Ordinance, it had once belonged to August. When he'd first dropped off the Necklace's radar, on the night Agrippa and Drake died, he'd abandoned his house in the Berkeley Hills, and the Necklace had moved swiftly to obtain his possessions. Whoever had driven that operation—it was before Tower's time with the cabal—had had the good sense to realize that they might come in useful one day, to their sorcerer.

Tower pulled up a chair and sat before the drum. The hide-covered top came almost even with his chest, and he knew at once that it had been used for decoration more than music. But there was the faintest of fiery essences around it. Fire was not Tower's native element, but it was August's, and so he began to beat on the drum. He was seeking the spirits that impressed themselves on it. There might be many of them, going back to long-dead shamans of the tribe that made it, but somewhere in there would be August's.

However, he came to realize that he couldn't raise any of them. The drum demanded a rhythmic, surging beat, to dance around a campfire in the African night, and it was a beat Tower couldn't muster. Maybe it was the precisely regular rhythm of his heart, maybe he was used to the steady rhythm of the zombi drums, but he couldn't build the surge, the rhythm in the rhythm, no matter how hard he tried.

1 SERPENT

Max sat quietly inside his car, readying himself for what lay ahead. He'd finally reached the edge of the savanna and come to one of the wide, wild rivers that so clearly marked the change from open country to lush jungle. Crossing the river on a rickety wooden bridge, he'd driven another three kilometers, then pulled far off the road down a dusty track. Not for the first time, he thanked Elohim that it wasn't the rainy season.

Two klicks farther on, if his sources in Para had been correct, was a checkpoint, at a fork in the road. Drivers wanting to turn left were turned away by men dressed as security guards, carrying sidearms. If they bothered to explain, the guards said they were protecting a bauxite strike, but with or without an explanation, no one was driving up that road who wasn't invited. So Max sat in his car two klicks away and studied his topo map.

When he was certain he knew the terrain, he carefully folded the map and slipped it inside his shirt. He got out of his car, slathered black on his face and hands, strapped a fanny pack and canteen around his waist, and slid his pistol into his belt; this time *he* had a CZ-83, thanks to Gert. He slung his rifle over his shoulder and hefted his machete. There was starlight, he was used to working in the dark, and he could *feel* a good twenty yards ahead. If he needed to, he could use the fire in his fingers, or his *wipe*. He was set.

Finding the trail heading in the direction he wanted was not hard. People had lived in this jungle for centuries, and they all tended to value the same places.

Whatever was actually in the valley he sought, others had sought it before him. All he had to do was find what they'd considered the best way to get there. Around him, he felt larger forces shifting in the night, but they didn't worry him at all. Rather, they reinforced the golden glow he found in action.

The trail crossed the road and started uphill. Well after midnight, it was almost chilly by Surinamese standards, but the humidity soon had him sweating. It was hard to avoid tripping over the vines that ran through the forest like so many cables, but it was instinctive in him to keep his center of gravity flexible. He might stumble but he would rarely fall. And the trail proved to have been chosen by men smaller than he was, so he was continuously having to duck. Mosquitos sang around him but, as usual, didn't land. He hitched his rifle over his shoulder and thought, *This is timeless, too.*

So he moved along at a steady pace, prowling through the jungle like a lion, or, in Suriname, a jaguar. The spotted cat was the hunter in the night here, and in Indio legend, the sorcerer. So even though the jaguar was a sharper energy than the lion, it was not a tough fit for him at all. Max fell into the jaguar's muscular grace as he padded along, and into the jaguar's clear-eyed watchfulness as he *felt* his way through the night.

It was oh so sad that he had to act like a thirty-five-year-old, he thought, but on the other hand, he *was* a thirty-five-year-old. He had the body, the stamina, the reflexes, the whole package. He might have been this good if he hadn't stepped off the merry-go-round, because his family had always been a hearty breed; his uncle Ed, conveyor of carved lions, had still been going strong in his eighties. But since Max actually was thirty-five, there was no question about it. It was good to be young, and to know he'd be just as young tomorrow, and to climb a mountain like a jungle cat.

DECEMBER 31, 1985 - 3:30 P.M. PACIFIC STANDARD TIME

6 STAR

He and Val were in Sibley, a regional park in the East Bay hills made of small mounds and valleys, jumbled together at random. Twenty years before, San Francisco hippies had begun constructing labyrinths in the valleys, each its own work of art.

In the little valley with the largest labyrinth, the winter wind was forced between high, steep hills and blew at a steady forty miles an hour. Max could lean into it at a ridiculous angle and remain standing, but he was sitting now at the base of a hill, watching Val. She was before him, bundled up like himself, stepping onto the beginning of the path.

Unlike mazes, labyrinths have a single path from the outside to the center and back again, albeit one that twists back and forth beside itself. They've existed since ancient times to provide meditators with simple rhythmic exercise while the mind concentrates itself, homing in on its object just as the meditator homes in on the center. But walking the labyrinth in this gale and staying on the path was not at all simple now. Val welcomed that struggle. She did not want to meditate; she wanted

.to fill her mind with nothing but the physical. She did not want to think about midnight, when Corny would die.

Max sat and watched her, but his mind was otherwise engaged as well. *Tonight I go into my own labyrinth. Cornelius will die and all the responsibility falls on me. I think I'm ready. Hell, I was born ready.* His mouth grew tight. *I'd better be.*

Val rounded the first reversal. It was not at all easy to do, leaning into the wind first one way, then readjusting to the other. The tip of her tongue was sticking out, her dark hair surged around her face, a strand across her eyes. Max thought, *She'll be my responsibility after tonight. It'll be up to me to bring her along the final turns on her own path. Cornelius taught me how, so I won't fuck it up. I won't let either of them down. I won't let any of us down. I love her so much, and when she's Timeless, when we're Timeless together, forever . . .*

Val was halfway in, maneuvering a back-forth-back twist. She was working with more confidence now. Max thought, *She's a star. Cornelius saw it when she was raw, and he managed her to the heights. Her new manager will have it much easier, she's so good. And so is he. Cornelius picked him personally. But she's nervous. She's losing her best friend tonight, and tomorrow she has to be a star without him. It's a one-two punch.*

Val was approaching the center, taking turns with a certain insouciance. Max thought, *She'll be fine. She's a little more dogged than I am—she puts her head down and goes—and that's why she's behind me in alchemy. I'm more free-form. But she'll get there. She's smart and she's strong and she loves life. She's not going to let me get away from her.*

Val reached the center. She hunkered down to examine the gifts left by previous walkers—beads, photos under a shapely rock, coins. She took the streaming scarf from around her neck and pinned it under the photos and rock. She took a single bead for herself. She looked up at Max, sitting on the hill, and across the labyrinthine distance she held the bead in front of her lips and blew him a kiss. Max felt it hit home; his heart surged with love.

Later, they would drive back to Marin, and go about their separate businesses until they got together with Agrippa for his final night. The best Max could determine in the months and years and decades that came after, this was the last time he had ever really looked at the real Val, in the full flush of her life.

NOVEMBER 3, 2007 - 6:50 P.M. SURINAME TIME

1 SERPENT

"You're an asshole, you know that?" Pam was stalking back and forth across the sisters' room, rattling the pottery on the wooden shelves. Steam was about to burst out of her ears. "A-S-S-H—"

He said reasonably, "I'm going places you can't come, Pam."

"I can go anywhere you can go!" she snapped.

"Ordinarily, yes. But I'm going to whorehouses. I need to talk with long-haul truckers, to see if there's anything going on in the interior, and you find them in whorehouses."

"I can go to whorehouses."

"In Paramaribo, you'd stand out big-time." He grinned

at her. "Or make a fortune. But we don't want to stand out."

She didn't grin back. "I don't want to be left behind. You wouldn't do it when I had the dart in my side. Couldn't even chance a separate room. And now I'm supposed to be the cowgirl! You were just telling me about Elohim and duality! 'That's how the world *actually works*,' you said! 'It's *simple*,' you said! 'There has to be a circuit—' "

He went and stood in her path. She had to stop but she turned her face down to the side. He took her chin gently and tilted it back up.

"Pam," he said, his hazel eyes looking straight into her blues, "I'm not dumping you. I'm setting us up to take the fight to the FRC, together. You'll be there at the fun times. Guaranteed. And I did split up with you when I played the beer man at the fights. Stay here, have that great meal I predicted. You can already smell it, and it smells good. I wish I could stay with you—I want us to be together. But I need to catch those guys before they head upstairs. A man's gotta do—"

"You're an asshole," she said again . . . but no longer with any vehemence. "All right. Go. I've got the three witches to protect me. We'll get drunk and talk about you. Who needs you anyway?" She leaned forward just enough and gave him a kiss, pointedly on the cheek. Then she left the room.

And that was the last time he'd seen Pam. In the full flush of her life.

1 SERPENT

Gradually Max became aware of elementals in the jungle around him. He couldn't make them out at first, even from the edge of his vision, but he knew they were there. He stopped in the next clearing and waited for them to come forward.

Soon their small, stocky forms stood up, shadows in shadows. Logically, of course, they were not the same elementals he had spoken with before, to the north, but elementals are really just forms of their element, in this case the Earth. They're all connected through the Earth. And they reported to him exactly as if they were the same ones.

There was no sign of Pam.

They had sought her throughout Suriname and the surrounding countries, deep into the common rain forest, but had found nothing.

Which to Max meant one thing: whoever Tilit had taken her to had put a magickal shield around her. It was unnervingly similar to Val's utter disappearance, but he didn't believe the FRC would kill Pam while she could be a bargaining chip, before the zombi plan played. Beyond that, Max believed that the man he was now, as opposed to 1985, would *feel* it if her spirit were loosed, and he felt no such thing.

There was always hope that she'd be held at the bauxite mine, and he'd find her when he arrived. Moreover, he could ask the elementals to try again, look harder— which he did. They agreed because once you had their trust, they'd do whatever you asked. So they melted back into shadows, on their way, and he resumed his hike to the mine.

It would end up taking six hours to go four miles, and he used the time to send *calls* through the night to Pam. Now and again, having no success, he changed it up and sent *calls* through the veil to Val. He had no expectation of success there, but he would never give up on either of them.

NOVEMBER 3, 2007 - 11:45 P.M. EASTERN DAYLIGHT TIME

1 SERPENT

Snow was falling hard in Wheeling, driven by a hard north wind, but Lawrence Breckenridge stood enveloped by the copse of witch hazels on Dick Hanrahan's dark estate, reviewing his options. He was satisfied that he showed no signs of his encounter with Aleksandra, nor would he have expected to. No one had seen his true face in forty years, not even his old friend Dick Hanrahan.

The real question on his mind was how best to present their current situation. The continued existence of Max August, despite the best efforts of good men—and the Luchtmacht—was not at all favorable. Their plan depended to a large extent on nobody noticing, let alone interfering, yet August stayed in the middle of it. The Necklace held the balance of power, but Breckenridge could extrapolate from Aleksandra, downward to be sure, to imagine how much power a Code Red wielded. There was a real chance that this could all go wrong. And then Aleksandra would destroy him.

But Breckenridge couldn't admit to knowing Aleksandra for any reason, not least because Jackson Tower was the official Necklace sorcerer. If the others knew Breckenridge was in contact with a higher power, some might well be afraid of where they were headed. It was better to plan in silence for what might have to happen if Suriname failed, and in the meantime, lie. Fortunately, whatever he told the others would have one certain backer, since Dick Hanrahan and he went way, way back—to the University of Chicago, and Professor Leo Strauss.

In one of the oddest twists of history, Strauss had been a Jewish refugee from Nazi Germany who'd come to believe that the Nazis had been on the right track. Even the part about sending guys like him—or him, if he'd stuck around—to the gas chambers was fine with Strauss because it enabled the Nazis to create a state unified around themselves, which was what a ruling élite was supposed to do. And Leo Strauss believed in a ruling élite with all his philosopher's heart.

Strauss's ideology was simplicity itself: the ruling élite had to do—had to be able to do—whatever they thought best. They were the ones charged with preserving the state against all enemies, foreign and domestic, so they could not possibly be hamstrung by laws, ethics, morality, or the whining of the masses. Especially not the masses, who would be the first to whine if the rulers *didn't* preserve their sorry asses. The problem was, the masses liked to whine. They knew a little bit about what was going on and thought it mattered, and of course, this was worst in democracies. So Strauss decided that the second job of any ruling élite was to flat-out lie about what they were doing. This was dressed up with rationalizations, that the people couldn't really understand what a ruler had to do and didn't really want to understand, anyway, but in the end, it came to "feed them shit and keep them in the dark."

So the élite had to live a lie in public, a complete fabrication meant to look like truth—and to live like that, without whining themselves, they had to see lies as no better or worse than truth—so they could say whatever they had to say with complete conviction and an untroubled conscience. An untroubled conscience was, to the masses, the best sign of truth.

But Strauss had a third job for the ruling élite, as important as the first two. For better or for worse, the masses are always with us, and simply deceiving them and leaving them to their own devices wasn't enough for a functioning society. The rulers had to have their support. The simplest way to get this, Strauss taught, was through religion. While morality should mean nothing to the élite, it should mean everything to the masses. If there were universal rules about what was and what wasn't permissible under the Almighty God, the ruling élite would have a much easier time of it (so long as they pretended that they obeyed the rules, too). Without those rules branded on the hearts of men, men would seek freedom.

And still, once you had the masses all dressed up, you had to take them somewhere, or they'd get restless and slack off. "Such governance can only be established," Strauss wrote, "when men are united—and they can only be united against other people." So the final job of the ruling élite was to lie to their pious people about the terrible enemies who would come after them if the élite weren't there to protect them, and to create those enemies if need be.

Then you had a smoothly running state. The kind the Nazis could have had.

Since Strauss was living in America while he refined this philosophy, and teaching at a major university, he got to practice it by lying to outsiders, telling them with untroubled conscience about the sanctity of democracy. But when he found a student he felt he could trust, he brought him (or rarely her) into an inner circle, his élite, where he taught his truth, that "those who are fit to rule are those who realize there is no morality and that there is only one natural right—the right of the superior to rule over the inferior."

Lawrence Breckenridge and Richard Hanrahan had been among his top students.

The midnight bells were ringing from Saint Alphonsus, far away across the fields, as Lawrence Breckenridge went inside to rule.

NOVEMBER 4, 2007 - MIDNIGHT EDT

1 SERPENT

"This is our last scheduled meeting before we control Suriname.

"Let me reiterate where we, the Necklace, stand at this time, and where we will stand in the future. We control the United States, and through it, we exercise broad control over the allies of the United States. That gives us reach, but the fact of the matter is, our reach is not certain. There are still elements in the world that can and do act against our interests. We have marginalized them to a great degree, cowed them, and moved aggressively against them wherever possible. Since 9/11 we've gone quite a bit farther than some of you believed anyone could in a democracy, but we still don't proclaim our existence openly. Study after study has shown that the American people would recoil if we proclaimed our real agenda—they simply don't want what we want—but by gradually removing their options we force them to adjust. In the next election, they will look for change, and we have candidates in place for that, as well as other approaches. Whoever they rally around, we will continue as before.

"So we operate through others. It's not completely efficient, but even in the clusterfuck of Iraq, we secured our foothold in the center of the oil region. In Suriname, though, we write a new chapter in our history by controlling events directly. Tower and Diamante will deliver the country to Dekker, and we will become, overnight, a voting member of the United Nations and over forty other international organizations. Suriname is small but it is sovereign, and as Archimedes said, 'Give me a place to stand and I will move the whole world.'

"Now, there will undoubtedly be questions about how Dekker came to power, but they will be few. First, Suriname is not on the world-media beat. I guarantee you ninety-five out of any hundred people have no idea where it is. Second, satellite feeds from the area will accidentally go dark, and Internet cables will be accidentally cut, so no communications will escape until we're settled. Third, anyone who survives in the death zone—there are bound to be some—will be interrogated, and anyone who took a photo or otherwise poses a threat will be eliminated. Fourth, we will announce a virulent outbreak of bird flu and quarantine the borders. An unassailable authority on bird flu will lead the only study team allowed in, and he works for us. Fifth, we'll have police outside the embassy in Washington, the mission in New York, and the consulate in Miami, to identify troublemakers.

"In the end, if a tree falls in the rain forest and no one is there to document it, it didn't happen. Everything will be presented to the world as a glad-it's-not-me story in some out-of-the-way place no one can find on a map."

Diana Herring nodded. "I can guarantee that the story will get no bigger than that."

"Poor Miller," Carole van Dusen said. "Meridian will make a fortune on flu vaccine."

"What about bloggers?" demanded Franny Rupp.

"*Are* there any with ties to Suriname?" Herring laughed.

Michael Salinan chimed in. "The political response team is in place. We'll have authoritative announcements from our end concerning the bird flu before the East Coast rolls out of bed."

"Surinamese assets will be frozen worldwide until the crisis is past," van Dusen added. "The diplomats will have an incentive to keep quiet."

"All cargo going in will be frozen as well," said Franny Rupp.

"Excellent," Breckenridge said, nodding. "As always." On the four huge plasma screens, a colorful satellite map of northern South America appeared, centered on Suriname. "So once the flu fails to spread, the vague disturbance will blow over. And once it has . . . eighty percent of our country is rain forest. We can create vast armies of zombis in that unknown territory, and when the time is right we'll take Guyana to the west, to stamp out their corruption or some such. Only then will the Venezuelans know that we're coming for them. That will no doubt lead to open war, but with America rushing to the defense of tiny beleaguered Suriname against that well-known lunatic Chávez, no one will seriously oppose it. After that, Colombia will see the writing on the wall, and Panama is already ours. . . . The continent of South America will have a new sheriff in town, connected at last to the continent of North America. Make no mistake, we will have control of the entire Western Hemisphere before we're done. And all this because tiny Suriname gets our nose under the tent."

There was a smattering of applause from Michael Salinan, Diana Herring, and Hanrahan, looking especially eager. But van Dusen leaned forward. "Have we, then, disposed of the Code Red, and Dr. Blackwell?"

Breckenridge had been waiting patiently for that one, like an angler on a drowsy day. "Jackson Tower has captured Dr. Blackwell, Carole, and has insured in his mystical way that August can't track her. So we have our Code Red by the balls. If he tries to interfere he loses his woman. We are absolutely certain that August loves Blackwell, and he lost the last woman he loved, his wife, which has affected him ever since, so he is effectively neutralized."

"That's great news!" said Glendenning. "Great!"

"But," van Dusen persisted, " 'effectively neutralized' is not as good as 'dead.' "

"Actually, it's better," Breckenridge responded gently. "You may remember that the killing of sorcerers releases vast amounts of energy, which we would not control. As we go forward, Tower is certain he can finish him off at his leisure."

"He's a Code Red; he could surprise us."

"Not according to Tower, who has studied him thoroughly, and is torturing Blackwell for her information as we speak."

Hanrahan spoke up. "I don't know how Jackson does what he does—and I know everything else"—chuckles ran around the table, none of them wholehearted—"but I trust him. I think we all do. And everything I do know from on site and around the world agrees with what you're hearing now. Our plan is proceeding perfectly, and with the very capable Rita Diamante at his command, I believe Jackson has everything under control."

Breckenridge added, "We are the Necklace, and the Necklace has never failed. For two hundred and seventy years, the people who have made up this Inner Circle have never been known to be wrong. That is because those who bequeathed this power to us knew the structure of history, and history has shown that what the Necklace does, works. We *can be failed*, yes, but *we ourselves can never fail.*"

Carole van Dusen nodded slowly. Others joined her. It was the truth that they lived by.

Breckenridge said, "Iraq is a success for us at the end of the day, but Suriname will be a success from its moment of birth. In Max August, we face a formidable foe, a terrible foe, but we will succeed with him as well. If anything, he is an opportunity for us to test our skills and procedures, and correct any fault we find on our way to crushing him absolutely. What we learn will make us stronger going forward, and that, my friends, leads to more *success.*"

All around the table, the members continued to nod in agreement. Salinan gave a surprised Hanrahan a high five, which Hanrahan completed gingerly. There were no more objections.

The meeting broke up into small discussions, as ad hoc groups vetted their final plans for the days ahead. One by one the members were called into consultation with Breckenridge and Hanrahan to go over their parts in detail.

When the last of them had left, glowing with the excitement of imminent triumph, Hanrahan led his old friend Breckenridge around his mansion and adjusted the clocks, including a grandfather built for the entry room that towered twelve feet tall, with a gong calibrated to echo from the high ceiling. Daylight savings time had finally ended.

NOVEMBER 4 - 4:00 A.M. SURINAME TIME

1 SERPENT

In Suriname, there was no daylight savings time, so the night went on as before. Jackson Tower ran along the valley floor for the second time, and this time he was completing the circuit. The drum had given him nothing, so he pursued his meditations in his preferred manner.

Diamante would be going back to her Miami empire, and if she held up her end, she might well be rising in the ranks of the FRC. But having already risen, Tower decided he would have this estate transferred to him. He dearly loved the north woods and the endless water of the Great Lakes, but everyone needed a vacation hideaway, and everything he saw here fit him perfectly. Including the spirits of ancient men.

As he neared the mansion he saw a modern man, Tilit, standing in the moonlight by the shimmering swimming pool. Tower slowed, reluctant to stop, but compelled to do so. Tilit moved forward and set off the message he'd been waiting to deliver.

DOC SAY BAJAN VOODOO WOMAN SENDING SUPPLIES. PLANE COME LATE THIS AFTERNOON.

"You're certain?"

Tilit just looked at him. But added, **AUGUST WILL CHANGE IT. HE WILL KNOW DOC TALKED.**

"Of course, but I'll have the ambassador send Calderón to the airport anyway, to make him think we're stupid. Meanwhile, you go back to where you found the doctor and search for August. If you can't find him, bring me more of these local witches. I want to know what they're planning to do with the supplies."

NEED STONE AGAIN.

"I thought you didn't like them."

WITCHES ON GUARD NOW.

They all need my magick in the end, Tower thought with strong satisfaction. He dug Omen's *stone* from the pocket in his robe and handed it over. Tilit regarded it reverently for a moment, before sliding it into his pants pocket beside its smaller sister. Tower could only approve of such devotion, because he knew Tilit was transferring it to him.

1 SERPENT

Pam lay more dead than alive on her small cot in the slave chamber. The drowning sensation had been horrible, terrifying. She'd held out as long as she could, but it wasn't long; no one could hold out against waterboarding. And all the while, Tilit's watchful eyes had told her he didn't care about her as a woman one way or another. He'd even dressed her once he was done with her. She was glad of that, though it couldn't matter too much in the end. She was certain that they'd never catch Max, and at some point he would beat them—but she was just as certain that they wouldn't leave her alive for that.

She thought about giving in, giving up. But it was only a thought, not something she could actually do. If they were going to kill her, she would make them work at it. She'd already made them work by creating the zombi antidote, by teaming up with Max. She'd said she'd take whatever fate that brought her, and she'd meant it. She wished it hadn't been such a short ride, but she'd known exactly what she was doing when she'd bought the ticket.

Her gaze was dull, unfocused. It seemed that things were swimming at the edges of it . . . and suddenly, she remembered elementals. But when she tried to see them, looking to the side, she realized that it really was just the swimming of her vision. There were no real shapes there. And of course, as spirits of nature, they wouldn't be inside a room.

But rather than depress her, it reminded her of what

she'd learned on her wild ride with Max through the world of the supernatural. The world that included vodou, where you could *call* to other people with the magick in your mind. The world where magick was everywhere if you only knew how to see it.

The world of Artemis, Establishing Internal Power, self-sufficient, part of Elohim.

For most of yesterday, she had had Miller Omen's *stone* on her person. She had felt its buzz when she'd held it, felt it now and again throughout the day. What if she'd absorbed even a little of its power? What if she could use what was left of her strength to *call* to Max?

She'd said she wouldn't believe until she'd verified. Well, now was the time to try. She would need all that energy outside her, because she had so little left inside. But it was just a skill set, he had said. It could be done, he had said, and now she would have to do it.

She would *have* to do it.

NOVEMBER 4 - 6:30 A.M. ST

2 DEATH

When the sun came up, the Mayans ticked off a new day. In his mind, Max imagined he heard Pam asking him, "What's special about today?" in her cheerful, adventurous way. He saw her big blue eyes looking into his, her blond head cocked slightly, her quirky smile. And in his mind he answered her. *November fourth. Nothing special magickally, but a national holiday for those of us who went through Vietnam. It's Walter Cronkite's birthday. He spoke for CBS News, and everybody trusted Uncle Walter because there was no question he was telling us the truth. Famously, he went to Vietnam himself and reported accurately on what he found there, and that turned the tide of that war. Most people today have never seen anyone remotely like that on their TV.* He smiled at her image in his mind. *I can tell you about him, Pam. I can be real with you.*

The Mayan day is Two Death. Two Death means Encountering Yin—Encountering External Power. Yáng and Yin aren't exactly Internal and External Power, really, but that's close enough for government work. He laughed silently. *Yáng and Yin were another discussion entirely; just because he knew a larger picture, he didn't need to burden her with it. And shouldn't, at this stage of her journey. External Power. Like death, to us. Like the FRC to us, and us to them. But people don't die in greater numbers on a Death day, any more than they do on the Day of the Dead; otherwise, every anniversary would be a slaughterhouse. It's just to remind us that we're not all there is. I think a lot of people are going to die today, but it won't be the Mayans' fault. And a lot more are going to live—you definitely included, Pam.*

The asteroid today is Dione, the ruler of her realm. Yesterday, Artemis was on her own in the forest, but after a day that's all changed, as the forest becomes familiar. The asteroid Dione is at home in her domain. The trick is, she has no idea what's happening on the outside. And with that cheery thought, his mind turned savagely back on itself. *"Well, what else can you tell me?" you asked me. And I, the all-knowing, all-seeing, I said, "You'll get to know Artemis." Meaning, as it turned out, you'll be on your own and I'll have no idea where you are. So what the fuck do I know?* He shook his shoulders angrily, though never breaking stride. *I predicted a "fabulous meal." I put things together completely wrong. I can look out into the future and spot probabilities, but never certainties. So what good am I?*

But the influence of Dione, a chunk of rock ninety-one miles across, twice as far away as the sun, kept moving him away from that mood. No matter how fucked up he was, he knew in his heart that anyone else would have done worse. This *was* his realm and he *did* have skills others didn't. And those skills, whatever they were worth, were not telling him Pam was dead. He was as sure of that as he could be of anything. So his usual confidence returned to him. He had work to do.

Now that the dawn's light revealed it, he found himself in the midst of some spectacular nature. The jungle clustered thickly around him, almost solid on both sides of the trail, so he was walking through a gorgeous corridor, broken only occasionally by some huge green room opening off to one side. The light from above was filtered, water dripped from the jungle ceiling, and the air was quiet in the leaves. But in that stillness the birds began to waken and sing their strange carols. Bird life was extensive, so that soon the world had its own sound track. Darting, soaring streaks of vibrant color weren't sylphs, but Amazon parrots. A fat toucan eyed him alertly from behind its huge beak, and a sun bittern stood in a shimmering mountain lake spearing frogs with its sharp, pointed bill.

He could no longer see the elementals in the bright light. Instead, the surrounding trees spat out squirrel monkeys, lurching from branch to branch. Neither could he see the howler monkeys, but their roaring filled the air, a harsh bass track to the birds' lilting melodies. And at one juncture he came upon a yagarundi, a small, fierce feline on its way home from a good night's work.

How could he not love it in here?

And that thought didn't change, even when he came upon a trail alarm—the same type as the one on Omen Key. It was the first one he'd encountered all night, and he had to admire its placement, so far from the road. Anyone who tripped it here would have no chance of escaping back the way he'd come before the FRC came for him; he would simply disappear in the jungle.

Max knew how to circumvent it, but he didn't for a moment believe that one alarm was all there was this time. They knew about him now, and there were only a finite number of ways in, through the thick forest. So before he passed the mechanical alarm, he was looking hard for a second alert.

He spotted it five paces ahead—a sort of mojo bag. Mojo bags were a staple of African-American folk magic, found wherever slaves had been. Max knew the ones around New Orleans and the Caribbean very well, but this version was new to him. For one thing, the designs on the bag were more rectangular than their northern cousins, which he attributed to Dutch influence as opposed to the French or Spanish. But whoever had made it, his walking past the bag, which hung mostly concealed from a chicle tree, would not be good for his health—if he were unprotected.

He put a gravitational wall around it and passed it by.

Finally, half a klick farther on, he reached the top of the ridge. As he stepped out of the forest onto the barren hilltop, the sound of the howler monkeys was replaced by a new sound: drums, from the canyon below. Directly in front of him was a viewpoint; it was why the long trail led here and not somewhere else. But of course, if Max could view from there, he could be viewed *from* there, so he went a little farther on, to where the vegetation picked up again, and slid in amongst that. He worked his way to the cliff edge and looked down, just as a chunk of the edge gave way into the abyss. Max moved back and crouched very still before anyone looked up.

Below was a rough valley, nearly a mile long. Half that valley was filled with zombis, picked out against the dark valley floor by the rising sun. There had to be five thousand of them, standing in silent rows stretching into the distance, like some Walpurgisnacht Nuremberg rally. Max slipped his rifle off his shoulder and used its high-resolution scope to examine them closely. They were all wearing old clothes and new canisters strapped to their chests—canisters of sarin. *There's some Yin,* he thought grimly.

Other zombis, identically equipped, were being marched around at the front of the valley. They were in groups led by uniformed mercenaries, with each group following a different pattern of movement. As Max watched the patterns unfold, they seemed random, but they were clearly well practiced; the marching was robotic and somewhat ragged, but still reasonably coordinated to the sound of the drums. Soon enough, he realized what he was seeing. The zombis were having instructions embedded in their nearly dead brains—instructions on how to make their way through whatever area they were intended to attack. The zombis couldn't follow a map, and no merc would want to be leading them when the sarin was released. But they could be programmed to walk, say, one hundred yards straight ahead, then turn right thirty yards, then turn again. . . . This was how they would end up where the FRC wanted them when they released the gas.

At the front of the valley, parked alongside the narrow bauxite road running up from below, were dozens of large, covered transport trucks. As each group of zombis finished its maneuvers, its guiding merc spoke briefly with a woman making her way among the throngs. Max was surprised to realize he knew who she was, and then surprised at his surprise. Rita Diamante was well known in the Miami drug scene and Max made it his business to know about bad guys anywhere. He'd closed down the magically-hipped coke that went through South Beach like a category-5 hurricane in 1998. It had been Rita's drug operation but he'd been focused on the refiner, and so hadn't crossed paths with her. If he'd known about the FRC then, though, he'd have understood what her involvement meant. Like Miller Omen, she operated at a high level—they, and certainly others like them, were the go-to people the FRC utilized. This was supposed to have been Omen's operation; Rita must be his replacement.

All this went through Max's mind as he watched, unseen, while the sun rose in the southeast. Even at this height, the heat increased perceptibly moment by moment, and in the close quarters of the clifftop vegetation, sweat ran down his face.

Through his scope, he saw that Rita was on top of the world, fully in command. From what he knew of her Caribbean roots, he was willing to bet she'd been less enthusiastic when she'd first encountered five thousand zombis, but running ten to twenty hired guns was her everyday job, so the rest of it would have grown on her. The magnitude of it and the chance to kick ass for her masters combined to make that magicoke look like baking soda. She dreamed big dreams.

Through the scope it was easy to read her ruby lips, speaking to each merc in turn. "Three A.M.," she said. "Three A.M."

From this distance, from this height, a kill shot was a simple matter of mathematics—how far to aim above her head to drop the bullet into her chest, as the wind blew and the earth turned. But that wouldn't stop the zombis; he could never kill all the mercs; and those who survived would send some of their number onto this mountain to hunt him down. Meanwhile, some of the zombis began marching toward the trucks at the command of their handlers. They stopped when they reached them and the mercs gingerly relieved each of them of their sarin before the zombis climbed inside. More went in than seemed possible; they must be jammed in like sardines. As each truck was filled, the canvas at the back was tied firmly shut. There would be no ventilation, and it was already eighty degrees. But what did zombis care?

The trucks began to rumble onto the bauxite road and head down the hill.

There was one thing Max could do right now, and he did it. He bowed his head, letting the sweat drip off his nose, and *called* to Mama Locha, telling her everything he knew.

When he opened his eyes, a cloud of red dust marked the spot where half a dozen of the trucks had stood. At this rate they'd be rolling out for hours yet, and it would take them time to get back to the road. They were surely on their way to Para, where they couldn't arrive in less than five hours. It was seven now. They could be back by five this afternoon, then take another load in by ten tonight. The question was, where exactly were they going? He could never make his way down the exposed hillside to find out, but he could catch the trucks back at the road if he got there fast enough.

NOVEMBER 4 - 10:00 A.M. ST

2 DEATH

Max took the trail back down the mountain at a deliberate jog. Gravity and daylight made it faster than the climb up, but the vines and branches still slowed him, and the snakes were out in this time between too cold and too hot. He could do his gravity wall to keep most of them at bay, as with the sharks, but a twelve-foot bushmaster was too stupid to take a hint. He had to keep his head on a swivel.

The rain forest had become a rippling green tent, with beams of sunlight like spotlights shining down through the leaf cover above; it was like orienteering through an ecological Disneyland, and he appreciated the beauty of it even as he ran.

It took three hours to get back to the main road, after six coming up. Even a thirty-five-year-old man would be tired after that, and he was. Amba's car was parked just a few hundred feet farther on, in the tangle on the far side of the road, but that wasn't the mode of transportation he needed now.

He picked a spot near the road and hid himself among the trees there. A stream splashed and gurgled down from the mountain, and he used it to wash the black camouflage from his skin. Ten minutes went by. Birds sang, different tunes from the dawn crew. A capybara crossed the road with its supercilious expression. Otherwise, nothing moved.

Until a truck descended in low gear on the bauxite road. Soon it rumbled past, closed up tight like all the others, trailing a cloud of pink dust. Max stepped out and swung onto its crumpled rear bumper, then climbed quickly to the top. If there had been a single normal human inside the canvas, he doubted he'd have made it without being noticed, but there was no reaction now. It would not be a fun ride atop this truck, if for no other reason than the blasting heat from the unshaded sun, but this, he reflected ruefully, was his ticket to ride. He changed gravity around himself to diffuse the sunlight and make sure he stayed on the roof for the duration, so he could take advantage of the time to catch up on his sleep.

Max remembered the last time he'd slept, in Pam's arms. Then he went out like a light.

NOVEMBER 4 – 3:00 P.M. ST

2 DEATH

The first hint of trade winds woke him. He found the temperature had cooled enough to make the day bearable. There was now a fair amount of traffic around him, but since he was atop a large truck, no other driver could see him. He cautiously poked his head up and found himself rumbling through the outskirts of Para. Soon, they drove onto an airfield, which could only be the Luchtmacht base at Zorg en Hoop, on the outskirts of the city. Coming out past them were two similar trucks, jouncing and bouncing enough to make clear they were empty. Well, he already knew the Luchtmacht was connected to the FRC. But what a brilliant place to stash the zombis.

The airbase had three large hangars. The first one they passed was for commercial craft; he saw several Cessnas and a helicopter. The second was military; parked in the open doorway was an Aviocar Max recognized as the one that had shot him down. He was pleased to see it needed extensive repairs. But as the truck continued across the expanse to the hangar farthest from the entrance, half hidden by a maintenance shed, he saw hundreds of soldiers milling around the base. Were live men involved in the FRC plot? That didn't seem likely.

The truck finally pulled to a halt before the last hangar and the driver got down, stretching hugely. A man dressed in a Luchtmacht uniform came out of the human-sized door in the front of the hangar and checked the driver's credentials, then rumbled open the main hangar door. The truck lumbered inside and the door banged shut behind it.

In the large, shadowed, but still stifling interior, zombis stood in the same neat rows Max had seen in the valley at dawn, only now they were pressed one against the other, maintaining their sardine approach. It was the only way to fit them all inside. But there were nowhere near the numbers Max had seen before. Clearly, this was only one place they were being kept as the FRC prepared to attack the area from all sides. The stench was intense.

The back of his truck was opened and drums began,

played much more softly than any time Max had heard them previously. That meant not everyone on this base was involved in the plot. Max wasn't naïve but he was glad the whole military wasn't corrupt; he was still regular Army in that regard.

The zombis stepped down from the truck to the beat of the drums, and were herded over to the mass of their fellows. They weren't programmed for this maneuver, but why would they be? Once the newcomers were in position, the drums stopped.

The mercs and airmen handling the hangar left the zombis to themselves, and went off to a coffee room. Max gave them one minute, slipped his CZ-83 into his hand, and climbed down from the truck.

As he started to lope across the hangar to the exit door, there was a movement to his left. He spun, prepared to make a fight of it, and saw a platoon of zombis coming right at him. Some final synapse firing had them moving without the drumbeat, in the wrong place. There was no place for him to hide, but thank God they weren't carrying sarin! That would have been no fun whatsoever.

He had no antidote, so he'd have to take them down magickally, silently—or try to. These soulless brutes would be resistant to power because they responded to so little, so slowly. But as he concentrated, forcing his building energy up and out toward his hands, the dead eyes swept over him . . .

. . . and marched past. Preprogrammed.

• • •

Outside, the base remained calm. With its dual status as a civilian airport, Zorg en Hoop made it easy for a man who looked like just another bush pilot to move around freely. That man strode confidently into the first hangar, where the civilian craft were based, and struck up a conversation in Sranan Tongo with an old man washing down a red Piper Cub.

"What's with all the damn soldiers?"

"There's some ceremony tomorrow. They've been coming in for two days." The old man spat in the bucket he was using to wash with. "Must be a general involved. Must be two. Because that could be the entire damn army out there."

All the better to be taken out with one blow, thought Max.

He chatted a few more minutes, then wandered over to inspect the three helicopters sitting on the tarmac. Two looked well washed, while the black one was covered in dust, but he ran his hands along the flanks of all of them. When he left again after five minutes, walking toward the base exit, he waved hello at men and women who sometimes gave him an uncertain glance in return, but mostly waved back. Then he went out the gate, looked around and saw the third hangar's door open again. His truck, empty, juddered out, and drove past him back toward the road leading south. Another truck was lumbering in, and the drivers waved at each other. It was a happy day.

NOVEMBER 4 - 3:30 P.M. ST

2 DEATH

Rita took another hit of blow and slid out of the truck, into the vastness of the hangar. Dope fumes followed her. She went back to survey the area around the building from a slot in the closed overhead door. It all appeared crystalline to her vision, bright and sharp as knives. If there were any flaw to what she was seeing, it would have been obvious, and there was none. She had to hand it to Omen. Staging the coup from the military's own base, with most of the military under her hand—she had to love it. And the base was right up close to the main target, making the strike unbelievably easy and sudden. The only possible flaw was a hitch in the trade winds and the direction they blew, but everyone without exception assured her that wouldn't happen, and they were in just as much danger as she was. She believed them, but she'd wear a hazmat suit when the time came anyway.

She looked around for Mérides. He was standing by a door with a combination padlock on it, and he nodded to confirm her thought. She went over to him and made sure no one else saw what she punched on the lock per FRC instructions. The door opened and she and Mérides went into the office Omen had set up. Against one wall was a communications console from which the attack could be coordinated. Above it on the wall were topo maps, of the area, of the country, with clear plastic covers so arrows could be drawn over them. The room was slightly dusty, slightly stale, unopened since Omen's last visit one week before. The maps indicated his final thoughts.

She stepped closer, as something in the curves of the channels in the Suriname River caught her eye. She cocked her head, then shook it. "Tell me what you think of this," she said to Mérides.

He came and looked where her red-tipped fingernail was pointing. He nodded. "The tide will fuck that up."

"Yeah," she said. "At last I got one up on Miller Omen. It takes Miami folk to know water. Let's see what else we need to adjust before I lock this down for dinner."

2 DEATH

Max caught a taxi to Para center. He had to get back to
Gberg and make certain everything was in place for tonight, and see if there were any news of Pam.

Even back in an urban environment, nature in Suriname was overwhelming. The short run into town passed
uncountable varieties of flowers, plus banana trees, apple trees, orange, lime, coconut, and Brazil nut trees. If
it hadn't been deliberately cut back, nature would have
filled every vacuum. One brick building they passed
had no roof atop its two stories, but the entire open interior was filled with trees, their leafy branches spilling
out and down the outside walls.

But where nature was nonexistent, where streets and
buildings held sway, crowds of people shopped and
wandered. The cab was driving down Heeren Straat,
past a YWCA that could have come directly from New
England, a synagogue that looked like a mansion, and
the Ahmadiyya Anjuman Isha'at Islam Mosque with its
towering minarets. It was late Sunday afternoon, the
Christians were kicking back, and the Moslems and
Hindus and Jews were enjoying the slackened pace. The
sheer mixture of people, with different clothes and different skins, struck Max forcibly, pleasurably. He'd forgotten how much he loved people until Pam had brought
it back, and he could savor it now. The numbers around
him, though dense, were nothing compared to Tokyo or
Manhattan, but the crowds of Paramaribo seemed more
alive than any that he'd ever seen before. And if things

went wrong, they would all—all—be dead in eleven hours.

From the mosque came the call to Asr prayers.

When the taxi dropped him off beside a statue of Gandhi, he made certain he wasn't being followed, by walking into the tide of humanity so that anyone tailing him "against the flow" would be easy to spot. The name for it was "surveillance detection run," or "SDR," and it had always struck him as a pretentious name for such a commonsense maneuver, but what the hell.

When he'd circled back to the ferry terminal without a nibble, he got on and took an aisle seat where he could keep an eye on people boarding after him. No one who did could plausibly have been an agent, of the FRC or the Surinamese police; they were all too old, too poor, too familial. Then the ferry pushed back and was on its way. Magic FM started blasting from the speakers.

NOVEMBER 4 - 4:30 P.M. ST

2 DEATH

The cargo plane coming from Barbados bounced hard on the tarmac at Zanderij, then skipped onward almost to the end of the runway before its brakes could fully take hold. It was obviously heavily laden.

It slowly turned and rumbled back toward the cargo bay, and the waiting customs agent . . . and the waiting men with merc faces.

The plane came to a halt, and after a minute the cargo door was released, revealing six large crates and a selection of other containers. The two mercs climbed up inside and began opening everything. The customs agents watched unhappily from the sidelines, and thought about the story they'd have for Sportie the next time they got in touch.

NOVEMBER 4 - 5:00 P.M. ST

2 DEATH

In Gberg, Tilit was prowling, as he'd been doing since mid-morning. Today was very different from yesterday. Then, he could move untouched through the people, but today, they all paid attention to a big white man. Not to him specifically; he had moved too quickly when he stole the woman, and the other two never got a good look at him. But they got *a* look, so he was fully aware that people were conscious of men that fit his general description. It ruined the pleasure he usually felt.

Just in case, he ran SDRs every so often, in case the witches had decided to *tail* people like him. But he never uncovered a soul. In addition, his *stones* were silent. Either there was no magick to be had, or it had all gone elsewhere. He suspected "elsewhere" because he had found the witches' house last night with one *stone*, but two were showing him nothing now. Based on that assumption, he was working his way away from their original neighborhood in a spiral search pattern, driving mostly, moving ever outward on the dusty streets. He was now out nearly to Speeringhoek. Once there, he would begin a spiral back inward along other streets. He could do this all day and all night if he had to—

though Mr. Tower had told him to be back at the mansion by 2 A.M. without fail.

The blonde had told him that the Code Red had gone looking for the location of the zombis. It was even money he was now in the southland, but if so, there were mercs there, all skilled and experienced. The other side of even money put the Code Red closer to home, looking for his woman. If that proved to be the case, Tilit intended to find him and kill him, Code Red or no Code Red. He owed nothing less to the Squire.

NOVEMBER 4 - 5:15 P.M. ST

....

2 DEATH

Max ran another SDR after departing the bus in Geertruidenberg, then took a roundabout route through side streets and alleyways toward the wharf. As he neared the spot where the sisters had told him they'd be set up, he *felt* as far as he could in all directions. It was only when he was certain no magician, no punk with a *stone*, no one of any kind who could compromise the evening's events was nearby, that he walked slowly across the final street and knocked briskly on the closed front doors. He didn't need to identify himself; the women inside would do that. In mere seconds, the door opened and he slipped inside. There were people on the street, especially down around the Chinese grocery, but none of them gave him a second look.

The warehouse was a large, drafty old building, weathered by years of tropical heat and rain. There were a number of gaps in the boarded sides, but Max didn't have to ask to know that no one could see in through them. At one side of the room lay a shroud. There had been no chance to bury Adyuba, and now, after nearly a day in the heat, the body radiated a distinct odor, mixed with spice-smells to disguise it. But no one present gave it any notice. What had to be, had to be.

Nearly three dozen men and women were standing or sitting in small groups, talking, drinking, commiserating with the sisters. Most were Maroons but there were also a few Indios, a few Creoles, a few Hindus, a few Javanese. The murder of Adyuba had run like lightning through the community. Most of the men wore jeans and hats, but a few wore thin cloth robes and hats. The women's garb was more varied by ethnicity: the Maroons wore dresses of intricate, clever patterns, the Creoles wore simple, striking patterns, and the Javanese wore bright solids. All wore straw hats or head scarves, with the Creole scarves wrapped like old-style nurses' caps. The room had the look and feel of a wake, with all the uplift of a good one, but there was a tension underneath it, concern about the threat looming over them.

Dividing the various groups were long wooden picnic tables, where the work would be done.

"It looks perfect, Amba," Max said. "How are you doing?"

"Well enough." The girl was solemn now, as if her vitality had drained with her sister's blood, but she was focused.

"And Kwasiba?"

"Well enough."

"No sign of Mama Locha?" Max asked.

"No. What about Pamela?"

"Nothing. I did find the zombis—and I left your car at the edge of the rain forest."

"That is the least of my worries," she said softly but without drama. "A greater one is, they're watching the airports."

"For our friends?"

"I don't know who else it would be."

"Well, Mama's the best at living off the grid. All we can do is give her time." He looked around the room. "Who are your friends, Amba?"

"I'll introduce you. And more will be coming as evening falls. Then you can bring us all up to date."

NOVEMBER 4 - 6:15 P.M. ST

2 DEATH

As the sun sank low and the Sunday evening church bells began to peal over the call to the Maghrib prayers, a spectacular moving van, painted with hippie sunbursts and melting flowers, trundled down the street toward the wharf. Max first became aware of it when he heard Mama Locha *call* to him, telling him to open the warehouse doors.

With the truck safely inside and the doors closed behind it, the rather piratical-looking driver shut off the engine and slid out, grinning. It was so much like the arrival at the hangar in Zorg en Hoop that Max reflexively *felt* the van's roof (and found no one lurking there). Meanwhile, several of the shamans greeted the driver as part of their network, as he went around, threw the lever, and rolled up the truck's back door. Inside were Mama and her eight priestesses, the same ones who'd rowed to Omen Key less than forty-eight hours before. And a dozen large crates.

"Worried about us?" Mama asked Max, Amba, and Kwasiba.

"Not you," said Max. "But the supplies . . ."

"They are watching the airports," Kwasiba blurted.

"And they would have caught us if they hadn't shot down this boy and his girl yesterday. Once I heard that, I decided I'd have to go back to the smuggling ways. Then Max *called* before dawn and said we needed to double the amount of material we were bringing. So in the end, we flew out by mid-morning and went to Guyana—a hellhole if ever there was one—so we could come in from the west, not the north. We landed in a jungle airstrip that my old friend Henrik, here, uses regularly, and he brought us the rest of the way. It took a little longer than we figured, but here we are."

"You're fantastic, Mama," said Amba, hugging her. Mama hugged her back.

"I brought everything you asked for, and more," said the mambo. "When mixing poultices, it pays to have extra. I've got all the makings for the smoke bombs, and I brought extra radios. I didn't know exactly how many people you'd have here."

"Thank you, Mama," Max said fervently. "I knew I could count on you."

She nodded her head at him, but she was anxious to turn to the Maroon sisters. "I'm so sorry to hear about Adyuba," she told them, beginning an intense conversation with her old friends. In the same way Pam had admired Max's ability to talk with anyone, he admired Mama's skillful movement of the talk to happier times.

Max drifted over to Henrik. "I like your van, man, but it's so vibrant you could see it from space," he said.

"Ah," said Henrik, "that's just it. First, what smuggler would use such a distinctive vehicle? And second, I rent it out regularly to visiting eco-freaks, so it shows up many places and often with tourists inside. You can set up cots, a stove, and pay me half what you'd give for a Volkswagen van. It has long since been considered part of the landscape here."

"Well, in any event, it worked."

Max gave the conversation between Mama and her old friends ten minutes to run its course, then touched Kwasiba gently on the arm. "Call them to order, will you? We need to get started."

Kwasiba raised her arms and called out in Sranan Tongo, to encompass the entire group. There were now over forty of them. "Please, everyone, listen to my *friend* Max."

"*Dames en heren,*" Max said, "in less than nine hours, an army of zombis carrying the deadliest nerve gas known to man is going to attack Paramaribo. I believe they intend to kill everyone in the city and its environs." He paused to let them react among themselves, before continuing. "The choice of three o'clock on a Sunday night/Monday morning catches everyone who's come back to the city from a weekend out, and everyone who'll be going to the country to work a few hours later. In other words, they've chosen the time when their kill ratio will be at its peak." The reaction this time was more aggressive.

"Fortunately," Max continued, "we have all we need to stop that plan in its tracks. We can bring the zombis out of their stupor and disrupt their programming, so that they don't set off the gas. To do that, we have to prepare the antidote and prepare the means of delivering it, and that's going to take hard work on everyone's part. Then we have to deliver it, which will be even harder. If anyone feels this is more than they signed up for, please speak up now."

A stooped but almost electrically alert man in the back stepped forward. "How do we make this antidote?" he asked in a cracked staccato voice.

"I will show you," Max said. Someone had left a piece of yellow chalk on a cross beam along one side of the warehouse. He picked it up and began to inscribe Pam's formula on the wall.

He wished it were she doing the writing.

Something began nagging at him, but he couldn't pin it down.

NOVEMBER 4 - 7:00 P.M. ST

2 DEATH

Rita Diamante entered the home of E. Emsley van Wilgen, the president of Suriname, as the friend of Wim Dekker, chairman of the country's one major television network. Also present was the American ambassador, Carlton E. Hughes. Dekker was a longtime supporter of the president and was often invited for a convivial supper; his goodwill was essential for government survival. He was also the FRC's man, and twelve hours from now he would become the new president. No one was gauche enough to mention this to van Wilgen.

The president's home was called the People's Palace. It was a three-story white building that actually resembled Richard Hanrahan's mansion in Wheeling quite a bit. It commanded a flat, well-kept lawn at the south end of a gracious park beside the river, which was called the Palmentuin. A low, dark-green hedge surrounded it, and streets ran in front and in back. Anyone could approach the president in his palace but he'd have quite a distance to cover and the Personal Guard detail was alert. It was much easier to come as a date.

The foursome ate on the screened veranda since the night had not yet begun to cool. It was surreal to Rita, but Omen had scheduled it (with himself as Dekker's business associate), and she continued to appreciate the man's balls. She would really have liked to have fucked him. Everything was now in place except for the last truckloads of zombis, arriving in three hours, so she could either sit in a small room on the air base and go stir-crazy, or she could shower and dress up and eat sea bass with the man she was about to kill. Like Omen, she liked the second way better.

In the soft candlelight, showered and made-up, Rita's angular features were intriguing, and both the president and Dekker were definitely intrigued. She herself had no interest in Dekker; once she delivered the country to him she was going back to Miami and get a promotion in the FRC. Her focus was President van Wilgen. She had killed men before, but that had usually been in some sort of war, her soldiers against theirs. Six times she had killed face-to-face. She was convinced that the man knew nothing of the menace sitting next to him. She let van Wilgen fondle her knee.

The only cloud on her horizon was Max August. They still didn't know where he was. But she put her faith in Jackson Tower on the one hand, and her army on the other, and led the president's hand a little higher. She did enjoy being a girl.

2 DEATH

Pam got up unsteadily. She'd been *calling* all day long, with no apparent result, and she was tired and weak and hungry. But she would not give up. She'd had to give up with her head wrapped in a sodden blanket, but she wasn't facing death now—just weariness and weakness. She would not give up. The *call* had become automatic for her, pulsing away in the depths of her mind like the zombis' drums, or the Mayan march of time. The longer she did it, the less alien it became. She began to walk around the aptly named slave chamber, moving to the rhythm of the *call*.

She thought of the stories she'd heard, just in passing, about sorcerers' apprentices. They must be the same for alchemists' apprentices; they all had to undergo some test. No doubt those tests were magickal in nature, but nobody gets the secrets without work. What good would the secrets be if they were just handed out like candy? Max said they were simple, but *seeing* what was simple wasn't simple at all. Well, she was no medieval novice undergoing a secret rite—she was just a twenty-first-century doctor focusing her mind. But she wasn't going to give up, however hard the work could be. The *call* kept sounding in the back of her mind, and she straightened her weary spine.

She could imagine the Dutch rancher with his slaves. There'd be a woman he fancied, or maybe more than one. He'd bring them into his house for easy access. This room was small and secure, but roomy enough for an occupant to make a home of it, if that was what was wanted. There was a toilet and sink in one corner, a bed in the other—no privacy between. The windows showed the world outside through heavy bars. The bars were set back a little, so once the windows might even have been openable, to let in cool air during the heavy summer, but they weren't openable now. They were some sort of clear plastic, unbreakable, that wouldn't allow a suicidal or vengeful prisoner a chance at broken glass. And the door looked like wood but had clanged when closed. The women here were complete prisoners.

But she could have been a prisoner when Ricky Holcomb attacked her in his empty house, and she'd kicked him in the balls.

She would not give up. She'd *called* to Max in the darkness, on whatever she could imagine as *the vibe*, for hours, and there'd been no response. Maybe there was no way for her to succeed; she wasn't even an alchemist's apprentice, let alone an alchemist herself. She'd touched a *stone* for half a day—less, really, because she'd been out of her clothes and in bed with Max for a chunk of it. But just as power was power, not good or bad, maybe she'd absorbed *some* power with that much contact. She didn't know. Max and Tower both believed magick existed; she believed it, too. She'd seen it. But maybe magick had no cut-and-dried answers. Maybe it worked at one time and not at another; maybe it worked for some people and not for others. Maybe maybe maybe.

She didn't know anymore. But it was all she had now. So she went back to the bed, put her back against the wall, and closed her eyes. She was exhausted, but she visualized her *call* going out through the deep black ether and arriving in Max's mind. She sent that *call* along that long, arcing path, again and again and again.

She would not give up.

2 DEATH

In the warehouse, a joyous celebration was taking place. Amba and Kwasiba's friends, seated at the long picnic tables, were working hard at preparing the antidote, and they were singing at the tops of their voices, having a wonderful time. Like the light that did not escape through the cracks in the walls, the sound was inaudible outside, but what was going on in this warehouse was still one of the most surreal sights Max had seen in a life that had seen a few. This was no part of a wake; this, as Kwasiba explained, was just what Maroons did.

"We love music," she said, that love seemingly helping her rise from her melancholy over her sister's death. "As soon as we're old enough to carry a tune, we're encouraged to create songs from our thoughts. Others hear and join in, and the best ones sweep through the entire village. And out of those songs comes our love of ceremonies. Getting people together, to work together, is not a problem for us. What you see before you is Maroon in every way. This is how we honor Adyuba."

"And when we have vanquished these witches," Amba added, her voice not quite singing but lilting nonetheless, "we will bury Adyuba with even *more* song and joy."

"I'll be right there," Max said. "Right there. You won't want my singing—but I will dance for her."

2 DEATH

Rita Diamante arrived at Zorg en Hoop, somewhat less satisfied with life. The after-dinner brandy had been surprisingly ordinary, and the cigars, which smelled extraordinary, were for men only. She'd been stuck with the second-hand smoke until finally Wim Dekker announced, regretfully, that he had to get going downcountry, and Carlton Hughes said he would be going along.

"You aren't in their party?" President van Wilgen asked Rita meaningfully, his eyes watching her closely.

"Oh no, Em," Rita said, meeting those eyes. "Wim and I are friends, but I have a place in the city."

"Then you need not rush away."

"Not at all, Mr. President."

So she'd allowed herself to stay an extra half hour and run upstairs with the most powerful man in Suriname. She had left him a very happy most powerful man. But he'd left her high and dry.

So she wasted no time in showering off and exchanging her evening gown for T-shirt and jeans. There were still five hours to launch, but she was ready to get back to being the one in charge. While she dressed, Mérides presented her with reports from the twenty-four staging areas. Not a one had been tumbled by the locals; Omen's plan was still showing its expertise.

"I want reports every fifteen minutes from here on out," she told him in their Cuban Spanish. "And I want everyone to be alert for any sign of resistance. We don't know where August is and we have to be prepared for whatever he might come up with." But she knew he knew that and had already taken care of it. She was just wired. She hadn't slept since dawn the day before. But she lit a Cohiba at long last and let the tobacco re-sharpen her mind.

At 3 A.M., the zombis would march on Paramaribo and its suburbs from the three landward directions. The most critical targets would be the People's Palace, the Nationale Assemblee, and the office and hotel district, with their computerized and telephonic abilities to record what was happening; Saddam Hussein's botched execution was still fresh enough in everyone's minds for the FRC to make certain no photos could possibly get out. But all twenty-four groups of zombis would loose their gas, in Gberg and Nieuw Amsterdam and Speeringhoek, everywhere within fifteen miles, and by 4 A.M., the only creatures left standing in that radius would be the zombis themselves. By dawn, they'd be dead, too, as they took their inevitable breath. Omen's notes had estimated that two hundred and sixty thousand people would die—more than half the country. When the two hundred thousand who were left awoke in their scattered homes, they would find their capital decimated, their government and no doubt many family members gone. But Wim Dekker would be calm and commanding from his home in the rain forest of Brokopondo, several hours to the south. His media empire would naturally give him in-country communication facilities, even though the satellites had gone dark overnight and would remain dark for another twenty-four hours. Fortunately, the American ambassador would be an overnight guest at Dekker's estate, so he could promise help from abroad. Cut off from the outside world, the survivors would have no one to rally around but Dekker. Everything would point toward him as the focus of the future.

Maybe he'll rename the capital the Federal Restoration Center, she thought savagely. *But it ought to be Ritaville.*

NOVEMBER 4 - 11:30 P.M. ST

2 DEATH

The Maroons and friends were deep in the rhythm of it now. Each shaman had his or her part down, and it made Max think of the zombis making the sarin in rows inside the airtight chamber—in that it was completely different. These people were still singing, chatting, and laughing as they sat inside the warehouse mixing ingredients. The only similarity was the care each group took with its components. Max was moving among the groups, checking their procedures, offering help if needed, but finding little to do, frankly—when he heard Pam *call* his name.

He looked at Mama Locha and found her looking back. She'd heard it, too.

He held up a hand, did his *wipe* to enforce quiet from everyone around him, and concentrated. But he didn't need that effort; he heard her clearly. Her *call* was ragged but driven.

"She's weak in body, but strong in mind," Mama told him, suddenly by his side. "That girl's tough."

"Have you heard it before?" he demanded.

"Not me."

"Then why are we hearing it now?"

"Maybe she's gained power," Mama said, but knew that was wrong even as Max voiced her thoughts. "Her *call* is the *call* of an exhausted woman," he said decisively.

"The elementals couldn't find her," Mama said. "There's a spell blocking us from her. Maybe it stopped blocking *her* from *us*."

Max grew very still. "Or something raised the energy around us." He touched her arm, looked around the room. "Keep an eye on the place, Mama."

"Where are you going, boy?"

"To have a look around."

He moved toward the doors at the back of the warehouse, which opened onto the wharf. He cracked them, *felt* outward with his mind. It was clear out there. He slipped onto the rotting pier and went left, to the side of the building. There was a narrow walkway running the length of the warehouse there, deep in shadows above the slick black water. The walkway looked to be in bad repair; there was no normal way to walk the length of it and not make some sort of sound, so he cast silence around himself. With that, he was able to sprint to the front of the building. From a distance a television muttered and reggae echoed. On the river a tugboat gave its low honk. Seabirds sobbed.

At the far end of the walkway, still in the shadows, he stopped, crouched, poked his head around the corner. Anyone out there looking for guards would be sensitive to a head six feet off the ground, not three.

Tilit stood across the narrow, deserted street, highlighted red by the grocery's neon, staring fiercely at the warehouse. He looked huge. Then he ran across the street, with the exaggerated soundlessness of a man who couldn't hear what sounds he might make. He looked like a Dr. Seuss elephant. And Max had to smile at his own alchemy of silence, utterly wasted on a deaf man.

Tilit came to a halt with his back pressed against the front of the building, facing away from Max. He carried a sawed-off shotgun, had a pistol in his belt at the back of his pants. He readied the shotgun, holding it with one hand, the butt against his hip, while he reached in his pants pocket and pulled out a *stone*. Even in the uncertain light Max recognized its shape as the one he'd taken from Omen and given to Pam. Now he knew why Mama and the others had heard her. Pam had only had the *stone* for a day but their energies had mingled— and Tilit had carried the energy with him as he approached.

Max eased off on his gathering magick. With Pam tied to Tilit through the *stone*, blowing his mind could have bad repercussions. But Tilit was moving the *stone* back and forth as if seeking a radio signal. Much more likely, he was seeking Max, and soon he would find him. Tilit was an external force, come to attack; all the energy of the day was behind him. But for Tilit, *Max* was an external force, and *Max* was behind him, too . . .

Max came around the corner in a rush. He had total respect for the *stone*, and he wasn't disappointed. Before he could reach Tilit, the man who couldn't hear him spun around, so Max's flying kick missed the kidney and took the hip instead.

Tilit dropped and rolled lithely, holding on to both the *stone* and the shotgun. He shoved the former back into his pants and, from his back, raised the latter. Max kicked it as it spewed a burst, plowing a trail through the weathered warehouse wood. Tilit held on to it, however, and used his strength to jerk it back toward Max. Max dropped, his knees crushing the deaf man's arms against his chest, taking the shotgun along with it. With his better leverage, Max yanked the gun from Tilit's hands and sent it spinning into the dark. But that left him somewhat off balance as Tilit rolled suddenly to his side. Max fell forward onto his knees and had to catch himself with a hand.

Tilit thrust his fingers at Max's throat, seeking the nerves there. He just missed, striking the muscles instead. Max grunted, feeling his chest go dead, but was able to grab the outstretched arm before Tilit could pull it back. From his kneeling position he had to use just his left hand, but he twisted his arm so his elbow was up, his hand grabbing the inside of Tilit's bicep. Max rotated his arm sharply, the upraised elbow coming down hard, as he pulled Tilit's bicep up and the forearm onto his own shoulder. Tilit's arm could not bend, and with a more studied grip Max would have broken it. But being off balance he couldn't get it right and the arm slid free.

Both men scrambled to their feet. In the tropical night, they were deep now in a primal world.

Tilit pulled a knife and came in fast. Max bobbed to the left, let the knife pass under his arm. He clamped his arm over Tilit's arm, and before Tilit could pull free, Max used the proximity to head-butt him. He thrust forward with his legs and put everything he had behind the eleven pounds of solid bone. It rocked Tilit back brutally. Max opened his arm. Tilit slashed wildly and nicked Max before crashing down hard on his back. The knife flew. Max kicked for the big man's balls, but Tilit somehow got his own leg going and slammed his foot into Max's knee first. It was only the ad hoc nature of the blow that kept it from ending the fight. As it was, Max's entire leg went numb to join his chest, and he was down in the dirt. He twisted, trying to find some room to get up.

Tilit grabbed Max's head from behind, his fingers clawing for the eyes. Max snapped his head back. Tilit's grip came loose. As he tried to tighten it again, Max thrust upward from his knees. Tilit's arms slid down Max's face, dropped to Max's mouth level as their grip tightened again, drawing blood from Max's lip but also giving him the chance to snap his teeth deep in Tilit's arm. More blood burst into the air. Tilit tried to hang in but had to yank his arm away, leaving a chunk of flesh in Max's jaws. Max spat it out, getting to his feet. Tilit got up as well, and with a soundless scream he charged.

Max olé'd him again and Tilit stumbled past. Both men were running out of gas. Tilit spun back but his head was low. Max grabbed it, with one hand on the back of the head and the other holding an ear. He jerked the head down onto his good knee. And again. Tilit spasmed, fought, tore himself free, his nose spurting crimson. He stumbled to his knees. Max kicked him in the face. His neck broke. He was dead before he hit the ground.

Max stood bent over him, hands on sore knees and panting hard in the warm night air. The tugboat sounded off again, farther downriver. Max looked up and saw for the first time that the Maroons and Bajans were massed in the warehouse doorway, watching wide-eyed.

He pointed to two of the men. "Drag him inside!" he snapped. He would have been nicer about it but he couldn't spare the breath.

Two men started forward but Maggie, Mama Locha's girl, beat one of them to the punch. She and the other man grabbed Tilit, and Max followed them in. Amba closed the doors behind them. "Take him to the back," Max said. "Where Mama and I were."

The group followed as the corpse was laid on the warehouse floor. "Lay him parallel to the river flow," Max said. He knelt beside the body and dug the *stone* from Tilit's pocket, and then, surprisingly, a second, smaller one. "There's a chance to read his spirit and find Pam."

"Necromancy?" asked Kwasiba.

"Vodou!" answered Maggie enthusiastically.

"Whatever," said Max. "I do it every year, looking for Val. All I need is a location for Pam, and he must know it."

"Then do it, boy," Mama Locha said. "I'll add my vodou."

"We'll all help," said Amba.

"No," said Max. "The rest of you stay with the anti-dote. I appreciate it, but Mama and I can do this."

Reluctantly, the others went back to work. It wasn't that they failed to understand the stakes involved in preparing the antidote, but their interest was piqued by what these great shamans were going to attempt. They went to their tables but kept looking back, to see what happened next.

NOVEMBER 5 2007 - MIDNIGHT ST

2 DEATH

Tilit's body lay sprawled on its back. Max sat cross-legged to the right of it, by the left shoulder, so he could look down into its face. Mama sat similarly on the other side.

Max held Omen's *stone* in his left hand, the smaller

stone in his right, as he began gathering his life force at the bottom tip of his spine—right where Pam had her tattooed fish. Consciously, he raised it like a serpent through the vertebræ, till it glowed within his mind. There was a flux in the air by his forehead, like heat waves on a hot desert day.

Exploding from his forehead, the serpent struck, driving deep into Tilit's forehead. It was something science could barely measure, and almost nothing words could express, but Max's consciousness went out-of-body, surging across the shadowed space, into the brain of the dead man. There it was black, and cold and still. But the serpent-light beat back the darkness, revealing a vast emptiness like space, with distant suns Max couldn't really pinpoint shedding soft midnight light. Closer by was the familiar landscape of the dead, with its sad canyons and dank trees. It was the valley of the shadow of death, where the walkers in the night should all be ghosts.

Max had almost always come here for Val, but tonight he was feeling his way toward Tilit. As he had told Fern, *"When your soul leaves your body, there's a period of ghostliness, where you see the world but the world does not see you. It's strange and disconcerting, but not scary; it seems perfectly natural, because it is. After a while you start to notice that time seems to be running backward. In fact, the years of your life are being stripped away like the skins of an onion."* The trick was to find Tilit while it was still Tilit. And the only way to do that was to attune his own mind to the newly entered ghostly mind.

Better men than Max had gone mad attempting this. The human mind known to us all is at least alive. Projecting it into the realm of death is a deeply disturbing experience, with fears of your own demise lurking on every side. Those who study necromancy have to face those fears and hold together—then go back for more and worse—until the realm of death becomes familiar to them. If the realm becomes familiar before the necromancer goes missing, the necromancer finally achieves comfort, or more accurately a lack of discomfort, like those who walk on burning coals and neither feel nor burn. But the cost is steep.

"Richard Kimble ponders his fate as he looks at the world for the last time. And sees only darkness. But in that darkness, fate moves its huge hand."

To his left sat Mama Locha. It was more than feeling her and less than seeing her, but she was clearly there, acting as an anchor, a solid, silent support he could use to orient himself.

"Give me a place to stand and with a lever I will move the whole world."

Max was here now, to the right of Mama Locha—not just his consciousness but he, himself. He walked forward, on the space, following a trail only he could see. He had had a reason to pursue this discipline, and after two decades plus he had his comfort with it. He saw the slight ghostly pale against the shadowed horizon that revealed a wandering spirit. He moved quickly, decisively, and he found Tilit.

The man was peering around, waving his right hand as if to clear away a spider's web before his eyes. There were no marks of his recent violence on his spirit, but there were many marks of accumulated pain. He was more solid than his surroundings—a ghost, but still a fairly simple one. He was more solid than Max.

"Tilit," Max called.

"Um?" the man replied, and neither he nor Max remarked on his ability to speak, now that his defective body no longer held him. But his voice was harsh and mechanical.

"Tell me where Pam is."

"No."

"Tell me, Tilit. I am master here."

"U R not. Jackson Tower is."

"Not here." *Jackson Tower must be an FRC sorcerer,* Max thought.

Tilit lowered his hand. "No," he said. "Not here."

"Where is Pam?"

A pale energy the color of new parchment slid from Tilit's head and shimmered in the dark. It was a sensory map, detailing every inch of his journey from the southern valley as he had seen and felt it. Rand McNally would never have recognized it, but Max plunged his hand into it and all those sights and sensations ran up his arm to his mind. They were as clear to him as his own thoughts. Although he had never been to the estate, he could now go straight there whenever he wanted.

There was just one more question. "What's happened to her?"

The energy brightened. She was alive. But Max considered the energy not as bright as it could be. She was hurt. Tilit had hurt her. A wave of anger surged over him, and Tilit stepped back, fading. Max mastered himself, refusing to let Tilit go. He realized he wasn't done.

"Where is Valerie Drake?"

Tilit stared at him. No response, and no pale energy. Well, it was a long shot.

"We're finished," Max said. "Go your way."

But the man stayed where he was a moment longer. "U R good fighter," he said grudgingly. Then he turned and, in the turning, grew younger. . . .

• • •

Max was sitting beside the corpse, in the warehouse, in Geertruidenberg, Suriname.

"You're good at a lot of things, boy," Mama Locha said respectfully. "That was like surgery."

"I'm into necromancy," Max said somewhat indistinctly. He was either shaking her off, or shaking off the Death World, as he got to his feet. Without a word, he stumbled out the back doors again, made his way around to the side, into the deep shadows of the rickety walkway. His energy had come back to him like a wave after the tide had dragged it out to sea. He was overamping—high on life—and he used it to call the elementals. Now!

Here on the pier, he got the earth elementals he'd had before, but also the water ones, naiads, and the flying sylphs. With one burst, he gave them all the map. "Tell me how she is." Instantly, the small shadows on the pier and on the waves vanished away.

Finally, he dropped down on the edge of the walkway and did what he'd wanted to do from the moment he'd heard Pam trying to reach him. He sat and opened his mind to her, and he heard her voice, *calling* him. It was faint; she had little technique and the magick she'd gotten from the *stone* was limited, but like a Chicago radio station he could pick up in the Everglades, fading in and out, he heard her. He did. So he sent an answering *call*, knowing she wouldn't hear it, hearing no sign in her continuing *call* that she had. But he sent it.

"I'll be there soon."

2 DEATH

Less than an hour later, men and women left the warehouse, headed in many directions. Each carried a heavily laden backpack or basket. They went to their cars, parked in various places but none closer than three blocks to the warehouse. They drove away. And soon the streets near the waterfront were once again empty and still.

Only when he was certain that the others had not been interfered with did Max August head out, his own pack slung over his aching shoulder.

2 DEATH

In the southern valley, lights were on all through the main house. It was only an hour until Paramaribo went down, and Jackson Tower was on high alert. He'd had no report from Tilit but that didn't worry him. Tilit had the *stones* but he didn't know how to send a report through the ether, so he'd be in the air, flying his helicopter back.

No, what concerned Tower, as it would concern any prudent man, was the sarin. Even though there was an hour to go, he went to the control panel Omen had built into the house, and began the process of closing the roof over the valley. It would take half an hour, he'd been told. Tilit would certainly be back before then, and there would be no question of their being fully protected long before any gas was scheduled to be loosed. But according to Hanrahan, they hadn't shut down Max August, and August could have already found one of the zombi lairs, set off the gas . . . some could be drifting Tower's way. Surely, Diamante would know if he had, and Tower would be alerted, but still—why not close the roof?

He stepped outside and watched as the sky began to be slowly eaten away. The roof was some sort of high-tech plastic that caught the glow of the house lights, pale tan against the sparkling darkness. A low rumbling echoed up and down the valley, like summer thunder. Interspersed were sudden thumps as the Filtration Reuse Canisters kicked in. *Science*, he thought. All that working with rigid reality made him dubious, exactly the way other people reacted to his magick, but that didn't keep him from using it.

Soon he tired of watching plastic crawl. Perhaps it was time to check in with Dr. Blackwell one last time.

He went to the slave chamber and found her apparently asleep. She was lying on the bed, her eyes closed, her hands neatly folded across her tummy . . . almost as if she were communicating with someone. He checked through the surrounding energies with his mind, and relaxed. The barrier against the outside was still in place.

Now she opened her eyes, becoming aware of his presence. He decided she must simply have been asleep. Well, it had been a long, hard day for her.

"We will win," Tower said conversationally, as if continuing their conversation from hours before. "You know in your heart that it's true, Doctor."

"So you people keeping saying," Pam said wearily. " 'Resistance is futile.' "

"Because you don't believe us," Tower replied. "Because you pretend not to understand. But I'm sure you know that we're an historical inevitability."

"Didn't the Nazis say that? Or was it the Communists?"

"Both, in point of fact—but there's a crucial difference. There are always new people looking to join *us*. The Communists offered power but little satisfaction in using it; their world was too circumscribed. The Nazis offered power and excitement, but they, too, were drawing from an ultimately limited base. Name any group you want. The Mafia? The Roman Empire? Even the Roman Empire ran out of leadership material. But the . . . Free Range Coalition draws from the entire world. Everyone knows that real power, real excitement, and real satisfaction lie in the world we inhabit. They may say they despise us when they first stick their toe in the water, and they usually do, but they want what we have, and are more than willing to jettison their scruples as they rise in the ranks. Miller Omen wanted in. So do many others. So even if our current rulers are swept away by time or trouble, the next rank will be right there. Future Reality Control will continue until we rule the world absolutely—and then people will *really* fight to join."

"If that were to happen—"

Tower waved her off impatiently. "There is no 'if' about it. No one will want to be under our thumb; they'll either join or die. There is no third option. When we rule the world there'll be no place to hide."

• • •

Outside, vague small shadows moved across the waving grass. The perimeter was marked with motion detectors, heat sensors, and mojo bags, but none of that was any good against elementals. They were part of the environment and couldn't be differentiated from it. They flowed up to the house and clambered silently up a side wall until they could peer in a window. There was no blond woman inside that window. So they kept looking, trying the next room.

• • •

Pam, looking wearily at Tower, with the bath out of focus behind him, saw a naiad pop up in her toilet.

NOVEMBER 5 - 2:07 A.M. ST

2 DEATH

Max was turning into the Watermolenstraat, deep in the peaked shadow of the Kathedraal, when Pam stopped *calling.*

He stopped, balanced easily, waiting. He encompassed his mind, expanded it, projected it, making himself completely available. But he could not hear her again. Had she simply fallen asleep? Had she been rendered unconscious? Had she been rendered . . . dead?

The enormity of the silence shocked him. He knew she was in danger but her spirit was so strong, so like his own, that it had seemed to him inevitable they would find their way back to each other. As the reverberation of that silence rocked him, he knew for certain how much he loved her.

They'd only been together for five days but in those

days she'd shown him everything she was, and everything she was was what he wanted. Strong, smart, beautiful, sensitive, inquisitive, athletic, heroic. He was a man perpetually in the prime of his life, and over time, his quest for Val and personal happiness had become two paths. It would have been easier if he'd known he was a widower, that Val was dead and gone, but he knew the exact opposite . . . and still, he was marching through Time alone. Part of that was his Timelessness. Part of that was his renegade attitude. But part of it was his quest, and that progressed by a series of All Hallows' Eves that brought nothing.

Then came Pam.

He loved her. And she might be gone.

NOVEMBER 5 – 5:00 A.M. GREENWICH MEAN TIME

2 DEATH

Eva Delia dreamt in the deepest hours of the Cambridge night. It was the time when the drugs grew less and the dreams grew more—a time she'd come to know in her life, when the dreams were all. It often seemed at this hour that the dreams were real. A doctor told her once they were *lucid* dreams, when a girl can be asleep and awake at the same time. But that never sounded right to her. She didn't even believe she was awake then. Awake was the bad place, or the no-place. Asleep, in dreams, was where she felt at home, and at peace. *Lucid! You got some 'splainin' to do!*

She usually flew in these dreams, soaring through the high sky like an airplane or an angel, all at home. The sky was her natural domain, full of white clouds and bright light. Sometimes she went higher, reaching out for the light, and if she caught it she flew into it and out the other side.

Tonight, the light was the light of a vast hall, shining all on her face. She was a Barbie doll, the most beautiful Barbie, brilliant and shining in denim and lace, and as far as she could see was an audience of girls and boys just like her, all applauding. All but one. There was a blond girl, she hadn't been there before, and she was pushing to the front of the crowd, pointing at Eva Delia, laughing at Eva Delia, yelling at Eva Delia. It spoiled the glorious music filling Eva Delia's ears and mouth. Eva Delia was singing it herself. Eva Delia was dancing. Eva Delia was flying. She was soaring to the top of the theater, and out to the rest of the world. She was out and away from the blonde. "Sorry, pal!" she shouted to the shrinking speck.

As she rose over London like Peter Pan, Eva Delia looked down and saw the marquee. There was a name on it like always, lit up like Christmas. But the letters were always jumbled.

NOVEMBER 5 - 2:30 A.M. SURINAME TIME

2 DEATH

Rita was beginning to wear down at long last. Her face was showing the planes of its age as they moved toward the shank of the night. If she'd been about to go into battle herself, the adrenaline would have kept her going, but all this was, in the end, just traffic management.

The zombis were preprogrammed. Her only job was to start them on their twisting journeys at exactly the right times.

"You want some loving before it begins, Rita sweeta . . . ?" asked Mérides, knowing her preferences from long experience. But to his surprise, she shook her head no.

"This is it, Alberto," she said tersely. "If I screw up, I for sure, and probably you, will go back to Cuba in the belly of a shark. I have worked too long and too hard for that to happen. I want the big-time."

"You have plenty already, *chica*. You have Miami," Mérides said, contemplating the changes this might lead to and worrying that she might be tired of him. "You sure you don't want loving?"

"No. Stop trying to help." She took in a deep breath, then let it all out again in an eloquent sigh. "It's time to get this show on the road," she said. They both took shiny gray hazmat suits from a rack on one wall— identical to those on Omen Key, had they but known it. Hers had a star on the front and the back, marking her as the commander. They were not the easiest outfits to get into, but when they had both snapped their helmets into place, she looked at the readout on the console, counting off another minute and forty-three seconds. At 2:45:00, she reached out with her gloved hand and decisively flipped a black switch.

In the barracks throughout Zorg en Hoop, filled with the sleeping soldiers of Suriname, sarin began descending.

2 DEATH

The Vlaggenplatform, two blocks from the People's Palace: Max stood deep in its shadow. The Surinamese flag whipped in the trades above his head. The Dixiebar loomed cold and empty to his left. Before him lay a deserted street, a sort of narrow park surrounded by a high mesh fence, more street, then the Palace. Several lights burned in the distant building but darkness lay heavily between; the moon wouldn't come up until nearly four. That was fine; it was the fenced area that interested him.

This afternoon, before leaving Zorg en Hoop, he'd disabled the helicopters, but he needed one for his end of things. So he would have to steal President van Wilgen's.

Fortunately, the president's Personal Guard was more concerned with his personal safety than with a machine inside a fenced area. Two guards were making their rounds but they weren't alert. This was not the FRC. Yet.

Max had Pam in the back of his mind, continually open to her *call*, but the rest of his mind was focused on the best way forward. It had to be that way; if Pam were alive, she was being held as a bargaining chip, so it was up to Max to make them use it. His eyes were on the guards, alert to every possible detail, and so he spotted elementals at the edge of his vision as soon as they appeared. Their shadowed shadows started popping up around his ankles, and their featureless faces turned up toward his. They were used to him now, even comfortable, and they were excited in their way to bring him good news. They had found the blond woman, and she was alive!

His heart surged with relief. His thanks were wholly inadequate, but he poured them out like a sun going nova.

Details like her condition were beyond them, but he was happy enough to get images of her location. For their part, they'd conveyed their images and that was it—so they wished him well in their rough-hewn way, and melted back into the corners of reality.

In the shadow of the Vlaggenplatform, Max longed to go get her, but there was no time before the attack came. And his lifelong goal was to make the future better than now; he couldn't break this off, even for her. And even if he *could* go, he needed the chopper to get there fast. And she'd used a *call*, hadn't she? He had to believe she could take care of herself.

In any event, he might be Timeless but his time was up. The guards turned a corner and strolled out of sight. Max ran silently across the empty street, to the high fence along the perimeter, the wire mesh singing in the winds. Soon those winds could carry invisible death, but now they were soft and slightly salty. He stood and moved his head back and forth, sweeping the area before him with a steady gaze, though his neck was still complaining in certain spots after his fight with Tilit.

When he was satisfied that there was no one sitting quietly he might have missed, he took hold of the mesh and created the fire in his fingers. Under strict mental control, there was no light to go with the heat that melted the metal links. Soon enough he had cut a door in the fence, and he stepped inside. Now, even running over open ground, the odds of his being seen were low. The darkness was deeper here.

He stopped behind a tree that one of the guards would pass in two minutes. When the man came by Max stretched the man's mind until he blacked out. Then Max ran back to meet the other guard and did the same to him. He did not want anyone calling for his chopper to be shot down.

Three more minutes and he reached the helipad. There were no guards there because there were guards at the fence. Max slid into the pilot's seat and took the controls with no trouble at all. It was a sleek Sikorsky S-92, the chopper choice of executives everywhere, and Max knew exactly how to hot-wire it. Back in '89, it was one of those things he'd learned with the idea that a lone adventurer might need to know it, and he'd used it a lot since then. So much of his life now involved either guns or transport.

But once he had the wires in hand, he sat silently, waiting. There were two minutes yet to go. . . .

NOVEMBER 5 - 3:00 A.M. ST

2 DEATH

The drums began at the crack of three.

The first people to hear them were the night-men, the ones who walk the darkness to do the jobs that others won't. The police and firemen and sanitation men. The invisible men. They heard them first.

They thought it was some idiot with a radio.

2 DEATH

Max touched the two wires together, and the engine burst into a roar. Across the lawn he saw men from the Palace turn at the sound as he pulled back on the throttle and the copter took him up in a hurry. If the guards fired at him, he was unaware of it. He couldn't imagine that Surinamese guards were trigger-happy enough to fire without more info.

Once above the nearby buildings, he put the copter in a long sideways slide, away from the Palace, above the Vlaggenplatform, out over the shimmering river. Unless fate had moved its huge hand, he would be the only one in the air tonight.

2 DEATH

The next people to hear the drums were the insomniacs, the paranoids, the spouses of the snorers. Easily awakened, alive to the darkness, they opened their eyes, narrowed them, and cursed the idiot with a radio.

Most people slept on.

2 DEATH

Below him in the river Max made out the wreck of a German ship, showing one side to the sky as it had since 1940. When the Nazis invaded Holland—then Suriname's colonial master—the German crew had sunk the boat to preclude the possibility of commandeering it. Afterward nobody'd had the equipment to raise it, or the interest, and since the river was wide at that point it was just considered an artifact, to be left where found. War happened.

Max had fought in seven wars so far. His skills as a point man had never failed him, and they never got old. But *wars* got very old very fast.

2 DEATH

The night-men and insomniacs tried to figure where that damned radio was. Most of the people who looked up their street or out their window saw nothing unusual. Only the few who lived on the wrong streets saw living dead men.

Maurits Tsong Fa saw them and decided it was some weird joke. Tsong Fa was drunk, yes, at the end of a forty-eight-hour bender, but he had a generally sunny disposition that took life as a joke. He went outside to see this joke better.

The zombis were marching three abreast, in rows. One stayed at the left edge of the road, another at the right edge, and the third in the middle. Behind them three more did the same, and behind them still more. They all moved like clockwork mannequins, right on the beat of the drums, with all their left legs pushing forward, then all their right legs. Their arms hung limp, their jaws hung limp, their eyes were blankly staring.

Tsong Fa thought it was the silliest thing he'd ever seen. He went up to the middle man in the first row and said in Sranan Tongo, *"Suma kan si yu now?"*

The zombi said nothing, but his right leg thrust forward, like all the right legs, and he bumped into Tsong Fa. Tsong Fa was generally sunny but the rum had made him prickly. *"Ei!"* he said. He reached past the can on the guy's chest and gave him a shove on the shoulder. The guy rocked a little, but not much, and when his left leg stumped forward, his foot came down on Tsong Fa's. Tsong Fa said, *"EI!"* and tried to pull his foot loose, but the guy's right leg came forward on the beat of the drum and nearly caught Tsong Fa's other foot. Tsong Fa danced backward, out of the way, but his one foot was caught and he was drunk and went down. The zombi moved his left leg and planted his foot square on Tsong Fa's knee, snapping it. Tsong Fa screamed and jerked and the zombi fell forward on top of him.

Tsong Fa fought his way free, and the zombi slowly got to his hands and knees, to get up and continue his march. But by that time, the zombi in the next row arrived and fell over both of them, knocking the first one back down. Tsong Fa couldn't pull his shattered kneecap from under the doubled weight, and then the zombi in the third row arrived. And fell.

As the drums beat on, the pile grew bigger, and Tsong Fa ceased his struggle.

NOVEMBER 5 - 3:05 A.M. ST

2 DEATH

From his vantage point over the river, Max saw groups of zombis in all directions, issuing forth from warehouses, old mansions, and the familiar trucks. He stayed high, looking for the pattern in their appearance, and relayed his findings by radio to his "troops." It was by far the strangest traffic report he'd ever done, and the most important. "They seem to be carving the city into two strips, and the suburbs as well. Those strips are made up of bands at the north end of habitations, bands in the middle, and bands at the south end. I see two of these deployments across Para, one group of three along the river, the other group cutting through the heart of the city to the west. I see two more groups along the south bank, through Gberg and Speeringhoek—another farther downriver, from Meerzorg to Boom Jachtlust— and two on the north bank, through Nieuw Amsterdam and Marienburg. Wait! There's another up by the ocean! That's a total of . . . eight. Eight groups of three."

He hadn't expected the one in the far north, but it could be handled. "Ramdien! Edmond! Get all your people on a line across the back of Nieuw Amsterdam now!" He saw car lights flick on in the center of Nieuw

Amsterdam, the lights start to move. Other lights were moving in other parts of the world below, following his directions into position.

They had time. The zombis wouldn't do anything until they were inside a perimeter the sarin could surely cover, a moment they'd been programmed for. It was Max's job to judge that moment.

NOVEMBER 5 - 3:10 A.M. ST

2 DEATH

The paranoids began to realize that whatever these blank-men in their streets might be, they were no joke. Michel Reynard ran out into his street and stared at the things, to be sure of what he was seeing. He'd seen zombis in Haiti; it was why he'd moved to Boom Jachtlust. He pulled his weapon, an old M1911 .45, and put a slug in the nearest one's leg. It fell over from the impact, but started to climb back to its feet. Reynard shot it again. This time the bullet penetrated its sarin canister. Then the night-people and insomniacs and people sleeping through it all, and everyone else downwind, died.

2 DEATH

Max kept up a running report of the zombis' locations until he saw his people's headlights stop their movements, establishing their choke points. He began a wide sweep over Para, looking for anything on the fringes he might have missed. There was little time to rectify it if he had, but he wasn't a traffic reporter and he wasn't a general. A detached, omnipotent eye-in-the-sky was not his style at all.

Finally, Max was certain there were no more zombis left to appear. He leaned forward in his seat and shouted, *"Now, everybody! Now, now, now!"*

2 DEATH

Amba slid her car to a halt half a block from her horde. They were still on the move, turning left onto a cross street, headed almost surely for the park a block away, where the gas could spread best. She leapt from the rattletrap Gert had loaned her, not ten meters away from them. It could have been ten miles for all they cared. She trembled, partly from primal fear and partly from primal rage. This was the result of the evil that had killed her sister. She began to hurl her canisters of antidote at them.

Her aim was bad at first, but soon she had the range.

She had more than enough bombs, thanks to Mama Locha's foresight, so she didn't have to be perfect. The canisters burst on impact, spewing yellow smoke that billowed thickly, filling the street like mosquito spray, enveloping the zombis. Some staggered, stumbled, collapsed, but those farthest from the bombs were less affected. For Amba, the creatures remaining upright, disappearing into the saffron mist to continue their march to annihilation, were the nightmare of all nightmares. For Max high above they were reminiscent of the zombis in the green mist on Omen Key. But those zombis had succumbed to the antidote quickly, because they'd been enclosed; it would take more time in the open air.

The front rows of the remaining creatures were nearing their destination. Amba grabbed her final bombs and ran alongside the marchers, trying to beat them to the park. She was all too aware of her rapid breathing and pounding heart, compared to their almost stately progress. But she passed them in time, racing out in front of them, putting herself between them and their goal. They did not slow down or attempt to go around her. They were programmed. But she was programmed in her own way. She lobbed the final bombs over their heads, into their midst.

The zombis kept coming. One turned her way, or so it seemed. He took one more step toward her, then another—then his legs gave out and he went down. His turning toward her had been the accidental result of losing his coordination. All around him, others began to collapse, at long last. They lurched, they clutched at each other in wonderment, they tumbled to the road. And when the smoke drifted away on the trade winds, the street was finally filled with men and women—

weak, confused, unhealthy men and women, but no longer zombis.

She looked at them sprawled on the ground, and suddenly her heart went out to them. They were pawns in this war just like Adyuba. But Max had told everyone to get out of there as soon as they were done, because a sarin canister could still break open. So she ran back down the block to her car. She jumped inside and left rubber in her wake. She had done what needed doing. She had avenged her sister!

"Mi lobi yu, sisa!" Amba screamed to the pure night air.

NOVEMBER 5 - 3:15 A.M. ST

2 DEATH

Along the river in Gberg, Kwasiba stood on a warehouse roof and lobbed her bombs in long arcs down on the zombis in the street. There was no way she could have heard Amba, and yet in that same instant, she, too, shouted, *"Mi lobi yu, sisa!"*

NOVEMBER 5 - 3:15 A.M. ST

2 DEATH

In the heart of Speeringhoek, Mama Locha mouthed the same words. Adyuba wasn't her sister but she loved her anyway.

2 DEATH

Max spotted yellow smoke blossoming like strange flowers all across the region. On one street after another they sprang up, until they began to flow together to form a single cloud. He soared back across the river, making sure nothing had gone wrong, and the cloud was solid as far as the eye could see.

But as he turned back to Para, approaching the Nationale Assemblee, he came upon a glaringly obvious hole.

"Harish!" Max used the copter's speaker to call the Hindu shaman whose area down there it was. And again, "Harish!" There was no response.

He dropped the chopper into the hole fast, cutting past the swirling yellow haze. Reaching two hundred feet, he saw what had happened. The Assemblee guards had opened fire on the zombis and shattered at least one of the sarin canisters. It had killed everyone for blocks around, including Harish, but not the zombis themselves. They were in the process of ringing the assembly building, still in step with the omnipresent drumming. Those whose canisters hadn't burst would complete their assignment, dumping far more sarin.

Max sent the Sikorsky flying around the ring, piloting with one hand, dropping four of his own antidote bombs out the open side with the other. He had always been the last line of defense and this was why. The bombs struck the ground below and exploded, filling the clear air with good yellow smoke. The zombis fell to their knees, and Max got the hell out of there.

2 DEATH

Rita huddled with her top mercs at Zorg en Hoop, wondering what the hell was going on. As each merc had arrived after setting his group of zombis on their course, he had donned a gray hazmat suit; there were now thirteen of them crowded into the command center. Rita thought furiously, *We look like a pack of ghosts—clustered outside the real world, unable to affect it! There are no mercs at the points of attack, so no one to tell me what the hell that fucking yellow smoke is! It isn't the sarin. Where is the sarin? I would kill for a satellite right now!*

Her secure circuit rang within her suit. It would be Hanrahan, wanting a report. She flipped a switch on the neck covering and began to give him the best one she could. "I think we've met the Code Red. . . ."

2 DEATH

Tower stood in the doorway of the mansion and pushed his thousand-yard stare into the darkness overhead. There was, of course, nothing to see except the dome now, but it was his way of participating. If all was going well—and there was no alert from Diamante to say it wasn't—two hundred and sixty thousand souls were surging into the spirit world. What he would give to be able to run through the middle of that! But the unfortunate part of a nerve gas attack was that the attackers—the sentient attackers—had to remain at a safe distance.

And if all was not going well . . . well, he was fully prepared to face the Code Red if it came to that.

His secure phone rang. It would be Hanrahan, providing a report.

NOVEMBER 5 - 3:30 A.M. ST

2 DEATH

"This is President van Wilgen. My private helicopter is being used in this attack! All surviving military are ordered to shoot it down! Again: shoot it down!"

Police below Max began to open up on the chopper. Other night-men joined in, official and unofficial alike. Yellow smoke began burbling in through a hole in his windscreen. A crack appeared six inches away and a section the size of a basketball let go. It was clearly time for Max to go get Pam. His work here was done.

Using evasive maneuvers he'd seen pilots try on the VC, he tilted over to blow smoke between him and the guards, blinding them for his getaway. But another bullet caught his tail section and the motor began to make an unpleasant sound. He wrenched the bird to point toward the southland and goosed it, leaving Para behind as fast as he could.

Someday Max would have to fly something that he'd be able to land. But he doubted his life would go that way.

2 DEATH

In her command center, Rita had waited too long for the silence that would proclaim her victory; she had to accept that the attack had been blocked. Because none of her men could go where the zombis went, the Code Red had brought Omen's whole house of cards down, and she had finally found the flaw in his plan.

The one thing she could say was, this was not her fault. She had made the best of a bad situation, taking Omen's flawed plan as far as she could. Now she and her men would have to flee toward the prearranged pickup spot on the western coast—prearranged for this evening at sunset, fourteen hours from now, but she had no actual choice. Whoever was left alive out there would eventually turn their attention to Zorg en Hoop, from which no reinforcements had come. They would discover the hundreds and hundreds of their dead comrades. They would hunt those responsible with implacable fury. Rita and her people would have to gather what they could, make sure there was nothing to connect this to the FRC, and run like hell before that happened.

As soon as she and her men got their rumbling trucks outside the ghostly base and pointed them toward Guyana, she called Hanrahan to lay out her position. As always, she was going on offense.

2 DEATH

Max had kept the president's chopper in the air for half an hour since leaving Para, and now he was doing everything he knew to keep it there long enough to get to Tower's estate. Even from the air, the destination the elementals had given him was crystal clear in his mind. But the Sikorsky was shuddering with every stroke of the engine, and the savanna stretched far and away before him, fitfully lit by the Virgo moon climbing crab-like in the east.

2 DEATH

In Wheeling, Lawrence Breckenridge told Hanrahan he had to step outside, get some air, and clear his head. It was an excuse he'd used several times before in times of crisis, and his old friend, the last man in the world to believe anybody, believed him.

Breckenridge strode swiftly to the grove of witch hazels he had used before. He disappeared into the absolute shadows and put his back against the strong central tree. Extremely old, it leaned in the direction of the wind, so that he was looking upward through its high branches.

He freed his mind and found Aleksandra.

"The Code Red has screwed us," he said. "Can you help?"

But his beloved was standoffish now, her crimson flame burning with a cold and bitter light that threw no shadows. La Fée Dangereuse.

This is your work, Lawrence.

"Yes, and I'm examining all my options, Diabola."

Don't tempt me to do the same. I am not an option. I chose you and you chose Jackson Tower. Trust him as I trust you.

He reached out for her, but there was nothing.

EXACTLY *as I trust you.*

NOVEMBER 5 - 4:30 A.M. SURINAME TIME

2 DEATH

Finally approaching the site of Tower's estate, yawing badly from side to side, Max made out the roof and wall covering the valley. At first he didn't know what he was looking at—it looked like a giant caterpillar chrysalis—but soon enough he understood. If there were a butterfly in that equation, it was Max in his failing helicopter. And it wasn't as if they wouldn't be expecting him. Since he needed to get through the chrysalis, he finally gave up fighting the bullet-riddled engine. . . .

The Sikorsky came down hard on the roof. The plastic it was made from was unexpectedly resistant, but the first impact split it and the copter's rebound ripped it out. The copter lurched downward, caught the blades on the struts of the roof, snapped them, and dropped Max nearly two hundred feet to the ground. There might have been one second when he could have leapt from the copter to grab at a strut in the roof, but he was thrown violently sideways even as the thought hit him. Then he was collapsing into the canopied world.

In the six seconds it took to fall, Max took the gravity that was causing him to fall and surged against it, pitting his personal power against the mass of the plummeting copter. When the copter hit, Max was four inches above the seat, riding his own personal "airbag." He hit hard, bounced, but didn't die.

Struggling up out of his seat, he lurched from the crumpled side of the copter before it could blow. He fell to his knees, got up, staggered onward; he had to find concealment in the nearby orchard before Tower's guards got down here to investigate. He ran to the trees' leafy shadow-bank, stopped just inside it for a moment to let his eyes adjust—

Something grabbed both his biceps implacably. Stunned, he tried to twist free and couldn't, couldn't even get some slack. He looked to one side and saw he was held by a zombi, standing quietly in the shadows of the grove, as still as any tree. A glance to the other side showed a second zombi, just like the first. And he couldn't mindfuck them because they had no minds. He was locked down good.

A glance straight ahead revealed a man running down the row toward him. At first he was simply a shadow of shadows like a giant elemental, but he ran into a ragged patch of moonlight pouring through the hole in the canopy and was momentarily revealed. He wore a jet-black robe, unmarked, with curiously roomy shoulders and short cuffs. He wore a crown of many jewels.

He came to a halt before Max and stared through him, or so it seemed. "I saw the elementals," he said in sepulchral tones that didn't disguise a deep-seated pleasure. "I knew you'd come. I'd have hated to end this

fiasco without pulling something positive from the
wreckage. I've had zombis waiting on all parts of the
estate for you these last two hours."

"You're Jackson Tower?" Max asked, matching the
other's calm to mask the excitement surging through
him.

"Of course I am."

"How's Pam Blackwell?"

But Tower was no longer listening. Max tried to mindfuck him, but where the zombis' minds were too empty,
Tower's was too well guarded. The sorcerer searched
Max's pockets, dumping their contents on the ground,
keeping only the two *stones*, which he slipped into a
pocket on his robe. "Now I have even more power, and
you have even less," he said matter-of-factly. He turned
and *ran* away down the row of trees. Max stared.

The zombis, maintaining their hold on Max's arms,
began to march, following Tower back toward the mansion. Max was just along for the ride.

2 DEATH

Max was taken into the main house, through the foyer
to the library. As they entered the room he heard Pam's
voice: *"Max!"* He looked and she was there, alive, inside Tower's ceremonial circle. Strapped to a chair, yes,
face and arms bloody, yes, sharing the circle with a
headless, gutted corpse, yes—but alive. Emotion surged
through him; he could see she'd kept her spirit, just as

he'd thought she would. And, he saw, she'd kept her faith in him.

"Hey, Pam," he said casually. "You got a little something on your chin."

She laughed, released—a laugh that broke at the end, but was unstoppable to start with. That was all he needed. His faith in her was secured.

The zombis took him into the triangle beside the magick circle, and stopped. Tower snapped his fingers three times in succession and lambent sheets of energy rose from the three lines, coming together at the high ceiling. Max was inside a triangular pyramid, seven feet per side at the base. He tested the pyramid with his fingers and his mind. Both reported he lacked the power to break free of it. That was not what he was used to. Not what he'd hoped for.

Tower entered the circle and moved behind Pam in her chair. Energy began to rise from the circle. Max could see the demons in it.

"That was a good idea on your part," Tower said disinterestedly, "having elementals scour the country. But they alerted *me*. I was fully ready for you, August, as you can surely understand. And, of course, I had continuing reports of your progress." The last was a lie, but what matter?

"Fine, you win a pony. Now what?"

"Now you watch Dr. Blackwell die, and then you watch yourself die."

"Don't you want to torture her a little?" Max asked curiously.

"You mean, don't I want to give you some time to think? I think not." Tower snapped his fingers once and blue flame splashed from the tips. He crouched so his head was just above Pam's, looking at Max over her shoulder, and moved his fingers toward her throat. "I *have* tortured her. She was bait. Now she's nothing."

Max! He heard it again, but this time her mouth did not move. It was her vodou *call*, stronger than ever with the *stone* right beside her.

I hear you, baby, he responded.

"I love you, Max," she said out loud, her lips stiff. "I'm not sorry at all." The demons in the energy curtain fluttered and chittered, crowding to watch the next move.

"Tower," Max said quickly, "don't you want to know what I know about the FRC?"

Tower stopped his hand but just to make his point. "No, because you don't know enough." His hand closed on Pam's throat. "She would have told me."

"I know about Michael Salinan and Diana Herring. Strange bedfellows."

Use the stone, Pam! Sweat was beading on Max's face, but he thought the glow of his pyramidal prison was hiding it.

Tower said, "I have no idea what you mean."

"Salinan and Herring. Having an affair. Didn't you know?" He saw the flash of calculation in Tower's eyes. "Yes, you do know, on some level. You just never put it together before."

Use the stone, Pam!

Pam blinked. Tower's burning hand moved back a few inches. *The stone?* she thought furiously. *What stone? The stone I got from Omen? Tilit has it!*

Tower has it now. But it still knows you. Use it!

She blinked again. Then she closed her eyes.

Tower, looking over her head at Max across the room, said dismissively, "You heard a few names somewhere."

"And yet I did hear them, so I've come at you from a way you never suspected. You *don't* know all I know."

"Tell me what it is or Pam dies."

"Now she's a bargaining chip again."

"Talk."

"That's what I was trying to do. But you didn't want to listen."

"Quit wasting time. Talk or she dies. Right now."

"Okay, Jackson. It all started the last time I saw Aleksandra. You know Aleksandra, don't you, Jackson? Maybe you call her Madeleine."

"No!" snapped Tower. He clamped his hand on Pam's throat.

Max was surprised, and it showed. "How the hell can you not know Aleksandra? She's the demon running the FRC. Holy shit!" He leaned forward inside the pyramid. "You're not in the loop!"

"Listen, you," Tower said dangerously, "I am our *sorcerer*. If we were 'run' by a demon I would know it. If we had *contact* with a demon I would know it."

Max?

Focus!

He said, "Aleksandra is a demon. Above your level, Jackson. She came to me in 1980, came again in 1985, and then again in 1991."

"When your resolve was tested," Tower responded. "I know all about those three encounters, and there was no Aleksandra, and there's no one above my level, I assure you."

"She can assume any form, but she likes being a hot redhead."

Shockingly, Pam suddenly spoke up. "That's why you don't know about it, Tower. You're not interested in redheads."

FOCUS!

Okay, okay.

Tower said slowly, "If I don't know . . . someone else is higher than I am, and hiding it." His hand tightened on Pam's throat; her eyes began to bulge. "Who is it, August?"

"That I don't know. Why don't you give me some names?"

"Allenby," said Tower; then his eyes grew wide and his mouth grew small.

"Oops," said Max.

"She dies!" Tower shouted. But his hand was frozen. He tried to close his grip, but it gradually opened instead. It moved away from Pam's throat. Tower stared at it in anger, turning to horror. For the first time he realized the power of the man he'd caught. He stood up, spasmed.

Well, good luck!

Max's pyramid exploded outward into glowing shards.

To Tower's eyes, narrowed in unaccustomed pain and confusion, it was a golden jaguar who surged through his circle, scattering the demons in the crackling energy mist. They howled their alien rage, but Tower struck at his attacker with his own unsurpassed power. Max was knocked off his stride, all the pain he had suffered tonight reawakening, but he plowed ahead, driving into the magus. The two men crashed to the ground together, rolling and grappling, as bursts from their hands lit up the room. The books on the shelves threw regimented shadows up the walls, sweeping back and forth in unison as the witch-lights below moved and swirled.

For all his vitality, Tower was weaker than Max physically, but Tower had the *stone*. His arms pumped, knees gouged, feet kicked and stomped. The air was filled with the stench of incense, ozone, blood, and sweat. But finally Tower, finding a moment of good balance, flung Max across the room to strike the shelves and spill books to the floor on all sides. Tower climbed to his feet, started forward, both his hands extended palm outward, his power palpable, shaking the room. He was rocky but he was doing fine.

Max stayed where he fell, but not because he couldn't move. He gestured with his hand, turning it over as if to receive an offering. Above his palm, a sphere of light appeared, floating. Inside was the sarin he'd put away on Omen Key, just before they'd vented the rest. He flipped his hand at Tower as if tossing a stone across a lake, and the sphere flew. Tower staggered back, unsure what it was but knowing it couldn't be good, but his tired legs weren't working well enough. He threw up his hands to block the sphere magickally, but too late. It struck his outstretched hands and burst. He took one gasping breath, and spasmed volcanically. Sweat burst from his twitching body, soaking his black robe. He vomited once, wet himself, shit on his black leather shoes.

MAX!!!

"It's okay," he said, directing his voice toward her but never removing his gaze from Tower. "It's okay. I focused the gas on him like I focused the fire. We're okay." He started to get to his feet.

Tower was convulsing, clawing at his mouth. He started to collapse, in sections, like a demolished building. As he hit the floor, his power exploded into Max, driving him to his knees. Tower's body arced backward and landed sprawled across the large drum. Incredibly, the beating of its mechanical heart continued unabated, magnified by the drumhead.

Ga-dumm, ga-dumm, ga-dumm, ga-dumm . . .

Max forced himself to his feet, though the reaction to his magickal exertions had left him drained. He had to forge through the next few minutes, like a sleigh over snowless ground, and get Pam free. "It's over!" he yelled, though it came out more like a croak. "We did it, Pam!"

"Then get me out of this!" Pam responded. And followed that with a mental *Now!*

He went to her, knelt beside her, and brought the goblin flame to his hand. It went nowhere near her throat as he sliced through her bonds, and as the first one parted she gave a long, shuddering sigh of relief.

"The *stone* knew you," Max told her, cutting as fast as he could. "You didn't have it long but you made a bond. When you started *calling* for me, I couldn't hear it because I'd been blocked, but eventually I got it as Tilit brought your *stone* closer. At last I had a way to find you, but I had to fight the zombis first. Sorry it took so long." Now she was free but she still couldn't move as circulation began to reestablish itself in her limbs, so he began to chafe her hands and feet.

"Think nothing of it," she croaked, filled with sparkling pain. "Is everyone okay?"

"Almost. Some neighborhoods died. We did the best we could."

"I'm sorry." A thought struck her. "Tower got the *stone* back, from you. Didn't that increase *his* power?"

"Yes, it did, which is why it took us a while to get him. But our power was greater than his."

"He said he was your master."

"He wasn't *our* master. You and I together were stronger."

"I couldn't have added much," Pam said.

"Oh yes you could. You just had to be you. Since there were two of us, we set up a field between us. Together, we were Elohim."

"Elohim is God, Max."

"And God is energy, between two poles. It's gravity, it's magnetism, it's sex, it's love. It's not Pam and Max their very selves, it's what's between us. We had it, and he didn't. We were riding the flow of the universe."

"Oh, Max!" she said, and dropped her tingling arms around him. She couldn't tell how hard she was holding him but she knew just exactly how hard he was holding her. Everything she'd had bottled up since Tilit took her came surging through her, and she could hardly breathe. So much emotion, and one emotion over all: *love*. She loved Max August, and she knew he loved her. She said so, and he answered her, and they stayed like that, hugging, murmuring, kissing deeply, with the inhuman heart of Jackson Tower drumming behind them, for what seemed like eternity. Timeless.

Finally, she pulled her arms away, no longer tingling, and he rocked back on his heels. The moment was gone, like all moments. She stretched her recovering muscles, settling back into this world—and he looked at the drum. His brow furrowed. "That's my drum," he said, peering at it closely.

But that meant nothing to Pam. She followed his glance, and, still with the gentle tone known only to lovers, asked, "What happened when he died, Max?"

He stared a moment longer, then answered. "All his power went into us. Mostly into me, because I can encompass it, but some into you, because you earned it."

"I did, didn't I? I tried to *call* and I did *call*."

"That's exactly how I started, back in the day. And you know what? If there *had* been some way to take

you to the whorehouses, you'd never have had the opportunity."

"Oh, you're still—"

*At which point the room exploded in a million jag-
ged shards of light!* It was like Max's attack on Miller
Omen to the power of ten. The reality around them itself shattered, collapsing in upon itself in slow motion.
As the shards, each one reflecting a shred of real life,
dropped into an abyss below their feet, a new reality
was revealed. It was space, stars and darkness, but Max
and Pam weren't falling along with the shards. They
were standing on an invisible something, in the midst
of eternity. Looking down past their feet, they saw one
of the stars pulse, a dull, angry red. It began to move
toward them.

"Stay right with me!" Max snapped.

"Are you kidding?" Pam shouted, holding tight to his
belt. "Where would I want to go?"

The star's light grew dazzling as it grew closer, a vast
sphere of flaming power, scarlet beams slicing through
the night. It was rushing up at them and for all the world
they were falling into it. But they didn't burn, and as
the star engulfed their feet it shattered in its own way,
the shards exploding harmlessly up and through Max
and Pam, to reveal its own hidden reality.

Rising to their level was the most striking woman
Pam had ever seen. A burnished mass of hair so red as
to shine velvet black, eyes blue as noon but showing
midnight behind, and blinding white flesh wreathed in
scarves of hazy rouge. Her figure was not only revealed,
it was flaunted. Tall, lean, young, firm, her only true gar-
ment was a narrow girdle crusted with sparkling rubies, covering only her hips, accenting everything else.
She was a sculptor's ideal of a woman, perfect, but just

too perfect, and the flesh just too white. Pam knew she was looking at a *mask*. The mask of a demon, named Aleksandra.

Beside her, Max was almost growling with excitement.

He snapped his hands up and hurled his golden power at the demon. She came back instantly with a cloud of lightning, spitting flame-red blasts. A convulsive wave of burning power burst over Max and Pam. *This is what happened to Val* started to flash through Pam's mind, her last living thought—but then she realized the thought had been completed. She was still alive. They were still alive!

Max!! He was still blasting his golden light. *No,* she thought, *our golden light!* Deep in her soul, where she'd *called* to Max, she felt the gold, too. She threw all her newly won confidence into the battle beside him. She raised her own hands, willed her own power to surge, and saw fire waver forth. It was thin compared to the others', useless on its own, but it was there.

Their light beat against Aleksandra's flame, forming a wall. The demon crouched ferally, hurling crackling power at them, straining to hurl more. From her scarlet lips came words in languages known and unknown. Max stood like a tree in the wind, leaning into it, palms outstretched. He had waited sixteen years for this! She'd killed his master and his wife, and this was what he'd prayed to all his gods for. He was praying now, in words never meant for human speech, roaring at the top of his voice, conjuring the power from a dozen sources at once. His voice and her voice slashed like chain saws through the shriek of their sorceries.

Suddenly, Max snapped his hand over, changing the way his power struck hers, rocking her like an unexpected wave on the shore. She countered it, coming up from below, driving him one awkward step back, then two, before he recovered his balance. Pam clutched his belt, willing him everything she had. He leaned into her strength, pushed off and drove Aleksandra back a step of her own. In the instant of her resettling, he whipped his fire across her legs, sweeping them out from under her. He strode forward, pinning her to the invisible floor. But she laughed and dropped back *through* the floor, out from under his pressure, and surged back three feet to the side to catch him unaware. He came free of Pam's grip, hit the floor, rolled, and came up firing.

It's magick as mixed martial arts! Pam realized giddily. *Magick with a K-1!* But her joy congealed as Max loosed a tremendous golden blast to disperse Aleksandra's power, then charged forward to grab her wrists. Thrusting her hands wide, not breaking stride, he slammed hard into her perfect body and drove her over backward. This time she didn't have time to erase the floor and she hit hard.

But her body was a mask. Whatever she was inside ignored the concussion and fought back like a wolf. Max fought like a point man as they rolled back and forth, both seeking a moment when they could get their hands free to fire more magick. But as they rolled, auras joined at the breast, Max found Aleksandra's so-familiar sexuality unbelievably intense. She was so exquisitely beautiful, so perfectly molded to him, that it all but tore him apart. To his disgust he found himself responding. The only consolation was, Aleksandra was clearly feeling the same thing. It had been like this on New Year's Eve 1980, when they'd fought for the fate of the world. He had forgotten.

Come with me, Max! I need a man like you!

"Pam! The sword!" he shouted, his eyes looked with Aleksandra's.

"What sword?" Pam stared at him dazedly. She, in her own way, was feeling exactly what he felt, and she was disoriented. But turning around, she saw, of all things, a sword lying on the invisible floor. She recognized it— Tower's ceremonial sword, carved with runes, covered in blood. She picked it up, turned back, held it out. But if Max took his hand off Aleksandra's wrist to grab it—

He did. Aleksandra slammed her hand against his side. He ran her through.

For a moment, nobody moved, as all of them stared at the steel blade in her stomach . . . and then Aleksandra, unhurt, laughed in his face. Until his golden power rocketed down the steel.

Her perfect body blossomed with patches of expanding rot. Parts of it winked out of existence, returning only to flicker like embers in the darkness. She yanked herself free from the sword blade, jumped up and back, but the golden light continued to pour through the sword and bridge the gap to her sternum, twitching and bucking in its fury like a Jacob's Ladder. She, too, was spasming. Her scarlet power crackled on her fingers but threatened to go out. Instead, through a monumental act of will, she forced herself to ignore the distraction of her crumbling form—forced her soul to fight back. But today was a day of *external* power. Even a diabola had to fight that wave. The struggle built a nimbus around her hands, then her forearms—then, so slowly, her entire form. A scarlet bubble formed around her, choking off the golden light. She sank to her knees. The rot dissipated. She stayed on her knees.

"You can't have us, Aleksandra," Max said, his voice ragged but steady. "You evolve, but I evolve, too."

No! You only stole Tower's energy! She looked up from under her dark red hair, eyes flashing in shadow, and her voice still battered him and Pam in waves.

"Shit happens when an artist dies," Max said sharply. "That's why you don't kill Code Reds. But I've got it now, and that's evolution, too."

We kill Code Reds if we have to, Max.

"But you can't kill me. Your problem is timing, Aleksandra. You always come too late."

She laughed, increasing the battering. *I needn't kill you to control you.*

"Same old song."

I control the most effective humans in the physical world. I will control you. You kept my people from Suriname but our next moves are already in play. You can't set yourself against me forever, Max.

"Keep telling yourself that."

You think you're tough! The 'point man.' But how tough are you when I tell you—Ha! Val lives!

That rocked him, and both women felt it viscerally. But he fought to keep control as he answered her. "I don't have to be tough because you're lying. She may not be dead but she's not alive."

She is. She's just not Val.

It rocked him again. He couldn't ignore it this time. ". . . She's reborn?"

Exactly. But she has no more memory of her previous life than anyone else. You'll never find the woman she is now. You will walk the earth, scheming your simple schemes against me, but knowing you might pass her in the street, unaware, at any time. The world changes for you here and now, Max. Unless you join with me.

"Everything you say is a lie, Aleksandra!"

She's a little young for you still—but she'll catch up to the Timeless man. And meanwhile, Pamela Black-well will turn forty, then fifty, then sixty, seventy, eighty—maybe even one hundred and ten if she's lucky. But eventually she'll leave you. You'll have lost two, and if you ever dare to love a third, you'll lose her, too, and so on forever. The only woman who can stay with you through Time is me!

"It's a lie!" He was out on the ragged edge. Aleksandra's thrust was just too deep. Pam had to step forward. "Maybe so, Allie," she shouted, her voice a thin reed compared to the demon's. "But I'm going to devote my life as it is to kicking your pasty white ass, right along-side Max."

Aleksandra's voice dripped disdain as she cut to the chase. *What if he finds Valerie, blonde?*

"According to you, that's impossible. So it probably isn't. But I don't care! I'm in this now for myself as much as anybody."

He'll never love you like he loves her.

"Bite me, bitch!"

So, Max. You have a new priestess at your side. But if you want the old one you'll align with me. And soon, because who knows what will happen to her in this cold, cruel world?

Aleksandra vanished, as completely as the night she left a hole in the rain. All around Pam, shards of reality flicked into view like elementals, falling together, an egg uncracking, until the room in the mansion in the jungle on Earth was their only reality once again, and there were just the two of them.

They stood there in utter silence, putting their minds back together. Until Pam's legs gave way and Max was forced to grab her, dropping the sword with a clang.

"Sorry," she gasped, surprised at herself. "Sorry. That was just a lot."

"I noticed you didn't collapse until it was over," he said.

"I couldn't, could I?"

"No," he said, "*you* couldn't."

She wanted to stay in his arms, but she wanted more to stand up again. So she stood. It might be a struggle, but she still felt she could do anything. Except ask what was foremost on her mind. So she said, "Where did that sword come from?"

"It was always there. Ceremonial swords exist in two worlds at once—two edges, two worlds; that's their ritual purpose. So it wouldn't vanish like the rest of our world. And because it joins two worlds, I thought it'd carry my power directly to her, bypassing her defenses. *Once* I thought of it, which I should have done from the start."

"You are so hard on yourself! Couldn't *her* power have come back at *you*?"

"Not tonight. Because that energy between two worlds—that connection between two poles—wasn't just between two poles. Just like when we faced Tower, *my* pole had an additional connection; I was the focus of her energy and yours, and yours was nothing to sneeze at. We had something she didn't and she couldn't match it."

"She *almost* killed you. She almost killed *us*," Pam said suspiciously. "I know I'm not wrong about that."

"Can't argue with a doctor. And that's *why* I'm hard on myself. But she didn't kill us. We seem to be doing things right." He was cheerful. Too cheerful. He was doing it for her.

"But won't she track us from here on out, now that

she knows where we are?" Pam demanded. "She's got magick, she's got the FRC. . . ."

"No. Another aspect of energy being nothing but energy. She can't track us specifically."

"Even though she's a demon?"

"You have too much faith in demons, Pam. They're more powerful than humans but also more rarified. She can't be involved on this level too much now—it's too brutal, for want of a better word—and her powers can be blocked by a smart brute, which I hope I am. She has to work through her FRC in this world."

"That is not a good thing. They're brutal and they're smart."

"But not smart enough. We've done good work against them tonight."

"Meaning—?"

"Michael Salinan and Diana Herring are confirmed. Somebody named Allenby's in the mix. Tower will have to be replaced. The whole thing involves a golden necklace. And I know for certain that Val is alive."

Pam kept ignoring that. "You seemed very sure about Salinan and Herring, whoever they are. I felt it."

"You had to feel it if Tower was to believe it. I didn't know it until he confirmed it."

"But then why did you say their names?"

"Aleksandra told me once: people inevitably make one slip. It's human nature." He walked her back to the chair she'd been tied to, but understandably, she didn't want to sit there. She sat on the floor. At least her limbs were back to normal; fighting demons was one way to kill time.

"In 1991," Max said, "Aleksandra confirmed that a group like the FRC existed. But all my attempts to prove it came up empty. Still, my guy Dave, my computer guy—I had him doing data mining to the extent the Internet and home-brew technology allowed it, and the extent grew steadily over time. Two years ago he was scanning for five hundred names I'd identified as possible group members, and his algorithm turned up a credit card receipt for Michael Salinan at the Amangani in Jackson Hole. No big deal, except that on the next sweep through American Express, four hours later, it wasn't there. Dave was looking for anomalies, and it made me wonder not only why such a top-shelf politico had to hide that visit, but how he hid it. So I booked myself into the lodge and soon enough determined that he'd been there with another name of that list, Diana Herring. With her controlling half the radio, half the television, and ninety percent of the newspapers in the United States—a fact I was all too painfully aware of, since her predecessors bought KQBU in 1980—it made sense that a media tycoon and an advisor to presidents needed to be secret. If their affair were known it would affect the world. So that only left 'how,' and the probability that they were part of what turned out to be the FRC. But I never could find anything to prove it without tipping them off that I knew about them. They're too good.

"So I changed my tactics, and let them come to me. If I had done *anything* to reveal myself to them, somebody there would have wondered if it was a setup. But Aleksandra had told me that people inevitably make one slip, so she would have told them, and they would wait patiently for the day when they would overhear someone make a slip by contacting me. So I just did other things, year after year. But when Fern called on All Hallows' Eve, I knew from the second I heard her voice that the slip was being made—and a path to

Aleksandra was finally opening for me. All I had to do was keep them thinking that they were the cat and I was the mouse."

Pam looked stricken. "You're saying, saving me— was just part of a plan?"

"I have to admit that it was," he said soberly, looking at her directly. "But then I fell in love with you." He squatted down beside her, laid his hands on her arms, kissed her. "I knew this was my chance at Aleksandra's cabal. I didn't know it was also my chance at a cowgirl."

But there was one more question she still had to ask. "Did you expect to learn Val was alive, with your little plot?"

"Did I expect it? No. But I did at least hope that if I defeated the FRC, Aleksandra would come out of the woodwork again, and I thought she might want to try to hurt me in the best way she knew."

"A lot of ifs."

"There are no cut-and-dried answers." He smiled. "Magick is constant verification."

She didn't smile back. "I verify that you used me, Max."

"For about ten minutes. Then I saved you, and then you had to stay with me, and then everything else. That's why I told you my name, right from the start, when I never tell anyone else. I knew it was right. Alchemical intuition." He searched her face. "I do love you, Pam."

"So, if you love me . . ." She tightened her lips, steeled herself, looking directly back at him. There was no other question left. ". . . What about Val?"

He shook his head. "I won't abandon her; that's never changed. But everything else has. I'm different from the man I was in 1985, and you're a different woman.

Val herself is different, if Aleksandra was telling the truth. Everything's different now, because you brought me back to the world."

Pam looked deep into his eyes, seemingly searching for his soul. "But she might come back. I don't know if I can form a long-term relationship . . . under those circumstances, Max," she said slowly. And then: "But you know—I will if you will."

"I will," he said, and somehow those words seemed to echo off the high, vaulted ceiling.

Val might be "Susie" now, Pam thought. *Val might never be found.* Should they lose this chance at happiness over possibilities? Should they live in fear of the unlikely? Her alchemical intuition said no. They were going to live for the future, and not the past.

She got to her feet, and he followed her, looking around the room, at the scuffed circle, the shining sword, the fallen books, the blistered walls. She asked him, "Do you want to take that drum?"

"I don't think so. I gave it up for lost a long time ago. And besides, I don't form long-term relationships with *things*." He took her hand. "You ready, Pam?"

"I was *born* ready, Max—to get out of *this* place." She laughed. "Thanks for being patient, and honest, with me."

"Hell, you're my cowgirl, aren't you?"

To his astonishment, she threw back her head and shouted, " 'YES! YES! Say it! He vas my . . . BOY-FRIEND!' " She laughed again, harder. Released. "Cloris Leachman, *Young Frankenstein*. That's one pop reference *I* know." And then she kissed him back. "I love you, too, Max. I *grav* you."

They held hands as they left the room, each taking

one final look at Jackson Tower, one final listen to his beating heart. Max, the deejay, found himself thinking he could dance to it.

Found himself thinking that he *wanted* to dance.

2 DEATH

Richard Hanrahan sat back in his chair, turned off the monitor, and removed his earphones. He dragged his fingers across the bridge of his nose. He had bugged Miller Omen's—now Jackson Tower's—Surinamese mansion as a matter of course. No one outside his area knew that he'd done it, not even Renzo. But Hanrahan made it his business to know as much as could be known about as much as he could, and his team had been down there installing covert surveillance equipment not half an hour after Omen first chose the place and left.

Once Rita had called to tell him her end had fallen apart in the face of the Code Red's assault, Hanrahan had sat down to witness what Tower would do. And in due time, he had witnessed it: the death of their cabal's sorcerer at the hands of a former disc jockey and a doctor he'd known for less than a week. The final destruction of their plans for Suriname, South America, and the world. Followed by a mysterious power surge that overwhelmed both video and audio. He had sat and waited with an old hand's patience for the signal to resume, while subjecting it to detailed analysis, but when it resumed, August and Blackwell were leaving the building and the analysis had revealed nothing.

It was very disturbing, and made more so because he had seen that power surge before. Twice. When he had bugged Renzo's helicopter.

Hanrahan removed the flash drive containing the record of the last hour in Omen's mansion and locked it in his personal safe, next to four other drives that were for his eyes only. He would make use of the information he'd gathered as needed, to help Renzo lead the Necklace in an effective way, but he would never reveal the full extent of it to anyone.

He picked up the midnight-blue phone.

NOVEMBER 5 - 3:35 A.M. EST

2 DEATH

Carol van Dusen was awaiting Hanrahan's call in her den, watching Miriam Hopkins in *The Story of Temple Drake*. She paused the player, answered on the second ring, and listened with tightening lips as he gave her his report. At the end she said simply, "I understand. Thank you so much, Dick," and hung up. She'd been right about Rita Diamante: not up to Miller's standards. But that was water under the bridge.

She turned to her computer and began moving stock through London, Zurich, and Tokyo. There was a lot to move and little time.

2 DEATH

Diana Herring was awaiting Hanrahan's call, with her laptop right beside her bed. After hearing his report, she responded, "There'll be tales of an attempted coup, with all the dead soldiers. Those don't matter; nobody knows where Suriname is, let alone cares. It might as well be Darfur. There'll also be some reports of people claiming to be zombis. I'll get a dispatch from South Africa about a witch doctor exploding a village—didn't happen, of course, but if any editor finds that kind of stuff interesting, he'll figure his readers know South Africa better than some place he's never heard of. Most editors would never touch zombis in the first place. It'll be at worst a digest footnote."

"What about all those people you've got lined up to air?" Hanrahan asked.

"I'm sure they'll have plenty to talk about without mentioning . . . what's that place's name again?" She laughed engagingly. "It's covered, Dick."

2 DEATH

Michael Salinan was awaiting Hanrahan's call, and took it with a grave demeanor. "That's very disappointing news," he told the spy chief. "My shop was looking forward to the contract for advising the new government.

But don't worry about U.S. politics. When we stage the immigration debate this morning, I'll have Pluscher call brown people 'sewage,' and that'll tie up both Congress and the media for at least two days."

He hung up. "Still foolin' 'em," he told Diana, as she resumed tapping away on her laptop. "But why did he call you first?"

🦁

NOVEMBER 5 - 3:41 A.M. EASTERN STANDARD TIME

2 DEATH

Lawrence Breckenridge lolled halfway off the toilet, shoulder against the sink, hand dangling. His heart was beating strongly—that was part of his deal—but he was weak as a kitten and breathing shallowly, raggedly. Consciously. If he didn't force himself to breathe, it might well not happen.

At last, rolling just enough to slide himself completely off the john, he fell to his side on the rug, where he lay trying to regather his strength. He needed to get up and go to work. But it wouldn't happen soon.

Aleksandra had not been happy.

She had come to him with a force she'd never shown before, like a dynamo, shooting off scarlet darts. She had swept through him like electrical shock and blasted his brain with scarlet outrage.

But she hadn't destroyed him.

And as he lay there, Breckenridge thought about that. The Necklace hadn't destroyed Max August, he'd personally failed her—but she still needed him. That meant there was no one else to take his place.

In their admittedly deteriorated relationship, he felt he had gained another edge. There was no question that she could snuff him out any time she chose, but the more hooks he could put in her, the less likely she'd be to do it. And he would not fail her again. He would win her back.

It would be his task to find a new sorcerer for the Necklace—another person of great accomplishment but not quite great enough to know about him and the Diabola. There were not many like that, and fewer still who would come or could be brought to the inner circle, among the Nine. But there would be someone, eventually, and he would find him, or her. There was no one out there who was better at running the Necklace. When you came right down to it, he was the *man* who ran the world.

He could master any situation, and he would master this one.

Once he got off the floor. She had really not been happy.

"Renzo! You in there?" It was Hanrahan, through the door.

"Occupied," croaked Breckenridge. Fortunately, Hanrahan wasn't listening for anything more than confirmation.

"Suriname's gone to hell," he said crisply. "I've alerted Carole, Diana, and Michael, but I can't raise Jackson."

Breckenridge chuckled, and in so doing realized that the crisis was past. He could breathe, he could talk . . . he could chuckle. He rolled over and started to get, slowly, to his feet.

No one could raise Jackson now.

But he, Lawrence Breckenridge, was standing on his

own two feet. He, Lawrence Breckenridge, would not only restore but *strengthen* the Necklace, to focus all its power on the obliteration of Max August and Pamela Blackwell.

Then she would be *very* happy.

NOVEMBER 5 - DAWN SURINAME TIME

3 HAND

Tower's former zombis sprawled stupefied on the lawn, far away from his mansion—human again now that Max had retrieved the antidote from his copter. Pam had administered it, then given them all water, and food if they could stomach it. She had stabilized any injury she could handle with the rudimentary supplies on hand at the ranch, and made them as comfortable as she could. Like their predecessors on Omen Key, they suffered from gangrene, faced amputations—but unlike their predecessors, they would be fine until better help arrived. No one would change that this time. Tower was dead, Tilit was dead, and the other bad guys were long gone from Para. Max had gotten the *call* from Amba.

Pam had also used some water to wash the blood and sweat off herself. So now she and Max were lounging in the seats of a sparkling clean Range Rover, still with that new car smell—the last legacy of Miller Omen's dreams. It was parked at the first crest of the road leading out of his plantation, looking back at the grounds and valley. High above the hilltops, the first rays of dawn were coloring the sky, even as the mansion exploded in white flame below. Max was using the same alchemy he'd used on Omen's lab, keeping the flames concentrated in the building, sparing the people and things surrounding it. He was taking Tower's power and Omen's *stone*, but the rest of the magick that had passed this way was going back to the universe, out through the valley's opened roof. The smoke up there turned a gorgeous crimson in the dawning light. Pam was remembering Harmakhis, lord of the dawn, lord of endless new days, when Max murmured, "Here we are now, entertain us."

She burst out laughing.

And the longer she laughed the funnier she found it.

It was release and she knew it and went with it . . . all the way to its gasping end.

Then she took in a breath, and let out a sigh. "Oh, man . . ."

Max asked, "Second thoughts about all this?"

"No way," she responded. "No way. But I *really* understand *better* what 'all this' *means*."

"There's a lot left, and a long way to go," he said.

"Always the realist." She smiled.

"Always trying to be real," he agreed.

"Well, I'm game for it, Max. It's so much bigger than I knew, and I thought I'd been *out there*, working with *tetraodontidæ*. So much to see and to do that I didn't believe existed." She rolled to her side in her seat, looking at him. "And I'll lay that to Jackson Tower and his friends. Their whole thing is beating people down. But I didn't get beat down. It was hell . . . but it was swell."

"How old are you? Twelve?"

"I'm seven years younger than you," she answered.

"And before those seven years are up, I'll be Timeless, too, so I'll never be older."

"Seven years will take some doing, sweetie."

"You did it in five."

"I got lucky."

"No . . . and you think it's swell, too." She poked him on the thigh. "Do you mind if I say something now?" she asked.

"No, of course not. Professional deejay—get it all the time. I'll shut up."

"It's not that. I just have something to say." She squared up in her seat, and pointed at the zombis. "Look at them. They're all people, but they had no life force, so they were zombis—I'm not saying this real well."

"I'm think I'm keeping up so far."

"Well, there's a difference between zombis and people. The difference is life force. People without their life force are zombis. Lumbering bodies. Working stiffs. But all the real *people*—they're just zombis *with* life force. You need a body and a life force to be a real person. And you—you're the total *opposite* of a zombi, Max. Your life force is too strong to be removed—"

"Maybe."

"Well, it's strong enough. You don't age because your life force won't let it happen, and your life force won't let it happen because you made a better connection with Elohim, the two-in-one energy between us all, that Moses said created the universe.

"So being alive means establishing reality and having relationships and all that. Your two hundred sixty asteroids, representing two hundred sixty types of rela-

tionships with two hundred sixty types of people—
that's a lot of types, but just one life force. One thing to
rule them all. And all of them have it, until it goes away,
and then their body dies without it. So the life force is
key." She laughed at herself. "So, duh. But even though
each of my relationships is with an individual, each
one has the same life force. So if I pay attention to the
people around me, and look for whatever the energy
is that's the same in all of them—the light in the eyes
that's the same in all of them—eventually I could come
to recognize the life force, in and of itself. The thing that
runs through all two hundred sixty types. Through
hundreds of thousands of types. And when I do that,
I'll know it in myself, too—the force I can use for
alchemy—and I can use alchemy to make it stronger,
right up to the point where all my energy will be in the
life force, and my body will just be along for the
ride—a Timeless ride, like yours. So I'm going to look
at every person I meet from here on out, and see what
makes them alive. While you tell me what goes on in
your *Codex*."

He nodded, smiling broadly. "Pam, first and foremost, that was fabulous. You're putting it together like
a champ. If it didn't sound patronizing, I'd say I was
proud of you."

"You can say it," she said.

"And it was *almost* right on the money."

"Almost?"

"There's one part in there where you confuse me
with somebody great. I don't have any first-name acquaintance with Elohim. All I did was learn a skill set;
other people can, too. That's sort of the point, actually,
since you want to learn it. But I'm not some chosen one,

and neither will you be. Moses says Elohim came to him, but I happened to run into Cornelius Agrippa, and you happened to run into me. We're not chosen people. We're just alchemists."

"'*We* are just alchemists,'" she echoed. "It sounds good enough for me."

"Well, get used to it. Because the way your mind is going, you're on the way, and I can guarantee you, you're in for an amazing ride."

Below them, one of the mansion's side walls collapsed inward, onto the flames. The mansion was burning furiously but not a single ember fell outside its footprint. The former zombis were all huddled around the fire, feeling warmth after so much time feeling nothing, but none was in danger. Sunlight was creeping down to them, over the rolling hills.

"And meanwhile," Max said, rolling around to face her, "back in the real world, you and I are going completely off the grid. We're not going back to San Francisco, or Bridgetown, or even Para. Amba and Kwasiba will go to their people, deep in their jungle, to bury Adyuba, and we can join them for that. But then we'll sift south with their people, to Brazil and beyond. You can't ever contact anyone you knew before—not Phyllis, not your boss, not your old college roommate, not anyone."

"Well, five days ago—*five days?*—I would never have said this. But that sounds *great* to me." She stretched in place, rolling her shoulders. She couldn't sit still. "Of course we have to be smart, Max, considering who we're up against. But you know what? To know we can go up against them and *win*?! That's what I didn't have before Hallowe'en! I was just keeping my head down, hoping for change—and that's over! We're alchemists with guns!"

Below them, the roof of the ranch house collapsed, shooting a spectacular display of flaming embers high overhead. Max and Pam both watched them rise, and peak, and slowly fall, twinkling red against the sunny sky. From the former zombis came a collective sigh.

"Another day in paradise," Pam said. "What do we know about this one, Max?"

"November fifth." He considered. "It means nothing particular to the Celts—in fact, we can forget the Celts for a while. Their next big time is Yule. But the English, tonight, will mark Guy Fawkes Night, complete with fireworks. Interestingly, the asteroid today is Camilla, which means the same as the Mayan day Three Hand—Advancing Assertion."

Pam rolled back toward him. "That Mayan part could happen, Mr. Deejay," she said with a devilish grin. She leaned closer. "Hell, it's happening *right now* . . ."

All history is one immortal man who continually learns.

—BLAISE PASCAL

3 HAND

She sat on the narrow bench in her little room and looked out through her open window. She had to admit it was going to be cold, but she wanted to feel the fireworks, and she wanted to feel the cold, because the cold made her feel her skin—all those millions of little goosebumps up and down her arms. This strange scrawny body. The sky looked like a mother's sad gray veil, darkening as she watched, and from the street outside she could hear the other children heading out to get their candy and potatoes. The blond girl was out there, somewhere in the darkness, trying to steal the children's potatoes. She wanted to fight the blond girl.

But she mustn't get excited.

Now the strong must live through Darkness until the Light returns, she thought. It was just one of her random thoughts, something she'd heard somewhere. She'd learned not to care, tried to learn not to notice strange words in her brain. Strange worms in her brain. But she spied in her mind's eye the sun, burning on the far horizon, and just the thought of that sun warmed her blood. Wouldn't it be wonderful when the sun came back, and all the golden flowers bloomed again? Eva Delia had just had her birthday, the dark day, Halloween, sweet sixteen. But what was so bloody wonderful about *now*? NOW was cold and dark and wrapped her up like meds.

But she mustn't get excited.

The fireworks began all at once. She started delightedly, and another random thought fired random words from her lips like rubies. She didn't know what they meant but who cared?

"My name," she whispered to the dark now, "isn't Eva Delia Kerr."

And she went out the window.

Appendix

An excerpt from the *Codex*, as it existed at this time.
Interesting dates:

Alexander the Great born	-356 July 15	11 Tooth	Owning Cohesion
England founded	1066 December 25	8 Dog	Connecting with Embodiment
Leonardo da Vinci born	1452 April 15	3 Night	Advancing a Private World
Cornelius Agrippa born	1486 September 14	2 Corn Stalk	Encountering Unison
The New World discovered	1492 October 12 before dawn	11 Tooth	Owning Cohesion
Benjamin Franklin born	1706 January 17	13 Earth	Managing the Universal
George Washington born	1732 February 22	3 Moon	Advancing Transcendence
Thomas Jefferson born	1743 April 13 before dawn	1 Candle	Establishing the Matrix
United States of America founded	1776 July 4	9 Corn Stalk	Being Unison
Ceres discovered	1801 January 1	11 Milky Way	Owning Alchemy

Abraham Lincoln born	1809 February 12	11 Night	Owning a Private World
Richard Wagner born	1813 May 22 before dawn	10 Wind	Personifying Possibilities
Giuseppe Verdi born	1813 October 10	9 Corn Seed	Being the Public World
Karl Marx born	1818 May 5 before dawn	12 Monkey	Fulfilling Divergence
Sigmund Freud born	1856 May 6	10 Corn Stalk	Personifying Unison
Confederate States of America founded	1861 February 8	7 Tooth	Engaging with Cohesion
Carl Jung born	1875 July 26	10 Corn Stalk	Personifying Unison
Aleister Crowley born	1875 October 12	10 Monkey	Personifying Divergence
Albert Einstein born	1879 March 14	11 Sun	Owning All
Franklin Delano Roosevelt born	1882 January 30	11 Corn Stalk	Owning Unison
Adolf Hitler born	1889 April 20	9 Dog	Being Embodiment
H. P. Lovecraft born	1890 August 20 before dawn	1 Candle	Establishing the Matrix
Leo Strauss born	1899 September 20	5 Eagle	Empowering the Storyline
Ansel Adams born	1902 February 20 before dawn	3 Earth	Advancing the Universal
Orville Wright flies	1903 December 17	6 Night	Responding to a Private World
John F. Kennedy born	1917 May 29	4 Eagle	Encompassing the Storyline
Bettie Page born	1923 April 22 before dawn	12 Star	Fulfilling Devotion

Lenny Bruce born	1925 October 13	8 Jaguar	Connecting with Clarity
Hugh Hefner born	1926 April 9	4 Tooth	Encompassing Cohesion
Marilyn Monroe born	1926 June 1	5 Serpent	Empowering Yáng
Martin Luther King, Jr. born	1929 January 15	2 Corn Seed	Encountering the Public World
James Dean born	1931 February 8	2 Flint Knife	Encountering the Unique
Elvis Presley born	1935 January 8	2 Star	Encountering Devotion
John Lennon born	1940 October 9 before dawn	9 Star	Being Devotion
Dick Cheney born	1941 January 30	6 Wind	Responding to Possibilities
Atomic bomb tested	1945 July 16 before dawn	8 Moon	Connecting with Transcendence
George W. Bush born	1946 July 6	13 Serpent	Managing Yáng
Bill Clinton born	1946 August 19	5 Moon	Empowering Transcendence
Flying saucers sighted	1947 June 24	2 Flint Knife	Encountering the Unique
Roswell UFO incident	1947 July 2	10 Death	Personifying Yin
Hillary Rodham Clinton born	1947 October 26	9 Wind	Being Possibilities
Tony Blair born	1953 May 6	13 Nipple	Managing Reality
Playboy established	1953 November 8 before dawn	3 Death	Advancing Yin
First man in space	1961 April 12	12 Milky Way	Fulfilling Alchemy

Barack Obama born	1961 August 4	9 Corn Stalk	Being Unison
Martin Luther King, Jr. speech	1963 August 28	9 Hand	Being Assertion
JFK assassination	1963 November 22	4 Corn Stalk	Encompassing Unison
Star Trek premieres	1966 September 8	11 Jaguar	Owning Clarity
Moon landing	1969 July 20	4 Sun	Encompassing All
Watergate breaks	1972 June 17 before dawn	13 Wind	Managing Possibilities
Pong debuts	1972 November 29	10 Star	Personifying Devotion
Microsoft established	1975 January 2	7 Tooth	Engaging with Cohesion
AIDS identified	1981 June 5	13 Flint Knife	Managing the Unique
The Internet established	1983 January 1	3 Corn Stalk	Advancing Unison
The X-Files premieres	1993 September 10	8 Flint Knife	Connecting with the Unique
Princess Diana dies	1997 August 31	3 Moon	Advancing Transcendence
George W. Bush presidency	2001 January 20	6 Hand	Responding to Assertion
"Bin Laden determined to strike"	2001 August 6	9 Serpent	Being Yáng
World Trade Center attack	2001 September 11	6 Nipple	Responding to Reality
Euro debuts	2002 January 1	1 Corn Stalk	Establishing Unison
USA attacks Iraq	2003 March 19	1 Eagle	Establishing the Storyline

Worldwide financial crisis erupts	2007 August 9	6 Milky Way	Responding to Alchemy
Pam meets Max	2007 October 31	11 Wind	Owning Possibilities

The magical fantasy thriller that launched Max August

THE POINT MAN

STEVE ENGLEHART

Trade Paperback • 978-0-7653-2501-3

Max August was a point man when he served during the Vietnam War, the guy who had to lead his patrol through dangers he couldn't possibly anticipate. Now he's a disc jockey, at one with the music and his faithful audience…until the day when he is swept into a battle invisible to all but the participants.

"Steve Englehart comes up out of nowhere to explode on us with a first novel that places itself way up there with some of the finest in the genre. *The Point Man* is as exciting a slam-banger as you'll find this year. But it's much more than that. The magic is most magical, and enormous to boot, and the mystery and the tension will not release you."

—*Twilight Zone Magazine*

TOR®

tor-forge.com

TOR